Praise for *The Perfect*

One of Ms. Career Girl's "10 Spring and Summer Thriller and Mystery Must-Reads"

One of The Nerd Daily's "Most Anticipated Thrillers"

"A tenacious, loving mother fights to prove her daughter is innocent of murder in this well-crafted psychological thriller from Palmer. Palmer digs into the fraught family dynamics of the Francone household, [and] alternating points of view . . . ratchet up the suspense. Palmer's take on a complex psychological disorder will keep readers in its grip."
—*Publishers Weekly*

"What starts as a slow-burning thriller ends in a crescendo of intensity as D. J. Palmer's newest thriller, *The Perfect Daughter,* explores the often-terrifying intersection of mental health disorders and the criminal justice system. . . . Full of twists and turns, [this book will keep readers] busy trying to guess just what is coming around the corner. But much like the poorly funded state psychiatric facility where a lot of the story takes place, there are some surprises that you will never be able to anticipate, and you better be on your toes and ready for them!"
—The Nerd Daily

"One of the most thrilling books I have read all year, *The Perfect Daughter* by D. J. Palmer is a book you won't want to miss."   —*Seattle Book Review*

"Readers will find themselves caught up in a bewildering and delightful maze as Palmer slowly reveals the layers of this Russian doll of a book."   —CrimeReads

"A thrill ride with a shocking ending you don't see coming."
—Red Carpet Crash

ALSO BY D. J. PALMER

The New Husband

Saving Meghan

D. J. PALMER

The Perfect Daughter

ST. MARTIN'S GRIFFIN
NEW YORK

Published in the United States by St. Martin's Griffin, an imprint of St. Martin's Publishing Group

THE PERFECT DAUGHTER. Copyright © 2021 by D. J. Palmer. All rights reserved. Printed in the United States of America. For information, address St. Martin's Publishing Group, 120 Broadway, New York, NY 10271.

www.stmartins.com

The Library of Congress has cataloged the hardcover edition as follows:

Names: Palmer, Daniel, 1962– author.
Title: The perfect daughter / D. J. Palmer.
Description: First edition. | New York : St. Martin's Press, 2021.
Identifiers: LCCN 2020048622 | ISBN 9781250267924 (hardcover) |
    ISBN 9781250267931 (ebook)
Classification: LCC PS3616.A33883 P47 2021 | DDC 813/.6—dc23
LC record available at https://lccn.loc.gov/2020048622

ISBN 978-1-250-26794-8 (trade paperback)

Our books may be purchased in bulk for promotional, educational, or business use. Please contact your local bookseller or the Macmillan Corporate and Premium Sales Department at 1-800-221-7945, extension 5442, or by email at MacmillanSpecialMarkets@macmillan.com.

First St. Martin's Griffin Edition: 2022

10 9 8 7 6 5 4 3 2 1

For Jennifer Enderlin, with my deepest thanks and gratitude

CHAPTER 1

AT THIRTY MINUTES PAST eight o'clock, red and blue strobe lights lit up the sky outside Grace Francone's modest Cape house with the frenzy of a fireworks display. A quick check out the window revealed two cars parked in her driveway, one a sedan, a single twirling red light mounted to its dashboard, and the other a black-and-white from the Lynn Police Department, lights also flashing.

A wave of fear clutched Grace hard.

Not more than two hours ago, she had returned home from a run to find her sixteen-year-old daughter, Penny, gone. Since she was a teenager, it was no great surprise her daughter had left the house without a text or a note to say where she was going. Out of habit, Grace had checked the garage to find the burgundy Chevy Caprice, still registered to Penny's deceased father, was also missing. Grace assumed Penny, who had the car keys and her license, had taken it. The house rule was to always ask permission before taking the car, and to give a destination and return time. The lack of any such communication put Penny's driving privileges in jeopardy.

Naturally, Grace had texted Penny to check on her whereabouts. When she didn't get a reply, she figured Penny was trying to avoid a conflict. Now, Grace had a different thought.

The unexpected arrival of the police filled her with a dark vision of a twisted knot of steel, parts of it resembling what was once that Chevy Caprice. She imagined the vehicle had veered off a road somewhere, and now lay crumpled like a balled-up piece of paper. Penny was either still pinned in the wreckage, rushed to a hospital . . . or worse, much worse.

Grace opened the front door before the police had time to exit their vehicles. Outside, a crackle of indecipherable radio chatter momentarily drowned out the night-calling insects. Even though she lived a mile from the ocean, the air carried a tinge of salt, that special seawater smell that normally she found so rejuvenating. Not tonight.

Of the two men who strode up her walkway, only one was dressed in a police uniform. The other gentleman, a heavyset fellow, sported a thick mustache and wore a dark suit to match his hair. This one greeted Grace with an inscrutable expression, which set her somewhat at ease. At least his eyes didn't carry the weighty look of someone about to crush her soul.

"Ms. Francone?"

He had a deep, gravelly voice, good for coaching or getting hardened people to follow his orders. The best Grace could manage was a quick nod.

"I'm Detective Jay Allio from the Lynn Police Department, and this is Sergeant Brent Adams. Is your daughter Penny Francone?"

"Yes," Grace said, shifting her weight from one foot to the other, feeling her anxiousness fire back up.

"We came here to tell you that we've arrested her. She's at the Lynn Police Station right now."

Grace's field of vision blurred momentarily. "Arrested? For what?"

"We believe she killed a woman," Allio said, showing no emotion in his voice or face.

Grace used one hand to grip the doorframe while the other went to her chest, where she could feel her heart beating way too fast.

"Killed as in . . . what? Was it a . . . a car accident? Is Penny hurt?"

"No, it's not that," said Allio. "No accident. And Penny is uninjured. We believe it was a homicide."

The matter-of-fact way he shared this information made it hard for Grace to process his words.

"I'm sorry, what? Say that again."

"We believe Penny committed a homicide this evening."

"A murder?" Grace stammered. "You think my daughter *murdered* someone?"

Her words came out with a sharp edge as her grip on the doorframe tightened. She felt like she'd slipped out of her own body and was observing these events from some higher vantage point. Part of her wanted to slam the door in the detective's face, imagining that doing so might make it all untrue, but she resisted the irrational urge.

"When was the last time you saw your daughter?" Allio asked. His delivery seemed dispassionate, but Grace reminded herself that his job was to remain even-keeled when delivering seismic news. The other officer continued to hang back, giving Grace the distinct impression he was there simply to assist should she become unhinged or hysterical, either of which were real possibilities.

"A couple hours ago. When I'd gone for a run, and when I came back, she was gone," Grace said, fighting for every bit of composure she could muster. "When was she arrested?"

"She's been at the station a half hour or so."

A sharp twinge hit the back of Grace's neck, which she tried rubbing away with her hand.

"So have you talked to her? Asked her what happened?"

"We checked her license. She's a minor. It's our policy that we talk to you first."

Grace thought: *And I need to talk to a lawyer.*

"When we arrested her, she was covered in blood—it was all over her body, in her hair—so when you come to the station, you should bring a change of clothes."

"She's still in bloody clothes? You left her like that?"

"It's evidence," Allio said as explanation. "It takes time for us to collect the samples we need before we can let her get cleaned up."

"I need to get there—I need to leave right now." Grace felt the ground tilt beneath her feet.

"I understand," Allio said, continuing to radiate calm. "You need to take this a step at a time, okay? I have some more questions I'd like to ask."

"Blood," Grace whispered. "Oh my God. And you said she wasn't hurt?"

"No, there are no visible wounds on Penny. But the victim was found deceased at the scene, and we believe it's the victim's blood on your daughter's body."

Grace got the impression the detective was holding something back.

"She's calling herself Eve, but that's not the name on her license."

Again, a chill ran through Grace. *Eve.*

"She said she doesn't remember anything that happened before we showed up. We think maybe she's in shock, but we're not sure," Allio went on. "Is Eve a nickname?"

Grace paused, deciding how to answer. "It's more complicated than that," she offered sparingly, thinking that oversharing wouldn't do Penny any good. Thankfully, Allio decided to let it go.

"And you had no idea where Penny was headed when she left the house?"

"No, none," Grace said.

"Had she done that before?" Allio asked. "Taken the car and not told you where she was going?"

"No, it's against the rules," Grace said again, thinking *less is more.* "She likes to take walks. I thought maybe she took the car to go to the beach or something and forgot to tell me."

"Any reason she might have gone to Lynn? Does she have a friend there?"

Grace shook her head, reminding herself that Allio wasn't on her side. He had her daughter in custody and his agenda was different than hers.

"Have you noticed any changes in her behavior lately? Have you seen any anger, withdrawal, anything different?"

Grace mulled it over before answering. She was barely holding on. A slight breeze could totter her off some invisible edge into full-blown hysteria. For a moment she worried she was going to be sick.

"No," Grace finally managed. "Everything has been fine. I think I need a lawyer."

Allio's eyes danced across her face in an unsettling way, as if he knew much more than he was letting on.

"Let me ask you one last question, if I may. I'm sure you want to get down to the station. Do you know a woman named Rachel Boyd?"

For Grace, it felt as though time itself had come to a stop. Her body went numb, mind a blank.

"Rachel Boyd?" Grace repeated in a quiet voice.

"Yes. Do you know her?"

"Not personally, no. Is she . . . is she the victim?"

"Yes, Rachel has been murdered. Is there a connection between Penny and Ms. Boyd?" Allio asked.

Grace nodded insensibly. Her legs were shaking, barely able to hold her upright. "Yes," she said, her thoughts fading as her vision grew dark. "Rachel Boyd is my daughter's birth mother."

CHAPTER 2

GRACE WENT TO THE kitchen to retrieve her phone. She had a lawyer in mind, one who had become a regular at her restaurant, Big Frank's, an oceanfront pizzeria Grace had inherited from Arthur after his death.

Grace wasn't certain if Greg Navarro, attorney-at-law, would answer her call, what fee he'd charge, or if he'd even want to take the case. She also wasn't at all sure if he was as good as he presented himself to be; however she liked him a great deal. Which, given how they'd met, a fender bender over a month ago, could easily have gone the other way.

* * *

Grace had been driving in Vinnin Square, a highly congested area near the Swampscott Mall, when she felt a sharp jolt from behind. She heard a loud crunch before her seatbelt locked as she lurched forward. She was shocked at first, wondering what had happened, but a check in her rearview mirror revealed a blue car that was basically conjoined to her bumper. She pulled into a nearby Dunkin Donuts parking lot to escape traffic, and the blue car followed.

A survey of her Mini Cooper—which had a hundred and fifteen thousand miles on it and was nearly on its last axle—revealed a large dent in the bumper. Minimal damage aside, Grace was grateful not to be at fault, or else she'd have to pay the hefty deductible. Her small car fit the size of her life as well as her budget. Everything had shrunk in the wake of Arthur's sudden passing.

The man who'd struck her with his Ford Focus had the stocky build of a former jock, with sandy brown hair kept neatly trimmed above his ears. He was dressed nicely in a blue suit and white oxford shirt, unbuttoned at the top, no tie. His brown eyes brimmed with embarrassment. Below a broad forehead his eyebrows stayed noticeably arched, as though he were still surprised he'd struck her vehicle. Soon Grace realized it was a feature of his appearance and nothing more, as if he were perpetually questioning everything.

After making sure Grace was physically unharmed, he surveyed the damage.

"I was on my way to meet a client at a restaurant," the man said by way of explanation. "Took a wrong turn, went to check Waze, and . . . bam!" He smacked his hands together to reenact the impact. "Serves me right for taking my eyes off the road." He shook his head in utter dismay, clearly still upset with himself. "I'm just glad you're okay."

They exchanged insurance information, which is how Grace learned his name.

"I'm really sorry about this," Greg Navarro said, apologizing for the third time. "Such a novice move. I never get into accidents. Look, if you're ever in need of a lawyer—defense, personal injury, family, wills, estate—just give me a call. I have a practice here on the North Shore. I'll cut you a deal on my usual rate to make it up to you." He gave her his card, on which he had his mobile number listed.

* * *

Grace had hoped and prayed she wouldn't need a criminal defense attorney for Penny ever again. Once was enough. In the kitchen catch-all drawer, where she kept a business card holder, was the card of the attorney Arthur had hired when Penny and her friend Maria Descenza got arrested in ninth grade. Penny had been doing wonderfully well in the years since that awful incident, no trouble with the law, and Grace felt confident she had outgrown that disturbing behavior. Everyone, nobody more so than Grace, was shocked that girls so young could face such serious criminal charges for using words, not weapons, but the law was quite clear: if you threaten somebody's life, you will be arrested.

While Penny was complicit, a willing participant in the crime, Grace had no doubt Maria—or Firebug Maria as she was known around town thanks to a childhood habit of setting small fires, a nickname that carried over into her teen years—manipulated her daughter into writing those death threats.

The DA eventually agreed to drop the charges and seal Penny's record, but that privacy extended to schools and employers only. These detectives certainly had access to the case file, so they knew everything about her daughter's criminal history.

The descriptions of murder and mayhem, the horrible, dark violent fantasies that the girls secretly shared with each other included a "hit list" of targets—a list that Grace had no doubt was about to come back to haunt her daughter with a vengeance.

Penny's psychiatrist back then had played a critical role in the plea deal her daughter was given—far more so than the lawyer they'd hired, who Grace didn't like one bit. She found him unresponsive, sometimes taking days to get back to her with a simple answer. There was a reason she had deleted his contact information from her iPhone—and even Arthur concurred he was overly dismissive of their concerns.

Thankfully, though, she had a new lawyer to call, one who had proven himself to be kind and coolheaded in a crisis, and whom she'd come to know well enough to make him a grilled chicken Caesar salad for lunch without his having to place the order.

"I thought I'd make up for hitting your car by buying a few lunches, and I've honestly become addicted to the food," Navarro once said with a laugh.

She called Greg Navarro using a number in her phone's contacts, and to her great relief he answered after a couple rings. She didn't need to make an introduction, but still found herself saying, "It's Grace from Big Frank's," then, albeit breathlessly, broke the news about her daughter, recounting as quickly as she could the detective's visit and what he'd told her of Penny's arrest.

Navarro's first words back to her were delivered with quick and decisive precision.

"Tell the detective she can't be interviewed, and get yourself down to the police station soon as you can. Don't forget to bring her a change of clothes and a towel. They may not have one. I'm not sure they even have a shower. I'll call the station myself, soon as we're off the phone so they know she's not to talk to anybody, not until I get there. Give me thirty minutes, max. And Grace . . . "

"Yes?"

"Don't talk to the police either."

"Got it," she said.

He'd barely done anything to help her and already Grace liked him better than Penny's last lawyer. At Navarro's instruction, Grace handed the phone to Allio, who was waiting patiently outside. A moment later, Allio gave the phone back to Grace.

"He made it clear we're not interviewing her. But, if she wants to make a statement, it could definitely help her in court."

Score one for Navarro, who had anticipated she'd be pressured.

Grace followed Allio's sedan to the police station in her Mini Cooper, which had a new bumper thanks to her daughter's new lawyer. Allio had offered her a ride, but Grace declined. She needed to be alone with her thoughts, her fears. The only person's company she wanted had half his ashes dumped in the ocean, the other half stored in an urn on a shelf in the home they had shared for twenty years.

The police station was a fortress-like three-story brick structure. Allio directed Grace to a visitor's parking spot in the back of the building, where he waited for her before using a key card to open a metal door. He escorted her down a series of austere hallways until they came to a cramped, windowless room, which contained a small rectangular table pushed up against a soundproofed wall, some round-backed plastic chairs, and nothing more.

Pacing felt like the only way she could pass the minutes before Navarro got there. The younger officers who came to check on her called her "ma'am," offered to get her water, coffee, or tea, something to eat from the vending machine if she preferred, all of which she declined. Her stomach felt too unsettled to take in anything other than air, and even that wasn't going down smoothly given how tight and dry her throat had become.

Greg Navarro entered the room while Grace was responding to a text from her sister-in-law, Annie. She was making it clear to Annie not to tell Grace's two boys, Ryan and Jack, both of whom were attending college in Boston, anything other than what she had shared: that their sister Penny had been arrested, and details would be forthcoming.

Navarro came dressed in a blue suit and tie, similar to what he wore whenever he dined at Big Frank's. Seeing him made it easier to breathe.

"How are you?" he asked, taking a seat at the small table and encouraging Grace to do the same.

As she settled herself into the uncomfortable chair across from him, Grace managed to muster the lie: "I'm fine, thank you."

Navarro returned a look of encouragement. "Hang in there, all right?" he said. "We're going to take this a step at a time."

He handed Grace a plastic bottle of water, which he'd brought just for her, and she took a generous drink.

"Before we go on, we've talked some about your cases, and I know you're a very good lawyer, but I need to know that you've handled murder cases before." Grace couldn't believe she'd uttered those words in connection with her daughter.

"Trust me, you're in good hands, Grace," Navarro answered with assuredness. "I provide the gamut of legal services, but I specialize in criminal defense.

"I guess I haven't really shared my professional background with you, so let me do that now. I believe I told you that I grew up in Weymouth, graduated from Weymouth High. I gave the navy four years of my life, and they helped me pay for college. After I got out of the service, I went to law school at Suffolk and became a public defender here in Essex County. Worked in that office for fifteen years, and was chief public defender for eight of them. Plenty of lunches with the mayors. It was a great job, and I defended a lot of murder cases. Too many, sadly. The ones I couldn't win outright, I always got the best deal for my client.

"After my divorce I decided I needed a change, so that's why I went out on my own. I had a good reputation, and unfortunately a lot of past clients of mine were serial offenders. Some could afford a private attorney and they wanted the best, so they came back to me."

Navarro fixed Grace with a look that somehow managed to convey both empathy for her plight and confidence in his own ability.

"Okay, then," Grace said shakily. "Good. That sounds really good." Conversations about money and her concerns over how she'd pay for Navarro's fees could wait. "I guess though, well, there's something you should know about Penny before we speak to her. She's . . . been arrested before."

If the reveal were at all concerning, it did not register on Navarro's face.

"Okay, but is it relevant to these charges? Otherwise—"

Grace cut him off quickly.

"It think it's pretty relevant," she said. "A few years back, when Penny was only in ninth grade, she exchanged messages with a friend from town. A girl named Maria Descenza, who, like my daughter, has some mental health troubles."

"What kind of messages?" asked Navarro.

"They were dark, violent fantasies. Murder fantasies. Worse—dismemberment. It was all awful." She took a deep breath, then dove in. "They were really graphic and quite unsettling to read."

Grace didn't bother to share the weighty guilt she still felt for not keeping closer tabs on what her daughter did online. But did every parent read each text, track down every secret place kids went to hide private correspondences? True, she had more responsibility than most parents, given her daughter's illness, but still, Penny was a teen and entitled to some privacy.

"The girls wrote about how to commit the perfect murder, the methods of killing, all of it described in gruesome detail, the weapons they'd use, how they'd get away with it, that sort of thing, and they kept their exchanges hidden using Snapchat, Kik, and some vault app called KMSS—that stands for Keep My Secrets Safe."

"If it was so secret, how'd they get caught?" Navarro asked.

"Maria accidently sent a Snapchat message—a hit list the girls had made of potential targets—to the wrong person, another classmate at school. That girl shared it with her mother, who called the police."

"Naming specific targets is going to get you in a lot of trouble with the law no matter your age."

"Exactly. The police had no problem getting warrants to search the girls' phones and they found all the other messages, all the details."

"So was the charge attempted first or second degree murder?"

"Yes," said Grace, pleased to see Navarro had no trouble pinpointing what law they'd violated. "Second degree was the initial charge, got plea-bargained down to reckless endangerment, but that's not what's most relevant here, I think. The potential targets on that hit list included my son Ryan, who had a difficult relationship with his sister for reasons we don't have to get into right now, and also . . . Rachel Boyd."

Navarro blanched, and his Adam's apple jumped as he took a gulp of air.

"Rachel, the victim? Your daughter previously threatened the victim's life?"

Grace nodded grimly.

"Oh wow," he said, scratching at a spot on his scalp while reining in a grimace. "That's not great news for us," he said, a dip in his voice. He took a quiet moment to collect his thoughts, and Grace could almost see him get centered again.

"Okay," he said. "It's good information to have, and let's leave it at that. We're not going to focus on it right now. First thing I need to do is speak with Penny—alone. This is an attorney/client room, no recording devices, no cameras. The officer outside can take you to another room while Penny and I converse. Then I'll come get you after we're through."

"Another room? No," Grace said forcefully. "That's not happening. I need to see my daughter. I need to be in here when you talk to her."

Navarro took in Grace's demand with a tight-lipped expression, but he didn't look like he was about to acquiesce.

"Grace, I understand your desire here," he answered calmly. "But I don't want you to become a witness. I have no idea what's going to happen or what she might say. I have attorney-client privilege with Penny because she's my client, but *you're* not, so that privilege doesn't extend to you. It's possible you could be asked to testify *against* your daughter in court. It's too great a risk."

"That's my problem, not yours," Grace said, having no second thoughts about her stance. "She might be your client, but she's my daughter and I need to lay eyes on her. Either I stay in here with you, or I'm getting myself another lawyer."

Navarro took a moment to think it over, and Grace liked that he was listening to her, really listening. She also liked the relaxed manner in which he seemed to process his options.

"Okay, okay," he said eventually, letting his broad shoulders relax. "Let's bring Penny to you. You talk to her. See her. Give her a change of clothes. I'm assuming they've got the DNA they need. But no talking about the case, about what happened. Promise me that, Grace. You can't go there with her."

"I promise," Grace said.

"I'll do my interview in private, then come get you when it's over. If she gives me permission, I'll tell you what was discussed. Sound good?"

"Nothing about any of this sounds good to me," Grace answered bitterly. "Greg . . . there's something else you should know, something about Penny. When you see her, you may have to address her as Eve."

"Eve . . . is that a nickname?"

"Not exactly," said Grace, feeling an anxious flutter in her chest. She wasn't sure how this news would be received.

"My daughter has a disorder called DID, dissociative identity disorder." Nothing registered in Navarro's eyes.

"You probably know it as multiple personality disorder," Grace clarified.

"Oh," he said, and those arched eyebrows of his raised a notch higher.

"She's one person, and different people. I'm sure it was Eve, one of my daughter's personalities, who wrote those terrible things with Maria. And if she's somehow involved in the murder of Rachel Boyd, if she did it, I'll bet anything it was Eve, not my Penny, who committed the crime."

"I understand."

Grace gave a sad little laugh. "Then you may be the only one. Now, please . . . tell the police to go get my daughter."

CHAPTER 3

WHY DID YOU KILL?

That's the question I keep asking myself. That's what I have to figure out. It's the only thing that matters to me.

I'm working on a film about you. What I'm writing here are my memories, my musings—call it a diary of sorts—on the subject of you. According to Warren Brown, my film teacher at Emerson, these recollections and thoughts will help me separate feelings from facts, and allow me to put the events into some sort of logical sequence. Professor Brown says until I finish the exercise I won't know for sure how to structure my movie. He also said it's for my eyes only, he won't read a page of it, so I can be completely honest here.

I can tell my secrets, too.

Professor Brown thinks the film will get picked up for some big festivals, but I'm not making it to see my name, Jack Francone, on the big screen. I'm doing it because a jury isn't going to tell me what I need to know.

Are you ill . . . or are you evil?

I have no doubt in my mind that you are a murderer. The evidence against you is irrefutable.

You were alone in the house with the victim when the police arrived.

They found you with blood all over your body, sticking in your hair, caked on your hands, on your clothes, *holding* the murder weapon—a massive, bloodstained kitchen knife. That knife was used to stab Rachel *twenty-five* times. Twenty-five! It cut her throat so deeply, she'd almost been decapitated.

I've read all the reports, Penny. Mom got them from the lawyer and gave them to me to study when I told her about this project. I've also listened to the 911 call from Rachel's apartment so many times, I've got the transcript memorized.

"Nine-one-one, what's your emergency?"

On the recording the dispatcher's voice sounded calm and professional. She had no idea this was the call that was going to dominate headlines in Boston and around the nation for months to come. Sensational. Unprecedented. It was a newspaper's dream come true—and our family's worst nightmare.

"Nine-one-one . . . what's your emergency, please?"

All anyone could hear on the other end of the call was heavy breathing. It was a sound to make your skin crawl—in and out, slow and tortured, like each breath was going to be the last. The sound of death.

The dispatcher did her job admirably, tried to get the pertinent details, but to no avail.

"Can you talk? Can you tell me your name or location?" she asked. "What's the nature of your emergency?"

Now we know it was Rachel breathing heavily on the phone, but she couldn't answer, not with blood pouring through the opening you cut into her windpipe.

"Are you there?" the dispatcher asked, her voice betraying increasing concern. "Scratch or tap the phone if you're in trouble. Can you do that?"

In the recording you can hear a *tap, tap, tap,* like the sound of footsteps, only softer.

Tap. Tap. Tap.

"Are you bleeding? Are you hurt? Tap the phone again for yes."

Three more taps sounded.

The call came in at 7:08 that night. Police have to respond to all 911 calls—even the ones that are silent, or disconnected.

The dispatch system in Lynn has an automatic location identifier, so the operator knew where to send patrol cars. The cops had to break down the front door using a ram—a pared-down version of the same battering rams from the days of knights and castles, like the one in the picture book I used to read to you when we were little.

When the police entered the home, they found you standing in the doorway to Rachel's bedroom, bathed in her blood, holding a blood-stained knife in your hand.

You say you don't remember anything about that night, but it wasn't all blackout time for you though, was it? You shared a fuzzy memory (as Eve) with the police: looking out Rachel's grimy apartment window, trying to figure out where you were, why you might be covered in blood. You thought you saw somebody standing across the street, someone who seemed familiar to you, but you couldn't say more. You couldn't say if it was a man or a woman. You couldn't see a face or describe height or weight. None of it was stored in your memory bank, but you did recall checking again. When you did, nobody was there.

That's your mind, though, isn't it, Penny? How confusing it must be to live like that, with your thoughts and memories always shifting, like the sandcastles we loved making together on Eisman's Beach: here one minute, gone the next. Who can trust that brain of yours?

I was the closest to you growing up. In a way, I'm the one who found you, the reason we adopted you, and I was the first to see that you could be different people at different times.

So who is this person that could commit cold-blooded murder? I again ask: Are you truly evil?

I didn't know about dissociative identity disorder back then. According to the DSM-5 (the bible for psychiatric disorders), the condition can be diagnosed with the presence of two or more distinct personalities, or "alters," shorthand for alternate personalities. In cases of DID, there is the primary self and then there are the alters. You certainly presented that way, or so we all believed. Day to day, we never knew which Penny you'd be.

When you first got diagnosed, you were what? Thirteen, or thereabouts. I thought it explained all of your strange behaviors: those frequent memory gaps, your bizarre moods nobody understood. But what explains the violence, the death threats you made with Maria, the brutal murder of Rachel Boyd? DID doesn't explain any of that. The idea of an "evil alter" is a myth. It's the stuff of movies—and if there's one thing I know about, it's movies. So if there's no such thing as an "evil alter," how can I understand what you did that night?

Maria told the police she was sick in bed on the night of Rachel's murder, and her mother backed up that story. She insists you acted alone. Maybe. Maybe not. But let's say she's not fibbing and you went to Rachel's house alone and you lost control, that you were (as your lawyer intends to argue) legally insane at the time of the killing. I can imagine it. You saw Rachel for the first time since you were a little girl, and it triggered a memory buried deep inside your subconscious; some traumatic, unspeakable horror of what she did to you in the years before you came to live with us. We don't know anything about that time. You would never speak of it. But in that moment when you finally met face-to-face, terrible memories came at you like a flash flood.

Maybe it was you, Penny, holding that knife, or maybe it was one of your alters—a new one even, an avenger-type personality we haven't yet met, keeping in their rage for years like a powder keg awaiting a match.

Was Rachel that match? I read the Facebook messages that she sent you.

Hope it's okay to contact you this way . . .

Hope you don't mind . . .

I know this is hard for you, but I had to reach out . . .

Was she feeling you out, Penny, testing to see how'd you respond? You were hardly upset in your replies.

OMG! It's so crazy. I'm freaking out, you wrote to her.

Rachel wanted her messages to you to stay a secret. *You can't tell anyone we're in touch, not yet. Okay??*

And you were all for it.

Yes. Okay. Promise.

And you posted a picture of the fingers crossed emoji.

Did Rachel interpret your giddy glee as indication you'd forgotten how you'd suffered at her hand? Was that the last mistake she made in her messed-up life?

All this is just one possibility to consider: you, or your avenging alter, took vengeance on your past abuser. And if it can be proven in court that you couldn't control yourself, then you, Penny, will be found not guilty due to your mental illness. They'll sentence you to a secure psychiatric hospital where you'll receive the kind of care you need, and maybe one day you'll get better. Maybe all of your alters will go away, become integrated (that's the clinical term) into you, Penny, the host person. You may even get out of the hospital in time to have some sort of independent life.

But there's another possibility, one that I've considered carefully, as have many others, according to the blogs, social media posts, opinion pieces, and news reports about you and your crime: that you don't have DID, and you never did. That's not to say there isn't something wrong with you. Clearly there is. You might just be a psychopath, a person who chooses evil for evil's sake, a violent individual who doesn't care, who shows no remorse, the sort of person who deserves a lifetime behind bars.

It's not a stretch to think a psychopath would *invent* alternate personalities to justify and explain away all sorts of crimes, including murder.

So which is it? Have you been playing us all along? Was DID your invented excuse to do as you wished, until your wish included murder?

Or is your condition real, and you took Rachel Boyd's life in a fit of un-controllable violent rage to avenge some abuse you suffered long ago?

Are you deranged or damaged?

Sick or evil?

In the end, I pray my film will help me answer these questions.

CHAPTER 4

AT THE SOUND OF the doorknob's metallic jangle, Grace took in a breath and held it. She dreaded this moment and yearned for it at the same time. She had to see her daughter, to set eyes on her, but would it be Penny who greeted her, or somebody else?

A young uniformed police officer brought Penny into the room as nonchalantly as if he were delivering a package. Grace had to suppress a gasp of utter horror, as it looked to her as if Penny had crawled through a slaughterhouse on hands and knees to get here. Dark blood was everywhere—on her jeans, soiling her blue tee, staining her hands as if she'd dunked them into buckets of paint. The pungent smell of death that followed her into the room was something Grace thought she'd never forget.

"How could you leave her like this?" Grace seethed to the baby-faced officer, who/merely shrugged his shoulders in response.

"Sorry, nothing we could do about it. She didn't have a change of clothes."

"Well, someone could have found her something to change into, for goodness' sake," Grace scolded him.

"This isn't Walmart, ma'am," he said, in a calm and even voice that be-lied his years. "We're a police station; we don't have clothes to give her."

Or compassion, thought Grace.

She turned her attention back to the girl standing by the doorway. She certainly looked like Penny, tall and thin-limbed, with thick bands of straight hair held together in sticky clumps of dried blood. If someone were to scrub off the damn blood, she'd look like a normal teenager: round, smooth face unworn by years of experience, cheekbones on the cusp of being enviable, glimpses of the beautiful young woman she'd become.

For a fleeting moment, Grace allowed herself to believe it *was* Penny. But no, that was an illusion. This girl had a menacing stare that radiated anger.

So familiar. So heartbreaking.

So damn Eve.

Penny was the child Grace had raised, but she was perfectly attuned to her daughter's many mannerisms, speech patterns, moods, and behaviors. A squint of her wide eyes, a dip of her delicate shoulders, or an upward tic of her full lips might signal the arrival of someone new within, transforming her in a blink from friendly to sullen, from easy to anxious.

Each alter—and there were three Grace knew of, well below the average number of ten—was as distinct as any two people. There was Eve, the darkest and most outspoken of the lot; Chloe, the perfectionist, always striving for straight As in school; and Ruby, who spoke with a British accent. The alters were so different from each other, and from Penny, that Grace had come to view and treat them as individuals in the same way she did her two sons.

Right away, Grace noticed that something was missing. Her daughter always wore a necklace with an anchor pendant that Grace had bought for her. Penny never took off that necklace except to clean it, but now it was gone, probably stained with blood and bagged and tagged as evidence.

"About time you got here." Her daughter spoke in an acerbic tone. "Like Officer Charming here said, I could use something to change into."

Despite the coating of blood, Grace couldn't resist the urge to hug her daughter. As she approached with her arms outstretched, however, Penny raised her hands like two stop signs.

"Please, Mother," she said, grimacing. "I'm absolutely disgusting. I wouldn't think of hugging me. Get a grip, will you?"

The officer, who had remained in the room, spoke up.

"She needs to come with us to get changed. A female officer will take her clothes for evidence. We have a shower she can use. Your lawyer said I'm to escort you to another room so he can meet with your daughter in here, in private, after she's cleaned up."

"Okay, does that mean you can leave now so I can be alone with my mother?"

"Not right now, no," said the officer. "When your lawyer's here, I'll wait outside the door. But not before."

"Okay, after can I go home?"

The officer shook his head. "No, you need to be arraigned. Can't do that at least until morning."

"So I have to spend the fucking night in here?"

She spit the words. Most girls Grace knew, most anybody, would be quaking with fright in this situation, but Eve was hardly a typical girl. Her nature was to lash out and defend at all cost, which is why Grace intervened before her daughter could launch the protest she knew was coming.

"It's okay," Grace said, trying not to gape at her daughter's horrific state. She thought of Navarro, strong and steady, his advice to take it one step at a time, and found comfort in that mantra. Keeping a short distance between them, Grace handed her daughter the plastic bag Detective Allio had already searched.

"Here's your change of clothes, Penny," she said. She wasn't thinking when she spoke, but regretted it the moment the word left her mouth. *Penny.*

Her daughter looked as though she'd been given an open-palm smack to the face.

"What the hell, Mother?" she snapped. "I've got blood all over me," she gestured to her body, "I've been arrested, my wrists hurt something awful—the *least* you can do is get my damn name right."

She presented her wrists to Grace as if that were the worst part of her deplorable condition. Sure enough, there were bright red rings marring her skin where handcuffs had been. Penny then turned to the officer standing close by and whispered loud enough for Grace to hear: "My mother might be on something . . . you know . . . something *e-legal*. You may want to check her purse before she leaves."

The stoic young officer failed to restrain a reluctant smile.

"And just so you know, Officer Charming," Penny continued, "my name is Eve. Eve Francone. I'm seventeen years old. I can tell you that, and I can tell you where I live, but I don't *have* to tell you a damn thing if I don't want to. I know my rights."

Grace shivered at the precision of her daughter's speech. It was as if she'd rehearsed the words in advance, knowing she'd need them. Then again, that was her job. Eve had always been full of aggression and rage. (*Stay away! Back off!*) In that capacity, she functioned as Penny's guardian.

"We all have 'Eves' inside of us," Grace had told Penny's brothers in an attempt to put their sister's DID condition into a more relatable context. "She's the angry one who lashes out when you get cut off by an inconsiderate driver. Or the revenge fantasy of what you'd say or do after you get your heart broken, or you're fired from a job. Eve is the girl you'd *want* on your side when you need someone to look after you. Now I'm counting on you two, her brothers, to look after her."

Penny was always so reserved, so unsure of herself, and, at least according to one of her elementary school teachers, painfully timid. She would have shriveled like a raisin in the presence of any uniformed officer, talking in a voice so soft she'd have been asked to repeat every word. But this girl had no trouble holding court or expressing her needs. Now that Grace knew for certain one of her daughter's alters had taken over, she would no longer think of this girl as Penny. No, this was Eve.

Eve removed the items from the bag. In Grace's rush to get to the police station, she had grabbed dirty pajamas and a blue sweatshirt out of the laundry room hamper.

"Oh my God, these clash horribly, Mother," said Eve, holding up the clothes with a scornful look, which Grace found utterly chilling.

Thanks to plenty of therapy and practical experience, Grace knew Eve's antics were merely a mask, a protective shield, nothing more. Underneath that false and misplaced bravado lurked a terrified young woman trapped in an utterly foreign, incomprehensible situation. Eve had taken over for Penny as was her duty and obligation, because Penny couldn't survive in here—and nothing Eve said could be taken personally.

Grace had done her duty as well. She'd laid eyes on her child; seen that she was okay and appeared uninjured. She could let her go and sit with her thoughts and the profound ache of helplessness that was sure to be her new constant companion.

"Just know I'm here, okay?" Grace said, hoping her words meant something. "I love you, and I'm not going to leave you alone. I'll be with you every step of the way."

"They said I killed somebody. Who did I kill?"

Grace wanted to know everything—to ask her what happened, how she'd reconnected with her birth mother, what triggered her rage. She wanted to know it all, but then thought of Navarro.

"We'll talk later, okay?"

It took incredible restraint to muster that simple response.

"Why don't I take her now," the officer in the room said, perhaps sensing things were about to head south, and fast. "We'll get her changed and cleaned up, and I'll bring you to a room where you can wait in private for your attorney."

"Oh, don't look so glum, Mother," Eve said, putting her bloodied hands together in a prayer pose. "Think about the bright side. You won't have to worry about paying for my college now."

The smile that overtook Eve's face held nothing but malice.

"Go get changed. I'll see you soon. I love you . . . Eve," Grace said, catching herself before she used the wrong name again.

* * *

After meeting with Penny, Navarro entered the small room off a kitchen area where Grace was waiting. He wore a solemn expression, and his complexion appeared to have gone a bit ashen. It was disturbing to think that Eve could drain the life force from even the most seasoned defense attorney.

"Well?" Grace asked nervously.

"Well, we've got our hands full, that's for sure," said Navarro. "Thanks for that warning, by the way. She was quite upset that you called her the wrong name, but she did give me permission to talk to you about what we discussed, so I'm free to share some of what we talked about."

"Thank goodness for that," said Grace, feeling a mix of relief and anxiety. "What did she say?"

"She said she doesn't remember taking the car, how she got to Rachel's house, or even why she went there in the first place. And she told me definitively that she doesn't remember killing Rachel Boyd."

"Is she devastated? It's her birth mother."

Grace braced herself, unable to fully grasp how shattering that news would be.

"No, and I suspect we need some professional guidance in that regard. I'm surprised, though, at her lack of memory. It doesn't strike me as a convenient memory gap."

"It's not that. It's a major symptom of DID, but it's far more severe than being forgetful." Grace hated the sinking feeling in her bones. "When she switches alters, it's possible, probable really, that she can't recall specific events, people, things she's said or done, even something like this. Sometimes those memories belong to someone else—to another alter, or to her primary self, to Penny. But it could be, if the event is truly traumatic, she might enter a dissociative fugue state, a type of amnesia that could last for minutes, hours, months . . . even years."

"Wow," Navarro said, setting a hand on his chin. "Clearly I've got some research to do."

"I have a lot of information I can give you," Grace told him. "With time, when it's less stressful, she may have new memories to share."

It felt good to stay proactive. Her other option was to do what, become immobilized? Useless? Catatonic? That simply wasn't Grace's way. The more time she spent with Navarro, the more comfortable Grace was with her decision to move on from that other attorney. She felt certain by the end of the evening they'd work out a formal agreement and she'd remind him of the rate cut he had offered. She imagined there'd be a lot of free lunches in his future.

"What now? What happens next?" Grace asked.

"Next she'll be arraigned. We're still sorting out the indictment, but given her history, I'll petition the court for a full psychological evaluation."

"Do you think we can win on an insanity verdict?"

Navarro raised a hand as an indication to proceed slowly and with caution.

"One step at a time, like I said. This is a marathon, not a sprint. But the court should grant a request to have her hospitalized at a secure facility for the evaluation period, twenty days to start, and it could be extended from there."

"A hospital," said Grace. "That's good, right? It's better than jail."

Navarro's face harbored a cryptic look. "There's only one state hospital with the strict security the court will demand that takes patients of the same age and gender as Penny."

"And that is?"

"Edgewater State Hospital," Navarro said, his voice carrying evident dismay. "It's part of the Mass Department of Correction."

"But it is a hospital, right?" Grace asked.

"Yes, but Grace, I'm just being honest here, knowing Edgewater, its reputation . . . I have clients who are sentenced there, and, well, it's not the best place in the world. It's less healthcare facility and more housing for the criminally insane. In fact, part of me thinks prison would be better."

CHAPTER 5

WE DIDN'T GET ALL the details until we gathered at the kitchen table in Swampscott. It was just the three of us—Mom, me, and Ryan—though I'd swear I felt Dad's presence like a ghost hovering in the room. Mom told us what happened, starting from the detective at the door to seeing you as you were, covered in blood, like that scene in the movie *Carrie*—the one starring Sissy Spacek, forget the remake.

Mom's a stoic, doesn't like to show her vulnerable side. But that night, her dazed look, the way her jaw was set tight enough to crack the bone, told me the burden was more than even she could bear.

I was shaken to the core, couldn't believe my ears, but Ryan's reaction, well, it sort of surprised me. He looked—I don't know exactly how to put it—but I guess smug is the word, sitting there, sipping an icy Coke, like he knew all along that you were dangerous and one day something like this would happen.

As your alters became more apparent Ryan couldn't take it, wanted less and less to do with you, stopped trusting you entirely. I don't know how much of his distancing was your DID, which he didn't believe was real, or that he continued to blame you for Dad's death.

You know what, I worry about Ryan. When you carry that kind of resentment around long enough it stews inside, cooking blame into a foul-tasting anger.

But nothing compares to your anger, does it? After your arrest, you put someone else in charge. Your switches have lasted days, maybe a month even, but *never* for this long. Almost a year and a half now since you've been gone, the entirety of your time locked up in that psych hospital while awaiting trial. It feels a bit like you abandoned us, ran away, leaving us with the harshest, cruelest, most caustic and hard to handle of all of your alters.

You left us with Eve.

I still don't know if you were excited to see your birth mother or if all that was just an act. Did you know from the moment she made contact with you what you were going to do? What you wrote to her in your first exchange was either quite tender or quite cunning. All this time later, I'm still not sure.

I am sure that I miss you, Penny. I really do. You're my sister and I love you, and I always will, no matter how the court eventually rules, in your favor or not.

Over the year and a half you've been away, I've amassed pages about your case for my film diary. I know all the maneuvers Attorney Navarro has made on your behalf. I also have a detailed inventory of all evidence gathered. I can tell you this: the prosecution has a lot more of it than the defense.

Mom won't say it often, but she's mentioned it on occasion, the possibility that somehow you're innocent. I call it wishful thinking, but there was a guy—Vince Rapino is his name—who piqued my interest early on. Rapino was something of a two-bit criminal from Lynn, same town Rachel lived in, who allegedly put crime aside to start an auto repair business. His name was on the lease to Rachel's apartment, which is how the police found out those two were having an affair. Rapino was married at the time, but he wasn't a suspect because he had an alibi, thanks to his wife. That is a bit unfortunate for you, because from what I've read of him he's a real dirtbag.

Nothing about your case has produced any big surprises. You were determined fit to stand trial. The forensic psychologist who did the assessment wrote that you were manipulative, clever, quick-witted, and potentially quite dangerous.

Hard to disagree there.

The court ordered you hospitalized at Edgewater for your psych evaluation for twenty days, and that got extended another twenty, as the law allowed.

Your shrink at Edgewater was a guy named Dr. Dennis Palumbo, who we all despised. Well, maybe all but Ryan, because Palumbo thought the same thing he did: that you didn't *have* DID. According to Palumbo, DID wasn't even a real condition, and didn't belong in the DSM. Turns out that what you have (or I guess allegedly have) is quite the polarizing diagnosis. There are no lab tests to confirm a case of DID, no genetic or hereditary component to use as a marker, and some experts believe the amnesia barrier, those vast memory gaps of yours, belong to the world of fiction, not fact. It's thought that DID is just a variant of a borderline personality disorder, or in your case an antisocial personality disorder, and that the appearance of your alters is akin to fantasy play rather than a verifiable neurological state.

In short, Palumbo thought you were an expert liar.

You did take a polygraph test and passed. Later, I found out that those tests aren't indicative of anything in your case. In your deluded mind you might believe, and hence convey it as truth to the machine, that you have no memory of killing Rachel Boyd. You're lying, but you believe it, so it's true to you, even though it's really a lie.

It's enough to make your head spin. Or at least mine. I guess you're used to it.

When it came to your chances in court, Navarro wasn't nearly as gloomy and despondent as Mom. Juries have believed the DID defenses before, he told us.

He was right, too. I've studied those cases, a few examples at best.

The highest-profile and most recent was the murder trial of Thomas Huskey, which ended in a hung jury. According to Huskey's public defender, an alternate personality named Kyle had done the killings, not Thomas, who Kyle claimed to hate. Huskey was convincing too, employing different voices, mannerisms. Even his dominant hand varied depending on the personality. Kyle was left-handed, Thomas right A if it had been Mom or me on that particular jury in Tennessee, undoubtedly we both would have believed him, for his condition was chillingly similar to yours.

You were facing fifty years in prison, maybe more, and that, Penny, is only because of your young age at the time of the murder. Navarro, to his credit, understood his job wasn't to add weight to Mom's worry.

"We're taking things a day at a time," he kept telling us.

One day turned into another, and eventually it became a year and a half of your life spent in Edgewater State Hospital, locked up with the crazies, the violent offenders who didn't belong in a regular prison. That didn't make them any less dangerous, though.

While Edgewater may have been an ailing institution, a deplorable place to be, you asked to stay there, and Mom agreed. At least Edgewater had the veneer of a hospital, and you could receive consistent psychiatric care there.

That's why Mom had Navarro petition Ruth Whitmore, the facility director, to allow you to continue your care and treatment there while the proceedings against you were still pending.

It was the lesser of two evils, Mom concluded, but I've visited you, Penny, and five minutes inside is five minutes too long. How you've survived all this time in that hellhole is beyond me. I guess you have Eve to thank for that.

Aside from your defense, the biggest worry we had was money. Navarro was good, but he wasn't cheap. Not to make you feel worse, but Mom had to take out an equity loan on the restaurant to afford the forty-thousand-dollar retainer. And that was not nearly going to cover the rest of the charges she'd accrued. I'd offered to drop out of school, but Mom put her foot down.

Ryan, though, he didn't give her a choice.

That August, a few weeks after your arrest, Ryan was supposed to go back to Northeastern for his senior year and start taking those law school classes he'd been dreaming about since his high school days as a star on the debate team. Getting accepted into the PlusJD program—Northeastern's prestigious fast track to law school—was no easy feat, and I thought he couldn't wait to begin. Instead he dropped out, quit, no word of warning, just announced that he wasn't going back for his last year of school. He wouldn't say why.

Mom had a meltdown, of course. It was hard enough having you living in Edgewater, but add to that a son working the pizza ovens at Big Frank's, following Dad's footsteps instead of his own dreams—it broke her heart. But Ryan's an adult, he can make his own decisions, and Mom wasn't about to deny him employment. The restaurant is a family business, after all. Since he's been working there, Ryan's become the general manager, and he's done a good job of it, too, though business is down because of the notoriety around your case.

The whole family has suffered, Penny, and we're not any closer to understanding you or what you did not for lack of trying, though. Since I'm something of a film buff, I've watched all the movies I could about multiple personality disorder. *The Three Faces of Eve,* which put Joanne Woodward on the starlet map. Funny enough, your Eve alter came out even though you've never seen the film. *Sybil,* a story we all know, but maybe more have seen the movie than read the book. You were even dubbed "The Sybil of Swampscott." Cruel, I thought, but people don't understand DID, and sadly Hollywood doesn't do a great job explaining it.

More recently I watched that movie *Split,* from the mind of M. Night Shyamalan. James McAvoy gave a good sense of what having a chaotic and disorganized mind might feel like, but that's not the mind of a cold and calculating psychopath.

That's what Palumbo thinks you are. Remorseless. Ruthless. Totally lacking empathy. Faking your alters to do as you please. And maybe he's right. Maybe you're more like a heartless killer than you are Kevin from *Split* with his twenty-three personalities.

One thing I know for sure—Edgewater is the sort of place where you can't get better, but you sure can get a whole lot worse.

CHAPTER 6

FROM THE OUTSIDE, EDGEWATER State Hospital—approached via a series of wide, tree-lined streets—looked exactly like a prison. A tall chain-link fence topped with rows of razor wire enclosed a series of three-story square brick structures Houses, they were called, with thick iron rods fronting dingy rectangular windows. Inside one of those second-floor windows was the room where Grace's now-seventeen-year-old daughter slept.

Good as it would be to set eyes on Penny, it would be Eve whom she'd visit today. It was always Eve in here.

Since her daughter's arrest, Grace's harried days were filled with running the restaurant as well as meeting with Navarro whenever developments required her attention, or her pocketbook. Soon, maybe today, she'd have a sit-down with Dr. Mitchell McHugh, Penny's new doctor here, to discuss strategy—not only for her daughter's treatment, but for the upcoming trial as well.

She was glad Dr. Palumbo had finally resigned. Good riddance to him. Her primary hope was that Dr. McHugh would not only believe DID warranted its own classification in the DSM, but that her daughter *had* the condition. While Palumbo was out of her life for good, Grace would see the ghost of him soon enough. The assistant district attorney, Jessica Johnson, had an expert witness prepared to testify that DID wasn't a valid diagnosis, and that Penny suffered from a severe antisocial personality disorder.

Would McHugh be an ally or an adversary? She'd find out soon enough.

Trudging across a parking lot turned scorching hot under an unrelenting July sun, Grace made her way along a curved walkway leading to the secured entrance of Abbot House. Weeds sprouted up through the many cracks in the paving stones. In her mind, everything about this godforsaken place, from its decrepit exterior with its chipped brick and nonexistent landscaping to its bile-yellow interior walls, was cracked. Jack would say if you weren't crazy when you came in, that's what you'd be when you got out.

My daughter is here . . . my girl . . . my heart.

Off in the distance, Grace spied the tops of two other units poking up from behind Abbot House. When taken together, these three buildings and the series of tunnels that connected them comprised the entirety of the Edgewater complex. One building housed the men, another the women, and a third, the oldest building of the bunch, provided residency for the most violent, volatile, and difficult-to-manage patients. The names of these structures—Crane, Hartwell, Abbot— seemed fitting for a college campus, but these weren't dorms. The rooms were cells.

At the visitors' entrance, Grace pressed a round door buzzer so that someone peering through a camera mounted above her head could grant her entry. There were five people in the spare and uninviting waiting room, none of whom she recognized. Good. Nobody, including the paid employees, wanted to be here, so eye contact and small talk were avoided at all costs.

Accustomed to the routine, Grace handed her ID to a stone-faced woman working the screening desk in a cubby-sized space secured behind Plexiglas. After completing the check-in procedure, Grace stored her purse in an empty locker, closing it with a lock she'd brought from home. An armed guard emerged from behind a heavy steel door secured with a biometric apparatus and keypad. Grace found it ironic that the "hospital"—and she used that term lightly—had elected to upgrade their security systems before they addressed the insufferable "patient" accommodations—"patient" being another word she used lightly.

Grace endured yet another pat-down before clearing the metal detector and finally gaining entry to a long, windowless corridor that had the stale smell of a bus station. Two armed guards escorted her to a private visiting room that was no more than twelve feet from door to wall.

Normally lawyers used these sparsely furnished rooms to confer in private with their clients, but the overcrowding necessitated a creative use of space. Grace preferred these private quarters whenever she could reserve one. Her daughter didn't behave as well in a crowd.

A powerful ammonia aroma hit Grace with force the moment she set foot inside. The miasma of harsh chemical clung to the air, stinging her eyes and making them water. *What the heck happened in here?* she wondered. A number of disgusting possibilities necessitating fumigation flittered in and out of her mind.

Resting on top of a table in the middle of the room was a pizza, steaming inside a corrugated box (the sort Grace could have assembled blindfolded). Opening the box, Grace observed tiny ovals of pepperoni spread out evenly across a molten landscape of bubbling cheese. Her daughter had grown up hating pepperoni, even disliked the word, but it wasn't Penny who'd be eating this lunch. It was Eve, and that girl happened to love, simply love, meat on her cheese.

Even though Grace owned a pizzeria, she'd preordered this meal from a local establishment. The rules about food were clear and reinforced with ample signage:

All takeout food must come from an approved restaurant.

You cannot use a patient's name on a food order.

You cannot order food with bones, beverages, chopsticks, glass, plastic or paper bags, or metal of any kind (including aluminum foil).

Beverages may be purchased in the shared visitation room.

You must clean up the room after a visit.

Grace had her own set of rules for these visits:

Don't talk about her father. It always upsets her.

Try to smile.

Don't talk about the case.

Don't give her any reason to become more hostile.

But how could her daughter not be angry in a place like this? Everywhere she went, every corridor she traveled, mournful wails and constant chatter ricocheted off the concrete walls, blending into one great squawking like an aviary out of a nightmare. This was no place for a young woman to be, but here she was.

The door soon opened. Grace took in a breath and held it. This was the moment when hope dies: first contact, those initial few seconds that always gave way to disappointment. Once a week Grace would make the hour-long drive to Edgewater, each time praying to see Penny's guileless eyes beaming back at her, only to encounter the angry, cold stare of Eve.

Her daughter stomped into the room, took a whiff or two of the ammonia-heavy air, and paused. She wrapped her arms around her chest, suddenly looking unsure, and tottered on her feet. The change in her bearing happened in an instant, leaving Grace utterly perplexed. She considered the girl standing before her, so unsteady that she seemed drugged.

They've overmedicated her, Grace fumed.

From memory, Grace recalled the drugs her daughter was taking: 225 milligrams of venlafaxine for anxiety and depression along with some dosage of lurasidone, often given as a stabilizer or antipsychotic for teens with bipolar depression. In her daughter's case, these were mood boosters, not treatments for psychosis. The grim fact remained that no medication on the market specifically treated dissociative identity disorder.

Physically, nothing appeared amiss. Her daughter was dressed in her usual attire, something akin to dark green hospital scrubs. She'd lost weight in here, and the uniform had become so loose it was as though she'd slipped on a garbage bag.

Her daughter shuffled forward in a daze. Up close, she looked even more hollowed out.

Damn medications. Damn doctors. Maybe this McHugh fellow will actually have a clue.

She hadn't scheduled a meeting with McHugh for today, but seeing her daughter so off-kilter made her think she couldn't delay.

Grace waved away the correctional officer, or CO for short, a man named Blackwood, according to the nameplate pinned to his shirt. Blackwood's close-set eyes narrowed, and he smiled tightly, but made no protest. Except for Crane House, the rest of Edgewater was a medium-security facility, affording Grace some privacy during these visits. She closed the door.

"Are you okay, Eve? You don't seem yourself."

Thinking back to that night so long ago in the police station, aware how triggering it could be, Grace did not hesitate to call Penny by another's name. Except this wasn't Eve whom she'd helped guide into a seat at the table, and it wasn't Penny either. This child was an empty slate, with dead eyes and the expressionless face of a mannequin, giving no clues as to who might occupy the consciousness within.

Grace saw her daughter blink several times in rapid succession before touching her head, as if suffering from a headache.

What the heck did they give her?

It occurred to her that Dr. McHugh may have in fact caused the problem, prescribing new meds or doses on a whim, trying to make his mark without first knowing the patient or the case. This place was so backward it made Grace fume with anger.

Lifting the lid on the pizza box, Grace freed a cheesy scent that battled back the lingering aroma of ammonia.

"What's this?"

Out of nowhere, it was Penny's gentle voice asking the question, not Eve's harsher cadence.

A knot of concern formed at the base of Grace's neck before the shock and panic set in.

Oh no . . . what if . . . ?

"It's pizza, darling. Your favorite."

"I hate pepperoni," she said, sounding perplexed that her mother of all people could have forgotten.

Oh no . . . no . . . no . . .

The rest of the switch took place before Grace's eyes. There was a slight rounding of her daughter's shoulders as her body sagged forward, and as it did, Penny's familiar tight-lipped worried expression came into being.

"Where am I?" Penny asked.

Alarms rang out in Grace's head. She couldn't speak, didn't know how to begin.

"What is this place, Mom?" Penny's head moved as if on a swivel, darting this way and that, taking in her surroundings: the drab concrete walls, the scuffed-up table, the dirty floor, baffled by it all. She tugged on her uniform, her hands now trembling.

"What's going on here?" Her gentle voice shook with rising panic.

Her daughter wasn't drugged. She was in the middle of a switch from Eve back to Penny, a switch that had been triggered for reasons unknown.

She doesn't know. God help her, Grace thought. *Penny doesn't know what happened.*

From Penny's perspective, she'd come back from being Eve into a strange place, with no idea where she was, no memory of how she'd come to be here. A fugue state—that was how Grace had explained it to Navarro, who had asked about the memory gaps that occurred when one alter took over from another. The personalities were so distinct that some specialists speculated there wasn't any room for shared memory.

"Where . . . am I?" Penny asked again.

"Let me get Dr. McHugh," Grace said, her anxiety pulsing like a throbbing wound.

If she knew the truth . . .

"Who is Dr. McHugh?"

Grace had to think fast how to respond. "He's the person looking after you," she said.

And he's going to have a hell of a first week on the job.

"Looking after me? Where?" Again, Penny tugged on her uniform, which must have seemed so foreign to her.

"You're in a hospital," Grace said, still reeling.

"For what? Am I hurt?" Penny surveyed her arms, her hands, looking for signs of injury, finding none.

"No, darling. Nothing like that. It's not that kind of hospital."

"Then what? Mom, what am I doing here?" Desperation leaked into her daughter's voice. She clutched her sides tightly, as if holding herself together. "Please . . . please . . ." Tears seeped into her eyes. "Tell me what's going on."

Eve had never been a welcome member of the family, but Grace found herself desperately missing that girl's brash bravado and cool confidence.

You can't tell her, not now, not without guidance.

As much as Grace had prayed for this moment, for Penny's return, she wasn't at all prepared for her sudden appearance.

CHAPTER 7

"WHY AM I HERE, Mom?"

Mom . . . that's what Penny always called her, not Mother.

Sinking to her knees, in that pious position, Penny tugged urgently on her hair, one clump clutched in each hand, as if doing so could somehow pull the answer from her head. Bright color flooded her cheeks, red as a warning. Her mouth quivered before thick tears rained down.

"Relax, sweetheart," Grace said, stepping forward with the tentativeness of a rancher approaching a wild colt. She knew any effort to calm her would be in vain.

In response, Penny rose to her feet to face the wall behind her and began pawing frantically at the concrete as if to dig her way out.

Her futile attempt at escape was blessedly short-lived. Turning to face the only exit, Penny squared off with two guards who had appeared, summoned from the ether. One was CO Blackwood, who moments ago had escorted Penny to his room. Grace remembered his dimpled chin and those narrowly spaced eyes. She didn't know the name of his heavier-set companion, but both he and Blackwood lurked in the doorway, impassively watching the situation escalate. They had their guns holstered, while other implements used for command and control: handcuffs, sprays, Tasers, maybe chemical restraints—were secured inside the leather pockets and holders of their utility belts.

To Grace's utter astonishment, Penny held her ground, eyeing her adversaries with an uncharacteristic fiery stare. When it became evident that these professional guards weren't going to be intimidated by a young girl, Penny's arms fell limply to her sides as if accepting defeat. A flash of hope passed through Grace—perhaps this was an act of surrender. Then, without warning, Penny darted forward, generating a surprising burst of speed for such a short distance. She slammed into Blackwood, bouncing backward as though the man were made of rubber.

The larger of the pair came barreling into the room, a determined stare on his stern face. Blackwood followed him in, and the ensuing takedown was effortless, not a movement wasted, the outcome never really in doubt. CO Blackwood took hold of one of Penny's wrists, and with his palm pressed firmly against her shoulder, brought her arm back until she fell forward and facedown onto the floor. She hit the ground hard, striking her head on the unforgiving cement surface with a thud.

"You're hurting her!" Grace shrieked.

Penny groaned but couldn't clutch her injured head because the other guard had violently wrenched her hands behind her back and was attempting to click the handcuffs in place. Resisting as best she could, Penny grunted while straining to pull her arm away. It wasn't until Blackwood unclipped his baton that Grace intervened, latching on to the man's beefy shoulders with two hands and turning her fingers into talons as she tried to pry him off her daughter. She was no match for the man's muscle, though, and to Grace's horror, the baton came up to shoulder height, ready for a strike.

As she opened her mouth to scream, a stern male voice crackled from the direction of the open door.

"Drop it this instant!"

Grace turned her attention to the doorway, where she saw a gentleman with a shock of silver hair atop his head, his handsome face partially obscured by a trim beard speckled with brushstrokes of gray. He strode into the room carrying the authority of an Old West sheriff, eyes burning like two embers.

"What the hell do you think you're doing?" he asked of CO Blackwood. "Are you seriously considering striking her with that baton?"

Blackwood clambered to his feet, hovering over Penny with his head lowered, while the beefier CO tried to melt into a wall.

"Put that damn thing away," the man said. "Protocol allows batons only when you are in physical danger. Are you telling me that this unarmed girl posed a serious threat to you?" He pointed an accusatory finger at Blackwood, and away the baton went, back into its auto-lock holder with an audible snap.

The man with the silver hair and trim beard helped Penny to her feet. His focus went straight to the bright red mark now marring her forehead. He examined the injured area closely.

"Mom . . ."

Penny's strangled voice tore through Grace.

"Get her to the ER straightaway," the man ordered the guards through gritted teeth. Grace knew Penny wouldn't be leaving the premises. Like all prisons, Edgewater had its own emergency room.

"I'll be there in a minute," he continued. "And if I hear one word," he held up a single finger for emphasis, "that you two manhandled this patient in any way, you'll both be looking for a new job come morning. Now go."

In a flash, Penny was ushered outside. Grace knew she wouldn't be allowed to accompany Penny, so she focused instead on the thin man in the tweed blazer who had prevented her daughter from what could have been a grievous injury. Behind his tortoiseshell glasses were brown eyes the color of caramel, which now projected kindness and compassion. His face was open and friendly, but etched with enough lifelines to suggest that today wasn't the first time he'd come to another's rescue.

Grace extended her hand and officially made the acquaintance of Dr. Mitch McHugh.

CHAPTER 8

THIRTY MINUTES HAD GONE by since Dr. McHugh had escorted Grace to his cramped office, then left her alone to check on Penny in the ER.

Have they given her x-rays? Grace wondered. *Checked for head trauma? Or did they just dope her up with Haldol like Palumbo would have done?*

The walls where McHugh worked were the same drab yellow found in the patients' quarters, which made the space feel rather cell-like. It was a fitting aesthetic, Grace thought, because she was certain this doctor's new job here was a sentence for something he'd done elsewhere in life. She'd seen it on his face, caught it lurking behind his eyes—a look that hinted at secrets and unfortunate outcomes, a maze of decisions that had somehow conspired to bring him to this godforsaken place.

When Dr. McHugh finally returned, Grace got to her feet quickly, bracing herself for bad news.

"How is she?"

McHugh sent a look of pure and unfiltered empathy, as if a gaze could reach out and wrap her in a hug. She didn't detect a single whiff of arrogance about him, and allowed herself to think he might actually be an ally in this fight.

"She's going to be fine," he said, sounding a warm and encouraging note. "Dr. Bouvier is looking after her, and he's an excellent physician from what I can tell. She's resting in the ER right now. I'll go check on her soon, though I may require an escort. Not entirely sure I can find the place on my own." Grace had never roamed the halls here or visited the underground tunnels that connected the various buildings in the Edgewater complex, but she imagined they could be as confusing as a rabbit warren.

Grace said, "Is she drugged?" She hated to use the words "chemically restrained," but that's really what she meant.

"No, it's not advisable in cases of head injury," he said. "There could be a mild concussion. I've talked to her though, and she seems fine, emotionally, that is."

"Well, how could that be?" Grace's eyebrows shot up. "She must be sick with fright."

"We've kept the most damaging information from her," explained Dr. McHugh.

"Is it . . . is it still Penny?" Grace's voice was hopeful.

"When I asked her name, that's the one she gave me."

Grace let go a sigh. Her girl, her heart, was still here.

"We told Penny she's in a special mental care hospital, one related to her condition, and that seemed to suit her fine. She's accustomed to being treated and evaluated."

"Oh, thank goodness. What a nightmare. If Penny knew what really happened . . . if she had any idea . . . it's . . . it's never been Penny, you see. *She's* never been here before. It's always been Eve." Grace couldn't get her thoughts straight, but she sensed Dr. McHugh was following her just fine.

"Eve is the more . . . difficult of the alters, am I right?"

Grace returned a succession of resigned nods. "Yes, she's always been the angry one . . . filled with rage, really, so it makes sense she'd be the one to stick around in a place like this." Grace gestured at McHugh's office as though it were emblematic of all that was wrong with Edgewater.

"From what I saw today, Penny needed all the anger and rage she could muster to defend herself," McHugh said. "I'm surprised she didn't revert to Eve for protection."

"Me too," said Grace. "I don't know what triggered the switch, but maybe there's a reason Eve *couldn't* return."

"Could be," said McHugh. "As I work with her, hopefully we'll get an answer. I want you to know, I'm reporting that guard with the baton, Blackwood, for disciplinary action. Good gracious." He shook his head in utter dismay. "First week on the job and I'm already making friends and influencing people. Apologies for the mess," he said, gesturing to the towers of moving boxes, some piled three high, many with packing tape still in place. "Still settling in. Sit, please."

"So, do you think Eve will come back?" Grace asked once they'd both seated themselves. She heard a tickle of apprehension enter her voice.

McHugh tugged at his beard as he lowered his gaze. He took his time answering, and it pleased Grace to see he was a thoughtful man.

"I can't say for sure when or, if Eve will return," he replied. He had spoken Eve's name as though she were genuinely separate from Penny, and that small gesture meant absolutely everything.

"You believe her condition is real," Grace said with great relief.

Dr. McHugh nodded, and Grace could swear the lines on his face grew deeper in that moment, as if some of the burden he'd taken from her had burrowed into him.

"I'm a believer *in* the condition, but I can't say for sure that Penny has it. I know what's in her medical file, but I'll need to work with her to form my own opinion."

"That won't be easy if it's Eve. She won't talk to you. She doesn't talk to any of her doctors. I think that's why Palumbo labeled her with antisocial personality disorder. He didn't like being bested by a teen."

"He doesn't like DID as a diagnosis, either," McHugh replied. "I'm open to the idea though, Grace. Could be she's got DID, a real and true case of it, or it could be borderline personality disorder, or . . ."

"Or Palumbo is right, that's what you're going to say, and my daughter is a psychopath."

"Like I said, until I do my own work, I can't form an opinion. Who gave her the DID diagnosis, if I may ask?"

"Dr. Caroline Cross, do you know her?"

Mitch shook his head.

"She wasn't our first doctor, believe me, but she was the best. Passed away a few years ago . . . cancer. Heartbreaking loss. Such an amazing woman."

"I'm sorry to hear."

"Thank you. I'm not ashamed to say that Dr. Palumbo being gone isn't a loss for any of us. I'd like nothing more than to purge that man from my memory."

"Try not to be too hard on him," Dr. McHugh suggested. "He was doing what he believed was right. Dissociative identity disorder is a polarizing diagnosis that's split our profession into believers and non-believers. That's a fact."

"Well, I'm glad you're one of the believers," Grace told him.

"Statistically, it's thought that one percent of the population has this disorder, which puts it on par with schizophrenia. A case like Penny's has the potential to end some of the debate about the validity of DID within my profession, so I confess I've got a keen interest in your daughter's care."

"So do I," said Grace. "What do you think about our chances in court?"

"Funny you should ask. Your lawyer called me yesterday," McHugh said. "Wanted to introduce himself, a Navy man, former chief public defender, good guy to have on your side, I'd say. He was being diligent, knew I'd taken over for Palumbo. I think he was feeling me out to see if I'd be a good expert witness."

"And?"

Dr. McHugh rubbed his trim beard again. "And I'm sure you're well aware that the insanity defense is extremely difficult to prove."

"Maybe you can help us with that," Grace responded coolly. She had little room in her life for the negative. She gave herself plenty of that already. The guilt Grace hauled around, little links of it, were like the chains wrapped around Marley's ghost.

You did this, Grace would say to herself in the mirror some mornings when she couldn't put on eye liner because her eyes were still wet from crying. *You wanted this. You had it in your head you wanted to mother a daughter and you made it happen . . . for better, or for worse, you are the one responsible for this stress, for everyone's unhappiness.*

McHugh rose and made his way over to a black metal file cabinet pushed against a wall. The top of the three drawers was mostly empty of files, making it easy to locate the one he was after. He returned to his desk, and from underneath pulled out a large plastic container filled with colored paper and a variety of arts and crafts supplies. He removed the plastic lid and fished out safety scissors and several boxes of crayons before locating a pencil.

"I specialize in child psychiatry, and I do a lot more psychotherapy than most, so I brought this with me from my last job," he said, clearly feeling a need to explain items Grace would have stocked in her classroom back in her teaching days before the pizzeria became her work life.

"I might have said something if you had started taking notes in laser lemon or mango tango," replied Grace with something of a smile.

McHugh returned a smile of his own, opened the folder, and jotted something down, in pencil, on a lined piece of paper within.

"How old was Penny when you adopted her?" he asked.

"Five," Grace said, happy to step away from the legal morass that always stressed her out. "But we had fostered her before the paperwork went through."

The eraser end of McHugh's pencil vanished in his mouth, his attention focused on something in the case file.

"You found her, is that correct?" He glanced up with an endearing eagerness.

"Yes," Grace said. "In a park."

CHAPTER 9

IT WAS LATE OCTOBER, thirteen years ago, and the sun was setting earlier and earlier. Grace led her then-six-year-old son, Jack, through the park near their home in Swampscott. They had just left the Montessori school where Grace taught preschool, and where Jack and Ryan also attended. Ryan had stayed home from school that day with a little cold, otherwise he'd have been with her when their lives forever changed.

She remembered being in a hurry, knowing if she didn't arrive home soon, she'd be doing her training run not only in the rain, but in the dark as well. On her thirty-fourth birthday, Grace had given herself a year to prepare for her first marathon, and the race was fast approaching. Her long legs may have helped with the miles, but she'd found they could be a lethal weapon in a crowded yoga studio.

She'd given some thought to cutting her straight brown hair shorter for the race, but kept it long because it allowed for the perfect ponytail, and the rhythm of it swishing against her back helped set her run pace. Whenever she taught, she kept her hair clipped back with a barrette that exposed ears too large for her head. At one time they were her most embarrassing feature, but she'd long outgrown her self-consciousness from the days of 'Dumbo,' a taunt she'd endured back in grade school.

She had expressive brown eyes that sparkled with wonderment and joy at every mundane story she heard from her charges, and a small nose that fit her head a bit better than those ears. Although she was thin, she was also soft, easy to hug and hold, a warm and inviting presence in the classroom. She welcomed the children every day with a tender smile, exposing the dimples Arthur later confessed had made him fall in love at first sight.

Arthur was at home getting dinner ready with Ryan, who was feeling better as the afternoon wore on. While they owned and operated a pizzeria in town, Arthur made sure pizza was a once-a-week treat, and that night they were having hamburgers.

Grace had promised Jack a stop at the playground, but it would be a quick one, as the forecasted rain started to fall just as the duo arrived. As the rain became heavier, she thought of calling Arthur to come pick them up, but Jack was enjoying the mud puddles too much, and Grace couldn't get enough of his laugh. So what the heck, they'd be wet. They'd live.

If she had taken a different route home, hadn't promised Jack she would let him play, she never would have heard the sound. It was a plaintive, lonesome wail, high-pitched but mournful, definitely that of a child. The sound caused her to hurry around a sharp bend. There, standing alone and rain-soaked next to the slide Jack wanted to use, was a little girl. Knowing children as she did, Grace put the child at age four, no older.

It wasn't a shock at first. Grace assumed, having been to parks before, that she'd turn her head this way or that and see Mom or Dad, perhaps hidden beneath an umbrella, their focus on their phone. She might have politely educated them on paying proper attention, no more. But when Grace scanned the area, there was no one in sight. The park was completely deserted.

The rain had started to come down even harder, turning into thick, cold drops that completely camouflaged this poor child's tears. Her cheeks were splotchy red, and her bottom lip, delicate as a rose petal, jutted out from the top one as it quivered. She looked light as a songbird, in a sweet yellow dress with thin straps holding it up on her delicate shoulders, but it was far too little fabric for the weather. She had no coat—no coat in the rain!—and she'd been soaked to the bone, her blond hair matted down against her little head, white sneakers splattered with mud. Her small body shivered from an uncontrollable cold, or fear, or a combination of the two, Grace couldn't say. She knew only that every sob from this poor little waif broke her heart into countless pieces.

She didn't go to the Montessori school, otherwise Grace would have recognized her immediately. Still, she was familiar with many of the children from town. For all of the times Grace had come to this park to watch her boys play on the slide or the swing, this girl was one she'd never seen before.

Grace experienced an initial moment of fear, a feeling of icy dread that coated her in the same way as the rain. Somewhere nearby, behind the bushes perhaps, or next to the roundabout, she'd look and see two feet sticking out that belonged to this child's mother, a woman who had either suffered a medical event or maybe even an assault. Swampscott was a safe town, but it wasn't crime-free.

Grace clutched little Jack's hand tightly in her own as she approached the girl with hurried steps. Scanning the area for those feet, Grace had to wipe away the rain that stung her eyes, flattened her hair, but she saw nothing, no sign of any person, mother or father.

The poor girl, dirty and shivering, began crying even harder as Grace knelt on the ground to wrap the child in her jacket. Jack clung to Grace's leg as though she were a life preserver, which in a way she was. She knew without asking that her son was scared, nervous, and unsure as well.

"What's your name?" Grace asked the girl. "Where are your parents?"

The girl didn't answer, but pointed to the road.

Oh, thank goodness, Grace thought. There were steps leading up to the level of the street, and surely at the top of those stairs, she'd find this child's mother in a frantic search for her missing daughter. Grace ascended the concrete steps with Jack on one side of her and the little girl on the other, holding each child's hand as they went up. Having given her coat to the girl, rain plastered Grace's shirt and jeans to her body, making it uncomfortable to climb those stairs. When she finally reached the top step and had a look around, she did not see anyone searching for this lost child.

The sidewalk was empty and there were only a few cars on the road. None of them were going slow enough to suggest the driver might be looking for a missing child. As cars zoomed by, they sloshed through newly formed puddles, and the beat of car wipers matched the thud, thud, thud of Grace's heart.

"Do you know where your mommy is? Or your daddy?" Grace asked the girl, who shook her head forlornly.

She tried all the techniques she'd learned through years as a parent and teacher, but the girl refused to speak, not even to give her name. Soon the police and an ambulance were on the scene. Arthur came with Ryan and brought Jack home, but Grace wouldn't leave the girl's side, insisting that she accompany her to the hospital.

She was like a ghost, an apparition that had appeared one day out of the void. Grace had never been a believer in destiny, even though her name came from the Latin gratia, (meaning God's favor,"). but she couldn't help thinking that there'd been a touch of the divine in the timing of it all. The little girl could speak, she did speak eventually, but refused to say her name or explain how it was that she ended up alone in the park. She could not, would not, tell anyone who had left her there, or where she'd come from.

Doctors were quick to diagnose post-traumatic stress disorder, but thankfully found no signs of physical or sexual abuse. As for Grace, she couldn't forget the profound look of sorrow and fright in this child's eyes, the likes of which she had never seen before. Grace spent hours in the hospital, and told the girl, whose name she did not know, not to be frightened, that she'd be back in the morning to check on her. When the girl started to cry, Grace had a reclining chair brought in, got some blankets and a pillow, and spent a fitful night's sleep in the girl's room in the children's wing of the North Shore Medical Center.

When daylight came, Grace went home, but returned later with a huge stuffed animal, a bear she'd bought at a local toy store. Spent hours reading to the girl, drawing with her, playing games, and hearing her sweet little laugh for the first time. Whoever this child was, whatever her name, she was perfect and sweet as could be. That was the day, in the hospital room, with just the two of them, playing their games, as a patter of rain from the slow-moving weather system continued to fall outside, that Grace's heart burst wide open and love, profound love for this precious being, filled her from head to toe.

Tips came in soon, as the girl's face appeared on the local news, which was how Grace learned the child's name was Isabella Boyd. According to the many tipsters, the mother was a woman named Rachel Boyd, from Lynn, Massachusetts. Soon, police issued a warrant for Rachel's arrest. Rachel turned herself in to the authorities, and confessed to having abandoned Isabella because she couldn't care for both a child and her drug habit at the same time.

It was Rachel's idea to give up her parental rights. In exchange, police would drop the child abandonment charges. On her own, she had come to the difficult decision that her daughter would have a brighter future with a mother who had more means and no addictions. She didn't want to be an influence in her daughter's new life, and agreed to a closed adoption should a willing family come forward.

Grace was more than willing. She had always wanted a daughter, and God had seen fit to send her one.

* * *

"You named her Penny? Why didn't you keep her given name?"

"She refused to answer to the name Isabella, so Jack—my middle son, very creative and clever—came up with the idea of calling her Penny. We found her and picked her up, he said, so now she's our good luck. The name just sort of stuck and eventually Penny started answering to it. When the adoption went through, we got the privilege of making that name permanent. Now she is officially Penny Isabella Francone."

"The state didn't give you any difficulty with the adoption?" Mitch asked.

"No, not really. We just followed the process," Grace said. "Rachel was out of the picture early on. The Department of Children and Families told us she had moved to Rhode Island, but we weren't in touch, for obvious reasons."

"And the birth father?"

"According to Rachel it could have been any number of men. None of them wanted anything to do with raising a child. She was ours to love and care for."

McHugh was writing something down in the folder when his cell phone rang. As he spoke, she watched his expression register a deepening concern. He ended the call and his eyes focused on Grace.

"That was the ER. Penny said something to one of the nurses . . . something . . . well, I think we should both go see her right now."

In a flash, Grace was rising to her feet. "I didn't think I was allowed to go there."

"You're not, not really," Mitch said. "But I'm new here . . . I don't know all the rules yet." He winked.

"What did Penny say?" Grace asked.

"She told a nurse she remembered something from that night. Something important."

CHAPTER 10

DR. MITCHELL MCHUGH MADE his way to the ER at a pace a few ticks below a jog. With the patients outside in the courtyard at that hour, his fast footfalls echoed in the barren hallway. Grace stayed in lockstep with him, and he suspected they were thinking the same thing: *Will it be Penny we find? Or will Eve have returned? And what has she remembered from that night?*

Mitch was still unfamiliar with Edgewater, making the creepily similar corridors a maze to rival one of Daedalus's creations. Twice he found himself backtracking after making a wrong turn. Mitch was reminded of a time, years ago, when he got lost trying to find Adam's hospital room after his son's surgery to remove a ruptured appendix. Eventually, Mitch had to call Caitlyn, his ex-wife, to get directions to the room.

Shaken by the memory, Mitch refocused his attention on his job. By no means had he been enthusiastic about accepting a position here, but the bills were mounting and nobody else was calling, so he resigned himself to the equivalent of professional purgatory.

Regret.

Profound, heartbreaking, perspective-shifting, soul-searching regret.

That's what Mitch felt after his previous employer, MassGeneral for

Children at the North Shore Medical Center, decided that the time had come for them to part ways. "Heal thyself" made an excellent biblical proverb, but it was severely frowned upon when interpreted literally by a medical professional. Mitch knew he should have sought help for his depression before turning to his prescription pad, but he was stubbornly self-reliant, a tradition forged by family dysfunction that included an absentee father with whom he had no relationship and an alcoholic mother who gave her life to her disease. Mitch was a poster boy for "grin and bear it," having perfected the art of bottling up his feelings until they fermented into something unhealthy.

For years Mitch had told his patients there was no shame in seeking help for mental illness, all the while failing to heed his own advice. Technically what he had done—self-diagnosing and self-prescribing—was not illegal, but it wasn't exactly endorsed, either. Which was why a sharp-eyed pharmacist thought one personal refill was one too many and informed Mitch's employer of his actions. Two weeks later, Mitch got the boot, along with an invitation to become a client of Physician Health Services.

PHS, as it was more commonly known, provided support and monitoring services for doctors with mental illness, substance abuse, boundary issues, and behavioral problems. Most new PHS contracts required the troubled physician to enter some sort of treatment program or inpatient rehab, followed by regular meetings with their assigned PHS counselor and random urine screens if alcohol or other drug abuse were an issue. While they offered troubled docs a second chance, what they couldn't provide was freedom from guilt.

"Please, Mitch, please promise me you won't squander this opportunity."

Mitch promised his counselor at PHS, Dr. Steve Adelman, that he wouldn't squander anything, but a friend of his who was familiar with Edgewater didn't view the opportunity as the brass ring of second chances.

"It's a real hellhole in there, Mitch," this friend had warned over beers a week before his start date. "You sure you have no other options?"

Mitch had smiled back wanly. His buddy knew the answer well enough. It takes a lot less effort to dismantle one's life than it does to build it back up. It was a miracle he'd managed to crawl out of the hole he'd dug for himself far enough to land this gig.

One year. That's what Mitch gave himself. One year of intensive therapy, no more self-medicating, and then maybe he could work his way back to private practice, provide himself that second chance he'd promised Caitlyn.

"You're better than this, Mitch," she had told him. "I'm just not sure you see in yourself what others do."

What Mitch saw was a failure on his part to stop their son Adam's perilous descent into drug addiction. He saw his son in his bedroom, skin blue with cyanosis, his body unable to oxygenate the blood, a needle on the floor near his inert form. Like father, like son, Adam's method of self-medicating involved heroin, and it would have been a fatal injection, too, had Mitch not stocked a ready supply of Narcan for this very occasion. Mitch had talked to countless parents of troubled teens, instructing them on the warning signs for drug abuse, while those very signs were present in his own home.

He understood all too well the pain of a parent unable to help a child in need, which is why when Mitch and Grace found Penny resting comfortably in one of the ER treatment bays, he was already deeply invested in her case and care. She was dressed in a hospital gown, a thin white sheet covering her long legs. For all of the problems Edgewater had, the ER wasn't among them. The four treatment bays were modern and well-equipped. In addition to the monitors reading Penny's heart rate, blood pressure, intracranial pressure, and oxygen saturation, there were medical instruments to suture cuts, cast broken bones, and listen to lungs. Down the hall was a brand-new x-ray machine, which came with the staff to work it.

Grace took hold of her daughter's hand as she tried to make sense of the numbers on the monitor. Mitch wasn't a trained ER physician, but he knew the readings were all within the normal range. What was happening to Penny, the real issue, wasn't something any instrument could measure.

"Penny, honey, are you okay?" Grace asked, voicing palpable concern.

The confusion and fright on the girl's face wasn't because of the name. She was on the verge of a breakdown.

"Mom," Penny said weakly. "What's going on? Please, tell me."

Mitch stepped forward with a warm smile. *Easy does it,* he cautioned himself. Be relaxed and she'll relax. "Are you feeling any better?"

"My head . . ." She touched the gauze bandage a nurse had put over the bump she'd gotten.

"That's understandable," said Mitch. "You took a pretty nasty fall."

"You're. . . . you're . . . Dr. McHugh, right?" The fact that Penny remembered Mitch's name from his prior visit was a good sign.

"Yes, I'm Dr. Mitch McHugh," he said. "But how about you call me Dr. Mitch."

Penny seemed to like that, and she finally managed something of a smile.

"What's wrong with me, really? I've seen people come in here handcuffed, escorted by guards, strapped to their beds. Am I in a hospital or a prison?"

Mitch leaned in to whisper in Grace's ear. "Maybe give us a moment alone," he said.

Grace's initial reluctance to leave was only natural. Mitch felt the same pang every time he dropped Adam off at another rehab facility. Requesting privacy was an even bigger ask, because at any moment Penny could flee to make room for Eve, and Mitch understood what a devastating loss that would be for Grace.

"I'll let you and the doctor talk," Grace said apprehensively. "I'll be back in a few minutes, honey. Okay?" She gave her daughter's hand a gentle squeeze.

Penny's expression turned harder, and for a fleeting second Mitch thought the primary self might retreat like a turtle seeking the safety of its shell. But she simply nodded her head and Grace left—not, however, before planting a gentle kiss on Penny's forehead.

Now, thought Mitch, eager to get to work, *let's find out what memories you have.*

CHAPTER 11

AFTER GRACE DEPARTED, MITCH wheeled a metal stool over to Penny's bed. He kept a lookout for the nurse who'd summoned him here, and saw that she and Dr. Dan Bouvier were busy with the two patients occupying the other bays. No worries. He felt confident he could handle this on his own.

"Penny, you told a nurse you remembered something important, something from the night that brought you here."

"Well, I don't know if it's important, but I told her I remembered being in my bedroom, long ago. That's what I said."

"Yes, you've been here for some time now. I want you to tell me the last thing you remember before this hospital. Can you do that?"

According to Grace, the last conscious memory Penny would have would be from the night of the murder, before the crime actually. She closed her eyes tightly, and Mitch could almost feel the concentration on her face.

"I just remember being in my room," she said, her eyes shut tight, talking in a low voice as if in a trance.

"What were you doing?"

"Nothing . . . I . . . I was reading."

"Do you remember what?"

Details, those were critical. The more she recalled, the more likely it was she could go deeper into that night, following the scent of truth like a bloodhound hot on a trail.

Penny thought . . . and thought . . . then shook her head. She opened her eyes, looking dismayed.

"Close your eyes again, Penny," Mitch said in an encouraging voice, one he'd perfected during his years working with children in private practice.

He knew to be cautious. Memory retrieval could be a tricky business; there was always the potential for recovering false memories.

"You said you were reading. What's the book?" he asked. "Try hard to see the cover . . . a picture . . . the color of it . . . the author, anything you can recall. Think, now."

There was a deep, heavy thumping in Mitch's chest as he awaited her answer.

Penny, eyes still closed, took her time responding. Eventually she said, a bit dreamily, "It's dark blue, and there's water and boats on the cover. That's all I can remember."

Mitch tamped down his excitement as his thoughts branched off into multiple paths. Leaning forward, making sure not to crowd her, he contemplated the best way to further his inquiry without influencing Penny's answers.

"Do you remember what kind of boats?"

Penny shook her head solemnly like she'd been a disappointment. "No. I was just in my bedroom, reading that book. Oh, what was it?"

The desperation in her voice was raw. Even though she had her eyes closed, Mitch kept a neutral expression as he weighed different options to jostle her recall.

"Talk to me about your room," he eventually said. "What does it look like?"

Penny lowered her chin to her chest, still deep in thought.

"Oh yes," she said. "I see it now. My bed, all the blankets, I should have picked them up like Mom asked me, and—"

She stopped mid-sentence, and her eyes flew open like she'd been jolted awake. If ever a look cried out for help, it was that one, and the significance of the moment put Mitch on high alert.

"Penny, what are you thinking about right now? What are you remembering?"

Penny blinked rapidly as if dust had gotten in her eyes and she was trying to clear away the unpleasant sensation. Her hands flew to her mouth. She swallowed several shaky gasps.

"Blood," she sobbed. "I saw blood, so much blood."

"It's okay, it's all right." Mitch touched Penny's arm to soothe her. "You're safe here. I promise."

Her eyes closed again, mouth puckered as if enduring a bitter taste.

"I wasn't alone." She said it quietly, as if she were physically in the apartment where the murder took place and was trying to keep her presence in this memory a secret.

A sharp jolt ripped through Mitch.

"Say that again?"

"I wasn't alone," Penny repeated in a breathy voice.

"You weren't alone in Rachel's apartment?" he asked, seeking clarification.

Penny's eyes opened wide, more frightened than before.

"She's on the floor. I saw her. I saw her face," she said in a murmuring voice. "I was with her, but I . . . I . . . wasn't alone."

Mitch went blank for a few seconds. He was torn between several possibilities: probe deeper, run to Grace, or find the nurse to confirm exactly what had been said. Before he could decide, he saw something shift in Penny. The transformation came on so subtly that if he hadn't been laser-focused on his patient, he'd have missed it entirely. She touched her temples, as if enduring a headache. Her shoulders went back as she sank into her bed. He could see her body relax like the air had been let out of it.

"Penny, is everything all right?" Mitch asked hesitantly.

Tilting her head this way and that, she regarded Mitch in a curious, assessing manner, as if she did not know what to make of him.

"And you are?"

Her voice was different, deeper, more assured. The tone was somewhat conversational, though she breathed an air of mistrust into her question.

"I'm Dr. Mitch McHugh."

Instinct told him to forgo the informal moniker of "Dr. Mitch" he'd given himself moments ago. The girl's eyes brightened.

"So you're the new doctor I've heard so much about. Well, lucky, lucky me."

She checked him over from head to toe. Mitch managed a tight smile.

"Can you tell me whom I have the pleasure of addressing?"

"It's me, silly. It's Eve."

A dark gleam flickered in the girl's eyes. Mitch's heart sank. For a short time, he had stood on the precipice of discovering something truly astounding about the night Rachel Boyd was murdered, but Eve had come rolling in like a great cloud, summoned by Penny to sweep across the landscape of her subconscious, hiding everything within her protective fog. Mitch had to admit, if she were borderline and not DID, it was a brilliant bit of role-playing. Her switch from Penny to Eve, subtle shifts in body language that could easily go unnoticed, occurred in textbook fashion for how alters often appeared.

"Where's Penny? May I talk to her? We were having an important conversation."

Eve shrugged her shoulders. "How should I know?" she answered in a singsong voice. "I'm not her keeper."

"Do you know Penny?"

Mitch had experience with DID patients who could communicate with their alters, but oftentimes the patient wasn't aware they had alternate personality states.

"I know who Penny is, of course," said Eve. "We have the same mother, after all. But this is no place for a girl like her. Really, it's quite awful in here."

Eve had spoken confidently of Penny's existence, as if the two inhabited different bodies. Her response was consistent with what was in her case file. Eve knew she had DID and viewed Penny as one of her alters. In fact, all of the alters, Eve, Ruby, and Chloe, shared the same backstory. They'd grown up in Swampscott, had two brothers named Jack and Ryan, and a father who had died. If asked, each would say that they were abandoned in a park as a young person, and that Grace and Arthur Francone had adopted them.

Mitch cursed himself. He had pushed her hard on what happened that night, and surprisingly his probing, not the attack by the guards, was what had pushed Penny away. She was protecting something, that's the feeling Mitch got. He knew the barriers between alters could be as fortified as a border crossing, and as thin as a membrane. A rush of sympathy overtook him. *What a horribly disorienting, isolating, and confusing condition it must be,* he thought. The intermingling of different voices, different personas within a single consciousness, redefined the notion of self and had to be a hellish way to go through life.

Convincing as the switch had been, Mitch reminded himself that these alters might be nothing more than an elaborate invention. Until he made his own diagnosis, his sympathies must not occlude caution and careful observation.

"So, Eve, tell me, do you know why you're here?" Gut instinct told Mitch to embrace Eve rather than push for Penny's return.

"I do."

"Can you tell me?"

"Pretty sure you have a thing called a file on me. Have you read it, Doctor?" She smiled wickedly.

"I have. I just wanted to hear it in your words, get your take on what happened."

She appeared skeptical, a clear signal to Mitch that he had best move on to another topic.

"Penny was here, not long ago. Did you know that?"

Again nothing.

"She said she remembered something from that night that brought you here, but she didn't say what it was. Do you know what she remembered?" Mitch allowed a bit of desperation to leak into his voice, playing, he hoped, to Eve's ego.

"Maaaaaaybbeee."

The way Eve studied Mitch, a coquettish glimmer in her eyes, made him shudder. It was an alluring stare, one brimming with a poise that was startling to see in a seventeen-year-old girl just coming into her own.

"Can you tell me?"

"I think you'd best ask Penny."

Seeing the circular nature of this conversation, Mitch switched tactics.

"Do you remember the night you were arrested?"

"Hard to forget."

"So you know what happened, why you're here?"

"The file," she said, as if he was the one who needed a reminder.

"Was someone in the apartment with you that night?"

There was nothing in the police report to indicate someone else was involved with the murder. The police had found Penny alone with Rachel in the lower-level apartment of a multifamily home in Lynn. Mitch speculated that one of Penny's alters had leaked into her subconscious, giving her the *impression* that another person was present. But that theory needed to be verified.

"I can't remember much from that night," Eve said flatly. "A bunch of cops piled on top of me and they took me to jail."

"You don't remember killing Rachel Boyd?"

"I do not. And I told the police that, but they didn't seem to believe me."

Mitch wasn't sure what to make of Eve's conviction.

"Do you know who Rachel Boyd is?"

"I'm told she's my birth mother."

"But you've never spoken with Rachel before?"

"No."

"You exchanged messages with her online via Facebook. Do you remember that?"

From her case file, Mitch knew that Rachel made the initial contact, but didn't know how she'd learned Penny's identity. He made another mental note to get that detail from Grace.

"Wasn't me," Eve said assuredly, and Mitch thought it could have been Penny, or one of her alters who had those correspondences, but he'd have to reach them to confirm.

"Was Penny in the house the night Rachel died?"

"You'd have to ask her."

"Well, can I talk to her?"

Eve sat more upright in bed. "And what will you do for me? Will you get me out of here?"

"You know I can't do that," he said.

"Then I guess pretty Penny has to stay away."

Her tone was ice cold. Grace had returned to the treatment bay, taken one look at her daughter, and pulled back as if stopped by an invisible wall.

"Hello, Mother," Eve said languidly with false cheer. "I'm famished. What are we having for lunch?"

CHAPTER 12

GRACE SAT ACROSS FROM Mitch in the Edgewater staff cafeteria, drinking a cup of coffee that was going to compound her jangled nerves. The cafeteria's bright lighting vanquished all shadows, making the prepared food displayed in the under-counter refrigeration unit look as sickly as the patients. The coffee, however, was surprisingly good.

The news Mitch shared was less so.

"Explain it to me again," Grace said. "Penny only *thought* she wasn't alone at the time of the murder?"

"Think of it like signals in the brain getting crossed," Mitch explained. "The stimuli she was experiencing produced such an overload of information that it led to the bleeding of one persona into another."

"Like it broke down the walls in her mind?"

"Exactly," Mitch said. "The shock, the trauma, of Rachel's murder basically blasted a hole through the metaphorical bricks separating Penny's alters. I don't know which alter came through that night, but I suspect that was the other presence in the room."

Grace found Mitch's explanation heartbreakingly all too plausible.

"I thought you didn't believe she has DID?"

"I said I haven't drawn any conclusions, but I'm operating on the assumption that her diagnosis is accurate. To that end, I'd like to know more about Penny's alters . . . about how you met them."

"It began eight years after we found Penny in the park," Grace said, after taking a moment to collect her thoughts.

"So Penny was . . ." Mitch added in his head. "Twelve at the time?"

"That's right. She was twelve. And that's when we met Ruby."

* * *

Arthur had been at the stove, cooking up his weekend special. Ryan and Jack, Penny too, had all outgrown the days of Mickey Mouse–shaped pancakes, but Arthur made them anyway because some traditions were too hard to let go.

Arthur was thin, due to twelve-hour days spent on his feet coupled with the willpower to avoid sampling his wares. He had the sharpest blue eyes Grace had ever seen, keen as an eagle's, somehow capable of seeing everything happening at the restaurant, including things that took place behind his back.

Without any prodding, Arthur knew when the sausage sizzling in the pan needed to be flipped. He set the table, poured glasses of juice, cut the fruit, flipped the pancakes, the sausages, doing it all effortlessly because he took to the kitchen like a fish does to water.

After her bath, Penny came downstairs damp, still wearing her bathrobe, nose in a Harry Potter book. She was entering adolescence and all that came with it—new places for hair, menstruation, buds for breasts. She was reading book four in the series, The Goblet of Fire, *a thick and meaty tome that she carried with her everywhere she went. Penny loved her books, could get lost in them for hours, so it was no surprise to Grace that she fell hard and fast for the magical world of Harry Potter and the utter brilliance of his creator, J. K. Rowling.*

The trouble all started with a single word.

"I'm quite peckish this morning," Penny said as she took a seat at the table, speaking in a mock English accent.

"Peckish?" Ryan looked at Penny askance. "You mean 'pukish'?"

"No, silly," said Penny, keeping that accent going. "Peckish. Hungry." She elongated the word and her eyes went wide at the sight of the pancakes and sausage steaming on warm plates.

"Are you going to talk like that all day?" Jack asked.

"Like what?" Penny studied them, confused.

Jack and Ryan stared at each other, equally bemused.

"Like with your dumb English accent," Ryan said.

"What are you talking about?" Penny said, an edge invading her voice. "This is how I talk."

Jack rolled his eyes at his brother.

"Oh yeah," Jack said, and the brothers shared a laugh.

"Mom," Penny said to Grace. "There's a football game I want to watch on the telly later. Can we go to the shopping center this morning instead?"

Grace was about to say sure, as the day was remarkably under-scheduled, but Ryan had keyed in on several curiosities.

"First off, it's May," he said. "And football season is over. Second, 'telly'? And third, 'shopping center'? Do you mean 'the mall'?"

Penny rolled her eyes at her brother. Insolent being, her look said.

"It's real football, not dumb American football, dummy. Liverpool is playing Man City and I want to watch. Second, it is a telly, and okay, the mall, whatever. You say 'potaaato,' I say 'potahhhto,' but you understand me perfectly well, don't you, because you're not a complete idiot?"

Grace dropped the mail she'd been sorting onto the counter. Normally, she'd issue some sort of rebuke to keep the sibling peace, but she was too stunned at Penny's speech—how quickly the words spilled out of her mouth, the perfection of her accent.

Arthur didn't miss a beat as he moved a mouse cake from the pan onto Penny's plate. "'Ere ya go, luv," he said with a jovial accent, more Chim-Chimminy than Beatles. "And make sure you put your wand away next time. I sat on the couch and that thing turned my butt into cottage cheese." He gave his butt cheeks a squeeze with a free hand and bounded off with a smile and laugh. But Grace wasn't laughing, and neither were Jack or Ryan.

"You're so silly, Dad," Penny said.

With that, Arthur's smile faded. She always called him Daddy. Maybe this new accent was her way of moving into a different phase of their relationship; maybe some kind of maturing and distancing had just taken place. Quickly *regaining his composure, Arthur slipped right back into character and asked Penny if she was going to buy new trainers at the shopping center. Penny answered that she didn't need them, like he hadn't made a joke at all.*

* * *

"She talked like that all day," Grace said to Dr. McHugh. "Didn't break character once. And she watched that soccer game—sorry, football match—from start to end, riveted as could be, cheering for Liverpool like her life depended on it. When I went to her room before bed, I kissed her forehead like I always did and said, 'Goodnight, Penny.' She just looked at me like I was crazy and said, 'Mum, it's me. It's Ruby.'"

"In the accent?" McHugh asked.

"Yes, in the accent. It continued the next day, too. She had all these new words I didn't know she knew. *Knackered. Cheeky. Mate. Bloody.* Phrased things just like a British person might say them."

"What did Arthur say about it?"

"He wasn't concerned at all. He thought it was just imaginative play, probably inspired by the Harry Potter books. He told me not to worry."

"So at this point you hadn't met Eve?"

"No, both Eve and Chloe came later."

Mitch took out a small black notebook and jotted something down.

"I need you to believe in this, Dr. McHugh."

"Please, call me Mitch."

"Okay then, Mitch. I need you to believe in us, in the diagnosis. Eve, or some other alter, is responsible for what happened to Rachel. Not Penny. My daughter doesn't belong in prison, potentially for the rest of her life."

"You know if she's found not guilty by reason of insanity that the plea won't prescribe a limit to her stay here. It could be five years, ten, or decades. The mandate would be that she'd stay hospitalized until she's deemed safe to be released out into the public. I could be gone, and Penny could stay locked up here long after my departure, longer even than a possible prison sentence."

A chill raced up Grace's spine.

"As I understand the law, Penny can't just be punished for having a mental illness. If she gets proper treatment, she *could* be released."

"You're talking integration," said Mitch, referring to the therapeutic practice of bringing all dissociative parts of Penny's personality into one sense of self—in essence, killing Eve, Chloe, and Ruby. "For that we're going to really need to understand her past. Tell me, how did Penny and her mother reconnect?"

Color flushed his cheeks, and Grace realized that her pained expression might have caused him some embarrassment. "Birth mother," he corrected. "Rachel. How did they reconnect?"

As an adolescent psychiatrist, Dr. McHugh should have been well versed in the tricky vernacular that came with adoption. The common names—*birth mother, first mom, tummy mommy, natural mother*—all have a qualifier distinguishing the biological parent from the adoptive one, the one who carried the physical, emotional, and psychological weight required to love and raise a child. For her part, Grace was deeply honored by the role Rachel had played in the formation of her family, and always said a special prayer for her on Mother's Day.

"That's all right," Grace said, letting his slip bounce right off her. Lord knows, she was used to it by now. "Penny was arrested when she was fourteen—she'd just entered high school. She and her friend, Maria Descenza, who regrettably is still a friend of hers, were arrested together. I don't know if any of that's in her file."

"It is," said Mitch.

"Good, so I don't have to go into the details. It was a difficult time for us all, as you can imagine. Anyway, after her arrest, Penny put her personal story on the Internet for all to see, a Facebook post that went viral. Everyone has some fascination with DID, I suppose. By the time I read it, the post had already caught fire. There were at least a thousand shares in the first hour alone."

"She revealed her condition to the world?" Mitch asked.

"That she did," said Grace, her tone a little defeated. "She wrote it all out: how she was the Jane Doe from the park, her diagnosis, about Eve, her arrest, all of it. It was her coming-out party in a way, done on her own terms."

Dr. McHugh didn't bother concealing his grimace.

"I tried to put a bow on it," Grace went on. "Young girl, complicated history, expressing herself, needing an outlet to process her feelings, all that. I do think Penny felt terribly guilty for her arrest, deeply ashamed, and needed to put those feelings somewhere, get some support—which, by the way, she did. A lot of kids at her school commented on that post, and for the most part, they were very supportive and encouraging."

"So, prior to the Facebook post, her peers didn't know she had been diagnosed with DID?"

"No. We kept them, and most everyone except a few administrators, in the dark. Students thought Penny was obsessed with her grades and that she was high-strung as a result, which is why she got in so many fights. They didn't realize it was her alters—Chloe, the perfectionist, and Eve, whom you met—until she posted her story. Unfortunately, the Internet is a damn digital time capsule—which is how Rachel found Penny. She'd been back in Lynn for a few years, reconnected with old friends, and one of them forwarded her that post. She had no idea her daughter lived so close by."

"And you're sure it was Rachel?"

"Absolutely," said Grace. "Attorney Navarro got the discovery materials from the DA's office, and according to the forensic experts, those correspondences came from Rachel's computer, so it wasn't a setup, if that's what you're thinking. Penny never told us that Rachel had contacted her, and Rachel made it clear in her messages to Penny to keep it a secret—for a little while at least, in her words."

"How did she know it was her daughter?" Mitch sounded a bit incredulous.

Grace offered him something of a smile in return. "Doctor," she said, sounding as if he should know better. "There are only so many girls who can say they were abandoned in a park."

"Had you ever tried to track Rachel down before she and Penny reunited?"

"Yes, after the diagnosis we were curious about past history, but Rachel was living on the margins. She didn't want to be found."

"No arrests?"

"None recent. Rachel had been arrested *before* Penny was born. We knew that. It was a major possession charge, enough to slap her with intent to distribute. She pled guilty, but to a lesser charge, and didn't see any prison time."

"Where was this?" Mitch asked. "Do you know?"

"Lynn," Grace said. "She's from there, or somewhere on the North Shore, I know that for certain—ironically, the same district where Penny's trial will take place. I believe she was quick to cut a deal and give up her parental rights in exchange for having the abandonment charges dropped because, with her criminal record, she was looking at serious time."

"Makes sense," said Mitch.

The topic of Rachel led Grace to another question she often wondered about.

"Something happened to Penny before she came to us, didn't it, Dr. McHugh? Something Rachel did to her that caused Penny to develop DID. That's usually the case with the condition, isn't it? Maybe there was something in Penny's memory, in her subconscious, and when she saw Rachel—" Grace didn't bother finishing the thought.

"Yes, that's right," Dr. McHugh said. "Childhood trauma is a leading theory on the causes of dissociative identity disorder. The condition is thought to be an elaborate coping mechanism. Do *you* think Rachel hurt Penny?"

"The doctors who examined Penny at the hospital after she was found noted two long, narrow burn scars on her forearms that could have come from a curling iron," Grace said. "But Penny never talked about any abuse."

Grace often had to bury thoughts of Penny's childhood trauma, because it was far easier to believe that her daughter's formative first few years were filled with love, not pain, and that Rachel's actions were a personal sacrifice born of desperation rather than the continuation of a long pattern of abuse.

"Dr. Cross, who gave us the DID diagnosis, said that we all start out with multiple personalities when we're young. Is that something you believe?"

"I do," said McHugh, nodding. "It's like learning about life through committee. Those disparate voices in our young minds help us figure out the world and how different environments and stimuli affect us. Do we like things sweet or sour; what's funny to us; what scares us? By age nine, our experiences tend to mold us into the person we become, and all those likes and dislikes, our moods and disposition, solidify into a single identity—this concept of self."

"So why is it that childhood trauma doesn't arrest that process for every victim of abuse in the same way?" It was a question that had bedeviled psychiatrists and psychologists alike, and Grace wanted Dr. McHugh's take on it.

"Hard to say," he replied. "I mean, why do people have different responses to trauma? There could be a biological or genetic link involved, an overactive fight-or-flight response—we just don't know. What those in my profession mostly agree on is that children have different coping mechanisms, and in certain cases walls are built in the mind."

"Walls so that the abuse feels like it is happening to somebody else?"

McHugh nodded. "We dropped the name 'multiple personality disorder' because people with the condition don't have more than one personality. It's more like they don't have one whole personality, not yet anyway. Penny's alters aren't different people. They're fragments of her whole self—think of them like personality traits but in a concentrated form."

"Do you think integration is possible in Penny's case?"

McHugh dipped his head. "If I can confirm the diagnosis, that would be the goal," he said. "But it won't be easy. Alters function as added layers of security."

"I always worried that she'd been abused. Arthur, well, I guess he didn't like to think about those things, didn't want it to be true. In his mind, if he ignored it long enough, the problem would just go away."

"So there were warning signs early on?"

Disappointment washed over Grace. "Looking back, you know how hindsight is—I guess you could say those signs were flashing neon, but we were all too in love with Penny to notice them."

CHAPTER 13

AFTER WE FOUND YOU in the park, you were in the hospital for eleven days, and Mom went to see you every day you were there. Went right from work to Salem and spent the afternoon with you coloring, reading books, all that sort of stuff. Even though you got presents from strangers—stuffed animals, games, puzzles, you name it—she brought you a new toy at every visit. I have to say, Ryan and I were both a little jealous, but even though we were young, we still understood. After all, we *had* a mom and dad, and you had neither.

When the Department of Children and Families finally found out your real name was Isabella Boyd, you wouldn't answer to it. I guess that name was full of bad memories for you. You told everyone to call you Penny, the name I proudly gave you, and it stuck. Nurses, doctors, social workers—everyone looking after you started to use that name, because we all wanted you to be happy.

I know DCF tried to place you with relatives, but Rachel's parents were both dead, and your other relatives didn't pass muster. No idea why. I called the agency to get more background as part of my film research, but as you can imagine, they have a strict confidentiality policy.

With nobody else to claim you, you entered the foster care system. After getting Dad on board, Mom put in a request with DCF to take you home with us. I think she told them of her intention to adopt you before she told Dad. Not like Dad didn't want you, but Mom knew he'd be more cautious and resistant by nature. The special circumstances of your case allowed some processes to get sidestepped, some norms to be ignored, and DCF granted Mom's request to have you come live with us—on the condition that Mom and Dad complete the state-mandated procedures to become foster parents. Until those requirements were met you had to reside elsewhere, so a temporary foster family was arranged.

I saw Mom sizing up Ryan's room, imagining how she'd fit my bed, my clothes, and my toys in there so she could give you a room to yourself. I think she had the paint colors picked out even before she started filling out those forms for the foster parent application.

When you left the hospital, Mom couldn't visit you every day. You had a place to live and a nice older couple looking after you. DCF felt that it would be fine for Mom to see you twice weekly, but not daily as it had been. The limit was for your benefit—they said it would help you adjust to your new situation and hopefully, if all went well, it would only be temporary.

Mom was obviously sad. I heard her cry a couple times, and it freaked me out a bit. I'd come to this realization that the person I counted on most to keep me safe was actually a human being with *real* feelings— she wasn't a superwoman, she was vulnerable—which meant *I* was vulnerable, too.

The whole fostering process, with its training requirements, background checks, home visits with social workers and whatnot, took three months instead of the usual five to six. I'm sure Mom had a hand in speeding up that effort. You know how she gets when she has her mind set on something. Google "tenacious," and you'll get a picture of Grace Francone.

I mean, who else but Mom could have taken over for Dad when he died? Even Aunt Anne, who inherited part of the restaurant from Grandpa when he passed away, was happy to help out in the kitchen—but she didn't want to run Big Frank's. It's a lot of work, more than people realize, to make a place like that go. But Mom knew she could make more money slinging pies than delivering interactive learning programs, so she gave up her teaching job—which she loved, really loved with all her heart—to do what had to be done for the family.

That's who your mother is, Penny, tenacious as can be. And you were tenacious too, in a way. You weren't going to let your trauma destroy you. We praised your strength and resilience. You were just a little girl, but you were so brave. Looking back, your speedy, seamless adjustment to your new life should have been a massive warning sign to us all.

You didn't pine for your mother, didn't cry yourself to sleep at night—you didn't even ask about Rachel. You accepted without complaint what you were told: that your mother could no longer care for you, and that if all went well you were going to eventually come live with us. Social workers and therapists assumed that as the trauma lessened over time, you'd experience the expected feelings of loss and sorrow.

You never did, though. Why? I guess either Rachel hurt you more than anybody knew, or you were completely lacking in emotion—a character trait found in most psychopaths.

The day we brought you home to live with us was one I'll never forget. We were all so excited. Even Ryan. It was the year I turned seven, so I wasn't quite sure what to make of the frenetic energy in the days leading up to your arrival. Dad had gone from nervous to eager, though he was still a bit more reserved than Mom, who I remember being downright giddy with anticipation.

It was a marvelous homecoming. I know I was only a kid, but some memories have a way of sticking. There were balloons and streamers galore, fresh flowers everywhere, Our little home in Swampscott looked like it was a float in the Macy's parade. Dad, Ryan, and me spent the whole morning cleaning, vacuuming, doing the bathrooms, straightening every pillow, as if the queen herself were coming to visit. And in a way, she was—*you* were the queen of that day. And me? Well, I was as excited as I'd be on Christmas morning.

Dad went all out, cooking up a feast in the Italian version of *Eat Drink Man Woman*. There were savory antipasto platters, every kind of pizza you could imagine, meatballs, and lasagna. For dessert he made *bombolone*, a light and fluffy fried doughnut filled with raspberry mascarpone. The house smelled of great food for a week. On the kitchen table was a vanilla-frosted cake with your name written on it, and below that, in swirly blue frosted lettering, Dad himself wrote: *Welcome Home!*

Ryan might have devoured those doughnuts and the cake, but I think reality sank in for him that day. He hated sharing a bedroom with me, but what choice did he have? You were the girl and you got your privacy. I remember you had a look of pure delight when you saw your new bedroom for the first time.

Mom had spent a week getting it just right for you. She painted the walls a light shade of lavender, and in the center of the ceiling, she hung a mobile of winged horses circling a bright orange sun. In a corner of the room, where my Batman cave had been, she put a small desk, a perfect spot for doing arts and crafts. She found a colorful rug at a consignment store, along with a perfectly sized bookshelf that I helped her paint a deep shade of purple. She filled the bookshelf with some of our favorite reads and some of hers, including one she loved as a girl, *The Country Bunny and the Little Gold Shoes*.

As she walked you around the house, she showed you all the rooms and various things, pictures on the walls and such, telling you who was who. She made it clear that Mom didn't think of herself as a foster parent, but as your new mother, though the courts would have to make that official—and first, Dad would have to get on board.

The social worker we'd partnered with was there that day, same with your original foster parents, and there were friends, family, and neighbors, all there to welcome you to your new home. It had to have been a bit overwhelming, and nobody was surprised to see you behave like you had in the park that day—a reserved child, shy and demure, incapable of much eye contact.

But things changed when we were finally alone, when all the visitors had gone, leaving Dad to bemoan how much extra food there was, patting his belly as if anticipating its growth. We finally had a chance to play—you, Ryan, and me. I suggested hide-and-seek and your face lit up. I didn't know you loved that game, but you jumped at the opportunity to be the one to hide, and I volunteered to be the first seeker.

I went to the kitchen because nobody was allowed to hide in there and started my count.

One . . . two . . . three . . . four . . .

Ryan wasn't too hard to find. For whatever reason, he thought I'd never think to look between the couch and the wall. It was the fourth place I checked, and I found him curled up in a tight little ball. Then together we set out looking for you. We searched every room. Checked under every bed, every closet, every part of our house, from the basement to the attic, and we couldn't find you anywhere. It was as if you'd gone.

Eventually I started to get nervous. Where could you be? Mom heard me calling your name, and the look on her face when I told her we couldn't find you was like Shelley Duvall's Wendy Torrance character confronting the horrors of the Overlook Hotel for the first time. Mom went to the front door, certain you'd gone outside. First day with us, and she'd lost you, or so she thought. Maybe you'd run into the street, or worse, maybe you'd been taken—that's what had to be going through her mind. It for sure was going through mine.

We started calling your name, all three of us, because Dad had gone to the restaurant to help with closing.

"Penny! Penny, come out! Game over!" I remember shouting while we were outside, screaming your name to the winds, praying you had concealed yourself in a bush in a neighbor's yard.

And then I heard you giggling from *inside* the house. Mom rushed to you and wrapped you in such a tight hug I thought she'd break a rib.

"Where were you?" I asked, and your smile grew ten times the size.

"I'll show you," you said proudly, and you marched us down to your room. You got on your knees and lifted up the bedskirt to your bed.

"I looked under the bed," I told you.

"I wasn't under," you said to us. "I was in."

You reached under the bed and pointed up. In the dark my eyes needed a moment to adjust, but I soon saw it. You had pushed the wood slats to your box spring apart and crawled up into that tiny dark space, where you must have laid yourself flat on the other slats. We had checked under the bed, but we never checked *in* it.

Mom was shocked. We all were. She got down on her knees to look, and asked you how you came up with such a clever hiding place.

You said in a voice that carried pride, and I'll never forget: "I didn't make it up here. I made it up in my other home, because I needed to have a good place to hide when it got really scary . . . a place where nobody, no matter how hard they looked, could find me."

CHAPTER 14

GRACE RETURNED FROM EDGEWATER hours later than she'd planned, arriving at the restaurant in time to help Ryan with the dinner rush. She had much on her mind, much to discuss, but right now, it was all about making pies.

The familiar scent of yeast, flour, and tangy sauce worked as a hard reset. Even so, the implications of the day—Penny's sudden and shocking appearance, the possibility someone else had been with her daughter at the time of the murder—weighed heavily on her.

As Grace walked into the kitchen, she gave the food prep stations a quick once-over, pleased to see everything in its proper place. Ryan, who'd grown up working alongside his dad, didn't need any training to run the show. He was already an expert pizza maker and skilled restaurateur, able to step in and take the reins without missing a beat. It was a good thing, too. Grace had her hands full with Penny's trial, and her sister-in-law, Annie, divorced for many years, was keen on moving to Florida and fishing year-round now that her kids were grown and gone.

Across from her, on the other side of the counter, a half a dozen or so patrons dined happily on perfectly prepared pizzas made to Ryan's exacting standard. Before the murder and all of the negative media attention, that number would have been double.

Grace knew Ryan belonged in college, not working the ovens. To this day he wouldn't explain what had triggered him to drop out of Northeastern shortly after Penny's arrest. No one questioned that he could work at the restaurant—it was a family business, after all—but it was not something Arthur would have wanted for his son. He didn't even want it for himself.

Arthur's father, Francesco, had opened Francone's Pizzeria in 1968 with a three-thousand-dollar bank loan and a dream of leaving a legacy behind. Years later, Arthur would rename the pizzeria Big Frank's, in honor of his late father, and it continued to be a local favorite. After his death, Arthur's sister Annie returned to the restaurant she'd left in her youth to help Grace keep the family tradition alive. Everywhere Grace looked she saw signs of her late husband's legacy. Draped over the lattice that separated the wait staff station from the dining area was the flag Arthur's father had brought home from Italy. The walls were decorated with pictures of Italy and the Francone family over the years. It was hard to believe how close they were to closing the doors forever.

It was in this very restaurant that Grace had met Arthur. She was in graduate school doing her student teaching and she'd come into Francone's Pizzeria, as it was called back then, for a slice of cheese and a Diet Coke at least once a week. While it was love at first sight for Arthur, or so he'd later claim, for Grace it was a slower burn. Even so, Grace felt a "bump," a little dip in her stomach, every time she saw him.

Grace's parents had grown up on the low end of middle class, and hoped their daughter would partner with someone of greater means. But love is love, and they were quick to accept this pizza-slinging boyfriend as "the one."

On the day of her wedding, Grace had worn a simple white dress and a crown made of wildflowers. She said her vows under the watchful eye of Jesus at the same church where Arthur's parents had been married some thirty years before.

As far as Arthur was concerned, the pizzeria was merely a pit stop on the road to rock stardom. He played guitar (really, he played any instrument he could get his hands on) and wooed Grace with ridiculous pizza-making songs, which he layered with more double entendres than a deep dish had ingredients:

> Baby, you make my dough rise
> I'm the pizza pie to your oven
> Melt all over you like I am made of cheese
> You're the only topping that I'll ever need

Grace kept all of his guitars in their original cases in the basement, standing them up like suits on a rack. On occasion, she'd venture down there, and in a form of meditation and reflection, open the cases and sit on a foldout chair, admiring the instruments while hearing Arthur's songs play in her head.

Since Arthur's death, her friends, even Annie, had encouraged Grace to move on with her life, date again, find someone new. Oh, how she hated that phrase—move on. To move on meant to leave, to abandon Arthur's love, his devotion to her and the children, wasn't something Grace could simply walk away from. Arthur existed in her mind and in her heart in the present, not the past.

As if to put an exclamation mark on that sentiment, oftentimes Grace found herself speaking of him in the present tense.

Arthur loves this show. Arthur makes the dough like this. Arthur knows how to fix the refrigerator.

She owned a pizzeria now because of Arthur and because she'd lost him. He was present in Ryan's blue eyes, there in Jack's lanky build. She heard his laugh in things she knew Arthur would find funny, and saw his heart in Penny, whom he had welcomed into the family as warmly and with as much love and devotion as if she'd come to them via the delivery room.

So while Grace's well-meaning family and friends were wrong with their choice of words, they were right in the sense that she needed to move forward with her life, and that Arthur could and would forever remain part of that journey. In many ways, Grace's grief was like Penny's disease—incurable. No treatment, not even time, could make it go away entirely.

Tying an apron around her waist, Grace approached Ryan at the central prep station and gave him a quick peck on the cheek, catching the annoyed look in his eyes. In his mind, family affection didn't belong in the workplace. He wasn't wrong, but Grace loved her boy, so he'd have to endure.

Ryan was a tall, strapping twenty-one-year-old with sandy brown hair and a handsome dimpled smile. He should have had a girlfriend, a life path, been on his way to becoming a lawyer as he'd planned, but instead he'd retreated into himself, grown sullen and distant—except while serving his customers, who were increasingly scarce.

"How are we doing on orders?" Grace asked.

She scanned the tables covered with checkered tablecloths and realized there weren't enough people eating to make payroll.

"We need salads prepped," Ryan said as he ladled sauce onto pizza dough with the care of an artist applying the first bits of color to a blank canvas. He layered the pie with mushrooms and peppers as quickly as if he'd grown an extra set of limbs. It was in these moments, watching Ryan work with supreme confidence, that Grace paused to think that while Arthur might not have wanted this life for his son, he'd have been damn proud of the pizza maker he'd become.

"On it," Grace responded. She was good with a knife, but not as good as Annie, who could dice and slice veggies faster than any Earp brother could draw his gun.

"Where's Annie?" Grace scanned the kitchen but saw only Sarah and Dylan, two young people from town who made twelve bucks an hour serving customers. That alone would have given Arthur a coronary if he hadn't already had one.

"She's in the back, building boxes. I call it wishful thinking. Where have you been, Mom?"

"You know where I've been."

Grace did not elaborate. She gave no details of the day or Penny's surprise appearance. Ryan didn't like to talk about his sister, because of his dad. Arthur died not far from the new oven Ryan had purchased. Penny was sitting on the floor near his lifeless body, the cordless phone used to take orders clutched in her hand, busy signal sounding like an alarm—*beep, beep, beep*. Her expression was a blank, her eyes glassy, as if she were sleeping while awake.

An hour or so before that, everything was fine—relatively speaking, for it had been an extremely difficult and stressful day. Shortly after Penny and Maria were arrested for writing those horrid murder fantasies, Arthur began looking at inpatient treatment options. He and Grace had been away overnight, having made a six-hour drive north to visit a residential treatment facility in Maine and returned home numb and heartbroken.

"If you think this is easy for me, you're wrong," Arthur had said to Grace in bed the night before the tour. "I love that girl so much." His voice broke with grief, and it shattered Grace to hear him so distraught. "But we're in over our heads here, honey. We have our other children to think about." There were tears in his eyes. "What happens if it gets worse? Grace, you have to admit it. We can't control her."

It was true. Penny was on a variety of medications, but none suppressed her alters, and nothing dissuaded Eve from making thinly (or not so thinly) veiled threats. Honestly, life would have been manageable with any combination of Penny, Ruby, or Chloe, but with Eve in the mix, it was too volatile for everyone's comfort.

The thought of locking Penny away someplace was absolutely crushing. When Grace closed her eyes, she didn't see a troubled and angry teen, but rather a sweet little girl in a rain-soaked yellow dress, shivering and alone in the park.

Grace would never forget the guilt that consumed her on the drive north to tour the facility. Annie had agreed to stay at the house to look after the kids, because Penny, who grew up working with Auntie Anne, wasn't a problem for her, which meant Eve wasn't either.

There were no programs that specialized in DID, but Moose Creek was ranked near the top of treatment centers for teens with bipolar disorders. They seemed best equipped to take on Penny's unique case, though at a price that would put quite a strain on them financially.

"There are varying levels of care here," Arthur had said, trying to sound encouraging as Grace reviewed the intake forms. "As Penny gets better, we can visit her more frequently."

Arthur had just sunk an arrow into what troubled Grace the most. It could take more than a year for Penny to be deemed well enough to return home for a two-week stay. Grace's fear and shame about abandoning her daughter came barreling at her in one great rush.

There was no delaying the inevitable when they got back from Maine. "We'll tell her together in the morning," Arthur said as he pulled into the driveway. Grace didn't contradict him. Annie reported perfectly behaved children, which meant no sign of Eve—making tomorrow's announcement about the treatment center all the more painful.

The manager had already closed Big Frank's for the night, but Arthur wanted to go to the restaurant to review the receipts and place some orders for the morning. Penny asked to go along. She was hungry and craving an Italian sub, but wanted to make it for herself just the way she liked it. Given all that was going to happen, Arthur couldn't say no.

When they didn't return at the hour expected, and phone calls went unanswered, Grace went looking for them. It was ten o'clock at night when she pulled into the parking lot. There were lights on inside, and Arthur's was the only car there. Ryan and Jack had accompanied Grace because they, too, were worried about their sister and father. It was Ryan who found his dad sprawled on the floor next to the oven, dead from what the medical examiner would later determine was a heart attack. Then he saw Penny was slumped on the floor nearby, a blank stare on her face, the phone clutched in her hand.

Grace screamed Arthur's name as she fell to her knees beside him and started CPR, even though she knew it was a wasted effort. Jack went to Penny.

"What happened?" he asked her, distraught. But like that day in the park, she wouldn't speak.

Ryan went ballistic. He started screaming at his sister. "Why didn't you call for help? Why didn't you call nine-one-one? Dad might still be alive if you did! You killed him!"

The medical examiner had made it clear that Arthur was probably dead before he hit the ground, but Ryan refused to accept that explanation, and his resentment toward his sister never left him. Now, without Arthur's support and encouragement, Grace's willingness to send Penny away to Maine left her.

Annie emerged from the back storeroom carrying a load of boxes in her outstretched arms. She was pixie-small, but full of wiry muscle from years of reeling in bluegills and tommy cods on the Cape, where she still fished the spots she'd once fished with her father, holding his blessed memory in her heart.

Showing her sun-loving tendencies, she had a weather-beaten and salt-scrubbed face, but the elements had not worn away her pleasant aspect and cheery smile. Her eyes were big and expressive, lips thin, and for a hairstyle, she went with something short and low maintenance.

Annie dressed oddly for someone who loved the ocean, preferring cowboy shirts and dark jeans. She was also a collector of unique belt buckles. Today's showpiece was a horseshoe-shaped rhinestone buckle that looked like a million bucks and probably cost eight fifty at TJ Maxx. Annie could be as frugal as Arthur, but they were both lightweights compared to Big Frank.

"What gives, sis?" Annie said, sending Grace a friendly smile after depositing the boxes she carried onto a stainless steel table. "How was the visit?"

Grace always warmed when Annie referred to her as her sister. The death of her mother from a stroke years ago had left Grace in need of female family. Her one brother, who lived in California, never came to visit. Grace called her dad in Florida once a week, but she didn't discuss Penny's case, fearing his weakened heart couldn't take the stress.

Grace reviewed the day for Annie, who had no trouble talking about the case. She listened with quiet attentiveness, and held Grace's hand when she became teary about seeing Penny again.

"Dr. McHugh thinks the person Penny saw in the apartment is one of her alters."

Ryan called out for a Mediterranean calzone (spinach, olives, feta cheese, onions, and tomatoes). Annie grabbed some pre-balled dough from a plastic bin and began flattening it out on a floured pizza peel. Grace cued in on the strain in Annie's face.

"What's up?" Grace asked as she set about prepping a garden salad for a phone order.

"Nothing. It's great that Penny showed up." Annie, who had baked enough calzones in her day to make one in the dark, locked eyes with Grace as she added ingredients to her creation. "I'm just wondering."

Ryan was flittering about the kitchen, so Grace kept her voice low to avoid upsetting him. "Wondering what?"

"What if . . . what if it wasn't one of her alters?"

"What do you mean?" Grace raised her knife, using it as a pointer, but lowered it when the implications occurred to her: knife, Rachel Boyd, the slice to Rachel's throat, blood all over her daughter's body.

"I mean," Annie went on, "what if there *was* somebody else in that apartment that night?"

"Like a witness?" Grace leaned over the prep table, her gaze burning bright.

Annie leaned closer. There was a glimmer in her eyes, too, a sense of excitement dancing there.

"Maybe that . . . or . . . maybe . . . an accomplice."

Grace let out a slight gasp.

"Penny's vulnerable," Annie continued. "Could be she was manipulated, maybe someone was playing around with her, playing head games, who knows? Or it could be Penny was the accomplice, not the killer." Annie rattled off the potential implications like she was reading from a grocery list. While the notions were intriguing, Grace didn't know what the legal consequences would be.

She'd find out soon enough. Tomorrow she'd call Greg Navarro and ask for a meeting. Then she'd call Dr. Mitchell McHugh to see if he could join her, because some journeys were best not taken alone.

CHAPTER 15

It took a special request for Mitch to have a copy of the medical examiner's report of Rachel Boyd's autopsy sent to the records room at Edgewater. He was on his way to his office to give a review when he sent a friendly wave to a woman named Amanda, a patient of his, whom he passed in the hallway. Amanda had the haunted look of a castaway, and her frail body didn't appear to have a violent bone in it. But Mitch knew she'd taken a hammer to her husband's head as he slept because she was certain that aliens had abducted him and left a doppelgänger in his place. Edgewater was full of stories like that.

Seeing the lost look in Amanda's eyes felt like gazing into a mirror of sorts, reminding Mitch of his own sadness. He knew that the hollow sensation entering his chest was a precursor to the start of a deepening depression. And he knew exactly what had set him off: his ex-wife Caitlyn had called last night with the news that Adam had relapsed and was back in rehab. The protocols were all too familiar. It would be days before Mitch would be allowed to visit his son.

Damn drugs. Damn them all to hell.

Adam, a boy with every opportunity to succeed, chose a dark path over a bright future. *How could he do this to me?* Mitch thought, paraphrasing a line from a familiar Beatles song. What a waste, what a crying shame. Mitch took four deep breaths using a technique he'd picked up from a nascent meditation practice, and soon he calmed. Anger so often got in the way of his being able to support his son, as did the guilt that he could have done more to prevent Adam's descent into addiction.

Mitch knew the brain science behind his son's struggles, but that wasn't enough to make him entirely forgiving. And it wasn't just Adam he needed to forgive—it had taken Mitch's divorce for him to realize he needed more help than the Celexa could provide, but he didn't start seeing a therapist until Physician Health Services mandated it as part of his contract with them. The shame and stigma he felt in helping patients overcome their depression, while he struggled with his own, continued to weigh on him.

He'd given Caitlyn fifteen years and plenty of reasons for wanting out of the marriage. In return she gave him plenty of opportunities to change his ways. Instead, he had stonewalled her about his depression, as if not acknowledging it would make it go away. Then came Adam's addiction. The marital foundation wasn't nearly sturdy enough to withstand a hurricane of such force.

Mitch had suspected his son was still using. They'd fought just the other day, when he brought up meditation as a potential tool for Adam's addiction management toolkit. In response, Adam gave his father a dismissive wave before pronouncing he wasn't at all interested in any of that "New Age crap," as he put it.

"Meditation and yoga have been around for thousands of years," Mitch countered, "so it's hardly new."

He launched into a detailed explanation of the bidirectional link between substance abuse and depression, how those with the illness were more prone to addiction and those with addiction more likely to become depressed, but Adam refused to consider it.

That was when Mitch lost his temper.

"You know people are trying to help you here, but you're just committed to flushing your life right down the toilet, aren't you, Adam?"

Adam threw up his hands before walking away from Mitch, out the apartment door, and into his car, without a word of good-bye.

Those were, in fact, the last words he'd spoken to Adam before getting the news from Caitlyn, giving Mitch more reason to feel anger and guilt. When he raised his voice to his son, demanding better of him—more effort, more conviction, more fight in his fight—he knew he was really castigating himself for not having intervened sooner.

Some doctor.

Some father.

All thoughts of Adam and regret faded when he got to his office and could settle in to study the ME's report. The images in the file were gruesome. There were photos of Rachel on the floor, propped up against an unmade bed in an untidy bedroom. Behind her a table and lamp had been tipped over, indicating a struggle. Her dark blond hair was matted together in sticky clumps, limp and lifeless as the rest of her, and blood covered her shirt. She sat with her legs splayed out in front of her, head tilted back to reveal a long gash running from one side of her throat to the other in the shape of a gruesome smile. A cordless phone was clutched in her lifeless hand.

Mitch scanned through the report, keying in on certain passages that made him take special interest.

> The deceased was a Caucasian female stated to be forty years old. The body weighed 134 pounds, measuring 65 inches from crown to sole.

Not a body, he thought, a person, a woman, a mother, someone with a past but now no future. Rachel.

There were pictures of Rachel's eyes, milky with death, but he knew from the report that their true color was hazel. The pupils were fixed and dilated. The sclerae and surrounding tissue were unremarkable, with no evidence of petechial hemorrhages due to trauma on either. The ME observed no injuries to the gums or cheeks. Mitch read on.

> Sharp force injury of the neck, left side, transecting left internal jugular vein. It appears to be a combination of a stabbing and cutting wound. The wound path is through the subcutaneous tissue and the sternocleidomastoid muscle, with transection of the left internal jugular vein. The coloring below the subcutaneous fat that was observed bulging from the open wound to the neck area was pale yellow and with significant blood collection around the edges, indicating this wound was most likely delivered while the victim was alive.

The image of Penny slicing open Rachel's throat while she was alive was too much for him to process. *Could it be?* He visualized Penny clutching a large kitchen knife in her hand, dragging it across Rachel's throat, severing the carotid artery, sending a spray of blood that soaked her like a fire hose. Mitch read on.

> Seven stab wounds appear on the left side of the abdomen, about 35 inches above the left heel, measuring three-quarters of an inch in length. The wound path is through the skin, the subcutaneous tissue, and through the retroperitoneal tissue, terminating in the abdominal aorta, approximately one and one quarter inches proximal to the bifurcation.

In those wounds Mitch saw a dark, profound rage, a pure hatred, as though the cuts themselves projected the emotions preceding them. What else could have driven someone to such violence?

In his reading, he found what appeared to be the fatal wound, one of them at least.

The ninth stab wound, measuring 2.0 centimeters in length, went through the right side of the thorax between the sixth and seventh rib, puncturing the pericardial sac, allowing blood to flow freely into the thoracic cavity. This wound appears to have interrupted the normal action of the heart.

Final cause of death was listed as a homicide involving twenty-five sharp injuries: two wounds to the neck, eighteen to the chest and the abdomen, and five to the upper extremities. Two of the wounds—the one to the abdominal aorta and one to the chambers of the heart—were determined to be rapidly fatal. There were no slicing wounds to the hand, no effort made to grab the blade, suggesting the attack had come as a surprise.

Not an attack. A vicious, ruthless, bloodthirsty murder.

The question running through Mitch's head was how a girl as thin and lacking in muscle as Penny could deliver so many devastating blows. The wound to the neck alone would have required tremendous force. Adrenaline was what the ME had cited. Could be possible. But he was thinking, too, of her odd claim: *I wasn't alone.* Could someone else have been in the room with her at the time of the killing? Mitch didn't see how. The only other DNA found at the crime scene belonged to Vincent Rapino, the secret lover, and he had an alibi.

The forensic report documenting the blood splatter found on Penny's body and the accompanying images suggested that, indeed, Penny was a monster. The blood came not only from arterial spray, but was "painted on"—those were the exact words used in the report—after the fact, meaning Penny had dipped her hands into the victim's blood, then smeared it in her own hair, on her face, her clothes, like she was applying war paint.

The only marks to Penny's person were shown in a photograph of her upper extremities, taken after the blood was rinsed off, which revealed quite clearly two oblique, incomplete rings around her wrists, dark brown in color and accompanied by a red band on both sides. The marks were roughly several millimeters in diameter and in the same general location as handcuffs would be applied, so Mitch assumed they were the result of Penny's arrest.

He remained primarily interested in the viciousness of the wounds, and decided Ruth Whitmore, the facility director at Edgewater, should take a look at the files. She'd been there for quite some time, seen a lot of crazed patients over those years. Perhaps she could offer some insight, maybe an example of another female patient of Penny's stature who'd inflicted injuries like the ones that had been administered to Rachel's body.

Before Mitch could take that thought any further, his cell phone rang. The number was one he did not recognize, but when he answered the call, he was only somewhat surprised to hear Grace Francone on the line. She spoke for five minutes before Mitch agreed to her request.

"I'd be happy to meet with your lawyer," he said.

CHAPTER 16

THE LAW OFFICE OF Greg Navarro occupied two rooms in a former industrial complex in downtown Salem that had been converted into an office park. His tidy, nicely appointed conference room featured views of boats gliding across the slate-gray water of Salem Harbor and seagulls levitating above it in search of a meal.

Grace kept interactions with her attorney to a minimum. Every minute in this office or on the phone with Navarro was a drain to the pocketbook. Soon, the equity line she had secured would run out and Grace might have to mortgage the house, maybe start a GoFundMe campaign or seek donations elsewhere. Whatever it took, she would find the money to pay for Penny's defense, no matter if it meant baking pies well into her eighties.

"Hello, Grace. Good to see you," Navarro said, looking dignified in a blue suit, blue shirt combo. "And Dr. McHugh, nice to meet you in person."

Everyone took seats at the circular conference table.

"So, how are you doing this morning?" Navarro asked.

"Good," Grace said without elaboration, because it was a much easier answer than the truth. "I think we should get right to it." She resisted the urge to add that in this case, time was literally money.

"Have you given any further consideration to what we discussed on the phone?"

Navarro glanced down at a blank page on his legal pad.

"I have, and I think it's probably not in Penny's best interest to pursue it." His tone was matter-of-fact.

"Why not?" Grace pleaded. "If there was someone else in the house that night, couldn't it lessen her culpability?"

"In terms of *mens rea,* a guilty intent, an awareness of a crime being committed, understanding the crime was wrong, then no. I mean maybe we hope for murder in the second. Could be that," Navarro admitted. "But Grace, there's no proof your daughter was with another person. None whatsoever."

"There was other DNA at the crime scene," Grace reminded them.

Navarro said, "Right. Vincent Rapino, the boyfriend—or the cheating asshole, if you ask Vincent's wife—but he's not a suspect."

"Well, maybe he should be," said Grace. "After all, isn't it always the husband or the boyfriend? And Rapino is hardly a saint."

Grace was familiar enough with Rapino's impressive criminal resume. A onetime petty thief, Rapino graduated to grand larceny and assault and battery, and even did time behind bars before straightening out (allegedly) to become a car mechanic and small business owner in Lynn. Grace didn't get the impression he was flush with cash, but Rapino made enough money to keep his paramour sheltered in an apartment rented in his name, which gave them a safe place to enjoy their liaisons.

"What if Vince *was* there?" Grace said to the faces staring back at her. She pushed on. "Penny went to Rachel's place and didn't tell me because Rachel told her not to say anything. That was clear from the Facebook messages they exchanged, and I get it, it's complicated— birth mother, her mother, it's a tricky dynamic. Anyway, they're together in Rachel's house, reconnecting, doing whatever. Vincent shows up, maybe unexpectedly, and there's a fight. Maybe he killed Rachel and Penny doesn't remember any of it. She has no memory of being in the pizzeria when her father died. No memory of what happened to her before I found her in the park. I'm just saying, it's not such a stretch given her history. If that's the case, she'd be innocent."

Navarro sent a questioning glance Mitch's way. "Dr. McHugh, is it possible that one of Penny's alters is suppressing some of her memory?"

Mitch massaged his beard in thought.

"Possible, yes," he said. "Likely, no. I think it's as I told Grace, an information overload, one alter bleeding into another. It made Penny *feel* like someone else was in the room with her when in actuality, she was alone." Mitch took a long pause. "I guess given the gravity of the situation we shouldn't discount anything, but I wouldn't pin our hopes on it."

"Understood. Regardless of what we think of his alibi, Rapino's ex-wife insists they were together that night, and the police bought it. Let's change gears," Navarro said to Mitch. "We could really use you as an expert witness at the trial."

A dark cloud seemed to pass before Mitch's face as he shifted uneasily in his chair.

"Yeah, I've been giving that a lot of thought."

"And?"

"And . . ." Mitch let the word hang in the air, while Grace, sensing trouble, curled up inside. "And I keep coming back to the fact that this case was lost when it was allowed to *go* to trial."

"It's just not a very high standard for competency," Navarro said. "The forensic psychologist gave Penny the evaluation at the court-house and later again at Edgewater. She understood the charges against her and could assist with her defense—like I said, not a high standard. We argued that one of Penny's alters might have been responsible and that alter might not meet the competency criteria, but Judge Lockhart was concerned we were elevating her personalities to the status of persons."

"Which is exactly how it should be," Grace replied bitterly.

"The judge doesn't agree, and there's no room for negotiation there," said Navarro, offering his assessment in a neutral voice.

"Right," said Mitch. "Which puts us back to the trial and an insanity defense—which, to be perfectly honest with you all, no psychiatrist I know could argue and win."

For Grace, it felt like the air had been sucked out of the room in a single rush.

"Why do you say that, Mitch?" Navarro asked. "The murder appears disorganized, frenzied. Penny didn't bring a weapon, made no attempt to escape even when Rachel called nine-one-one. It shows lack of planning and total lack of awareness on her part."

"She wrote a hit list that had Rachel's name on it," Mitch reminded the room, as if everyone had forgotten the obvious. "Rachel abandoned her, and there will be no shortage of psychologists willing to testify that long-simmering resentment could have triggered extreme violence. Penny may have gone there with murder on her mind, and in the aftermath, she froze. You're the expert on the law, Attorney Navarro, but that seems like a winning argument for the prosecution to me."

"Our focus is on her different personality states," Navarro said. "We know the Eve persona is dark. She's the one who wrote the hit list, not Penny. We've got witnesses to testify to that effect, and I've got an expert lined up to talk about DID, because I know the ADA will argue it's not a valid diagnosis, but I'd rather it be you, Mitch. Having Penny's doctor on the stand, someone who is also an expert on the condition, would help us tremendously, I think."

"I could be convincing about DID being a real condition," Mitch said. "But I can't at this time give Penny that diagnosis until I work with her some more. She could have a borderline personality disorder . . . or . . ."

"Or you think she's psychotic," Grace said in a sharp tone. "That she just . . . what? Murdered Rachel in cold blood for the damn fun of it?"

Grace could feel the anger well up inside her.

"I can't get on the stand and simply go by what's in her medical file unless I am in full agreement. I need to have time with Penny to form my own conclusion, which could be that she has DID, or . . . it could be something else."

Grace bit her lip to keep from saying something she'd later regret. Mitch wasn't telling her anything new, he was simply confirming her worst fears. She also understood that the insanity defense was rarely used, and for good reason—it seldom worked. Of all court cases, only 1 percent attempted that defense, and of those, it was successful only 25 percent of the time.

"Where is your comfort level with helping us?" Navarro asked the question Grace was thinking.

Mitch drummed his fingers rhythmically on the conference table before turning his attention to Navarro.

"The standard for being put on trial might be quite low, but it's a high bar to win an insanity case. To do that you'll need to show that Penny was unable to understand the criminality of her conduct or unable to conform her conduct to the law. That's the standard set by the MPC, the Model Penal Code Test.

"Even if you argue that Penny committed the crime while in a dissociated state, and that Eve is the most likely perpetrator of the violence, those old correspondences with Maria are *proof* that Eve knows right from wrong. Why else keep them secret? All the prosecution has to do is show that Penny, or any of her alters, had partial comprehension of their actions. That's why those murder fantasies deeply hurt this case."

And there it was—the big rub, the thing that kept getting in the way. Maria. Damn Maria. Firebug Maria.

That's when a thought struck Grace, jarring as a splash of cold water. A tingle started in her feet and worked right up her body as a new theory came to her and began to take root.

"Look, Penny told us she wasn't alone," Grace said, her voice and eyes both pleading. "Forget Vincent, okay, forget about that for a second. Doesn't it make the most sense that *Maria* was with Penny that night? When you read those documents, Mitch, you'll see Maria is as twisted as they come. Could it be that Penny didn't kill anyone, but Maria did?"

For Mitch's benefit, Grace recounted Maria's troubled past. At five years old, Maria started setting fires in the woods around her house, and then started setting them *inside* her house. She was on all sorts of medications to control her impulse behaviors. She and Penny went to school together and they'd bonded over their mental health struggles. At the time, Grace had thought it was good that the girls had each other—Lord knows each needed a friend—but she had no idea how toxic that friendship had become until they were arrested.

"Why wouldn't Penny tell us about Maria's involvement?" Navarro asked.

Grace had her answer at the ready. "Maria and Penny—really, Eve—were extremely close," she said. "Best of friends. We tried to keep the girls separated after the arrest, but it was impossible. They reconnected as virtual friends . . . what am I going to do? Ban Penny from the Internet? Then, as they got older, more independent, they started seeing each other again. I could see Eve sacrificing herself to protect Maria. Don't you get it? That's what Eve does. She protects. It *had* to be Maria with Eve that night. Had to be."

"What's her alibi?" Mitch asked.

"The mother says she was home sick in her bedroom," Navarro answered.

"Mother lying for daughter," said Grace. "Or maybe she just *thought* Maria was in her bedroom. I could go hours not checking on my kids when they were teens. How difficult would it have been for Maria to sneak out, catch a ride to Rachel's home with Penny, and then walk back after the murder? It's a two-and-a-half-mile trek at most, which would have taken her maybe an hour. She could have been gone three or four hours and Maria's mother—assuming incorrectly that her daughter was resting in bed the entire time—wouldn't have had the faintest idea."

"Grace, I hear you, but there's no evidence linking Maria to this crime," Navarro said.

Grace was buzzing. Connections she hadn't made before were coming to her fast and furious. "That's because Maria researched how to pull off the perfect murder. She must have known Penny would go catatonic under extreme stress. It all makes sense now—we never knew the whole story because Eve didn't know it. But Penny does, and she's remembered. She told us the truth. 'I wasn't alone.'"

"No, what we have is Penny's word versus Maria's, and let's face it—your daughter is not the most credible witness." Navarro delivered that kill shot with stinging authority.

"Jessica Johnson will pounce all over that argument, if she's half the prosecutor you say she is," Mitch added. "And either way, even if Maria was there, Penny was too, and she'll argue that Penny and her alters all knew right from wrong—and we'll still lose."

Nobody seemed to disagree.

"Our choices here are limited," Navarro said somberly. "We'll keep Vince and Maria on the table, explore them as possible perps. Fine. But we have to try for the insanity defense because it's our *best* option."

"But you said that defense is hopeless, Mitch." Grace's voice sliced through the room sharp as a knife's edge. "We need to do better for my daughter. What Penny said changes everything."

"No, really, it confuses everything," said Navarro.

"So, what then? We're going to let the prosecution steamroll us at trial and try to fight on appeal?" Grace was outraged. "That's not good enough for me—and it shouldn't be for you either." She directed her ire at Navarro. "We have new information here, and we have to act on it. Now!" Grace punctuated her demand with a slap of her hand against the conference room table. The thunderclap turned the room silent, but nobody seemed ruffled by the outburst. Open emotions were to a law firm as an open wound was to an ER.

"You make a good point, Grace," Mitch said, "and I think if we hadn't talked it out, I might have missed an important angle."

"The two-killer theory?" Grace asked, sounding hopeful.

"No, something else," said Mitch. "Except for that one glimpse of Penny we just had, from the night of the arrest on, it's only been Eve. From my understanding—and Greg, correct me if I'm wrong here—to win in court, it depends on whether the personality controlling Penny was unable to appreciate the criminality of her conduct or conform to law."

"Not exactly. We need to prove in court that Penny has DID and then make the case that one of her alters did the crime, which is why she has no memory of the murder. There's precedent for that sort of strategy, but it's no guarantee we'll get the verdict we're after," Navarro clarified.

"What if we can strengthen the case by finding the killer?"

It took Grace a moment for the implications to sink in. "You're talking about getting through Eve, aren't you? Reaching her other alters."

Mitch nodded. "If I can observe this other personality—maybe it's Eve in an altered, psychotic state, or it's Chloe, Ruby, or someone we haven't met yet, a fourth alter. If I can observe them under the right conditions, I could testify that one of Penny's alters meets the test for lack of criminal responsibility, which really means that Penny meets the standard."

Navarro steepled his hands together, looking intrigued. "Go on," he said.

"I looked at the ME report of the murder. The crime scene photos . . . they were utterly savage." Mitch screwed up his face in a grimace, as if seeing those pictures in his mind.

"I didn't think a girl of Penny's size and stature could inflict such carnage, but I'm making some inquiries to see if it's possible. It's also possible she has a male alter, or an avenging personality that we've never met, one that not only gave her a feeling of rage-enhanced strength but changed her physiology during the attack. There are stories of an entire-body stress response giving people superhuman strength in life-and-death emergencies.

"I guess what I'm suggesting is this: if I can demonstrate that Penny can enter a dissociative state in which she cannot conform to the law or reasonably know that killing is wrong, we might have a stronger case in court. But it means I'll need to connect with all of Penny's alters, including ones she may be keeping hidden from us."

"Can you do that? Contact them?" Navarro made it sound like Mitch was going to attempt some kind of séance.

"I can certainly try," he said.

"I'm good with that," Navarro replied curtly. He, too, understood that time was money. "Whatever I can do to support you, I'm happy to do it."

"Thank you," Mitch said.

"But Mitch," Navarro continued, "the trial is three weeks away. You'd better hurry."

CHAPTER 17

Mitch got lost on his way to the therapy room, making him late for what he assumed would be a session with Eve. Maybe Penny, Chloe, or even British-sounding Ruby would surprise him and show up in her place. Perhaps his efforts would be too effective, and one of them would snap, try to break his neck—but then, assuming he didn't die, he'd have what he needed for the trial. If Edgewater had taught him anything, it was to always expect the unexpected.

When he arrived, Mitch locked eyes with the guard keeping watch over his patient. In forty minutes, this same guard, or another like him, would return to escort Penny back to her cell—though Mitch could see at a glance that it wasn't Penny awaiting his arrival. The girl, seated at the table in her green uniform, projected a confident air, greeting Mitch with something of a cruel smirk. Her blue eyes held all the warmth of ice chips. Her hair hung loose, cascading well past her shoulders.

Before Mitch could take his seat, a strobe light began to flash and a familiar siren wailed. No doubt a fight had broken out somewhere in the complex. Guards, including the one keeping watch over his patient, were quickly on the move. Mitch covered his ears to block out the piercing sound, noting that Eve kept her hands rooted on her lap. The sudden noise and flashing lights did not unnerve her, perhaps because she'd grown accustomed to it.

"Fight in the cafeteria," Mitch heard a guard yell as he went sprinting down the hall, followed closely by half a dozen personnel surging in that direction.

"Another day in paradise," said Eve with a dull smile. "You're late, Doctor." Her tone was mildly chiding.

Mitch closed the door behind him, blocking out the noise well enough. Medium-security protocols meant his patient wasn't shackled or handcuffed, and she was permitted to be alone with him without any accompaniment. This was good for therapy but potentially bad for Mitch, should Eve make false claims about him. There were security cameras in the visiting rooms, but not in here. Since therapy was about building trust, Mitch had no issues giving his patient the benefit of the doubt, and he'd hope for the best.

"Sorry for the delay," Mitch said. "I'm still not good at finding my way around here."

"You seem smart to me. You'll catch on soon enough." There was a mischievous look about her as she leaned over the table, getting closer to him, her eyes narrowed a bit in an assessing way. "But if I were you," she added, talking now in a conspiratorial whisper, "I'd go and get a better job somewhere else."

Mitch's return volley was a smile that didn't convey any disagreement.

"According to the notes Dr. Palumbo left, you don't talk much during these sessions." He allowed his grin to widen.

"I talked enough for him to decide I was a whacko psychopath, so let's just say I've learned my lesson. It's best to keep tight-lipped here." She glanced at the clock on the wall, and Mitch noticed that Eve sat with her hands interlocked on her lap. For all her posturing, she was still quite defensive. Mitch made a mental note to pay close attention to her nonverbal cues.

"Let's wait until the minute hand hits twelve and then I'll start."

"Start . . . not talking?" Mitch sought clarification.

The minute hand rounded twelve, and she nodded her answer.

"I'm not of the same mind as Dr. Palumbo. I'm here to help, not to judge. But I'm not going to be of much assistance if you don't talk to me," said Mitch.

She said nothing. It was time to go hunting.

"At least tell me if you're Eve," Mitch said. "Can you do that? We spoke in the ER. You were friendlier then. Why the cold shoulder?"

Nothing.

Mitch cleared his throat uncomfortably. Connecting with Eve was challenging enough, but reaching the others seemed as insurmountable as scaling Everest in a blizzard.

For a time, he studied the girl, noting how her eyes stayed glued to that clock, and thought more about what she was doing. She was making a statement, that much was obvious. He might be the doctor, but *she* was the one in control.

Fighting for control was something Mitch understood and could relate to on a personal level. He controlled his sadness enough to get up and go to work each day, then come home and help with dinner and cleanup every night, wishing all the while for the darkness to somehow magically disappear. Much like Penny had done with her alters, he had also created different personas.

The lack of security cameras in the room actually gave Mitch an idea: Eve wouldn't talk to him unless she trusted him. She was the "host" personality, the one whose job it was to let others in or out. That decision applied not only to her alters, but also to her doctor. So how to build trust? Mitch mulled it over in his head. Perhaps he'd have to give to get. And what could he give her that would make her trust him? A possible answer came to him.

"I know you hate these sessions," Mitch said. "But you at least gave Dr. Palumbo a fair shot before you went silent on him. Why not extend the same privilege to me?"

Nothing. Not a flicker of her eyes in his general direction.

"I am, you may be surprised to know . . . a bit like you."

She didn't look his way, but Mitch sensed she was listening now.

"I'll tell you what." Mitch uncrossed his legs, his body forward on the table. A tiny pulse of energy beat rhythmically at his temples. "Let's make a deal."

Eve pointed to her ears. "Listening," she said.

"I'll share a secret with you, something about my life. Something personal. You can ask me questions about it and I'll answer as best I can."

Eve mulled it over, and judging by the slim smile on her lips, found it somewhat appealing.

"And the deal? What do I have to do in return?" she asked in a clipped voice.

"The deal is that you share a secret with me. Whatever it is, make it something substantial, something you might not want someone to know, at least not until you trusted them. So? What do you say? Do we have a deal?"

She eyed him suspiciously, though it wasn't for long. A resigned look eventually came to her face, which she followed with an indifferent shrug of her shoulders.

"Whatever," she said, somewhat overplaying her disinterest. "I'm curious to know if you have something good to give, because honestly, I don't think you do. I think this is going to be a big disappointment, but—" She cut herself off before shifting her gaze to the ceiling. She appeared to be mulling something over in her head.

"But if it's good . . . really good . . ." She leaned forward in her chair, closing the gap between them, close enough to give Mitch a whiff of the harsh cleansers used in the industrial-strength soaps and shampoos given to the patients. "I'll give you something *really* good in return."

A sinking feeling momentarily pervaded Mitch's stomach as he second-guessed his strategy, but there was no turning back now. "I have depression," he said, followed by a sudden pang of nerves when his confession did not draw her gaze. "It's a clinical diagnosis, and I take medication for it. Hasn't been easy. Depression treatments don't always work, and they left me feeling pretty discouraged." He saw her neck move, a little twist to the left, her head inching his way.

"I took different drugs, tried different therapies, and I'm not cured. Doesn't work that way. Some days it's better than others and I think I have it under control. Other days . . . well, not so much. It's been part of me for most of my life, but I've masked it well. I don't like talking about my mental health issues. I think I'm supposed to somehow be above it because I help people get over their illnesses. But I'm not my disease. I'd still go see a cancer specialist who had cancer herself if I trusted her to cure me. She's not her disease, and neither are you. I want to get to know you . . . *all* the facets of you . . . and try to help. That is, if you'll let me."

Now, she was looking him squarely in the eyes.

"I don't know much about you because what's in your file are thoughts, notes, and observations, nothing more. It's not you, the person."

Mitch wrung his hands together nervously. This was not an ordinary therapy session for him. He was being an open book with a patient, and for sure there was some ethical line he had crossed, but a deal was a deal—he'd have to give something to get it. Eve didn't budge, meaning he hadn't given enough.

"I sometimes wonder if I'd be a better doctor without depression, or maybe I'm good at what I do because of it," Mitch continued on. "Maybe I connect with my patients better because I'm intimately familiar with mental illness." He shrugged, his expression one of uncertainty. "All I know for sure is that having this disease makes it easier for me to blame myself when things don't work out."

This got Eve's full attention.

"What hasn't worked out?" she asked, sounding like the therapist in a role reversal.

"You next. That was our deal."

Eve eyed him nastily. "Everyone has mental problems, some are just better at hiding it than others. I expected more from you."

In for a penny, in for a pound, thought Mitch.

"What hasn't worked is that my son Adam—he's a bit older than you—is addicted to heroin. I keep asking myself: Did my illness prevent me from seeing what was happening right under my nose?"

"And what was happening?"

Mitch offered up an ill-prepared answer that came straight from the heart.

"Adam was experimenting with drugs on his own—booze, then pot, then pills—until he got to the really hard stuff. He did it and he hid it, and as much as I'd like to blame my depression, sometimes . . . well, make that most of the time . . . blame doesn't do anybody any good."

"Where is he now?"

"In a rehab facility. I can't see him for a few days. That's how they do it there. He needs to focus on his recovery, not on what his parents think or feel."

"Oh. So you're married?"

"Divorced," Mitch said, not sure when his secret revealing would stop; hoping it would be soon.

"Single?"

She smiled like a woman might at a bar, with a sparkle in her eyes.

"Yes."

"Hmmm . . ." she cooed. "Do you like *my* mother? Do you think she's pretty, Doctor?"

"I don't think that's why we're here."

Eve bit her bottom lip in an alluring way. "She was married, too, you know."

"Yes, to your father."

"He's dead." She said it curtly, but sadly, wistfully even, without a hint of venom.

"Yes, I know. And I'm sorry for that. You're Eve, right?"

"I'm Eve. The one and only." She made a flourishing gesture with her hands, like she was the grand reveal of a magic trick.

Score one for the doc! Now that Mitch had her, he wasn't about to waste the opportunity talking about his own life. "Let me ask you, Eve: Do you know a girl named Penny?"

She nodded tentatively, as if wary of where the question might lead.

"Can you talk to her?"

Another long pause.

"That's not such an easy answer. It's . . . all a bit confusing."

"Try. I really want to know."

Eve sighed aloud. "Sometimes . . . sometimes I hear her voice, like it's in my head, like a really loud thought, but then it goes away. I usually just ignore it."

"And you think it's . . . Penny?"

She nodded. "I hear them all."

If it weren't for therapy, Mitch highly doubted Eve would know anything about the others in her head. In cases of DID the primary identity not only carried the given name, but they were most often passive, dependent, guilty, and depressed, which matched Penny's personality, but in here Eve was the dominant one, and for good reason. People with DID could develop awareness of the mind's inside chattering at any time, at any age, and that was a key milestone on the path to integration.

Nowhere in Dr. Palumbo's reports did Eve ever confess to hearing the voices of her various personalities. The prospect of getting through Eve to connect with *all* Penny's alters no longer seemed so daunting, but Mitch realized there was another intriguing possibility. What if he could help Penny tap into the darkest places of her mind and gain access to the traumatic memory that preceded the splintering of her self?

Either way, for Eve to speak to him this candidly was a massive step forward.

"Can you name those voices you hear?" Mitch asked.

"Well there's Penny, and a girl named Chloe, and Ruby, and of course there's me."

No admission or even a hint at any hidden alter, Mitch noted.

He wasn't about to reveal that Penny was the host—the primary self—and that Eve was one of the alters. That would be too much for one session.

"And they all sound like loud thoughts in your head?"

"Sometimes, when I hear them, yeah," Eve said. "So, doesn't hearing voices mean I'm schizophrenic?" She sounded tentative for once, and her unexpected vulnerability felt to Mitch like another small victory.

"No, it doesn't, not at all. It's a common misconception actually. Schizophrenia is really a split between rationality and emotion, but what you have is different. It's a split within the personality. In both conditions a person may hear voices, but I do believe you have a grasp on reality. I'd like to know though if Penny—or anybody else speaking those loud thoughts—knows you're in Edgewater State Hospital?"

To demonstrate that different alters held different perceptions of reality would be helpful in court.

"I don't know," Eve said. "Hasn't really come up."

Mitch reached into his jacket pocket and took out his portable recorder. "Do you mind if I record our conversation? It will help me to remember it."

"Whatever," Eve said.

"What about the reason you're here? Do these other voices—your alters—do they have different views on that?"

Eve straightened, putting distance between them, and Mitch sensed he was losing her.

"Do they ever talk about what happened?"

She eyed Mitch darkly.

"Do you know why you're here?" Mitch asked.

Eve said nothing.

I'm going to trigger her . . . she may snap . . . or clam up.

"Do you know where you are, Eve?"

"Your questions are annoying me . . . Doctor," she said with contempt.

"You think you're ready to tell me your secret?"

A twisted grin graced her lips.

"Fair enough," Eve said. "A deal is a deal." She clapped her hands together and made a sound.

"So, let me tell you about the first time I took a life."

CHAPTER 18

Looking back, I should have been more alarmed about what was going on with you. I suppose that goes for us all. I mean, we all met Ruby—charming Ruby, lovely British Ruby—but nobody thought anything of it. We thought she was a character of yours, someone from the world of Harry Potter. We figured Ruby was you, just pretending, playing a silly, harmless game that would come and go.

But what nobody knew was that by then, I'd already met Eve.

You'd been living with us for a year and a half, so that would have made you six, and I'd have been eight. Ryan and I were still sharing the same bedroom, which Mom had painted a *manly* shade of gray, something we covered with posters of sports stars and superheroes.

I liked having you around from the minute you came to live with us. There wasn't a big adjustment period, not that I recall anyway. One minute you weren't living in our house, and the next it was as if you'd always been there. I mean, there were small things. At first you were all "thank you," and "please," and "may I," but little by little, as you got comfortable with us, and we with you, away went a "thank you," then a "please," then a "may I," until after some time you were just like me and Ryan: asking, taking, demanding, while Mom and Dad did what they could to keep us in line.

We'd gone from being two kids to three, and that was fine with us—better than fine. It was great. Honestly, the early years of you becoming a Francone would have made for a terribly boring movie. Nothing happened, it was all perfectly normal. There were school days, and you had homework to do, activities like softball, piano, and karate, TV, messing around, bike riding, basketball on the driveway with that hoop we held up with sandbags, and weekends spent doing whatever. The days all kind of blended into a great whirling blur of family life. Yes, you were shy in a crowd, shy at school, always were, but with us you could be your boisterous, laughing, fun-loving self, and we loved you for it.

Most mornings we ate breakfast together, more often than dinner, because of the restaurant. You loved Apple Jacks the best, which Mom never bought before you came. Once she found out you favored them, well, suddenly the pantry was never without a box.

In no time at all you became our little princess, though you weren't very princess-like when you showed up to the restaurant to "help out." All you wanted to do at Big Frank's was play with balls of dough, and Dad was more than happy to oblige you. Your giggles while you made pizza creatures, the delight in your eyes when Dad baked them into something you could eat—those are really sweet memories of a really sweet little sister.

At first I didn't know what it meant to *have* a little sister, but I became your protective big brother in no time. It was important to me that you were safe. After the hide-and-seek debacle, I was always checking up on you. That gave us a good taste of what it would be like if we ever lost you for real. For Mom, it was a great relief, because I was a second set of eyes, which came in especially handy during the weekend getaways down on the Cape, at that hotel with the indoor water park.

You'd never seen a water park before, and this one was tiny in comparison to most, but to you it was the greatest place ever. The chlorine was so strong it turned our eyes red just standing on the tiled edge of the pool. You didn't know how to swim, you'd never had a lesson in your life, but you didn't have one bit of fear either, not one. You jumped right in with your floaties latched around your arms, and it was my job (and Mom's, who hovered over you back then before those JCC lessons finally paid off) to make sure you stayed above the water line. Your lack of skill and experience didn't stop you from going down the slide—I remember that clearly.

I also remember waking up in the middle of the night to see you standing next to my bed holding Wally the Walrus in one hand, a big pair of scissors in the other.

Earlier that evening, Ryan had changed the TV channel from a show you were watching to one he wanted to watch. You got quite upset at him, didn't you? But he was bigger, older by four years, and you didn't get your way even when you pleaded with Mom. She thought you'd had enough TV for the day and asked you to do something else.

You were mad as I'd ever seen you, and you stayed mad when you went to bed in a huff, and you were still angry when you took Wally out of our bedroom closet. Ryan was ten, so he hadn't fully abandoned all his stuffed animals back then, and you knew poor Wally was his favorite, even though he stayed mostly in that closet.

I woke up because I heard a rustling sound and saw you in the moonlight, your eyes aglow like those of a panther. You put your finger to your lips—"Quiet," you mouthed to me—and then with considerable effort, you stabbed one of Wally's fins with those scissors (sharp ones Mom would *never* have let you use).

You began to cut. Snip. Snip. You cut and tore at that fabric until one of Wally's fins dangled from his fuzzy body as if a motorboat had struck him. Next, you jabbed the scissors through Wally's eye socket, twisting them around until a glass bead of an eye popped out of his stuffed head and bounced on the carpeted floor.

I was so shocked at what I'd seen that I lost my voice, but eventually I whispered, "What are you doing, Penny?"

You whispered back to me, in a voice that sounded different from the one I knew, harsher, colder, "Don't call me Penny. I'm Eve."

You looked different, too. There was a strange tilt to your mouth that was almost like a sneer, and a new way you carried your shoulders—thrown back, with more confidence. You had swagger, no other way to describe it. You collected Wally's eye and took him with you when you left the room.

The next morning you were Penny, the old Penny—head down in your Apple Jacks; your sad, sweet smile—back to the sister I knew.

As for Wally, he vanished, simple as that. I'm not sure Ryan even noticed he was gone. I never said anything because, well, I was your protector and didn't know what to make of that night. Eve stayed away, so I sort of let it go.

Then you turned twelve, and Eve returned. One day, you and I heard a horrific sound coming from a patch of tall grass as we were walking home from Eisman's Beach. Mom let me take you there because Eisman's had a lifeguard on duty, so it was safe—not that we did much swimming in those frigid waters. Even so, on a hot summer day, ocean water up to your ankles could cool you down just like an ice bath. We were heading home on Puritan Road, carrying two chairs and a beach bag, when we heard the noise.

We didn't know what to make of it. It was a hissing, anguished, high-pitched whine. When we finally located the source, we found a gray-and-black tabby cat lying in the tall grass, its back broken. That much was obvious from the unnatural bend of its body, a U-shaped curve that had almost folded the poor animal in half. Two of its legs were shattered, their bones sticking out from the fur, and it had a long gash in its abdomen that showed what was happening on the inside. The cat saw us standing over it, and I swear those green eyes were pleading with us to end its misery.

We were both in total shock.

"A car must have hit it," I said softly. "What else could have done that?"

"She's hurting," you said, your voice quivering with fright. You had tears in your eyes, as did I. "She can't be saved. Look at her."

I looked away instead.

"I should call Mom . . . or the vet. I have a phone," I said breath-lessly. "We'll call the animal hospital."

"It's going to take too long," you said with evident despair. "A min-ute of this is too long. Look at her. She's suffering."

You pointed. This time you *made* me look. And you were right—never in my life had I seen such torment. The cat was writhing on the ground, moving as much as it could with a broken back and bro-ken legs, making a gravelly, groaning sound like a door creaking open. Sometimes the noises were higher pitched, sharper, as if the animal were calling out to say, *Help . . . please help me.*

"What should we do?" I shouted my question out of sheer panic.

You searched the ground until your gaze settled on a big rock lying in a tangle of weeds. When I realized what it was you were looking at, what had to be on your mind, I started shaking my head vigorously.

"No. No. We can't," I said.

And you said, "It's hurting. It's going to take too long to put her out of her misery. She can't be saved. You know it's true."

And it was true. We didn't need to be veterinarians to figure that one out. So I guess that's why I didn't stop you, didn't say no, didn't ask you to drop it, didn't do anything at all when you bent down and stuck your fingers beneath the rock, tugging and tugging until you pried it free from the soft earth into which it had sunk. I didn't call Mom or the vet. There were no passing cars to flag down. It was just the two of us when you lifted up the rock and cradled it against your belly.

I heard you grunt before you hoisted it over your head. It was heavy, lopsided, and must have been difficult, but you had a strength that day that I'd never seen before. I watched you for a second as you swayed on your feet, the muscles of your arms straining against the heavy weight, fighting for balance. There was this look on your face, a kind of excitement—a strange satisfaction brimming there. I couldn't look at you, so I settled my gaze back on that poor cat.

You started the countdown.

"One . . ."

My stomach tightened. The cat meowed like a siren's wail, as if it knew what was coming.

"Two . . ."

My hands balled into fists. I dug my heels into the ground, bracing myself for the inevitable. When I glanced over at you, there wasn't a bit of fear in your eyes, not a single indication of uncertainty or doubt on your face. Instead of seeming nervous, to me you appeared eager, and I had to look away again. But, looking at the cat continue to struggle, hissing now, knowing that the end was near, I couldn't do that, either, so instead I just stood there with my eyes closed tight.

I heard you grunt, one final heave-ho effort, before you let out a scream like a war cry.

"Three!"

As sunspots danced on the lids of my shuttered eyes, I screamed too. But it wasn't loud enough to drown out the thud of the rock and the crack of bone. The hissing stopped, and the air was soon filled with the smell of blood.

When I finally found the courage to open my eyes, I went completely cold inside. First I saw the cat, its body as still as the rock lying on top of it. I turned my head slowly to look at you. There you stood, your arms limply at your sides, surveying what you'd done with a look of astonishment on your face. You'd shed no tears, and you showed no fear, no sorrow, no hint of remorse. Worse, your eyes held a strange sparkle. There was dark satisfaction glimmering there, and I couldn't help but think that you'd gotten a twisted thrill out of what you'd done.

That look on your face, in your eyes—I'd seen it before, when you had Wally in one hand and a pair of scissors in the other. I asked in a voice soft as the warm summer breeze that ruffled your long hair, "Eve, is that you?"

You turned your head slowly to look at me, as if you'd just realized I was standing right beside you. You kept your unblinking gaze fixed on me for a time as a slight grin came to your face. And without saying a word, your smile brightened as you sent me a single nod.

Leabharlanna Fhine Gall

CHAPTER 19

THE DINING ROOM AT Big Frank's was a quarter full, better than usual, but not good enough. Customers contentedly grazed on pizzas, calzones, and salads, but Grace had no appetite at all. She was busy in the kitchen, helping Annie prepare pies and such, thinking mostly about Mitch and their meeting with Navarro.

As she was layering sauce on a pizza, Grace layered more guilt onto herself.

"Maybe if we'd met Dr. Cross sooner, knew about DID sooner, got Penny better treatment, none of this would have happened," Grace lamented to Annie, who was slicing veggies next to her with the skill of a Hibachi chef.

She left out how frustrating it was that after all the effort to get a proper diagnosis it wasn't sticking, not with Palumbo and apparently not with Mitch either. Of course she was grateful that Mitch had a plan that might help keep Penny out of prison, but with the trial so close, and Eve so difficult, it was a long shot—or a moon shot, as Navarro had implied.

"I think you're being too hard on yourself," Annie said, her knife a blur against the cutting board. "Everyone thought Ruby was a routine. You couldn't have known it was *DID*. And then, well, when Chloe came, you didn't even know it was an alter. If it weren't for therapy, you wouldn't have even known *any* of these alters had names. One day Penny just announces that she wants to get straight As in school and you're supposed to think . . . what? It's not really Penny? I would have been happy as could be if my kids ever committed to their schooling like that."

Grace had to laugh, because that was just how she'd felt back then. Happy. Her concern had been only that Penny would be too hard on herself if she fell short of that goal.

"There were signs much earlier, is all I'm saying," Grace said definitively. "The rock incident, remember that?"

"Refresh, please," Annie replied with a slight grimace of embarrassment. "A lot has happened to you, and this old noggin has downshifted." She rapped her knuckles against her skull.

"I'm sure you remember that Penny and Ryan were always squabbling—*he said this, she did that*—that kind of thing."

"Oh yeah, that I *do* remember."

"And Arthur thought it was jealousy on Ryan's part. You know, Penny took a lot of the attention away from him."

"I remember that, too."

"Then one day, after a fight about some nonsense, Penny threw a rock that hit Ryan in the head. She was . . . what, twelve? Thirteen? Way too old for that behavior, but she said she was just messing around and didn't mean to hit him. Next morning, Penny found her confiscated phone and was using it like nothing had happened.

"I reminded her about her punishment, but instead of defending herself, she was utterly horrified. She had *no* memory of throwing that rock and burst into tears, poor thing, saying how she'd never hurt Ryan. Memory loss is a sign of trouble, plain and simple. It was one of her alters who threw that rock, and I bet you anything it was Eve. I should have known, should have done something sooner, and that's all there is to it."

Grace noticed Ryan hovering nearby. He was carrying a box of potatoes retrieved from the back storeroom, and sported a brand-new, plum-colored Big Frank's polo shirt, which he had custom made for the staff to wear.

Grace liked the shirts well enough, thought they looked sharp. She was especially fond of the embroidered depiction of Ryan's grandfather, the restaurant's namesake, spinning a pizza on his outstretched (and stitched) finger. It was the spitting image of Francesco, aka Frank, right down to the same bald spot that Arthur had inherited. Ryan hoped that a new look would attract new customers, but the dwindling receipts couldn't be the only explanation for the brooding look haunting his face. It all fell apart soon after Penny's arrest. What had happened between then and now? The question continued to bedevil her.

"Talking about my darling sister?" Ryan asked as he set the box down atop a stainless steel prep table. Standing upright, he wrapped his arms across his broad chest in a way that made his biceps pop in the sleeves of the polo.

"I had a meeting with her lawyer and new doctor today," Grace explained. "Dr. McHugh is going to try to reach Penny's alters. He believes if he connects with them, he might be able to demonstrate she wasn't in control that night . . . that she suffered some kind of psychotic break when she met Rachel for the first time in person."

"I thought Eve was all dug in. So he's going to free the hostages, is that it?" Ryan said incredulously.

"It's possible," Grace said. "If not, he doesn't think the jury will buy the insanity defense."

"That's fair. I don't buy any of this nonsense about alternate personalities." Ryan's eyelids lowered, and Grace saw something in him that reminded her of Eve. "It's so absurd," he went on. "She's crazy as a loon. Always has been. That Palumbo guy was spot on when he called her a psychopath. Psychotic break? Give *me* a break. She *wanted* to kill, wrote about killing, even wrote that she was going to kill Rachel Boyd, and then she went and did it. What more do you need to know?"

"Ryan, please," Grace said, invoking the mother tone that had worked well only when her children were young.

He was heading back to the cash register when Grace heard the tinkling sound of the little brass bell above the front door. From the kitchen, she peered around Ryan to observe three men entering the restaurant. They were definitely not regulars.

Two of the men Grace did not know at all: dark-haired, dark-eyed, greasy-looking fellows, both in grease-stained work clothes. They moved from the front door to the counter with a cocky indifference that would have sent her across the street had she encountered them on a sidewalk.

The man in the middle, however, Grace recognized without a second glance because his picture had been all over the scandal-loving news around the time of the murder—Vincent Rapino, Rachel Boyd's paramour, who had never before found cause to set foot inside Big Frank's. Rapino was tall and thin, standing a head above his two companions. He came forward in something of a prowl, catlike on his feet, head darting around, surveying the restaurant with probing eyes.

Ryan, who was manning the cash register, politely waited to take food orders from these men, not realizing who it was approaching him. Or if he did, he played it extremely cool. Grace undid her apron as she came out from the kitchen to join Ryan at the front counter.

"I've got this, Mom," Ryan said.

"No," Grace muttered to him, talking in a low voice. "I don't think you do."

"Well, well, well," said Rapino, locking eyes on Grace as he smacked a calloused hand against the red laminate countertop. "Gracie Francone. What are the chances?"

He had a voice hard and cutting as a saw blade, which sent a shiver through Grace's body. Although he wore baggy jeans and an untucked plaid shirt, Grace could tell Rapino was ripped with muscle. He had his shirt rolled up, revealing sleeves of tattoos that wrapped around his arms like growing vines. His lean, sharp-featured face was pockmarked and covered in a heavy five-o'clock shadow. Beneath his thick black eyebrows, his eyes gave off the same ominous feel as storm clouds.

"How are you, Grace?" Rapino asked. Grace could smell cigarette smoke on his breath, and booze too, enough that you'd want to keep a match away from that mouth.

"Hello, Vince," Grace said, trying to sound calmer than she felt. "What brings you here?"

Rapino sent his two companions an overly exaggerated look of surprise.

"I thought this was a place where you could get something to eat," he said with a derisive laugh.

Grace swallowed hard before doing a reset. It shouldn't be a total shock to see him here, she told herself. The trial was coming up, so Penny was back in the news. She knew his auto repair place was in Lynn, and he was from there—but while Lynn had plenty of pizzerias, there were no laws on the books preventing his patronage here.

Rapino rubbed a hand across his head and through hair the color of oil.

"What can I get you?" Grace asked, fixing the three men with something of a gunfighter's stare. She knew they had come to harass her, but she didn't know how it would play out.

Rapino scanned the menus behind Grace—a set of blackboards in varnished wood frames, arranged so that they blocked the view of some industrial ventilation equipment. Most of the lettering on the menus was done using decals, but Annie always wrote out the daily specials in chalk. Today's was any slice and a soda for $4.99.

Rapino let out an exasperated sigh that sounded forced. "I was hoping to get a birthday cake," he said, running his tongue across his lips like he was licking off imaginary frosting. "Don't see it on the menu."

A confused look bloomed on Ryan's face.

"This is a pizza place," he said curtly. "I think Whole Foods is open; you can get a cake there."

"Whole Paycheck?" Rapino sounded aghast. "I'll pass." And he barked a soulless laugh.

"You know why he wants a birthday cake?" the shorter of Rapino's two minions asked in an accent straight out of Southie.

"Tell him," said Rapino, keeping his ominous stare fixed firmly on Grace.

"It's Rachel Boyd's birthday today," said the other man, who hadn't spoken yet.

Ryan leaned his body over the counter, closing the short gap between him and Rapino, no fear in his eyes. Grace could see the muscles in Ryan's broad shoulders go taut beneath that plum-colored polo.

"What the hell is this about?" he asked. Rapino took a single step back out of striking distance—he was no dummy. Grace suspected that Ryan could give these men a go, but hopefully he'd stand his ground. Three-to-one odds weren't in his favor.

"Want to tell him, Gracie, or should I?" said Rapino, casting a chiding smile.

"This is Vince Rapino," Grace said to Ryan, somehow keeping a cool demeanor while her heart pounded wildly. "He was Rachel's—"

Grace suspected Ryan remembered the name, but she wasn't sure how to label Vince and Rachel's relationship. She didn't have to think long, because in her brief pause Rapino answered for her.

"She was my girlfriend—something like that, right? Girlfriend," he repeated. "But that really pissed off my wife." Rapino scratched at a spot under his chin with a neutral expression. She couldn't tell what this man really felt, or if he felt anything at all.

"Now, though . . . now I got divorce papers, child support, and all the crap that goes with it. And you know what I'm thinking? I'm thinking that my wife—we'd been married eleven years, two kids—thinking that she might not have known about Rachel and me if your daughter, Gracie—your crazy, bitch-ass daughter—didn't carve her up like a goddamn pumpkin." The bit of lightness that had momentarily come to Rapino's face emptied on the spot.

"What do you want, Vince?"

Heat flushed Grace's cheeks as a prickle of unease danced across the nape of her neck.

"No harm here," Rapino said, holding up his hands as a truce. "We were driving around, saw your big, bright sign, and thought, 'Hey, let's get some birthday cake to celebrate Rachel on her special day,' and we come in . . . and I'm like, 'Wow, Grace Francone, here you are, what a shock.' It's like Rachel herself guided us here."

He made a flourishing gesture to the heavens, but Grace wasn't deluding herself that Vince's trip to Big Frank's had anything to do with some mystical influence from the beyond.

"Like you didn't know my mom worked here," Ryan said. Grace could sense him getting hotter.

"Mama. This your boy?" Rapino appraised Ryan up and down. "Big fella. Fed him good."

Annie came out from the kitchen to see what was going on. Seeing her reminded Grace of the gun in the safe in the back office. Annie was a shooter. The number of 'Annie, get your gun' jokes made over the years were far too numerous to count. Grace had been to the range with her and could attest that she could group her shots into her initials if she desired. Hopefully those skills wouldn't get put to any test.

"Everything all right?" Annie asked as her gaze traveled across the hard-looking men lining the front of the counter.

"It's fine," Grace answered quickly, still holding on to Ryan's shirt. "Vince, what do you want?"

"So okay, no cake. So . . ." He checked the menu for a second time. "How about some fountain Cokes for me and my boys then?" he asked.

"How about you—"

Grace gave Ryan's shirt a tug, both to keep him quiet and to anchor him in place.

"Okay, and then you all go," said Grace, finding a measured tone at last. "Annie, please get them some Cokes, no charge."

Annie poured the Cokes from the fountain machine while Vince looked around the restaurant.

"Nice place you've got here," he said. "Can't believe we haven't checked it out before. So, where is big Frank tonight? He here? Can I meet the fella?"

"Frank is my father-in-law, and no. He passed."

Annie returned to the counter with the Cokes.

"Oh, I'm sorry to hear that," Rapino said, not sounding sorry in the slightest as he took his Coke and stuck a straw in the lid. "Your husband, he's dead too, right?"

Ryan tensed.

"Get out," he demanded.

"Just asking," said Rapino, faking his upset. He leaned forward, squinting his eyes at Ryan, and growled in a low voice, "Why so hot, bro? You looking for something?"

Grace knew what that "something" meant to these men. Ugly. Violent. No way would she allow that to happen.

"Ryan, it's okay." Grace tried to ignore a sour taste that had settled in her throat. "Please, Vince, just go."

Vince appraised Ryan for a beat, perhaps thinking maybe he wouldn't just go, but then turned his attention back to Grace. He sent a leering look that filled her with a fresh flutter of fear. Then something changed in him. Like a car downshifting, he seemed to suddenly relax.

"Happy birthday, Rachel," Vince said, removing the lid from his Coke as he took a big sip from the open top. He raised his paper cup skyward, holding an ice chip between his bared teeth. While sending Grace an angry stare, he tilted his cup to the floor, allowing all of the sticky, brown, syrupy Coke to spill out. It made a loud splash, mixed with the delicate tinkling of tumbling ice cubes. Vince let the empty cup fall from his grasp.

"See you in court, Gracie," he said. "Looking forward to watching your baby girl get marched off in chains. But I'll tell you this: one way or another, justice will be served—maybe even *before* the verdict comes." He made his final statement while looking Grace dead in the eyes.

Then he turned around, his companions following suit as if it were a choreographed sequence. Away they marched out the door, the bell announcing their departure, the three of them oblivious to the shocked stares of the diners who watched them go.

Ryan shook with furious anger and might have leapt over the counter if Grace hadn't maintained a hold on his shirt.

"Don't," she said firmly. "Let them go. It's nothing. We'll clean it up."

"Nothing?" Ryan's eyes glimmered with rage.

Sarah, a longtime employee who had watched the encounter from a safe distance, approached with a tentative air. She had a sunny smile, but she needed some natural sunlight and a polo shirt maybe one size larger to keep some of the customers from gawking. Grace liked her chipper personality and knew she was not one to easily get ruffled, but what she'd seen had rattled her good.

"I'll clean this up right away," she said hurriedly before setting off for the maintenance closet.

"What an asshole."

Ryan couldn't let it go as he kept his eyes locked on the door, maybe hoping for a return visit. Grace felt a wave of relief knowing they were gone.

"What did he want?" asked Annie nervously.

"To taunt us, I guess," said Grace as she came out from behind the counter to stand next to the spill, which had spread on the floor like a brown lake with a jagged shoreline.

"It's all right, folks," Grace announced in a loud but calming voice to the patrons, who were still chatting nervously amongst themselves. "Those men are gone, nothing to worry about. Free slice or a drink for anyone who wants one. We're sorry for any inconvenience, but everything is fine."

Grace found a folding *Wet Floor* sign tucked behind the counter and set it in front of the spill, wondering what was taking Sarah so long to get the mop and floor cleaner.

"Why would he come here to taunt us?" asked Annie.

"I don't know," said Grace, wondering when the anxious feeling would abate. "Add insult to injury, I suppose. Make us suffer."

"Because he's suffering? He didn't look too broken up to me," said Annie. "I didn't get one vibe off him that he gives a rat's ass about Rachel."

"Maybe that's because he knows what really happened that night and he doesn't care," said Grace.

"Yeah, because he was there at the apartment, murdering her," said Annie. "But then why come here?"

"Why does an arsonist return to the scene of a fire?"

Grace answered before Annie could.

"Because they get off on seeing the damage they caused, that's why. The trial is coming up. For a guy like Vince that's like a full moon calling out the crazies."

At last Sarah returned, with a bucket, mop, and the news that they were out of floor cleaner.

"No, we're not," Ryan said. "We have a box of ammonia in the storeroom. You just have to dilute it with water. Hang on." He managed to keep his tone a few tics from condescending. He headed off for the storeroom in a huff, Sarah following behind.

Grace was about to use the mop sans floor cleaner, but something held her back. She turned her attention to Annie.

"Penny for your thoughts," Annie said, then grimaced. "Oh, sorry. Expression."

"Actually, it is Penny I'm thinking of," said Grace. "Ammonia . . . it might not have crossed my mind, except Ryan just mentioned it. That's what I smelled in the visiting room when Penny suddenly reappeared. Someone got sick or something before I got there, and the place had been fumigated with ammonia."

Annie's blue eyes conveyed her curiosity.

"At first I was sure it was Eve who'd shown up to lunch that day because, well, that cold look in her eyes was there. Then I remember she sniffed the air and her whole expression changed. She got a strange, blank look, and before I knew it, it was Penny. She was back, with no idea where she was or what had happened."

"She also stuck around for a while afterward in the ER," said Annie, who knew the story.

Excitement blossomed on Grace's face. "Scent can be a powerful trigger," she said.

"Do you think smelling ammonia could bring back Penny again?" asked Annie.

"There's only one way to find out," said Grace.

CHAPTER 20

MITCH MADE HIS WAY (without getting lost this time) to the visitors' entrance, where he awaited Grace's arrival. He'd spent the night researching the innate power of the fifth sense—smell—and he couldn't wait to debrief her on all he'd learned.

A buzz rang out, followed by a loud clank as the steel door to the visitors' entrance opened. In stepped a burly guard, and close on his heels came Grace, with a determined stride and cool smile. Perhaps if he'd said unequivocally that Penny had DID, a friendly embrace might have followed that smile.

With a flash of his employee badge, Mitch sent the guard away, leaving him alone with Grace to walk and talk in private. They exchanged pleasant hellos before Grace took a step back, appraising Mitch anew.

"Is everything all right?" she asked, probing eyes narrowed on him.

"I'm fine," he said, mustering some conviction, though Grace did not look fully convinced. "Didn't sleep well last night," he added, which was a half-truth. He wasn't going to cloud the day with news about Adam and his return to rehab.

"Tell me about it," said Grace, pointing to a trace of dark circles that only now did he notice under her eyes. "Are we all set?"

"The room is reserved, and I've got maintenance swabbing the floor with ammonia as we speak."

On his way out of work yesterday, Mitch had slipped one of the custodial staff a twenty for the favor.

"Excellent," said Grace, her head bobbing eagerly. She seemed both nervous and excited, and for good reason. "Are we using the same room as before? I think it's important that everything be as close to the way it was when the switch to Penny took place."

"The very one," said Mitch, starting down the hall.

Guards and patients, all females in this building, crowded the corridor, some chattering to themselves, others making low groaning noises. Grace, deep in thought, didn't take notice of them. Because of Edgewater's confounding layout, the only way to reach the visiting rooms involved some interaction between patients and visitors.

Grace had done this walk plenty of times, but even seasoned visitors sometimes found it hard not to stare. Mitch noticed her gaze fixated on a bedraggled woman with short dark hair, squinty eyes, and a square build. She held a well-worn Bible in her right hand, which she carried on her person most everywhere she went. Her name was Darla, a patient of Mitch's. At one point Darla had a husband and children, but her disease—acute paranoid schizophrenia—caused impulsive and aggressive behavior, which was never a good combination.

Five years ago, Darla shot her husband in the face at point-blank range because she held an unshakable delusion that he was cheating on her—which, after his demise, proved to be untrue. Unfortunately, Darla still harbored delusions that women were after her long-deceased spouse, and her impulses, though tempered with medication, were hardly under control.

Mitch wasn't overly concerned when he caught the brief eye contact between Grace and Darla, but he was keenly on guard. The vast majority of people with schizophrenia are not prone to violence of any sort. However, a small number who do suffer from the acute symptoms of psychosis can become quite violent, with delusions being the most likely trigger.

As Darla passed on the right, Grace refocused her attention forward, then took two steps before coming to an abrupt stop. "I should have ordered pizza to keep it the same as it was. I forgot. Dammit."

"I wouldn't be too worried about the pizza," Mitch said. "We're focused on the right thing here. I'm sure of it."

Before they could resume their walk, Mitch's senses became acutely heightened by a sudden surge of adrenaline. He turned to see Darla coming down the hall toward them, eyes blazing, guards nowhere to be seen.

"She screwed him, didn't she?" Darla said, pointing an accusatory finger at Grace. "I saw that look she gave me. You whore. You bitch."

Spittle shot from Darla's snarling mouth as Grace recoiled from the sudden outburst.

Grace was too stunned to speak. Darla pointed her Bible at Grace's face like she was flinging holy water.

"'If a man commits adultery with another man's wife, both the adulterer and the adulteress are to be put to death.' Leviticus 20:10. Hear that, Missy Prissy? I'll snap your neck if you so much as look at my husband again. Snap it like a twig."

Darla mimed the promised breakage with a downward thrusting twist of her closed fists.

Survival instincts sent Grace backward, away from Darla, while Mitch, far more accustomed to these unexpected flare-ups, positioned himself between the aggressor and her target like a human shield.

"Darla, this is Grace," Mitch said, speaking calmly, but in a firm voice. "She did not sleep with your husband. She doesn't know your husband." While Mitch gave the outward appearance of composure and total control, his insides were as tightly coiled as a jack-in-the-box waiting to spring.

"I need you to back away, Darla, right now. That's an order from your doctor. Do you hear my voice?" He spoke in a commanding way to reinforce his position of authority over her. She didn't budge, so Mitch changed tactics. "Your husband is dead and Grace has done nothing wrong to you."

This got a reaction. Darla gazed wide-eyed at Mitch, looking profoundly confused. He knew the shocking information about Charles being deceased would require a moment's pause for her to puzzle it out, and would, he hoped, help subdue her.

Behind Darla were two guards, who had somehow let her slip away from their sight. They were moving in quickly, ready to pounce, and from their eyes he knew they'd make it an aggressive takedown. By now, Mitch had seen enough fights at Edgewater to know that a quick resolution often meant a violent one.

"Easy does it," Mitch said to the guards as he put up his hands to hold them in place. "I've got this."

COs took orders from docs, and these two held their ground.

"Darla, I want you to look me in the eyes," Mitch said. Instead, Darla kept her gaze and ire focused squarely on Grace, who continued to shelter behind Mitch. She was thick all around, squat like a tree trunk, and Mitch wasn't entirely certain two guards would be enough if the situation were to escalate.

"Look at me, Darla," Mitch demanded again, more forcefully than before, and that got her attention.

"I want you to calm yourself down now, right now. You have the wrong woman. Grace did not sleep with your husband."

That might work better, he thought. Rather than try to get her to accept the truth about poor Charles, it would be far easier for Darla to hold on to her delusion that her husband was in fact a cheater and convince her this was merely a case of mistaken identity. Since it wasn't an outright lie, Mitch had no qualms about employing a little bit of misdirection.

To her credit, Darla continued to glare but didn't charge. She took several deep breaths, as she'd been taught, to tamp down her rage.

"You've got the wrong woman," Mitch repeated. With a slight head nod, he implored the guards standing behind Darla to take a few cautious steps forward. They were close enough now for Mitch to read the nameplates pinned to their shirts, opposite their shiny silver badges. He didn't know the one named Steadman, but he should have recognized the other man right away: Correctional Officer Blackwood, the same Blackwood who had nearly clubbed Penny with his baton on the day Mitch had met Grace. He was a bit surprised to see Blackwood still had a job, but was nonetheless grateful that the guard was on hand to assist.

"Darla, CO Blackwood and CO Steadman are going to escort you back to your room now," Mitch said. "I'm going to come check on you in a little bit, okay?" *And probably up your dose of Clozaril,* he thought, recalling from memory the medications she was taking.

"I need you to go with them without complaint." He used a voice that would be good for someone hard of hearing.

"'Let marriage be held in honor among all, and let the marriage bed be undefiled.'" She held up her Bible so Grace would know it was the word of God. "If I find out she defiled my marriage, I'll tear out her eyes with my fingernails."

"That's absolutely uncalled for, Darla, and very rude," Mitch said, sternly but in a softer voice than before. "Go back to your room and wait for me there. Is that understood?"

Mitch set his hands on his hips, sending Darla a look that made it clear his order was not open to negotiation. Something clicked, a flick of a switch, and Darla seemed to deflate on the spot.

"I'm sorry about that," Darla said, going a bit red in the face while addressing Grace in an apologetic tone. "Guess I had the wrong person."

That was a big admission for her, Mitch noted. It meant she was willing to take responsibility for a mistake, let her ego take a bruise, and see for herself that she could endure it without any lasting damage to her psyche. It was a positive step that he could reinforce in her therapy sessions. The guards came forward and took hold of Darla's arms in a gentle fashion; guiding, not pulling her, away from Mitch and Grace.

"Thanks, Doc," CO Steadman said, relief evident in his voice and eyes. CO Blackwood didn't appear nearly as pleased, and even went so far as to send Mitch a glowering stare. Perhaps he was still stewing over having been reported for his mistreatment of Penny.

Grace and Mitch watched Darla depart. She looked as shaken as he felt.

"Second day in a row I've almost gotten in a fight," Grace said, reminding Mitch of the incident with Vince Rapino that had triggered today's experiment. "That was very impressive," she added.

"Not really."

Mitch started down the hall, and Grace fell in lockstep with him.

"Nobody wants violence," he said. "But it's rampant here, and honestly, having more guards than docs on duty is a big part of the reason. Most of the time there are ways to defuse situations. Unfortunately, I can't be everywhere at once. Are you okay? I know that was a bit unnerving. Darla can be . . . well, intimidating, and I can attest that her bark is *not* worse than her bite. She's a real brute."

"I'm fine," Grace said, shaking it off with a shrug. "It's sad, is all. There's so much suffering here. So many people battling their minds."

"Your daughter among them," said Mitch, resetting the focus. Today wasn't about Darla, but Penny.

"Do you think it will work?" asked Grace with a hopeful note.

"I've come across cases in my research where a dank smell reminds a victim of a basement where some abuse took place, which resulted in switching to a protective persona as a consequence," he said. "Of all our senses, smell is the one most closely linked to memory, so I think there's a good chance you found a way to trigger the switch from Eve to Penny."

"Why is the link so strong?"

"Neuroscience would tell you that smell skips the thalamus in the brain, which the other senses have to pass through—like a relay station—to get various inputs to the hippocampus or the amygdala, where our emotions are processed."

"Where does smell go?"

"Straight to the olfactory bulb, which we've only recently learned is a memory center where certain long-term memories get stored."

"I just don't get what significance ammonia has for Penny," Grace said while walking.

"Did you clean with it a lot at home?"

Grace's shrug didn't discount the possibility. "I mean, we used it in the restaurant for sure, but not excessively."

"It could be any number of things."

Mitch considered sharing how the smell of grass and rubber cleats reminded him of Adam's soccer games, or that the stench of marijuana conjured memories of his son's decline, but opted against it. Grace had her own cross to bear today.

"Did you ever check for the book she mentioned that day in the ER?" Mitch asked.

"I checked her bookshelf thoroughly," said Grace. "But I couldn't find any that had a dark blue cover with water and boats."

"Maybe she took it with her that night, tossed it away somewhere," Mitch suggested. "That book is significant to her, maybe something her birth mother read to her. Could be she'd bought it on her recommendation, or it was something Rachel mailed to her. We just don't know."

"I'll check our Amazon orders," Grace said. "If she did buy it online, there'll be a record of it."

"Good thinking," Mitch concurred.

All thoughts of books with boats on the cover, of Adam and sorrow, faded when they arrived at their meeting room. Mitch checked his watch: Eve would be joining them shortly. He opened the door and the scent of ammonia hit with force, burning his nostrils.

"Oh my God, the smell wasn't this strong," Grace said, entering behind him, squinting her eyes as she pinched her nose with her fingers.

Mitch closed the door, effectively trapping them in the fumes.

"I don't think the ratio matters, but we don't want to let out all the smell."

Grace continued holding her nose as Mitch took out his phone, launched the camera app, and set the mode to video recording. He wanted to capture Eve's reaction—and, hopefully, her transformation into Penny. He did not discount the potential secondary benefit of this experiment, namely advancing the acceptance of dissociative identity disorder among his profession's many skeptics.

"I think I'll wait in the hall," Grace said, making for the exit. Before she could take a single step in that direction, the door to the room opened and her daughter came in.

CHAPTER 21

GRACE'S GAZE FLICKERED FROM her daughter to the two uniformed guards who served as her escort. Both were thin and on the younger side, but she got the distinct impression they were quite capable of holding their own in a fight. At that moment, after taking big whiffs of the heavily scented air, each CO simply held his nose. The stench sent them reeling back out into the hallway.

"Whoa, what happened in here?" one guard asked in a young man's voice.

"Need a gas mask," said the other.

Grace shifted her attention to her daughter, who had come dressed in her trademark green uniform, baggy as ever. Her hair was pulled back in a loose pony, how Penny often wore it, allowing for an unobstructed view of her face. There was no trace of a smile, and in those sapphire eyes a cold fire burned.

Not Penny. Still Eve.

Sniffing the ammonia-scented air, Eve looked about as if trying to locate the source of the odor before advancing into the room. Grace held her breath with nervous anticipation.

"Is this a gas chamber?" her daughter asked in Eve's trademark snarl. "Are you finally putting me out of my misery, Mother?"

Grace deflated on the spot. It hadn't worked. Eve remained, and whatever had brought Penny forth that day wasn't triggered by scent. A feeling of hopelessness welled up inside her, and Grace wasn't sure if it was the ammonia or her disappointment making her eyes water. She tamped down her emotions in order to take Eve into her arms and give her daughter a proper hug hello. She didn't expect any resistance, nor did she expect her hug to be reciprocated—which it was not.

Putting her nose to her daughter's scalp, Grace inhaled deeply. Underneath the chemical fumes, her hair carried a familiar scent, calling up memories of a smiling girl in a bathtub with a hairnet of suds and one of her favorite mermaid dolls clutched in each hand. A sob broke from Grace's lips. It was a surprise, but a relief, too, that Eve allowed her mother's hug to go on.

Eventually, Grace gave up the struggle and allowed her tears to fall freely. They went rolling down her cheeks in salty rivulets, and it was a cry for everything—for Arthur, for Penny, for Ryan's wayward ways, and for poor Jack, who was all but forgotten in the wreckage of her life. She cried for Annie, soon to be departing for Florida, and the world she had manifested for herself that was no longer hers to control.

Grace held on to Eve as her shoulders shook and the ammonia burned. She was about to let go when something brushed up against her back, stroking and soothing her. It was a phantom feeling, she decided, because nobody—not Mitch, not Eve—could offer her any real comfort in that moment. The touch intensified until she felt herself being pulled into a strong embrace, and only then did she realize it was her daughter holding her close.

With a gentle push, Grace broke the hold to gaze into her daughter's eyes. They shone clearly like two pools of the purest water, not a trace of menace to be found.

As the smell dissipated into the hallway, Grace's other senses sharpened. Now it was Penny's stoop-shouldered stance and docile manner—chin tilted down, hands stuffed nervously inside the pockets of her Edgewater-issued pants, mouth dipped into a slight frown—on full display. Brushing a hand against Penny's smooth cheek, Grace felt a warmth Eve never could generate, and her tears came again.

"Penny," Grace said in a disbelieving whisper.

"Mom." Penny's voice came out rife with anguish. Grace kissed her cheek, hard.

"It's so good to see you," said Grace. She kept her movements controlled and to a minimum, as if anything sudden might scare Penny away like a deer sensing danger.

"What's going on, Mom? Am I still here? At the hospital?"

Of course. Penny's last memory would have been from her time in the emergency room.

"Yes, you're still at the special hospital," Grace said. "Let's sit and talk."

"It smells awful in here." Penny took several big whiffs of the foul air.

"It'll clear out, not to worry." Grace didn't want to leave the room and risk having Eve return. "Talk to me, tell me how you're doing?"

Grace looked at Mitch worriedly as she guided Penny into a seat at the same table where, days ago, they had tried to eat lunch together.

"You remember Dr. Mitch, right?"

Penny nodded. "From the ER," she said.

"He needs to record us for your treatment," Grace said in an encouraging way.

Penny's next nod was nearly imperceptible.

As she took her seat, Grace peered over at Mitch. Sure enough, he had his phone's camera lens aimed directly at Penny. The small device did not completely block her view of Mitch's face, and Grace interpreted his slack jaw and crinkled brow to mean that he, too, was struggling to process what he was recording.

Grace took firm hold of Penny's tremulous hands. She didn't know how much time they had together. A minute? Fifteen? A half hour? *How long had Penny stuck around in the ER that day?*

"Darling, it's important we talk," Grace said, her heart butting up against her ribs. "You told us some things the last time we were together, things we need to clarify."

Instead of answering, Penny flung her arm into the air, bringing her palm down against the table with a smacking sound loud as a gunshot. It was a gesture similar to the one Grace had made in Navarro's office. Like mother, like daughter. Concern tugged at Grace. Was a switch happening before her eyes? Had confusion and fear driven Penny away?

"I need to know why I'm here."

"Penny . . ."

"Tell me, Mother."

Mother. It was still Penny, but even shy, timid girls have their breaking points.

"Don't be upset," Grace said. "You're safe. Trust me. I'm working hard to help you."

"Just get me out of here," Penny pleaded, her lower lip jutting out in a pouty way.

"This is a long process," said Grace, "we have to talk first."

"Talk? Okay, let's *talk*." Penny slumped in her chair. "I don't even know why I'm here."

Grace sent Mitch a look that brought him forward. "You told us some things in the ER, things you remembered. You said to Dr. Mitch you weren't alone that night. Do you recall that conversation?"

Penny eyed Mitch with focused intent, and Grace thought she saw a flicker of recognition burst forth in her eyes.

"I don't remember that," Penny said, pulling her hand from under Grace's with a quick jerk of her arm.

Mitch stepped forward. "Your memories will help us explain everything to you," he said. "You told me about a book you were reading. Something with water and boats on the cover?"

Penny shifted her focus from her mother to Mitch and back again, frustration straining her unblemished face. She was so young to be dealing with so much. Grace felt an ache that only mothers with a sick and helpless child can know.

Penny returned a slow shake of her head. "I don't know about any book, and I won't do anything you ask me, not a single thing, until I get some answers." She'd issued her ultimatum with uncharacteristic authority, but Grace knew it was still Penny making her demand known. "I remember being in the ER," she continued. "There were people in handcuffs . . . patients in a *hospital* in *handcuffs*. Now, what's that about?"

Pride flooded Grace as she witnessed her child's self-advocacy. Perhaps she'd been underestimating Penny's resiliency.

Mitch was about to say something, but Grace raised a hand to stop him.

"There was a crime and the police think you hurt someone. The crime was a murder," Grace said somberly.

Penny's eyelids sank. "Do people think I did it? This is a prison hospital or something, isn't it?" Her soft-spoken voice belonged to the old Penny again, her short-lived vibrato gone as if it never had been. How Grace wished she had Arthur at her side. "Better together" was his motto, the phrase he'd always say about the family. That wasn't an option right now, so she pushed ahead, undaunted.

"Yes, it's a prison hospital specifically for people with mental health issues. It's called Edgewater. And yes, they think you committed a murder," Grace confessed.

Penny bit her lower lip, her head still downcast. "Do they have evidence against me?" A shaky voice implied she knew the answer.

"They do. A lot."

"Who was murdered?"

Grace turned to Mitch for guidance, but he shifted on his feet, seeming as unsure as she felt.

She waited a beat, then two, and finally said, "The victim is a woman named Rachel Boyd."

Grace braced herself for a volatile reaction that didn't come. Then something caught in Penny's throat, and an instant later, tears flooded her eyes.

"Mom—" Penny closed her eyes tightly. "She contacted me . . . Facebook, we exchanged messages . . . she told me . . . to keep it a secret, and I did. She wanted to meet. I remember now . . . I took the car to meet her . . . I know I shouldn't have, but I did, and I'm sorry—"

"It's okay, love," Grace said, reaching across the table to take hold of Penny's hands again.

"I . . . I *killed* Rachel?"

"That's what people are saying," said Grace.

"*Why* would I do that?"

"We're trying to get some answers," Grace replied.

Off to her left, Mitch kept the camera trained on Penny.

"Think about that book, okay?" he encouraged. Grace appreciated his redirection. It was similar to the way he handled Darla not long ago. "You said it had a dark blue cover, boats in the water."

For a moment, nothing happened.

"Go on, darling. Try to picture it," Grace implored.

"I can't." Penny made a frustrated sound, but Grace patted her hand to encourage her to keep trying. Soon Penny stilled, and Grace sensed something transpiring. "Wait, I do see it," she said in a hushed voice after a moment's pause. "The book."

"Oh good . . . that's *very* good. Can you see the title?" Grace felt her excitement growing.

"I'm not alone," Penny whispered. Grace knew it was no longer just a book she was seeing in her mind.

"Who's with you?" she asked. "Is it a man? Is it Vincent? Vincent Rapino?"

Penny opened her eyes as if jolted from a trance.

"You know that name." Grace sounded stunned, but quickly composed herself. "He was Rachel's boyfriend. Do you remember anything about him?"

"I didn't do anything wrong," Penny said, her tone apologetic. Her eyes were open, but it looked to Grace as though she were seeing beyond the Edgewater walls.

Grace leaned in closer, thinking she hadn't heard quite right. "Come again?"

"I didn't do anything wrong," Penny said, this time with conviction. "Nothing."

Her eyes soon filled, cheeks went rosy, and before long tears were streaming down her face.

"It's okay . . . I understand. You're safe," Grace assured her. "What happened that night? Can you tell me?"

"Someone hurt her, but it wasn't me," Penny said, speaking in a soft, almost dreamlike tone.

"I'll say a name," Grace said. "You don't have to answer, just nod your head if that person was with you."

Penny went still as a painting, giving no indication she'd grasped her mother's instruction. From her wide and frightened eyes it appeared she was still lost in the past, trapped in some terrible memory.

"Was Vincent there?"

The only movement Penny made was to close her eyes slowly.

"Was Maria with you?"

Penny gave no acknowledgment. Her body stayed still even as her eyes opened. She looked empty, the mannequin look again.

While her daughter remained motionless, inside Grace was revving up. These new revelations—*I didn't do anything wrong, I wasn't alone*—revived a hope in her long ago abandoned in the face of the overwhelming evidence.

Could Penny be innocent?

"You saw someone hurt Rachel. Can you give us a name?"

Instead of answering, Penny tapped her hand softly and rhythmically against the table.

Tap. Tap. Tap.

Three times those taps sounded in short succession, and then paused before she did it again.

Tap. Tap. Tap.

"I didn't do anything wrong," she said in a breathy whisper.

Mitch's recording captured every detail: the way her lips pursed together, the squint of her eyes, how her hands had balled into tight little fists.

"Penny, who are you talking to?" Grace asked. "To me? Are you telling me that you're innocent?"

It looked to Grace as though Penny had donned a virtual reality headset, and through its magical lens, she could peer into the past to confront a terror that felt visceral and real to her.

"Look at your room again." Mitch's words seemed to come out of the gloom, causing Grace to startle. "Do you see the book?"

"The book with boats and water," Penny answered in a dreamlike voice. "I love that book."

"Close your eyes and see if you can see it in your head. Tell me the title if you can."

Penny closed her eyes. "I see only the bucket," she said, unclenching her hands.

"Bucket? What bucket?" asked Mitch. He moved in closer, kneeling on the floor beside Penny, his attention focused on the patient more than his recording.

"It's a blue plastic bucket . . . filled with that stuff . . . it smells . . . awful."

"What stuff?" Grace squeezed Penny's hand gently.

"Ammonia. The bucket is full of ammonia. I'm going to get my head put in the bucket, too, but I didn't do anything wrong, so I shouldn't get the bucket."

Grace and Mitch exchanged horrified glances. Had someone tried to force Penny to inhale ammonia fumes on the night of Rachel's murder? That scenario was sickening to the core, but it certainly explained why the scent had triggered a switch. Thoughts flurried through Grace's mind as she tried to puzzle out possibilities.

Nothing about this made sense, but these were clearly her daughter's recollections.

"It happened to her, and it's going to happen to me." Penny sounded truly terrified. Her eyes were closed, but her head was turned to a corner of the room, as if seeing Rachel there, on her knees, someone standing behind her, pushing her head down, down, into a bucket full of ammonia. "I heard the voice say it. She has to be gone and gone for good. I'll get the bucket, too, if she's not gone and gone for good."

Grace was reeling now. Voice? What voice? Had someone pressured Penny to stab Rachel using the threat of torture? Gone and gone for good . . . dead . . . what other explanation could there be?

Then, in a quiet voice, so soft Grace had to strain to hear it, Penny began to speak.

"Alabama . . . Alaska . . . Chicago . . ."

"Penny?" Grace asked. "What are you talking about?"

Lost in this trance, Penny either didn't hear, couldn't respond, or she simply chose not to answer.

"Charlotte . . . Virginia . . . Ohio . . . Tennessee . . . Santa Fe," she continued.

Grace looked to Mitch, utterly bemused. He offered a shrug in response, for he too was baffled.

Before any more inquires could take place, Penny's eyes snapped open. Grace saw the transition happen—rare for sure, but it was not the first time she'd witnessed a switch. First Penny's arms crossed, then her legs, too, and she struck a defensive posture. She was leaving—Grace could feel Penny's presence slipping away, going, going, until the sapphires of her now-open eyes burned again with that cool heat and her daughter's delicate mouth contorted into a devilish grin.

"Oh, hello, Mother," said Eve coldly. "What a nice surprise to see you again."

CHAPTER 22

BIG FRANK'S HAD A round table to accommodate larger parties, and tonight everyone Grace loved the most—well, everyone but Penny—occupied the seats around it.

It was thirty minutes past closing time, and without the persistent chatter of patrons, Grace could hear the steady churn of ocean waves thrumming against the sandy beach across the street.

At the table sat Jack, slouchy as a teen, who had come home from college at Grace's request. He looked well, she thought; maybe a bit on the thin side. At least the mountainous calzone Annie had prepared would provide him some much-needed nourishment.

Jack had on a green and black flannel shirt, a birthday present Grace had gotten him a few years back. The shirt was a bit warm for the summer weather, but for someone who'd devoured Nirvana and Soundgarden albums in his youth, the grunge look was always in season. Jack's long hair was not in its usual ponytail tonight, allowing his dark curls to drape across his slender shoulders, and he had grown a goatee that all but completed his Seattle look. Even with the facial hair, Grace could still see the sweet-natured boy who had wanted to play in mud puddles on the day they found Penny.

Next to Grace sat Annie, dressed sharply in a blue snap shirt with embroidered roses on the collars and denim jeans tucked into her trademark leather boots. She had on a belt buckle with *Freedom* written in cursive and adorned in glittery rhinestones. Thematically the buckle was the perfect accoutrement, not just a random selection, because today they'd gathered to discuss how to convince ADA Jessica Johnson to drop her case against Penny.

The ammonia had changed everything. Grace believed in her heart and soul that her daughter could be innocent, but now came the hard part: proving it.

I didn't do anything wrong.

Grace heard Penny's voice in her head over and over, her desperate pleas sinking into the most primal of places in her heart.

Ryan, who sat between his brother and Annie, wore a scowl that couldn't be scrubbed off with steel wool. The contrast between Grace's two sons was stark. Jack was working on a film about his sister's case, while Ryan didn't show the slightest interest.

From the kitchen, Grace could hear a clatter of pots and pans, along with the muted chatter of staff on cleanup duty—including chipper Sarah, who was mopping the floor in anticipation of the next day's opening. At Grace's request, nobody was using any ammonia-scented products.

"All right, Mom," Ryan said, taking a tone. "You got us here, what now?"

It was the first time in several months Ryan and Jack had been in the same room together, and Grace could feel an icy chill between the brothers. They exchanged an occasional glance, and what few words they shared—pleasantries at best—felt completely foreign next to Grace's memories of the ribbing, the jokes, the smiles, that special sibling code. It used to comfort Grace to know that her boys would always have each other, but now the space between them felt hollow, emptied out by the wedge that Penny had driven between them.

"Now," said Grace, "it's all hands on deck. Penny may be innocent, and we've got to figure out our next move."

Ryan screwed up his face. "Why? Because she told you she didn't do it?" His retort came out harshly. "Sorry to burst your bubble here, but that's pretty much what every person in prison says."

The layered look Jack sent his older brother all but told him to shut up.

"Go on, Grace," Annie urged between sips of Diet Coke—which happened to be Arthur's preferred soda as well.

Grace sipped from her glass of water, her throat suddenly dry.

"The smell of ammonia not only brought Penny back to us—it's happened twice now, I promise you it's authentic—but it unearthed memories from that night, things we need answered, evidence we have to gather that might exonerate her."

"'I wasn't alone and I didn't do anything wrong,' that's what she said, right?" Jack asked.

"That's right," said Grace, confirming the little bit of information she'd conveyed to him over the phone.

"Well, there ya have it," Ryan said, clapping his hands together. "Case closed. Guess I should start planning her welcome home party."

"I think the police have it all wrong," Grace continued, ignoring her older son. Underneath his bluster and braggadocio she knew Ryan was a kindhearted soul, a boy who called home regularly when he was away in college, never missed a holiday dinner, and always put family first, taking his dad's motto—"better together"—deeply to heart. Whatever darkened his demeanor—grieving his father maybe, or seeing his dad's legacy on the verge of collapse—was a secret he kept as locked as Penny did hers.

Grace continued, "We know from the Facebook messages that Penny had been in contact with her birth mother for some time *before* the murder. There must have been more to their reunion than we know."

Jack said, "Did Rachel and Penny ever talk by phone?"

"No phone calls that we have a record of," said Grace.

"Wow," said Ryan, exaggerating the glee in his voice. "She's sounding more innocent by the minute."

"Just cut it out, Ryan, stop it right now," Grace snapped at him. "I've had enough of your comments, your quips, your attitude. It's *extremely* unhelpful and quite upsetting. Your hostility toward Penny has turned into disrespect of me, and it needs to end. Now. We need to work as a team here, and I need everyone's support. That includes yours."

Every word Grace spoke rang true, but in fact, she was also deeply concerned. She seemed to feel guilt at every turn. Ryan, who appeared contrite after her rebuke, was suffering, too.

Sarah came to the table, depositing a steaming basket of golden fries along with a round of beers frothing in chilled glass mugs.

"My question to all of you," said Grace, getting back on track after the fries were savaged and beers gulped, "is what now?"

"Now, we need evidence," Annie said. "Irrefutable, really, because anything less won't do. Not with the trial so close."

"I think that's right," Grace acknowledged, feeling a crackle of nerves near her heart snap to life. "But how do we get it?"

"Let's watch the video," suggested Jack. "I need to get a better sense of what went down."

Annie agreed, while Ryan kept silent.

Grace had transferred a copy of Mitch's recording to her laptop computer. The video replay was as unnerving and amazing as seeing it in person had been. Jack kept his eyes glued to the screen like a director watching dailies from a film shoot.

When they got to the part about the book, it was Ryan who chimed in. "That book again," he said.

Grace paused the video, gratified to see him engaged. She had told Jack and Ryan about the book, but neither of them recalled ever seeing it.

Grace said, "Blue cover, boats in the water. You boys sure you don't remember a book like that?" Jack shook his head, and Ryan did the same.

"It's important to her for some reason," Grace added. "But it's not in her bedroom. I've turned it upside down looking. Strange she says it's her favorite and we don't know it."

"Well, she does keep plenty of secrets," Ryan said.

Grace ignored him and continued with the playback, getting to the part where Penny whispered that she wasn't alone.

"You see that?" Annie piped up excitedly, right after Grace said "Vincent Rapino" on the recording. Grace stopped the playback. "She lit up when you said that man's name."

"I was thinking the same thing," said Grace. "What if Vincent was there that night?" Her eyes danced across the faces staring back at her. "The police spoke to him, but they never considered him a suspect."

"That's because he had an alibi," said Ryan.

"People do lie," Jack said, sending a look that barely concealed his exasperation.

Grace resumed playback.

"I didn't do anything wrong," Penny said in the recording. "Nothing."

"Maybe you're right," Jack said, sounding breathless. "Penny could have been an unwitting accomplice . . . or somehow she's innocent."

"Oh for Chrissake," Ryan groaned loudly before downing the final swig of his beer. He pushed his chair back with an audible scrape and rose quickly. "I'm getting another." He hefted his empty beer mug in his hand. "Anybody else want anything?"

Nobody answered, and Ryan was off.

"He's so angry," Annie whispered when he was out of earshot.

"I don't know what to do to help him," Grace said.

"He's a big boy," Jack answered assuredly. "He can take care of himself. Penny can't. I get that Vincent should get a second look, but what about Maria? Penny said she wasn't alone. Who else would she be with that is violent and disturbed? I've hung out with those two together . . . Maria had a lot more issues than her pyromania, I can tell you that. Maybe it was Maria who wanted to bring fantasy into reality."

"She was at home at the time of the murder," Grace said. "That's what Maria's mother told the police, and that's what Maria will tell the jury at the trial."

"But did Maria's mother actually check on her?" Jack probed.

"I made the same point to the lawyer," said Grace.

"It's a good one," said Jack. "And faking an illness is an easy way to get someone to leave you alone. If her mother did do a room check, a wig and some pillows would do the trick. If you're planning a murder, you're going to plan for that contingency."

Ryan returned to the table with a mug of ice-cold pilsner.

"Talking about Maria, are we?" he said with a smirk. "Real sweet gal. Penny sure could pick quality friends."

Grace eyed him but didn't take his bait. She had already spoken her mind.

"You think Maria did it?" Ryan looked dubious. "Come on. Why wouldn't Penny turn on Maria to save herself?"

"Eve's the protector," Grace said. "She'd sacrifice herself for her friend . . . or family. Her nature is to protect."

"For the sake of argument," Jack said, "let's assume she wasn't alone. It's either Vince or Maria. Nobody else has come up, right?"

"That's right," said Grace. "We focus on those two."

"So Perfect Murder Maria left a witness whose head she threatened to stuff into a bucket full of ammonia?" Ryan asked. "Hmmm . . . call me doubtful."

"Was there a bucket found at the crime scene?" asked Annie.

"No, but Maria or Vince could have taken it with them when they left," said Grace.

"What was up with Penny tapping the table?" Annie asked. "That was strange."

"It was in the nine-one-one transcript," Jack said. "Rachel couldn't talk, so the operator told her to tap the phone." He re-created Penny's rhythmic taps against the table. "She was back in the apartment in her mind. She's remembering."

"And then listing off a bunch of cities and states like she was in some kind of trance. I'd call that strange, too," said Annie.

"Yeah, I've no idea there," Jack admitted. "The book, the taps, those locations, the bucket of ammonia—I don't know how it fits together."

"I do," said Ryan. "One of the kooky voices inside your sister's kooky head *told* her to kill Rachel and she did it. You're trying to fit pieces together from a mind that's broken apart. Good luck with that. According to Penny, a voice told her Rachel had to be gone and gone for good. Who do you know that hears voices, Jack?"

"Boys, boys, please." Grace held up her hands like a pair of stop signs. "We need to support each other, not argue. There's a lot of work to do to figure this out. It's going to be all-consuming."

"You know you can count on me to help," Annie said.

"Me too," said Jack.

"As long as you keep your grades up," Grace insisted. "Here's the thing: we are running out of time, the trial isn't far off, and Edgewater is a dangerous place. I almost got attacked today."

Grace recounted the Darla incident, and Ryan seemed especially intrigued.

"Sounds like Penny's with her people," he said.

Once again, Grace summoned the willpower to ignore her son.

"If Penny's innocent she shouldn't be locked up a minute longer than she needs to be, which means that Annie, I'll need your full attention on this. You can't put in hours at the restaurant and do what needs to be done, not until we exhaust all the possibilities. Can you commit to that?"

Grace was extremely grateful Annie's Florida move wasn't happening until after the trial. Ryan cleared his throat loudly.

"Um, excuse me," he said, "but we do have a business to run."

"I know that, sweetheart," said Grace, "but I can't work here until this is behind us. My entire focus has to be on Penny. The trial is weeks away. You're just going to have to hire replacements for Annie and me for the short term."

Ryan sent a look of pure indignation. He took a massive gulp of beer, but it didn't seem to cool him down. "That's all well and good, Mom," he said angrily. "If you recall, you and Annie aren't drawing salaries at the moment because a big chunk of the money we have to pay staff is being funneled to Penny's defense. So where am I supposed to get the money to hire two new people?"

"I don't know that answer off the top of my head. We're just going to have to figure it out. We're all fumbling our way through this."

Ryan's expression soured. "You're going to fumble your way right into closing this restaurant for good. How would Dad feel about that? Huh? That his precious Penny cost us everything he and Grandpa worked so hard to build? We're already in debt to our suppliers. If I can't make the minimum payments, they'll cut us off, no question about it. A lot of our regulars have left us high and dry, and now you're doing the same."

"I hear you, Ryan, but I don't have a choice."

"Oh, bullshit," Ryan snapped. "You had a choice that day in the park to let the state take care of Penny, same as you had a choice not to give Dad a hard time about putting her where she belonged—which, by the way, happens to be where she is right now, in a loony bin. But no, you had to keep pushing, keep advocating for her, not caring a damn what it did it to me, to Dad, and now you don't care about the restaurant either."

Ryan got up so fast the chair he'd been sitting on toppled to the floor with a loud clatter. He stormed off, feet stomping as he went.

Annie patted Grace's hand in a placating way. "We'll figure out the money," she said. "We'll get more loans if we have to."

"No, we won't," said Grace, a whisper of defeat in her voice. "No bank is going to touch us, not with the debt load we're carrying." She sighed aloud. "But I don't have a choice, and I need your help, Annie."

"Mom, what if Ryan's right and you lose the restaurant?" Jack asked with concern.

"What if your sister goes to prison for life for a crime she didn't commit?"

Jack said nothing, because what was there to say?

CHAPTER 23

THAT WAS AN INTERESTING night at Big Frank's—tense to say the least. I couldn't blame Mom for taking a leave of absence, and I couldn't blame Ryan for his frustration. His concerns had merit. As for me, it felt like my film about you was evolving right before my eyes.

Vincent Rapino was a born dirtbag. He needed (and was going to get) more scrutiny. What I didn't realize was how much of a role Maria would play. I thought she was a footnote, mention-worthy only because of those murder fantasies in which you wrote about Rachel Boyd.

But after viewing Dr. McHugh's video, I had to rethink Maria's significance. It's no big revelation that Maria was not my favorite of your friends, but thanks to Chloe and her got-to-get-an-A perfectionism, you didn't have many to choose from. You'd sacrificed your entire social life for your grades.

Mom and Dad couldn't have been happier about your scholastic ambitions, but they worried you were putting undue pressure on yourself. Sorry to report, you were never *that* great a student. When your first science quiz came back with a B, you returned home from school that day utterly inconsolable.

"I don't get Bs anymore," you wailed at dinner. "Call the school! Tell them we have to get my grade changed. We have to do it now!"

Your face turned splotchy and wet, with thick tears streaking down your cheeks.

The situation only got worse as your grades didn't conform to your plan and the blame game got going. Everything and everyone (everyone, that is, other than you) was responsible for your imperfect scores. *The teacher is stupid. I never got the assignment.* And so on.

That's when Mom began to worry that your dedication to academics had moved from commitment into the realm of obsession. You demanded to quit concert band—no time to practice, you said. Next, you dropped karate and field hockey for similar reasons.

I overheard Mom tell Dad your behavior wasn't normal. Dad said, "Well, we don't exactly know what's normal for her, do we?" The unknown had always been his greatest fear about you.

Mom said she was going to take you to see a doctor, and I knew that meant a psychiatrist. O'Reilly, I think was his name—he diagnosed you with anxiety and depression, but Mom didn't think that was the root of your issues at school or at home. This behavior came out of the blue, she kept telling him. But you were entering the teen years, and adolescence can bring on rapid changes in brain chemistry.

O'Reilly's answer was a course of medication, and for a time, it seemed to help. You resumed playing clarinet, but when you couldn't master a new piece with ease, you once again announced your intention to quit concert band, this time for good. Dr. O'Reilly added OCD to your growing list of conditions, which went hand in hand with a growing pile of pills in all shapes, colors, and sizes.

Once you entered the world of docs and diagnoses, of pills and ed plans, Maria entered your orbit. She was one of those kids—a troubled, dark, disturbed loner type. You two ended up in eighth-grade Spanish together, and the connection was instant. It's like you each possessed some built-in radar for uniquely wired minds.

Even back then, Maria stood out. She dressed differently and didn't seem to care much what anyone thought or said of her. She wore all black, dyed her long hair black, and wore so much eye shadow around her eyes that she looked more like a raccoon than a witch, which I know is the look she was after. She always wore bright red lipstick, and I don't think any other kid in middle school had a nose ring, either. All this plus her whiter-than-white skin—she looked to me like a walking corpse. But you didn't care one bit about Maria's appearance, and honestly, that's admirable.

Her nicknames—Firebug Maria, Torchy, Burning Woman (a play on Burning Man)—never fazed her. Her give-a-damn was busted. Maria was into witchcraft, that Wicca thing, something I don't think you ever bought into—or maybe you did, who knows? Maybe there is an alter I haven't met who tried his or her hand at casting spells.

As the protective older brother, I would tag along with you two sometimes because I didn't trust Maria. Wasn't hard to see why she made me uneasy. Remember that day you took me up to her bedroom, the summer before you started ninth grade, six months before you two got arrested? Her room looked like the souvenir shop at the Salem Witch Museum. The walls were plastered with tapestries and posters featuring pentacles, the talisman used in magical evocation. One hanging in particular stuck out to me—a Star of David, with interior spaces decorated in a combination of Hebrew letters and weird rune symbols. I didn't know what to make of that, but it was eerie nonetheless.

She kept a collection of knives and swords in her bedroom (knives and swords at thirteen years old, and her mother said nothing about it—what gives?) but they were for "ritual purposes only," or so Maria said. Now I'm wondering what kind of rituals she was conducting up there.

Of all the strange items in Maria's bedroom—Tarot cards, weird jewelry, incense, melted candles (which blew my mind—she was a fire bug, and her mother allowed her to have matches?)—the strangest of all was her black metal cauldron. What teen girl has a *cauldron*? Your friend Maria, that's who.

Her bedroom smelled like potpourri from *The Twilight Zone*. We didn't stay long, thank God, but I did get a Tarot reading from her before we left. She said I was going to be very well known. I'm thinking if she's right, it'll be because of you, Penny, and this film of mine.

Once you got your new diagnosis of DID, Maria became even more enamored with you. I think she tried conjuring up new alters using eye of newt, or whatever herbs and spices were required to make her magic work.

You let Maria meet them all. Penny was too quiet for her. Ruby made her giggle. Chloe could be annoying but helpful with homework. The girl Maria loved the best though, without a doubt, was Eve. I couldn't tell if you'd bring out Eve when you and Maria were together because you couldn't control it, or if you were playing Maria the same way you may have been playing us. Either way, when you were with Maria, it was almost always as Eve.

I keep searching for moments of truth, proof that you aren't sick but twisted. Because let's be honest, proving you're innocent is more than an uphill climb. I was thinking recently about that time you, Maria, and me were being aimless around town. I was doing my protector thing, pretending I wanted to hang out, but really I was keeping an eye on you. And things got pretty weird. You were Penny that day, quiet and shy. You had something on your mind, don't know what, but it annoyed Maria, that much was obvious. She kept needling you.

"Where is Eve?"

"You're boring me, Penny."

"Come on, let's have some fun."

"Fun" for Maria usually involved some kind of fire, and we ended up behind CVS, where there was a trash can half filled with garbage. Maria took out a lighter.

"No cameras here," she said. I got the sense she'd led us to that location knowing that fact ahead of time.

"Let's burn it." Her eyes glowed in the flickering flame of the Bic lighter she'd produced from a pocket.

As Penny, you were having none of that.

"No," you said.

"Come on," Maria urged. "It'll be fun. You're so lame. You won't do anything cool. I wish Eve were here. I don't think I like you. You're boring, Penny. Dull. Dull. Dull."

"Stop it, Maria," I said angrily.

I was about to pull you away, take you home, when I saw the switch happen. There are movies that sensationalized multiple personality disorder, portraying it as a transformation from one person into another, like a lycanthrope going from man to wolf, but switching doesn't happen that way. It's not dramatic. Not like a seizure. A lot of times it takes careful study to tell when a switch has happened, but this time, I could see it clearly. The way you carried yourself with a more confident stance, a dark gleam in your eyes, that trademark tilt to your mouth—it was all there in a snap.

What happened next was snaplike, too.

You snatched the lighter from Maria's hand, flicked on the flame, and put it to some paper in the trash can. I watched it happen, I'm ashamed to admit, just like with the cat—I sort of let it go on because maybe part of me, that dumb teen part, a brain not fully formed, wanted to see the burn. And up it went in no time. Flames spreading quickly, fire catching paper, all in a great chain reaction that soon had the trash can fully engulfed.

You and Maria danced around the fire like two spirits of the night trying to conjure a demon. Then we heard sirens, and that's when we ran, you two laughing manically and me thinking what the hell did I just let you do?

Later, when I had time to reflect, another thought occurred: I realized how easily Maria had manipulated you into setting the blaze. A couple taunts, and you were part of the burn.

After your arrest, I got to thinking about those murder plans you two secretly shared, and wondered if she'd encouraged you the same way she got you to set that fire.

I've read all your secret correspondences with Maria, and all I can say is: What the hell, Penny? The hit list Maria sent in error to the wrong girl (big mistake there) had a lot of names on it, but the stand-outs were your brother Ryan, and your birth mother, Rachel Boyd.

But that wasn't even the most chilling part. Maria was very clear in her writings about *how* she'd commit murder:

Don't move the body. Leave it where it died. We should kill random people, too, because most of the time the victim is someone the killer knows. We don't want to leave any trail back to us. If we off a stranger, it will be harder for the police to identify a suspect. And we shouldn't do it in Swampscott. We need to pick a different town, a place that doesn't get a lot of traffic. I hope we do it, too, because I want to know what it feels like to kill someone. It must be the most incredible feeling of power.

But it wasn't just Maria doing the planning. You played along, too.

We'll buy anything we need a month before we need it, you wrote back. *We need ropes, gloves, buckets, and sponges. After we do it we have to live our lives like NOTHING ever happened. We'll ride our bikes because that makes it easier to get off the road so we can avoid the police.*

You two went back and forth with your planning, talking dismemberment, pulling teeth, burning off fingerprints, burying body parts, eliminating DNA, and eventually you wrote what is maybe the most incriminating piece of evidence against you:

How about we do in my birth mother? We'd have to track her down, but that would be some weird juicy shit for a Lifetime movie or something.

Hahaha full psycho, Maria wrote back, following that with four purple heart emojis.

You wrote: *I'd want it to hurt and to last. What that bitch did to me is unforgivable.*

Maria: *What did she do?*

Maria: *Helllooo?*

Maria: *You still there???*

You: *Never mind.*

CHAPTER 24

ON ITS BEST DAYS, Mitch found Edgewater to be a depressingly alien place. He felt a malignant energy here, one with its own life force, feeding off the patients and employees with equal voracity.

Many of the warnings Mitch had received from well-intentioned colleagues had proved prescient. But, to his great surprise, he found himself thinking he might not be quite so eager to depart when he reached the end of his one-year commitment. It seemed that battling dark energy—his depression, Adam's addiction, even his divorce from Caitlyn—suited him well.

Forget about leaving. He was right where he belonged.

It was early afternoon, hours before the end of the workday. He had charting to do, reports to write, and prescriptions to evaluate. Of all his cases, it was Penny's that occupied an outsized portion of his gray matter. What Penny had shared was helpful, but not enough to get a jury to rule in her favor. He needed more. Much more.

Mitch made his way along yet another bland hallway with deliberate steps. He was doing his best to walk without a limp from the pain in his lower back and knee, the result of yet another fight he had helped to break up only an hour ago. The aggressor was a mountain of a man who'd squared off with a slender fellow, surprisingly agile, who had been suffering from paranoid delusions when he shot his mother over a nonexistent inheritance. The cause of the scuffle between the two men was irrelevant. It was the frequency of these skirmishes that inspired Mitch to take his concerns to the highest authority he could access.

"The guards need to learn how to see patients, not threats," Mitch explained to Ruth Whitmore, a thin, no-nonsense woman in her early sixties with an officious air—which, given her responsibilities as facility director, was quite understandable. She favored good suits and quality perfume, and her office, Mitch noted, was a great deal nicer than his own, with a leather armchair, ornate rug, and no bars on the windows.

"Are you hurt?" Whitmore inquired in a raspy voice, which did not exactly sound sympathetic. She was probably thinking paperwork—or worse, worker's comp.

"I'm fine," Mitch said, getting that feeling he was wasting his (and her) time. "But the guards put the guy in a suitcase hold, knees pressed against his chest, which could contribute to heart failure."

Whitmore bit the end of her pen as she studied the incident report someone had placed on her desk prior to Mitch's arrival. *At least something got done efficiently around here,* he thought.

"That's John Grady you helped take down, all three hundred pounds of him." She gazed up at Mitch, wide-eyed. "I'm impressed. So, Dr. McHugh, tell me, how would you suggest we go about subduing someone like Mr. Grady when he starts . . . acting up?"

Mitch found her tight-lipped smile rather chilling.

"I'm not sure," he said. "But I think a dozen or so laws may have been broken during that mêlée."

"Good thing there were no video cameras nearby."

Mitch couldn't tell if she was kidding or not, but he went with not.

"I'm just saying the whole incident could have been avoided if patients weren't being overseen by people trained to be prison guards.

If we had more doctors on staff, I think we could put an end to these fights that keep breaking out. We're being *reactive*, not proactive."

He recounted the incident with Darla in the hallway. "If I hadn't been there to talk her down, that encounter would have ended with violence. Instead, we had a peaceful resolution and Darla went on her way. But I'm only one person."

"Doctor," Whitmore said, elongating the word. "I'm grateful you're a member of our team. Really, I am. Your credentials are impeccable."

She took a moment to access Mitch's personnel file on her computer.

"Doctorate of medicine from Albany Medical College; associate medical director of child and adolescent psychiatry at Boston Medical Center for thirteen years. Five years with the North Shore Medical Center. Board certified in psychiatry and childhood adolescent psychiatry through the American Board of Psychiatry and Neurology. Not to mention you've done a fellowship in forensic psychology, an expertise that has certainly come in handy around here. You've quite the diverse background and skill set, Mitch."

"Brings back good memories of lots of sleepless nights," said Mitch.

"Reminds me how lucky we are to have you," Whitmore said. "The fact is that Edgewater *needs* people like you to look after our residents. But there's a little thing in the way of your grand vision for how it should be done, and that is money."

She paused here to let the non-newsflash sink in. "I'm assuming you're not going to open your checkbook to provide the necessary funds, which I promise you are a substantial amount, so I suggest you speak to the guards involved and together come up with some new protocols for engaging our more—let's call them overly exuberant— guests like . . . what was her name?"

"Darla Miller."

She typed something else into her computer, and quietly read whatever appeared on her screen.

"Oh, she's a tricky one, that Darla," Whitmore noted with a sharp intake of breath. "Lots of demerits there, but thanks to you she's not getting one for her confrontation with Ms. Francone."

Mitch knew a demerit was code around here for solitary and he was glad he'd helped to spare Darla that pain.

"Speaking of Ms. Francone," Whitmore continued on. "I heard a bit about your experiment. Ammonia. Quite inventive."

Mitch had no idea how word of their ammonia experiment had gotten back to her, but no matter. He knew from her reputation that Whitmore kept a close watch on all happenings at her hospital, and no doubt any developments with one of her more notorious "guests," as she liked to call them, would attract her attention.

"We sort of stumbled on the ammonia idea and thought it might trigger a switch, which it did." Mitch rehashed the medical details on smell he had previously shared with Grace. "Penny told us things about that night she hadn't revealed before."

Whitmore's eyes sparkled in a most delighted way. "So did she confess?"

Inwardly, Mitch bristled at the glee in her voice. "No, sort of the opposite," he said. "She talked about there being an accomplice, maybe, or someone else in the house with her. She claims she didn't do anything wrong. The mother thinks she may be innocent."

"Oh dear," said Whitmore, tapping her pen against her desk like a miniature drumstick. "Optimism can be such a dreadful thing in these situations. I do hope you'll dispel that notion sooner rather than later. Save her the pain. How is everything else going for you, Mitch? I'm so glad you stopped by."

Mitch was about to take that as his cue to leave when he remembered the second purpose of his visit here. He had with him the medical examiner's report and wanted to get Whitmore's take on it.

"Everything is fine, thank you. But before I go, I'm curious to know if there are other patients here, females like Penny, of similar height and build, who have killed with such savagery."

Whitmore sent him a sideways glance.

"Are you suggesting a woman's not capable of the same sort of viciousness as men? Tsk-tsk, Mitch. When it comes to equality, we women deserve more respect."

"Right," said Mitch, almost smiling, though he was feeling a bit hot under the collar. "It's just I've never seen anything quite like it. I have the pictures in the file from the state medical examiner's office."

Whitmore took the file and flipped through the pages, pausing longer to study some of the more gruesome images.

"Are you trying to keep me from sleeping tonight, Dr. McHugh?" She turned the file folder around to show Mitch a colored photo of Rachel's nearly decapitated head.

"Yeah, sorry, I probably should have warned you it was extremely graphic."

She read on, flipping pages and studying photos, for a good five minutes. Judging from her sunken expression, it was more than enough time to gander.

"Well, this is not unprecedented. I could name five women off the top of my head that have done something equally violent. One who comes to mind used a hammer to do away with her uncle—who, by the way, had been abusing her. So, yes, with the right amount of combustible material, girls like Penny can kill just as savagely, or even more so, than any man."

"Okay, that's good to know," Mitch said, a bit disappointed not to have a bombshell new theory to work with.

"However," Whitmore said, tapping the file with one of her long, manicured fingernails. "This image sticks out to me."

It was, of all things, a picture of Penny—a close-up of her wrists after she'd been scrubbed clean of blood.

"If there's one thing we don't have a shortage of around here, Mitch, it's handcuffs. For all the times I've seen our guests, ah, secured, I've never once seen them left with marks like these. It's a bit odd. And, while you might think I've grown immune to oddities while working here, I assure you—there's an ordinary to the extraordinary.

This photograph very much falls outside my standard deviation of strange."

Mitch ruminated on her observation for a moment. "Interesting," he eventually said, pondering what to do with this new information. Then it came to him. "You know, I have a friend from a prior position, a medical examiner—one of the best in the state, in my opinion. Maybe I should get Penny's file to her. Get her take on it. It will get a faster look-see than going through the state lab."

Whitmore appeared to be in full agreement. "The mother's the medical proxy, I presume," she said. "I'm sure you'll need her to sign some release forms and whatnot, so see to it, will you?"

"Sure thing," Mitch said, still reeling. *Why does she care so much?*

"Penny's a potentially important case, Mitch," Whitmore said, as if reading Mitch's mind. "She can give us—and by us, I mean Edgewater—a lot of attention. If it's not an open-and-shut case as it appears to be, then selfishly, I think I can spin that straw into a bit of gold for this facility without violating any HIPAA obligations." She paused and sighed, as if she'd caught herself.

"I know what I'm saying sounds crass," Whitmore admitted. "But managing the money is in my job description, so yes, I'll exploit every opportunity that comes my way. And it's not all self-serving: more money means better care for our guests. If nothing else, your contact might give you some new insights to work with."

Insights.

The word struck Mitch, and no surprise it was in relation to Penny. What could possibly give him the insights he needed into her world and her life? Grace didn't have a diary of Penny's she could share, but Mitch thought of Adam, whom he'd be visiting tomorrow and hadn't yet seen since his return to rehab. As a child, Adam loved to draw and his pictures often reflected his mood. For a time he was something of a serious artist, and had what Mitch thought of as his blue period— sadder works done in a somber palette that in hindsight might have presaged his later turmoil.

Mitch thanked Whitmore for her time and made a mental note to call Grace and ask if she could rummage up some of Penny's past creations for him to study. It was too late to help Adam avoid his addictions, but the trial wasn't over, and until the verdict was announced, Mitch vowed he wouldn't stop trying to help. He wasn't fooling himself, however. Reaching his son had proved impossible, and getting through to Eve might be even harder.

CHAPTER 25

A FEW DAYS AFTER the ammonia experiment, Grace returned to Edgewater, this time accompanied by Attorney Greg Navarro. As the trial was drawing nearer, Navarro's workload increased—as did Grace's bill. They'd driven to Edgewater in separate cars, and the plan was for Navarro to meet with Penny in private, briefly. It wouldn't take more than a half hour, he said, then he'd wait for her—off the clock—to debrief.

While Navarro and Penny (though of course it would be Eve) conducted their business in private, Grace and Mitch headed to the cafeteria for coffee and a chance to talk. She considered asking Mitch's opinion about Ryan and his unrelenting hostility, but probably wouldn't. He had his hands full. They all did.

Of everyone in the noisy cafeteria, Grace believed she was the only one sporting a visitor's badge, which she had pinned to the lapel of her blue blazer. Mitch returned from the checkout counter carrying a steaming hot coffee for him and water for Grace. On the table Grace had put the leather portfolio case containing her daughter's artwork, collected and saved over the years. She was incredibly curious what the art might reveal to Mitch, who had asked for this special showing.

"Children communicate ideas and feelings through their art," he had explained. "If we can learn to interpret this language, we might be better able to understand Penny's inner world. Maybe it'll give us a way to get past Eve."

"I'm glad I had some work to share. Penny hated her art, always wanted to tear up her drawings after finishing them, but I managed to save a lot for posterity. Not all, but a fair amount."

She expected they'd dive right into it, but before Mitch unzipped the case, he announced he had something to share, a minor breakthrough with Eve that had come with a somewhat disturbing revelation.

"Did Eve or Penny—or anybody, for that matter—ever tell you about an injured cat?" Grace keyed in on the hesitancy in his voice.

"No," she answered warily. "Why?"

And with that, Mitch launched into a frightening account about Penny (or Eve) walking home after school one day, by herself—a point of fact she mentioned enough times for Mitch to think she might be covering up for someone (Maria, most likely)—and finding the injured animal on the side of the road.

"I can only share this with you because I asked and she gave me her consent," Mitch said. "Whether it's all true or a fantasy of hers, I can't say for certain." He accompanied that assessment with a shrug. "But I do believe she enjoys the feeling of having life-and-death power over a living being. And I suspect there may be a sexual component to it."

Grace tried to maintain a deadpan expression even as a sick feeling swept through her.

"I'm not saying that there was a sexual component to Rachel's murder," Mitch went on to say. "But there is something in Eve that correlates lustful desire with violence. It could help to explain those murder fantasies she exchanged with Maria. It was a form of exploration for her—a thrill, neurologically speaking. And there's potential there for a psychotic break."

"I don't have to tell you that gets very twisted very fast," Grace said.

"Agreed, but this revelation could help us understand why the murder was so frenzied. The brutal nature of the crime just doesn't seem to match with Penny, or Eve for that matter, but the cat story gave me a new avenue to explore. It's possible it wasn't even Eve who committed the murder."

Grace got his insinuation.

"The hidden alter theory," Grace said. "A fourth alter."

"Alters can appear at any time," said Mitch.

"You think it's an evil persona?"

"It's not that the alter is evil. It would be that Penny herself has a psychopathic personality, and the expression of that psychosis is through this vehicle, this alter that we haven't met. The bottom line is there are no hard and fast rules when it comes to DID, but there are a lot of unknowns. So yes, there could be a fourth alter that we don't know, haven't met yet, who is more psychopathic. It could even be a male persona with enhanced strength—there's really nothing entirely off the table."

Grace almost grinned.

"Are you saying that you now believe Penny has DID?"

"I'm saying nothing is off the table," Mitch repeated with a rueful smile. "It's all still an open question in my mind."

"Well, not in mine," said Grace, who felt something smoldering behind her eyes. She managed to tamp down the anger before it flared. It would do her no good to start an argument with Mitch. What she needed more than to force a concession from him was an ally in this fight. Besides, she had high hopes he'd come around soon enough.

"Before I take a look at the artwork," Mitch said, seeming to sense her need to change the subject, "I want to know how you're doing with all this."

Grace's mouth went dry, her face hot. It was as if some kind of internal switch got flicked, firing up a reminder that she existed, too; she was a person going through something traumatic as well.

"I'm doing the best I can," she managed. "It's hard, of course, but that shouldn't be shocking."

"You seem upset, I'm sorry if I—"

"No, it's fine," Grace assured him, waving off any concern. "It's just . . . other than my sister-in-law, Annie, nobody ever really asks how I'm managing."

"Well, I'm asking," said Mitch, whose friendly aspect encouraged her to share.

Grace tried hard not to dwell upon how she really felt, because going there summoned a host of sad, unpleasant, and confusing questions for which she still had no clear answers.

"You have to understand something, Mitch," Grace began in a voice loud enough to be heard over the cafeteria din. "What I feel mostly is a tremendous sense of loss . . . loss of Arthur, loss of Penny, sadness for Rachel, for everyone hurting from this. But I also struggle with guilt."

"Guilt," Mitch repeated. "For what Penny may have done?"

"For that, yes, of course. But also guilt for how all of this has impacted my family. *I* brought Penny into our lives. It was my doing, my . . . I don't know the right word. *Obsession*. When we found her that day, I had a *feeling* that this child came to us for a reason, like we were picked, and finding her made her my obligation. It's hard to explain, but I convinced myself of it, and from the first second I was with her, I just couldn't imagine not being with her.

"In my mind it was the perfect situation and she was the perfect daughter. And I don't mean to imply that she never did anything wrong or gave us difficulties, even before her mental health crisis. None of us are *perfect*, but she was perfect *for me*. That's what I'm trying to say here."

"In what way?"

Grace let go a weighty sigh.

"I've always wanted to mother a daughter," she confessed. "Arthur and I had stopped at two because of money concerns. But suddenly . . . we didn't have to stop. I loved Penny, and I *wanted* to be her mother more than anything."

* * *

"We have two children already," Arthur had said on the day Penny moved in with them as a foster child, long after the cake and guests were gone. Jack and Penny

were playing with toy trucks in Penny's bedroom, while Ryan was sulking in the bedroom he now had to share with his younger brother. "It's not like we had nine months to prepare the kids for our new arrival."

"No, we had four. What difference does it make how she came to us, Arthur?" Grace said a bit sternly.

Arthur folded his arms across his chest and returned a serious expression, one usually reserved for conversations about the restaurant's finances. "We barely know anything about her," he said in a hushed tone, as if Penny might hear. "Her past, I mean."

Grace could see his mind churning, his conscience telling him not to pass judgment, not to assume the worst. Trauma. Mental illness. Genetic disease.

"Arthur, darling, please, just listen." From down the hall came the sounds of delighted laughter, and the make-believe vroom-vroom *of a big truck engine. "She's a sweet little girl, and she needs us. Please give it some time with an open heart and mind, that's all I'm asking."*

"The money," Arthur said, wincing as he voiced what Grace knew was a valid concern. "We can barely make ends meet as it is. The foster system won't provide for her, not really, and if we adopt . . . well, then, it's all on us."

"Let's not think about the money just yet," Grace said. "I'll start tutoring on the weekends if need be. Whatever it takes, I'm willing to do it."

Arthur smiled, a little forced, but genuine.

"I'll keep an open mind," he said. "As long as you do the same."

Grace promised, knowing full well her heart and mind were already made up. She was going to mother a daughter.

* * *

"Were you close with your mother?" Mitch asked.

"Extremely," Grace said, feeling the familiar bite of sadness she experienced anytime her thoughts went there. "When my mom died, she left a huge hole in my life. A huge hole." Grace felt the need to make sure this point came across clearly. "I wanted to do the things with Penny that I did with my mother—the crafting, baking, cuddling, shopping. It sounds a bit Norman Rockwell or gender normative, I know, but those were great memories for me. Don't get me wrong, I love my boys so much, but there's something about a mother and daughter that's just, well, different."

Grace didn't have a purse with her, so she had to resort to using stiff cafeteria napkins to dab her eyes dry.

"I brought all of this into our lives," she said. "My family's struggles with Penny can all be traced back to me." Grace felt a slight hitch in her breathing, but she refused to have a full-on meltdown in front of Mitch.

"You don't adopt a little girl," she continued, "thinking that one day you'll be glad, on your knees *grateful,* that Massachusetts doesn't have the death penalty. That sort of thinking doesn't once cross your mind, I can assure you of that."

The cavernous cafeteria suddenly felt quite small to Grace, as if she and Mitch were in a therapy session together.

"For the past year, I've had hope—but no evidence—that Penny is innocent of this crime. But now . . . 'I wasn't alone.' It's not a lot, I admit, but it's something for me to hold on to. And right now, I *really* need something to hold on to, Mitch."

Grace's voice shook, for these were difficult words to say.

"It's not lost on me that Penny most likely *destroyed* a life. All the evidence points to that simple, terrible, truth. Either she's sick or truly deranged. And now you're telling me that she's *killed* before—a cat, but still. She's killed before, and she seemed to have *enjoyed* doing it. That's hard to hear, it really is."

Grace let go a second loud breath.

"None of this is your fault," Mitch said. "You provided a loving home. You took good care of her."

"Apparently not good enough." Grace dotted another napkin at the corners of her eyes. "Arthur was worried. We didn't know a thing about her . . . her past, her genetics, family history, none of it. And I brushed it aside because the truth is, you *never* know. I don't care how a child comes to be your responsibility, it's always a risk."

"There are *always* risks," Mitch concurred.

"Yes, but I'm not taking this risk alone. It's not just me getting hurt. There are other people tethered to my rope, so when I fall, they fall. And we've fallen pretty far, and yeah, sure, I'm alive, I'm in good health, but survivor's guilt . . . that's a real, real thing."

Mitch's lips creased into a tight grimace.

"I suspect that's our curse as parents," he responded. "No matter the circumstances, we always want to do more for our children, take away their pain and suffering if we can. But some things are simply not ours to control, so we get the guilt instead, the what-ifs . . . *should've, would've, could've*."

Mitch broke eye contact for a moment.

"I saw my son Adam at the rehab facility where he's staying for the first time the other day. It was harder than I thought it would be. He kept insisting none of it was my fault, but it's one thing to hear the words and another to believe them. He told me I couldn't fix it for him. He said just talk to me . . . be there for me . . . that he needed my support, not my expectations that he was going to beat his addiction this time."

Grace's heart broke for them both.

"I'm glad Adam's where he needs to be to heal," she said. "And I can relate to your pain, Mitch, on a very deep and personal level. When we found out for sure that Penny had DID—how we found out is a longer story that I'll tell you later, but suffice it to say, the diagnosis was utterly shattering. We'd known something was amiss for a while, but to have all the pieces put together for us . . . I couldn't help but feel responsible, like I did something wrong, that it was my fault."

"It isn't, and wasn't, but yes, I understand."

"Right or wrong, I wasn't going to let her down again," Grace said. "I did my research, read every study on DID I could get my hands on, and every one of them said basically the same thing: that I had to embrace *all* of Penny's alters, even Eve, or it could be like LGBTQ kids who get shunned by their parents. Denial or rejection of any of her personalities can be a potentially fatal affront to the self."

Mitch returned an emphatic nod. "Making Penny feel loved, safe, and supported is a vital precursor to encouraging integration, for her to become whole again," he said. "I guess in a way that's what Adam was trying to tell me. He once said a hit of heroin filled him with this incredible warmth, totally relaxed him, so he had no worries about anything. He said it was like taking hits of joy, which was hard to hear because I felt my son's joy was somehow my responsibility. But then when he got hooked hard that joy went away, and he didn't need the drug to feel good . . . he needed it to breathe."

"I'm so sorry, Mitch," Grace said, feeling heavy in her chest.

Mitch moved his hand across the table. For a moment, Grace thought it might be to hold hers as a gesture of shared comfort, but instead he undid the zipper of the portfolio.

"You've suffered a lot," he said. "And I don't want to add to it by giving you false hope here. I honestly don't know if I'm going to be able to help. I've never had a case like this before or dealt with someone quite like Eve. All I can promise is that I'll try my best."

"That's all I can ask," Grace replied.

"Okay, let's look at this art, shall we?"

CHAPTER 26

MITCH REACHED INSIDE THE sturdy portfolio case and took out the first drawing from within. When Grace saw which one it was, she got another lump in her throat, thinking of the day Penny gave it to her.

* * *

She was in bed with Arthur, he with some nonfiction book about the Civil War, she reading about attachment in adoption. Penny had only been living with them a few months, but already Grace couldn't imagine her small purple bedroom ever being empty again. Grace paid particular attention to the chapters detailing how grief and trauma could affect a child's emotional development, finding those especially important.

"If she regresses in any way, wants to use a pacifier even, we should let her," Grace told Arthur as she flipped through pages on the early years. "A bit of extra nurturing won't make her more dependent, but it could make her more trusting. Think about it, honey. She hardly knows us, poor thing."

Arthur put down his book with a look of resignation, anticipating what was to come.

"We need to sign those papers. Start the adoption process right away." Grace sent him an imploring look. "Penny needs to know she has a home here with us

forever." She didn't feel bad about playing the guilt card, not when it came to something as important as Penny. "The more secure she feels with us, the more she can rely on us, the better her emotional development will be. It's all in this book."

She showed him the cover.

"I need more time to think about it," he said.

"What's there to think about?" Her voice carried a note of desperation. "Penny came to us for a reason. I know it. I feel it in my soul."

Grace gave Arthur's face a gentle caress. This was a huge decision, and one he needed to make on his own terms. Before they could discuss it further, the bedroom door creaked open and in came Penny, wearing the penguin pajamas Grace had bought at Old Navy weeks before her arrival. She took quiet, cautious steps toward the bed.

"Mrs. Grace . . . Mr. Arthur . . ." She called them that because they weren't yet Mom and Dad. "I made something for you," she said in the smallest, most tender voice Grace had ever heard.

"Come here, honey," Grace said, patting the bed before opening her arms wide. Over shuffled little Penny, holding a piece of brown construction paper in her tiny hand. She handed the paper to Arthur before falling into Grace's embrace. Arthur had to unfold the paper to study it, which he did for a long time, saying nothing, until Grace saw his eyes had gone red and watery. He showed Grace the drawing Penny had done.

One look, and her heart burst open.

Despite Penny's rudimentary artistic skills, Grace had no trouble making out what she had created. There were five figures—clearly meant to be Grace, Arthur, Penny, Ryan, and Jack—standing in front of a house, their little stick-figure hands overlapping to illustrate a chain. Above, in a scratchy blue sky decorated with a lemon-yellow sun, she'd written the words My Famile in green crayon—misspelled, yes, but heartrending as could be.

Arthur bit his top lip and said to Grace, his voice cracking a bit, "We'll sign those papers. We'll sign them in the morning."

* * *

Grace didn't explain the significance of that particular drawing to Mitch, allowing him instead to look at it and the others without any narration on her part.

"What's this?" he asked after some moments of quiet contemplation. "I'm seeing it on her later artwork."

His finger indicated a drawing of an anchor, tucked into the bottom left corner of a street scene of New York that Penny had copied from a book.

"When she was little, Penny told me she had a necklace with an anchor hanging down—I'm sure she meant a pendant—but she'd lost it. It was something she remembered having from her life with Rachel. I know she wasn't wearing it the day we found her, so I bought her a replacement necklace after she told me about it, one with an anchor pendant attached. When she outgrew one necklace, I'd buy her another. Some years later, when she was probably eight or nine, she started drawing anchors everywhere—on notepaper, even on her walls sometimes—thankfully those were in pencil. Then she started to put them on her artwork, like it had become her trademark."

Mitch studied the design closely, and he seemed perplexed by it.

"It's not a normal-looking anchor," Mitch said. "It has two stocks coming off the shank below the crown. I've done some boating, and the anchors I've seen only have one."

He showed Grace the anchor drawing—as if she didn't know it from memory.

She offered him a blank stare in return.

"I don't know," Grace said. "Penny made up the design as a kid. I didn't really think much of it other than it was her take on an anchor, which she's always had a thing for."

Grace did a quick scan of the other pieces of artwork she'd brought. The quality of Penny's drawings clearly improved with age, but the anchor design remained essentially unchanged.

"Is this the same design as the first necklace you bought for her?" Mitch asked, stroking his beard in thought.

Grace tried to picture that necklace in her mind.

"I don't think so," she said. "I have a bunch of them at home. As I'm sure you know, only plain wedding bands and religious necklaces can be worn in here."

Mitch flipped to the last drawing in the stack, a seaside cottage done in acrylic paints.

"Was she doing much art in her teens?" he asked.

"No," Grace said, shaking her head once the answer came to her. "She was trying to master landscapes, and then one day she sort of stopped doing art altogether. It was sad, because she loved it. She wasn't necessarily a natural. Wouldn't take art lessons, though I encouraged it. I wasn't expecting her to be Rembrandt. I was just happy she'd found something she enjoyed, a creative, constructive way to express herself, that's all."

"Hmmm," Mitch said, studying the drawing of the cottage closely. "I'm wondering if *she* was expecting she'd be Rembrandt." He surveyed some of Penny's later pieces once more.

For reasons Grace couldn't fathom, Mitch placed his fingers over the two stocks on the left side of the anchor symbol. He turned the paper around to show Grace the result.

"Look at it closely," he said. "Get rid of the pointed flukes, and the curved arm forms a *C*. Covering the two stocks on the left side of the shank, you get the letter *F*. I don't think this is an anchor at all—or if it is, it serves a dual purpose."

"And what purpose is that?" Grace asked, still not seeing it.

"C. F. Initials. Chloe Francone."

A gasp rose in Grace's throat.

"I think in addition to being a perfectionist, Chloe here, for a time at least, was also a budding artist—until single-mindedness stifled her creativity."

Mitch fell silent for a time, long enough for Grace to ask what he was thinking.

"I'm thinking we might be able to stoke those creative fires once more, and maybe, just maybe, it'll give me a way to reach her."

CHAPTER 27

MITCH WAS CONCERNED THAT his next experiment might not go well in front of an audience, but Grace wanted to watch, as did Navarro. As a compromise, Mitch reserved a room with one-way glass, allowing Penny some illusion of privacy during their session.

Grace used the cover of that glass to take in Eve's every movement—noting first and foremost that it was still Eve's hard expression on display. The girl was seated at a sturdy wood table in the center of a bright white, starkly lit, wide-open space. She stared directly into the mirror across from her, anger seared on her face, as if she knew her mother was on the other side to receive her message loud and clear: *It's your fault that I'm here.*

At least that was Grace's interpretation. Mitch had stepped out into the hallway to answer a phone call, leaving Eve with nothing to do but wait—and stare.

On the floor beside the table was the same container of art supplies Grace had seen in Mitch's office on the day they first met. Eve stole occasional glances at the contents, visible through the clear plastic sides, but revealed nothing of her thoughts or feelings.

While waiting for Mitch's return, Navarro had another opportunity to review the artwork Grace had laid out on a table in the viewing room.

"The anchor symbol isn't on all of the drawings," he noted, examining an earlier piece of her daughter's—a lopsided house rendered in a variety of colors on a sloping green hill, all done in frenzied crayon strokes.

"No, that symbol came about later," Grace explained, happy to have the distraction from Eve's cold eyes. "Mitch thinks Chloe might have replaced her desire for perfection in art with getting perfect marks at school—which would mean we were living with Chloe for years and didn't know it."

"So interesting," Navarro said, flipping through drawings done on different shades of paper. "And drawing will get Chloe to appear?"

"There may be a subconscious response brought on by the tactile stimulus of the drawing materials," Grace explained. "Mitch is hoping that a reminder of youthful innocence, especially here in a scary place like Edgewater, might make Chloe feel safe enough to come out."

Navarro, who made his living with words, seemed at a loss for them.

"So it's like the ammonia," he said eventually. "Some sensory stimulus to encourage a switch, is that it?"

Grace nodded. The look of curiosity on Navarro's face deepened.

"Do you think she's . . . what, parsed out her memories from the night of the murder to her different alters?"

"It's an avenue Mitch is exploring," said Grace. "He's not sure. But I'm certain of one thing: Penny's trying to tell us something. Something she's too afraid to come right out and say, or something she's repressed, and she won't let us in unless we find the keys."

Navarro appeared nonplussed. "I thought Dr. McHugh wasn't sold on Penny having DID," he said.

"He's not, at least not yet. He still thinks the alters could be make-believe, meaning she's aware of all of them at all times, which is different from the truly distinct personality states of DID." Grace shuffled Penny's artwork back into the portfolio. "Either way, he's helping us, and that's what's important."

Navarro, who was helping Grace put the artwork away, held up a drawing of Penny's—one of Grace's favorites, a girl in a yellow dress wearing a blue hat.

"That he is," he said, studying the picture, his voice a bit distant. "And we can use all the help we can get."

After finishing his call, Mitch reentered the interview room, acknowledging Eve with a slim smile—one she did not return.

"I hope you brought a pair of sunglasses," she said, peering up at the lights blazing overhead. The white-walled room with matching linoleum flooring amplified the brightness. Eve directed her attention to the plastic container of drawing supplies on the floor. "What's all that?" she asked impatiently.

He hauled up the box, set it on the table, removed the lid, and gestured to the contents within.

"I want to try a little experiment."

Eve groaned. "I'd much rather do a maze with a hunk of cheese at the end. Is that why we're here in this room—aka the sun—and not our usual spot?"

Aware how Eve might try to dominate and direct the conversation, Mitch maintained a neutral expression.

"What I'm asking of you is simple," he said. "I'd like you to draw something for me."

"Draw?"

"Plenty of supplies to choose from," he said. "Have your pick."

Without further prompting, Eve thrust her hands inside the box and began sifting through the contents in a manic way. She shoved aside stacks of colored paper, yellow containers of Play-Doh, safety scissors, glue sticks, and eventually settled on two items that held some special interest for her: a large box of crayons and a sheet of white construction paper. She smoothed out the paper with her hands. For a time, she sat quite still, intently studying the open box of crayons as though she'd never seen such a glorious array of colors. After that period of silent consideration, she selected a blue crayon and put the tip to the paper.

On the paper, she wrote in large capital letters: *THIS IS DUMB!* She gave a throaty laugh that held all the drama of a silver screen starlet.

"Eve," Mitch grumbled dejectedly, letting it be known he was expecting it to be someone else.

"Oh, Dr. Mitch," Eve said in a placating tone. "You sound so disappointed to have me around. And here I was thinking we were becoming pals."

Mitch gave a loud exhale. "Eve, please, this is important. I want you to draw something . . . anything at all that interests you."

She brushed the air with a wave of her hand. "Chillax. You're *way* too serious."

She pointed at Mitch before her focus switched to the wall behind him. He didn't turn because he knew exactly what she was looking at.

"Is someone watching us through the mirror?" she whispered in an overly dramatic way, as if they were both part of some nefarious plot. "Are you going to get fired if this doesn't work?"

"No," Mitch said, in a loud voice to encourage Eve to stop using her hushed tone. "I won't be fired. And chances are if I can't help you, you won't be a patient of mine here anymore. You'll be in prison, Eve, for murder. For life. Do you hear me?

"Now, if you'll work with me, there's a chance—a slim one, I'll give you that—that I can be of some service. But I can do that only if you help me by taking . . . this . . . seriously." He slowed the cadence of his speech to drive home the last three crucial words.

Eve's expression turned a bit more somber as she appeared to contemplate Mitch's plea. "Okay, Doc," she said, throwing her hands up in the air in a show of surrender. "Let's get on with it then."

From the container, she took out a second sheet of white construction paper, picked up a green crayon, and began to draw, her hand moving back and forth in a rhythmic motion. After a few more hurried strokes, the pace of her hand movement slowed down, seeming to become more purposeful. She continued making those slow, intentional crayon strokes for a time, eventually lifting her head to meet Mitch's alert gaze. Right away, he detected something different about her: a calmness, almost a childlike wonderment, that hadn't been there moments ago.

She began moving the green crayon up and down at the bottom of the paper until it became evident she had drawn the green grass of a wide lawn. She switched colors, and on that lawn, she drew a large tree with many crooked branches. On one of those branches, she rendered a tire swing in black crayon dangling from a line of rope, done in brown crayon.

As she worked to create the rest of her drawing, Eve bit the side of her lip, tilting her head this way and that, appraising her effort with an artist's critical eye. He noticed her right leg bouncing to the rhythm of the crayon strokes, up and down, her focus intensifying with each pass. Instead of sitting shoulders back with Eve's world-be-damned posture, she was looser and more relaxed as she quietly assessed her creation.

She continued to draw, acting as if she were alone in this room, just her and her art.

"What are you making?" Mitch asked.

"Oh, you'll see," she said proudly. To his ears her voice had a different cadence, flatter and slightly higher pitched, too. "Younger" was a word that came to his mind.

To make sure Mitch couldn't see, not yet anyway, she hunched over the table, positioning her free arm across the top of the paper to block his view.

"Eve, I could leave the room if you want to work in private."

"No, it's fine. You can watch if you want."

She didn't flat out reject the name, which Mitch had used on purpose. Something told him, though, that it wasn't Eve he was addressing. He watched her work, saw her body grow increasingly still, her focus intensifying as the crayon strokes became more purposeful. Smiles came and went from a face that now looked sweet to him, almost innocent. Surely, the expressions she made were nothing like Eve's natural intensity.

She created in silence, eyes seldom leaving the paper, glancing up only to switch crayons. She kept her body hunched forward, arm strategically placed, to prevent Mitch from getting an early preview. There was a fierce determination to her effort, like she had to get whatever was in her mind onto the paper before it vanished.

When she appeared to have finally finished her masterwork, she leaned back in her chair to give it an appraisal. It took great restraint on Mitch's part to resist the temptation to look at what she'd drawn, even upside down. He knew to respect the artist's wishes and let her make the big reveal on her own terms. Eventually, her facial expression morphed from a contemplative look to a pleased one, and she spun the paper around, giving Mitch his first peek at her efforts.

She kept a hand over the lower portion of the drawing, blocking out whatever was underneath, but the rest of it Mitch could see. He had no trouble making out the cross-section of a house, one that allowed him a view inside its many rooms. It did not look like a drawing a seventeen-year-old girl would make, but it wasn't a young child's drawing, either. There was perspective and proper scale to the structure she'd made, though it was a bit lopsided. Some of the furniture, the windows, and even the doors were a bit too big for the rooms they occupied, while other pieces came out too small.

Everything about the work felt intentional. There was nothing to suggest she'd made it in a spontaneous creative frenzy. From what Mitch knew of the developmental stages of art, he would have said the artist of this piece was somewhere between the ages of eight and ten.

Scale issues aside, the contents within were easy to identify. Standing in the kitchen were two figures: a woman with large ears and a blue dress, shaped like a triangle, and a smaller figure, also adorned in a dress (this one red), who had pigtails for hair. The table between them was a simple line with legs descending down to the floor, as if

it were a one-dimensional object. For whatever reason, she had ne-
glected to draw the chairs.

Mitch concluded the large rectangle near the kitchen table was a
counter. On it, she'd drawn a coffee maker, a bowl with oranges in it,
and a small box, from which poured gray and black swirls drawn using
long, billowing strokes to represent smoke.

"This is really terrific," Mitch said, instinct telling him to offer the
kind of praise Eve wouldn't be receptive to hearing. "It's such a beautiful
house."

"I hate it," she said, sounding discouraged. "It doesn't look right. My
drawings *never* look right."

"I knew what it was," Mitch said brightly.

"It's tilted. It needs to be straight, but I can't draw straight lines
without a ruler. I *should have* used a ruler," she said with a sibilant vent
of anger, her face dipping into a frown.

Mitch couldn't help but feel a pang of sympathy for the child's harsh
self-critique.

"What's your name?"

She didn't answer.

"Where is this house? Is this your house growing up?"

She stared back at him blankly.

"Did you have a tire swing in your yard?"

Again nothing.

"Is this your mother?" He pointed to the woman with the triangle
dress and big ears. Still no response.

"Is this you?"

She nodded.

"What's this?" he asked, pointing to the smoke pouring from the
small box on the countertop.

"That's a toaster," she answered glumly, clearly disappointed that he
didn't recognize it straightaway.

"I knew that," Mitch said, trying for corrective action. "I meant why
is it smoking?"

"The toast is burning."

"Who are you?" Mitch asked again, his voice a bit pleading.

The girl eyed him crossly, like he should have known.

Too fast. Too much. Mitch pointed to a bathroom she'd drawn in the upstairs part of the house with a tub full of blue water. Strokes of blue crayon spilled from a faucet, an indication the water was still running.

"Is the girl in the kitchen going to take a bath?" Mitch asked.

She shook her head. "Not yet. She has to finish her dinner first."

There was a bedroom next to the bathroom, and inside she'd drawn a second little girl who also had pigtails. This girl was given a yellow dress, done in the same triangle fashion as the outfit of the other girl. She had on a silver necklace with an anchor pendant attached. The pendant was supersized, but that was probably due to the challenge of drawing to scale. In one hand, she held a blue rectangle, a book, Mitch presumed.

"Who's this?" Mitch asked.

"That's me," she said, as if the answer should have been obvious.

"I thought you were downstairs having breakfast," said Mitch.

"It's just a dumb drawing," she answered testily. "I should rip it up and start again. It's terrible."

"No, no," Mitch said. "I like it very much. You're a very clever girl. Now, will you tell me your name?"

She hesitated, but eventually said, "I'm Chloe. See, I signed my initials."

She moved her index finger to a patch of side yard, below the tree with many crooked branches, and touched the anchor symbol she'd drawn. Then, using blue crayon, she went over the lines until they darkened, making clear the letters *C* and *F* in her stylized signature:

"C. F.," she said proudly, in case Mitch hadn't seen them for himself. "See? Chloe Francone."

"Chloe. That's a nice name."

While this wasn't definitive proof in Mitch's mind of Penny having DID (she could have known what he was after, which alter he thought he might reach) it was certainly a compelling demonstration. Either way, make-believe or not, Mitch wasn't fazed at meeting Chloe, nor was he shocked that she'd regressed in age. It could be the stimulation of the crayons opened the gateway in Penny's subconscious for a switch to take place, and the alter that appeared was of an age where those crayons would have been appreciated and enjoyed. She was acting ten years old, or thereabouts, the same age that Grace said the anchor symbol began to make an appearance on her drawings.

"Chloe, do you know your mother's name?"

"My mama's name is Grace. My daddy's name is Arthur. He makes pizza for a living."

Is Arthur . . . makes pizza . . . all present tense, because in her reality, at her age of ten or so, Arthur's still alive in her mind.

If this is make-believe it is certainly very consistent.

"What's that under your hand?" Mitch asked, pointing to the lower portion of the house. He could see she'd drawn a basement in black and gray crayon, but she was hiding what was in it.

A slip of a smile came to Chloe's face.

She lifted her hand slowly, eyes never leaving his. Mitch's focus went to a figure Chloe had drawn down in the basement: a woman on her side, two black *X*s for eyes. Dead. Although this woman wore the same triangle-shaped blue dress as the woman in the kitchen above, only one of them had Grace's trademark ears.

Mitch thought: *Rachel.*

Next to the body, Chloe had drawn a crooked jug filled with a liquid depicted in yellow crayon.

Ammonia.

"How old are you, Chloe?" Mitch asked.

"I'm nine," Chloe said sweetly. She got up from her seat. "Who are you, anyway? Where am I?" she asked, looking anxiously around the stark room as her calm veneer faded like a mirage.

Oh, no, thought Mitch.

CHAPTER 28

GRACE, WHO'D BEEN WATCHING through the one-way mirror, bolted from her chair and entered the interview room as quickly as her legs could carry her. She knew her presence was supposed to remain a secret, but the moment she heard her daughter's confusion, motherly instinct took over. With a beaming smile on her face, arms open wide, Grace approached her daughter, who stood still, timid as a mouse. It had been a long time since they were last together, but she had no doubt Chloe would remember her mother.

"Chloe," Grace said, embracing her daughter in a tight hug (which Eve would never have allowed). "Let me have a look at you."

She pulled back to appraise Chloe at arm's length.

"Mama?" Chloe's sweet voice tumbled out, shaky and uncertain.

Grace had no idea why her daughter had regressed in years, but for sure Mitch would have some explanation. Her immediate concern was for her child's well-being. Grace imagined it would be like waking up from a coma surrounded by bright lights and strange faces. "What's going on?" she asked nervously. "Where am I?"

She spoke in the clipped, pressured tones that Dr. Cross had first observed some years ago. It was her default way of talking when agitated about schoolwork, but this was a pressure of a different sort.

"Chloe, please sit down," Grace said, placing her hands lovingly on her daughter's shoulders. Accessing that inner place that allowed parents to keep calm in a crisis, Grace coaxed Chloe gently onto a chair. She knelt down beside her. "Don't be scared, sweetie," she said, taking Chloe's hand. "Everything is fine. It's hard to explain, but you're going to have to be brave and a little patient, okay?"

Chloe gave a nod. "Okay," she said, anxiousness showing in her voice and on her face.

"I'm going to ask you a question. There's no wrong answer . . . I just want your honest one. Can you do that?" Grace knew to offer reassurances that whatever answer she gave, it couldn't be incorrect.

Chloe returned another nod.

"Can you share with me a memory that you have before I came into this room, before you made your drawing, even?"

Grace gestured to the picture. Chloe sent her mother a pleading look, then turned her attention to Mitch, who stood nearby. "Who's he?" she asked.

"I'm Dr. Mitch McHugh," said Mitch, stepping forward.

"A doctor . . . what for? Am I hurt?"

With a glance, Grace made it quite clear to Mitch that she wished to be the one in charge. "You were in an accident," she said calmly. She hated lying to her child, but felt the end would ultimately justify the means. "You weren't hurt, but you did suffer a head injury."

Chloe touched her head gingerly as if expecting to feel pain.

"The injury—sweetheart, it's actually *inside* your head. In your brain," Grace explained.

"So my brain . . . is . . . it's broken?"

Grace heard: *So I'm not perfect?*

"No, love," she said. "You're not broken. And you're safe here." Grace dragged over a chair to sit beside her—less painful on the knees. She retook Chloe's hand.

"What was the accident?" Chloe asked.

"Well," said Grace, pausing to think how to respond. "Honestly, we're hoping you could tell us."

"Tell you what? I . . . I don't remember any accident." Chloe focused her attention on Mitch, an understandable choice given how doctors were supposed to have all the answers.

"This is a tricky question," Mitch said, coming around the table with his phone out, recording the events as he'd done before. "Think of it like a test and you want to do well on it. Close your eyes, and give it some *real* hard concentration. Do you remember a house with a tire swing? Having breakfast? Burning toast? What do you remember last?"

Chloe's nature was to perform perfectly, whatever was asked of her. Through counseling, Grace had learned that failure, in Chloe's mind, was an affront to her identity—though really it was Penny's fears manifested, augmented, and presented in the form of this girl alter.

"Is closing my eyes a part of the test?" asked Chloe.

"Yes," said Grace. "Now close them and try to remember."

With that, Chloe shut her eyes tight.

"What were you doing before you were here?" Grace asked.

Chloe's whole face was a picture of concentration. Grace observed the muscles around her jaw and eyes slowly began to ease. *Is she remembering something?*

Then Chloe made an audible gasp. "I was looking at a book," she said, astonished that a memory had actually come to her. Grace got Mitch's attention as she tapped her finger on the drawing of a blue rectangle clutched in the hand of the little girl upstairs.

"The title of the book," Grace said hurriedly. "Can you see it in your mind?"

Chloe shook her head.

"No," she said. "The cover is blue . . . and there are boats . . . boats in the water."

She spoke in a dreamy, faraway voice, almost a whisper. Grace turned to Mitch, who stared back as if disbelieving his own eyes and ears.

"You're doing so well," Grace said brightly. "What else can you tell us about that book? What else do you remember?"

At that Chloe's eyes flew open, her gaze fixed on the picture she'd drawn. She put her finger on the toaster, tracing the black and gray crayon lines of smoke spreading out in all directions.

"Burned it all up," she said in a trancelike voice, similar to the one Penny had used in the room flooded with ammonia.

Grace was puzzled. "Burned what up, Chloe?"

"It all burned . . . burned it all up . . . but she didn't go away."

"Who?" Grace asked. "Who didn't go away? Who burned it up? What burned?"

Instead of answering, Chloe tapped the table rhythmically with one hand . . . *tap* . . . *tap* . . . *tap* . . . and with each tap she said the name of a place:

"Michigan . . . Florida . . . Key West . . ."

Tap. Tap. Tap.

"I'm bad," she said.

Tap. Tap. Tap.

"I'm a *very* bad girl."

"Chloe?" whispered Grace.

"Alabama . . . Alaska . . . Charlotte . . . Chicago . . . bad girl . . . very bad girl."

"Chloe, can you hear me? Answer me, darling!"

Grace's voice cut through some fog, reached some place in her daughter's mind. Chloe blinked once, blinked twice, before her face went slack. She lowered her head, avoiding Grace's probing stare. When her daughter peered up at her, Grace knew without a doubt that Chloe was gone. She sat in her chair with her shoulders pulled back, chest out, head cocked to one side, looking rather annoyed.

"Hello, Eve," Grace said, feeling a pit in her stomach.

"Mother," Eve said, making her greeting extra saccharine for effect. "Are we to have lunch here?" Eve, blinking rapidly with her tongue sticking out, indicated her displeasure, before her gaze shifted to the drawing on the table.

"What's this?" she said, knocking her knuckles on the picture.

"You tell me," said Mitch, coming forward—still recording, Grace could see. "You just made it."

Eve's whole face screwed up.

"Don't mess with me," she said darkly. "I think I'd remember drawing this." She sent him a look of disdain as she put her finger on the dead woman in the basement. "Are you going to play head games with me just like Palumbo did?"

"No," said Mitch. "I'm not. I promise."

Grace sent Mitch a look as if to say: *How could this be made up?*

"Then who drew this?" answered Eve defiantly. She was behaving more frightened than upset, but that was understandable to Grace. To disassociate from the self meant to lose that time. To slip out of one's conscious personality and return to it later was naturally disorienting. For Eve, it was as if she'd blinked and the drawing had suddenly appeared.

"Do you know a girl named Chloe?" Mitch asked.

"Are you saying an alter of mine drew this?" Eve answered, skeptical.

"I'm not entirely sure who made it," said Mitch while rolling up the paper to keep it safe—and Grace thought that was the truth, at least in part.

Eve turned her attention back to her mother.

"I think I've lost my appetite," she said.

Grace was feeling the same. She kept thinking about the smoke billowing out from the toaster in the drawing and what Chloe had said.

Fire. Burned it all up. Didn't go away.

She didn't know the meaning of the places Chloe had recited, still didn't know what the rhythmic tapping was about either, or that damn book she couldn't find at home, but she did understand a thing or two about fire. And only one person Grace knew of had a pyromania problem.

Maria.

CHAPTER 29

THE MOMENT EVERYTHING CHANGED, the start of your journey and ours into DID, was a sunny Saturday in September when you were thirteen years old. The scene is one that will definitely feature prominently in my film. Picture the shot:

```
EXT. Wide pleasant street. Bright blue sky.
  Typical suburbia.

CUT TO: Cute boy on a BMX bike.
```

He showed up at the house having arrived on that bicycle—I remember that detail vividly. I was in the living room watching TV, and emerged only when it started getting loud and weird. He was a good-looking kid, about my age, so I put him at fifteen. He stood on our front doorstep, and I heard him ask very specifically for Chloe.

Naturally, Mom told him he had the wrong address, and he replied that he was from Marblehead, had recently moved to town, and had met a girl named Chloe at our restaurant. She'd invited him over to hang out and do math together, something like that, and she'd given him this address. My guess is, knowing boys of that age, that he didn't have just numbers on his mind when you, *Chloe,* told him where to meet.

How do I know it was Chloe in the restaurant talking to that boy, inviting him to our house? I can't be sure of it, but I was at Big Frank's that day, and I distinctly remember you sitting at a table, math books splayed out in front of you, being very diligent about your work. So I guess when the cute boy—pretty sure his name was Troy—came over to talk to you, you gave him the name of your most studious alter.

Now that Troy was standing on our doorstep, Mom was as confused as I was. She called you to the front door, asked if you'd ever seen this boy before, and you said no, never. And then, well, then he started laughing. He pointed at you and he just kept on laughing, but not in a mean way. It was an awkward thing, more like he was the butt of some joke.

Troy said to Mom—and to me, because I'd come out from the living room by this point—that *this* (here he pointed at you) is Chloe. *This* is the girl he met at Big Frank's. He stood there like he was waiting for this ridiculous joke of ours to end. It got quite uncomfortable, as you can imagine, I remember that clearly. And you, Penny, well, you just kept shaking your head, saying, "I don't know who this boy is, tell him to go away, Mom."

I've learned a few things about your alters over the years. As Penny, you say Mom, but as Chloe you'd say Mama; Ruby was Mum; and Eve says Mother.

Looking back on it, that's how I can be sure it was you, Penny, upset as could be, screaming at that boy to go away and leave you alone.

"I don't know him! I don't know him!" you shouted, clutching your head as if your brain was on fire.

Mom panicked, which made perfect sense because you were out of your mind, truly frightened. She slammed the door in that poor boy's face. He must have been beyond confused, and so was Mom, but me? I'm not sure. I was thinking of other people you've pretended to be, about Eve, and Ruby. And now Chloe? Remember, we didn't know about DID at this point.

I figured either you were embarrassed about inviting a boy over without permission, or you were an amazing actor, or you really *didn't* remember ever meeting Troy. To this day I'm still not sure. I wish I'd captured that look on your face, though. Such profound shock and horror—it reminded me of the way Mom looked that day we thought we'd lost you and you were hiding *in* the bed.

After the boy left, Mom made a dozen phone calls. With that you got yourself a new psychiatrist. Dr. Caroline Cross.

I think without Dr. Cross, you'd still be getting treated for OCD and depression, but the signs were there all along. Different types of memory loss . . . different personality states . . . anxiety . . . depression . . . and those were the symptoms we could see.

Your other doctors weren't incompetent; it's just that the whole Chloe incident made it easier for Dr. Cross to diagnose you. She was very methodical, patient, or so Mom would say when singing her praises. Dr. Cross observed things about you that we didn't, like how you'd sometimes talk faster, in a tighter, more nervous voice when you discussed schoolwork and grades, especially when under pressure to perform.

One day, not long after your diagnosis, Dr. Cross met with us as a family. She wanted us to understand DID so we weren't frightened of it. It was more common than people realized, she said. First and foremost, you weren't different people. You were one person with multiple personality states, each identity expressing a part of a whole. If we could integrate those different states, she said, you would be Penny—who sometimes got angry like Eve, who obsessed like Chloe, and who could be as fun-loving and carefree as Ruby.

"It's not something to be scared of," Dr. Cross assured us, mainly addressing Ryan and myself, because this meeting was our primer into the condition.

"What Penny has is a very elaborate defense mechanism," she explained. "It's quite possible that before your sister came to live with you, she experienced some sort of extreme trauma—something very difficult for a young mind, still in its formative stages, to process. Think about it like compartmentalization. Do you know what that means, boys?"

We nodded like we did, but I'm not sure that was true. I mean, I got the concept of a compartment where you put your stuff, in this case your personalities, but that's about it.

"For Penny to get on with life, to be fully functioning, she needed to create those compartments in her mind. It allowed her to escape those painful feelings, to hide from the trauma mentally when she couldn't do it physically."

"So what happened to her?" Ryan asked. You may think Ryan's always against you, Penny, but I can attest that on that day he was scared, confused, and cared for you deeply.

Dr. Cross looked to Mom, unsure how much to share. Mom spoke up.

"It's possible that Rachel, Penny's birth mother, hurt her, abused her in some way. We don't know for certain, but it would have taken place before she came to live with us." Mom waited to let that sink in before she went on.

"We don't know what Penny's life with Rachel was like. So there's reason to think it wasn't a safe environment for a child. But the good news is that with Dr. Cross's help, we can work on integrating the different parts of Penny's personality into a whole again."

That was a very informative session, to say the least. Since then, I've bolstered my knowledge about DID. Yes, there's a chance you have it, but I keep coming back to the idea that you've been playing us, Penny. Your alters, all of it—it's just a game to you, a built-in excuse to do exactly as you wish. It explains everything, doesn't it?

Who invited this boy to our house? Not me.

Who hit Ryan with a rock? Not me.

Who took Dad's car? Not me.

Who killed Rachel Boyd? Not me.

Ever heard the excuse "the devil made me do it"? Well, what if *you're* the devil?

These are hard questions, and I guess Dr. Mitch is going to try to find some answers. He's going to play detective. If he can unearth an alter who couldn't understand that killing Rachel was wrong, or maybe one who couldn't conform to the law, then I guess you'll be found not guilty by reason of mental defect. Not sure the legal ramifications of revenge—if some alter of yours felt aggrieved for abuse you may have suffered at Rachel's hand, would that make you not guilty because you snapped? That's a question for Navarro, I suppose. In some ways, he's a detective on your case, same as Dr. Mitch.

I think about the best detectives from the movies. Jake Gittes from *Chinatown* . . . Hercule Poirot . . . Marge Gunderson from *Fargo* . . . they examined every angle, not just the obvious. They followed logical paths and illogical ones alike. So, if you have DID, and DID is thought to occur from childhood trauma, then we should be looking at your childhood to give us a motivation for your crime. That's what I'm thinking. But we don't know anything about your life before you came to us, so that means the next best place to check is with your birth mother, Rachel Boyd.

Of course, Rachel can no longer speak for herself. But I've a friend at Emerson, someone who knows her way around a computer, who might be able to speak for her.

CHAPTER 30

MARIA DESCENZA LIVED WITH her mother, Barbara, on a cul-de-sac at the end of a hilly rise. The backyard offered an unobstructed view of Swampscott's famed Civil War monument, and beyond that loomed the ocean. The house where Maria lived was far too big for a family of two, but two were all that remained after Maria's brothers had gone off to college. Her father, Bill, had left Barbara for a younger man, which at least was a little less of a cliché.

According to town gossip, Barbara had no intention of selling the property, as it would have meant splitting the profits—if any—with her ex. The house and landscape both appeared to be in a severe state of disrepair, with patches of bare dirt the size of a pitcher's mound on the lawn and the remaining green consumed with clover. The front steps were in desperate need of a fresh coat of paint, and the side of the tool shed looked like the worst yard sale ever, with the only items for purchase being coils of old hose, a rusted grill, some random buckets, and a blue wheelbarrow with one wheel missing.

Over the years, Arthur and Grace had made friends with the parents of most of Ryan and Jack's friends, but such was not the case with the Descenzas. Barbara was a bit hard to take in big doses, always complaining about some injustice she'd suffered. She played the role of the aggrieved party with Oscar-like caliber.

Even before the arrest and darker truths about Maria had come to light, people tended to keep their distance from the Descenzas. There was something off about the family, as though they didn't *want* to integrate, and were happy just occupying space, taking up land and water, without being an active part of the neighborhood.

Maria, with her witchy ways, was hardly a perfect match for Penny, but for a while, with Penny's social life dismal as it was, Maria was a godsend. Only now, after much time and heartache, did Grace understand it wasn't that Penny had befriended Maria—it was Eve who sought out Maria's dark energy. Apart, the girls were probably harmless, but together, dangerous chemistry took place.

Grace had come to the Descenza house with a faint hope that she might reach Barbara, help her see the flaw in Maria's alibi, and consider the possibility that Maria might well have been at Rachel Boyd's with Penny on that terrible night—and that Penny could end up paying the price of this deception with her freedom.

It was easy for Grace to put herself in Barbara's shoes, imagining what she would do if someone came at her with accusations about her daughter. Of course she'd defend Penny to the end, but later, in the quiet moments after the dust settled, she'd ask questions of herself, and if she didn't like the answers . . . well, maybe, just maybe, she'd do something about it.

It was Barbara who answered the door. The green top she wore and matching tight pants called attention to the considerable weight she'd gained since Grace last saw her. Her skin was sallow and wrinkled, eyes drooping. She ran a sun-spotted hand through her short, wiry hair before her gaze hardened. All in all, Barbara looked tired, drained of life. Even though her daughter would be testifying for the prosecution—the girls' past crimes being relevant to this new case—Grace could not help but feel some empathy toward her.

"Hello, Barbara," Grace said.

"Grace," she answered coolly. "What are you doing here?"

"I just need a minute of your time."

From the kitchen, Grace heard Maria's familiar voice echo down the hall. "Is that the pizza? I'm starving."

Grace suppressed all reaction. She would have to check the receipts, but something told her the promised pizza was coming from her restaurant. All that empathy fled on the spot. *How dare she!* This twisted girl who had, at a minimum, led her daughter astray and quite conceivably, for the thrill of the kill, might have set her up to take the fall for Rachel's murder—she had no business eating her food.

Grace heard clomping footsteps, and Maria soon appeared in the hallway, dressed like she'd come from a funeral, looking like it had been her own. Her skin was colorless, and her eyes were ringed with so much makeup it was as if two black moons were peering out from behind a pale cloud.

"Hello, Maria," Grace said.

Maria hovered at the end of the hallway, arms sliding into the same defensive posture her mother had adopted.

"What's she doing here?" Maria asked. "Is Eve all right? Did something happen to her?"

Grace didn't bother correcting her. Of course Maria would think of Penny as Eve.

"I don't know about that," said Barbara. "I just know you shouldn't be here, Grace."

"I only need a minute of your time . . . alone, if I may," Grace answered calmly.

Barbara glanced back at Maria. "What you say to me, you can say to her."

"Very well," said Grace. "May I come in?"

She peered beyond Barbara into the dark hallway. She could smell the dust and stale, trapped air. Somewhere exotic incense was burning. It was a home without joy, and even if the shades hadn't been drawn, Grace doubted sunlight could brighten the gloom.

"We can talk here," Barbara said, placing one hand on the doorframe, as if Grace might try to force her way inside.

"As you wish," Grace said. "I'll get right to it then. There's a possibility that Penny is innocent. She's working with a new doctor, and her memory is slowly starting to come back. Either she was hiding in Rachel's house at the time of the murder, or she was present but threatened physically, scared for her life if she interfered in any way."

Maria came storming down the hall, feet stomping, worry creasing her near-flawless skin.

"So? What's that got to do with us?" Maria asked.

"I think you may know something," said Grace.

"Are you saying I did it?" Maria's death stare said it was possible.

"I'm asking for the truth," Grace said. She peered up at the second-floor window—which she knew looked into Maria's bedroom—and at the lattice entwined with ivy, which Maria could have easily descended without Barbara's knowledge.

"She made a drawing," Grace continued. "It wasn't Penny, it was her alter, Chloe, who drew it. She drew a toaster on fire and said that something burned up, but 'she'—I guess Rachel—'didn't go away.'

"'Burned it up.' Do you know what that means? I believe it's a message to you, or about you."

Maria glared at Grace indignantly from her safe perch behind her mother. "Just because I've lit a few fires, you think I'm a murderer?"

"I really don't think you should be here making insinuations," Barbara said scornfully. "We're on the witness list. We're not supposed to talk about the case, especially with you."

"But there's new information here, Barbara," Grace said, invoking her name with hopes it might also evoke some sympathy. "We don't have all the facts."

"Don't have the facts?" Maria said, feeling brave enough to poke her head over her mother's thick shoulder to confront Grace. "Blood all over Penny . . . a knife in her hand. I think there's plenty of *facts,* and I had nothing . . . *nothing* to do with it."

Penny now, Grace noted.

She wasn't about to bring up the vile murder fantasies and hit list Maria had been a part of, nor was she about to make any more accusations. She'd come here with one purpose and one purpose only—to plant a seed of doubt in Barbara's mind.

"I'm just wondering if there's more to this story than we know," Grace said.

"What are you getting at?" Barbara snarled, her face going red with anger. "Are you saying Maria was lying to me, to the police?"

Grace returned an *oh come on* kind of look.

"If she said she was home in bed, sick, then she was home," Barbara insisted.

"I just want you to give it some consideration. Think back to that night. Maria, I'm not saying you committed the crime, but maybe you were with Penny. Did you see something? Did someone intimidate you?"

"*You're* intimidating me," Maria clapped back.

Grace had a second theory she was willing to consider: that it had been Maria's head someone threatened to stuff into a bucket full of ammonia, not Rachel's, and that someone could have been Vincent Rapino. With Penny in prison, Maria had good reason to keep her mouth shut—at the risk of having Vince or one of his cronies shut it for her. Why Vince had let both girls live was an open question.

Grace's other theory, of course, was that she was currently asking questions of a killer.

"The prosecutor told us not to talk to anybody about the case," Barbara said.

"Barbara, these questions need answers."

"And you got them. Now, I'm asking you to go, Grace."

Grace and Barbara had something of a high noon moment during a lengthy stare down.

"Please," Grace said, her voice pleading, her chest growing heavy. "Ask your daughter the hard questions, make sure you have the full story. Penny's life is at stake."

"I'm sorry," Barbara said. "You've been through a lot. But don't come back here. You're not welcome." She removed her hand from the door and gently closed it. Grace could hear the lock click into place.

As Grace made her way to her car, she spied another vehicle coming down the road, this one with a Big Frank's custom car topper on the roof. She flagged down the driver, a high school student named Pete who'd been working for them for a year. Pete came to a stop a hundred feet from the Descenzas' house and rolled down the window.

"Hi, Ms. Francone," he said in a cheerful voice.

"Is that order for 38 Outlook Road?" she asked.

"Yeah, Barbara Descenza," Pete answered.

"She canceled," Grace said. "Bring the pizza to a friend's house, any friend you want."

Pete said a friendly good-bye, rolled up his car window, put the vehicle in reverse, and drove away.

CHAPTER 31

Mitch waited in the therapy room, his iPhone camera ready for recording, and used the time between appointments to study the picture Chloe had made. If there were any connections to infer from a child's drawing of a house, a toaster on fire, and Rachel dead in a basement alongside a jug of ammonia, they weren't evident to him. Grace had confirmed they didn't have a tire swing at the house in Swampscott, so that image, along with the rest of the drawing, probably had come from the same place—Penny's imagination.

Navarro didn't think the drawing was helpful for the DID case, but Grace thought otherwise. She remained adamant that the smoking toaster, coupled with what Chloe had said about "burning it up," made Maria, a known pyromaniac, not only a person of interest but quite possibly the one responsible for Rachel's death.

"Maria wrote about murder, about killing, about hiding bodies and getting away with it, as much as Penny did," Grace had said to him on her way out of Edgewater that day. "She deserves a closer look, especially now."

Where Grace saw connections, Mitch saw symbols. Chloe, who had presented as a young girl, was probably taught that ammonia was poison. Many of the stories and fairy tales Mitch had read to Adam as a young boy had poisons in them. It could be the jug of yellow liquid stood for death in a child's eyes, as poison was something a young person like Chloe could grasp.

Had Penny got the ammonia idea from Chloe through the subconscious bleeding of one alter into another? He thought there was a fascinating paper he could write on the subject of consciousness leaks between alters. He wondered if Penny was aware of these leaks and plugged the holes. At yesterday's therapy session with Eve, he had tried to trigger another switch—either back to Chloe using the crayons again or a strong ammonia scent to see if that would get Penny back—but those efforts had gone nowhere.

Mitch had extensive experience with treating a wide range of conditions in adolescent psychology. He'd written several peer-reviewed papers, even one on dissociative identity disorder, but for all his skills and background, he could not seem to break through Penny's defenses.

Best way to beat a good defense, Mitch knew, was to use a better offense.

From a canvas workbag, he withdrew a small white plastic bottle of a nasal-injected medicine. Spinning the dispenser around in his hand, Mitch reviewed the tiny print on the label, trying not to think of Grace out there chasing down leads (or more likely ghosts).

He felt a spurt of anger at himself for the fantasy Grace had latched onto; one he'd had a hand in helping bring about. He had nothing, no proof that the reveals from Penny or Chloe were anything other than an elaborate fantasy—in other words, something Dr. Palumbo would argue that a person with borderline personality disorder might construct to distract and deflect blame.

Someone with professional credentials as impressive as Palumbo's would take the witness stand and state that Penny suffered from a severe antisocial personality disorder, and the alters were an excuse to behave as she wished and nothing more. With testimony like that, Mitch had no doubt an experienced attorney would be able to convince a jury that this young woman was a psychotic killer, through and through, and had ended Rachel's life brutally, intentionally, and with total awareness of her actions.

"Intentional" was the word Mitch turned over and over in his head. He didn't see Penny as a true psychopath—someone without empathy, guilt, conscience, or remorse—but which of her alters either couldn't resist the urge to kill or didn't think killing was wrong?

None of them was the answer he kept coming back to. They'd all pass the MPC test with flying colors, which left him with one disturbing possibility: she was faking DID and Palumbo was right. The thought gave Mitch a pounding headache. After rubbing his temples, then his tired eyes, he picked up the vial once more.

Will this work?

Not only did he feel a great responsibility to help Penny avoid a lifetime in a max security prison, he felt a tremendous burden to aid Grace as well. He had a full slate of patients to attend to, other cases to manage, but no question about it—Penny now occupied an outsized portion of his gray matter. And Mitch was pretty sure he knew why.

Guilt.

Mitch felt that personal connection to Grace's suffering and guilt that she said she felt for him. He also blamed himself for Adam's struggles in a way similar to how Grace reproached herself for Penny's. For those reasons alone he wanted more than anything to ease her pain. Even so, Mitch had grave doubts that he could help Penny—or Adam, for that matter.

The latest news from Clean Start was really no news. Adam was in recovery, again; going to meetings, again; doing group therapy, again—and chances were this was another ride on the opioid merry-go-round. That had been something Caitlyn did not want to hear when Mitch made that exact point on a phone call with her the other night.

"Have some faith, Mitch," she had said. "You of all people know there's no magic pill for this; no off switch he can just flick. I wish there was, but there isn't. So this is all we get, okay?"

"You're right," he said. "Adam deserves better." And so did Penny.

He was about to find out if better was possible.

At the designated hour, Eve showed up (at least, he assumed it was Eve). The correction officer who brought her gave Mitch a big smile along with an equally enthusiastic thumbs-up. He'd been part of that scuffle when Mitch took on three-hundred-pound John Grady, aka the Mountain Man. In a place like Edgewater, respect wasn't given—it was earned.

"Afternoon, Doc," the guard said. "I'll be back in an hour to take her to her room. You need anything, just press the button or give a holler." The button—affixed to the underside of the table in every therapy room—sounded an alarm in the event a patient became violent, though Mitch expected no such trouble from Eve today. "How's the leg?" asked the guard.

"Couldn't be better," Mitch said, extending the appendage and feeling an unpleasant twinge at the side of his knee.

"Hey, we got your back here." The CO sent a wink. "You're all right in our book."

Mitch decided not to tell him about the retraining seminar he was organizing at Whitmore's suggestion. He thanked the man for his support, and as he settled into his seat for his session, Mitch began to feel better.

After gesturing to the chair across the table from him, Eve took a seat with a sullen look on her face.

"Are you talking to me today, Eve?"

He used her name, seeking acknowledgment that he had the right alter.

"Sure. Whatever," she said. "I've got nothing better to do."

"Mind if I record?"

"No, fine," said Eve.

"I'd like to try something today, if we could," Mitch said. "I'm going to give you a new medication."

Mitch had carefully examined Penny's medications and saw no risk in adding a low dose of ketamine into the mix—and lots of potential upside. At a higher dose than Mitch was using, ketamine would inhibit glutamate signaling and function more like a traditional anesthetic. But at a low dose, the drug—best known in the club scene and newly FDA approved—was actually one of the biggest breakthroughs in depression treatment in recent years. Mitch had tried it himself with positive results, which is why the idea had come to him. More and more doctors were using it in therapy to allow the mind to make free associations, even unlock blocked memories.

If administered properly in a low dose, Special K, as the club kids called it, acted like a flash mob—flooding the brain with NDMA receptors that actually ramped up glutamate signaling. The effect was to produce feelings of euphoria and reduced anxiety. It was also thought to help fire up dormant pathways in the brain, which could give Mitch access to another one of Penny's alters, much like the crayons and drawing paper had coaxed out Chloe. The question was how to find the right corridor in the maze of his patient's mind.

Mitch had spent much of the night thinking about Penny and her alters, what each represented. From what he understood, Penny, the primary self, subjected her needs to those of others. Ruby was like Teflon. Spoke in a British accent. Appeared one day when her father was making breakfast, around age twelve. She was free, happy, delightful, witty—in many ways the opposite of Chloe, who compensated for her worries about judgment and failure with excessive effort. And Eve—Eve was all about maintaining power and control. *And why is control so important to her?* Mitch had given that question careful consideration. It was Adam, of all people, who had unwittingly supplied him with a potential answer. The drugs muted Adam's pain—like taking hits of joy, as he described it.

Hits of joy, that is, before the drug took complete control over him.

The need for control often starts off as a healthy response to anxiety before it morphs into something all-consuming, following a trajectory not unlike that of Adam's drug use—first a little, then a lot, and then too much. If Mitch could lessen Eve's anxiety, and therefore her need for control, he felt he might increase his odds of reaching Ruby.

The effects of ketamine were short-lived, especially in the dose Mitch would give her. He handed the small vial to Eve and explained his request, giving her a brief primer on the drug. He left his objectives intentionally vague, anticipating Eve would take countermeasures, even if subconsciously.

"I think this will be a useful tool for us to get more out of your therapy," he said, and it wasn't a lie.

"Whatever."

The compact spray bottle made it effortless for Eve to self-administer the narcotic. The effects of it were almost immediate.

"How do you feel?" Mitch asked.

"Yeah, feel good," she said. "I mean . . . yeah . . . kinda nice."

"Okay," said Mitch.

He had Penny's file folder on the table, from which he produced a grainy photograph, taken by the police on the night of the murder. The image focused closely on the red rings surrounding her wrists. He was thinking of what Whitmore had said about the unusual marks, wondering if ketamine might help release a memory to explain them.

"Do you recall being handcuffed on the night of your arrest?" he asked.

Eve focused closely on the image. "Oh God, my wrists are so fat and ugly," she groaned. Then, looking up at Mitch, said, "Yeah, I remember."

"Did it hurt? Did you say anything to the police about the handcuffs being on too tight?"

Mitch put the picture away. There was no way he'd show her any of the other images from the crime scene. Eve contemplated the question, seeming more relaxed by the second.

"No," she said quietly with a shake of her head. "Don't think so."

"Got it. What do you remember from yesterday?"

"Yesterday?" She sounded unsure why yesterday would matter at all.

"Yes. Can you tell me about your day yesterday?"

"Well . . ." Eve began. "I did the morning stuff . . . breakfast, clean up, a little outside time . . . oh joy, oh rapture. I had a meeting with you in here and it smelled terrible . . . ammonia or something. The help really needs to be more careful with their cleaning products."

The help? Mitch barely stifled a laugh. She remembered his second attempt with the ammonia, the one that failed, but she'd omitted the crayons, which had also failed to trigger a switch after that first success. He'd have to go back further.

"What about the day before? Anything stick out in your mind?"

He was thinking of Chloe and her drawing.

"Hmmm," said Eve. "No . . . I had group in the morning. God, I hate group. So many people here have *really* big problems." She paused to send Mitch a playful smile because she understood she was one of them. "I met with my lawyer, and then I met up with Mother in that bright room . . . and you were there."

"And?"

"And we talked and that was it. No, lunch, now that I think about it."

"Nothing unusual?"

"Nope. After Mother left I got something from the vending machine, went back to my glorious cell, and hung out until dinner. It really is action-packed around here."

Either Chloe was lodged in some compartment deep in Penny's subconscious, or this girl was a marvelously deviant liar.

"Do any of these places have special meaning for you, Eve?"

Mitch read from the list of locations Chloe had recited in her trance, ones he had transcribed into a small black notebook.

"Michigan . . . Florida . . . Key West . . . Alabama . . . Alaska . . . Charlotte . . . Chicago . . ."

Eve shook her head at them all.

What could it mean? he wondered.

"Do you ever think of yourself as a bad girl?" Here he was quoting Chloe.

She sent him a lopsided, somewhat mawkish grin.

"I don't know," she said. "Do *you* think I'm a bad girl? Do *you* think I'm a brutal killer, Dr. Mitch?"

Mitch gave it some thought, happy to see the ketamine was still working. Everything about Eve appeared more relaxed.

"My job isn't to judge you, Eve. It's to help you."

He fired off some questions from the Competency Screening Test, curious to know if she'd pass.

"Do you know what you're charged with?"

"Murder in the first."

She was far too cavalier for any jury's liking.

"Do you understand what you're alleged to have done?"

"I killed my birth mother, Rachel Boyd, with a knife. Or was it a candlestick in the billiard hall?"

Clue.

Eve.

Lord help me.

Mitch could go on, but all the answers she'd give would confirm what he already knew. She could stand trial for murder and she understood right from wrong. She could resist the urge to kill. But could Ruby?

"I'd like to try something else, if I may," he said.

Eve eyed him apprehensively. "News flash, I'm not into that," she said sharply, and Mitch's face immediately reddened.

"No, no . . . nothing . . ." He bumbled for the words, and Eve sniggered.

"I'm just kidding around. What do you want to try? You're fun, Dr. Mitch. I like you. Really. So . . ." She clapped her hands. "Let's have some fun." Her eyes gleamed wickedly. She leaned forward in her chair, and Mitch got that cat-playing-with-a-cornered-mouse vibe. "What is it you want?"

Again, Adam's words came to Mitch.

Just talk to me . . .

"I'd like to speak to Ruby if I may. Is that possible, Eve?"

Eve did not look eager to accommodate.

"Why Ruby?" she asked, sounding confused.

Mitch heard a subtext in her question: *Do you like her better?*

He knew not to treat any alternate identity as more "real" or important than any other. He had to make Eve believe that Ruby was significant in Penny's psyche, but no more so than anyone else.

"I think she's an interesting person, from what I've read of her," he said. "But she's so hard to reach, and I was hoping you could help me. Honestly, it can't happen without you."

More subtext to Eve: *You are in control here.*

Eve went silent for a time.

"You think it could help me? Really help?"

Mitch heard: *I'm open to it.*

"I do."

"I'm coming back," she announced.

Translation: *I still dictate the rules.*

From Mitch's understanding, some people with DID could switch on command, some couldn't. He wasn't sure where Eve was on that spectrum, but he'd soon find out.

"Wouldn't want it any other way," said Mitch.

Eve looked down at her lap, head bowed, but Mitch could see a smile grace her lips, one that was tender and warm. When she looked up at him, he knew she was gone.

"Hello," the girl said in a British accent. "Who are you?"

"Well, hello there, Ruby," said Mitch with a broadening grin.

CHAPTER 32

"WHO ARE YOU?" RUBY asked again. She languidly scanned her surroundings, didn't act or sound the least bit concerned, which Mitch figured was the ketamine still working its magic.

"My name is Dr. Mitch," he said.

"Okay, Dr. Mitch," Ruby answered cheerily. "So . . . um . . . where the heck am I?"

Is this a game? Is it real? Mitch could only speculate.

"You're in a therapy room at a hospital. You've been here for some time."

"A hospital? Am I okay?"

"You're fine. More than fine."

She assessed him warily. "Well . . . if I'm so fine, why am I here then?" Her cocked eyebrow all but said *gotcha*.

"We can get to that in a bit," said Mitch. "First I was hoping we could talk. I'm recording the conversation, is that okay?"

Ask Eve . . . ask Ruby, treat each alter as an individual and with respect.

"Yeah, fine to record," she said in that lilting accent. "Okay, then . . . what do you want to talk about?"

"Maybe tell me a little bit about yourself for starters?"

She looked a tad uncertain. "Well, name's Ruby. I'm sixteen. I live in Swampscott, Massachusetts . . . love the ocean, like roller coasters, and want to be a VSCO girl."

"A VSCO girl?" Mitch asked, eyebrows arching. "What's that?"

"Like you don't know?"

Judging from her surprised voice and expression, Mitch might as well have said he'd never heard of dinosaurs.

"Honest, I don't," he confessed.

He couldn't place her accent. To his ears she sounded like Hermione Granger, and it was possible that Ruby came from Penny's interactions with the world of Harry Potter. Grace had said she was a fan of the books and movies beforehand, so it wouldn't shock him if some amalgam of them gave rise to Ruby. No matter her origin, she fulfilled a very specific purpose in Penny's psyche.

"VSCO girls are girls who favor crop tops, like their shorts *short,* and *always* have a scrunchie on the wrist."

"A scrunchie?"

"You know, for the hair," she said, tugging on her own long locks, which came free from the band used to hold them in a ponytail. She spun her head from side to side, flinging her hair from shoulder to shoulder, carefree and wild, which put a bright smile on her face.

"They know all the hot trends. Hydroflask bottles, I mean where do you think that got started? VSCO girls, that's where. Whatever they post or share, it goes viral. Just how it is."

"So *are* you a VSCO girl?" asked Mitch.

Ruby tossed back her head with a laugh.

"I *will* be," she clarified, a determined look coming to her face. "I'm starting a YouTube channel. Got Insta of course, just need more followers is all."

"Instagram?"

"Yeah, if you think I'm gonna work a desk job, you're plumb *mad.* I'm going to be free of all that. All I need are good pictures, build me a following, and then I'll get the ad dollars. VSCO girls are no dummies. Don't care what the memes say about them. They know what they're doing and I'm going to do it, too. I told Mum all that, so she knows my plan. She's not happy, mind you, but it's my life, right?"

Unlike Chloe, who'd regressed in age, Mitch put Ruby at the same age as Penny, though perhaps a bit more refined than a typical American teen.

"Your mom is?"

"Grace . . . Grace Francone," Ruby said proudly. "She adopted me when I was little, so Ruby wasn't my original name."

"Oh, what was your original name?"

"Isabella Boyd, I'm told. But Mum and Dad wanted me to feel like I had a new name for my new family."

Mitch wished he could delve deeper into Ruby's mix of fact and fantasy, but didn't want to risk upsetting her in a way that might summon back Eve.

"And who's your dad?" he asked.

A misty look swept into her eyes.

"My dad's name was Arthur, but he's dead," she said softly.

"Oh, I'm sorry."

"I was there when he died," she added. "He dropped to the floor at the pizza shop he owned. I called nine-one-one, but there was nothing anyone could do to help him. He'd had a heart attack, you see, so it wasn't my fault."

Mitch heard: *I still blame myself.* As he remembered it from Grace's retelling, no 911 calls were made until she arrived on the scene. It was more fact and fantasy colliding in Penny's mind, mixing up truths, and Mitch could not help but be reminded of the manipulative prowess of a sociopath.

"What about your birth mom, do you know anything about her?" he asked.

Ruby shook her head. "No. Nothing. But don't go feeling sorry for me there, Dr. Mitch. I mean, whatever. People will say stupid things like, 'Those aren't your *real* parents,' Arthur and Grace and all. I've heard that before, and it's a bit stunning at first, but then you realize it's just ignorance. They don't get it. So whatever. My mum *chose* me. She found me, right, and could have left it at that, but she *fought* to get me, she wanted me so much—"

Unable to finish the thought, Ruby bit her bottom lip, swallowed hard.

"Because . . . because she loved me."

Her voice broke, but after one deep breath it seemed her composure returned.

"It's not like I don't think about it, you know—my past, my birth mom, all that. But there's a difference between being curious, wanting to know where I got my eyes, or my hair, or whatever, and being devastated about it. Want to know what's devastating? My dad dying, that's what. He's gone. I can't talk to him . . . can't ask him for help with my homework, or just . . . I dunno, watch a show together, or eat his silly mouse cakes again."

Ruby's gaze softened as if she were back in that memory.

"He'd make pancakes shaped like Mickey Mouse, even though I was like, whatever, Dad, I don't need my food shaped funny to eat it anymore, but he kept doing it because that was him. He just had a silly way about him, and now he's gone. That's hard. Being adopted." She shrugged. "What's wrong with having more than one set of *real* parents? Who says it has to be one way over another? I don't have to fit someone else's mold. I can *choose* whichever mold works best for me, for my life, like Mum chose me, right? Same as I can *choose* to be a VSCO girl. You read me?"

"Loud and clear," Mitch said.

He was about to take the conversation on a darker turn, engage Ruby on matters of the law, see what she thought of the crime of murder, if there were circumstances in which it might be justified. Before he could get going though, an alarm rang out. The strobe lights went flashing, and that meant guards were on the move. None of this was jarring to Mitch, who'd grown accustomed to the noise, but Ruby looked quite surprised and unsettled.

"It's nothing to worry about," he said. "Probably a little incident in the hospital is all."

"What kind of incident, like a fire?" She sounded nervous at the prospect.

Fire . . . fire makes her nervous, thought Mitch.

"Probably more like a fight," he said, thinking the truth would be less alarming than a blaze. "There are guards on duty, it'll be handled."

Hospitals had security, so Ruby didn't seem to mind that explanation. While Mitch was looking at his notes, readying his questions, the door to the therapy room—one he didn't lock in case a guard needed access—flew open. Shock replaced surprise on Ruby's face, a look that Mitch shared as his gaze traveled to the doorway and he made sense of what he saw there.

Darla, looking strong and sturdy as a tree trunk in her Edgewater greens, filled the doorframe to the therapy room with her substantial girth. Her face was a knot of rage, mouth twisted and snarled, hair wildly upended. She glared not at Mitch but at his patient, pressing her sizable hands against the doorframe, leaning her body into the room.

"You," Darla said in a growl, pointing at Ruby. "You slept with him, you bitch!"

Mitch half expected the blast of adrenaline that hit him might have sent Ruby scurrying away to make room for Eve, but no, the sharp-edged voice that answered retained an English accent.

"What do you mean I slept with him? Who are you?"

"You know who I am," said Darla. "Don't play games with me, missy. I don't care who you say you are. Penny, Eve, whatever—you're a piece of shit whatever your name is." Foamy spittle flew from Darla's mouth. "You had sex with my Charlie and now I'm going to rip your head off."

Darla removed her hand from the doorframe, and that's when Mitch saw the knife. It was a crude weapon, long and thin like a needle—a shank, as it's known in prison parlance, fashioned from scraps of metal that she'd acquired from who knows where.

Out of instinct, Mitch hit the panic button as he rose from his chair and came around the desk to confront Darla head on. The gap between them was now no more than seven feet, a distance she could travel in under a second. The sight of Darla's eyes swimming with madness tightened Mitch's chest in what he could only liken to a heart attack.

He managed to get out two words—"Darla" and "no"—before the full weight of her body crashed hard into his. Mitch saw the shank in Darla's right hand come at his left side, the blade slightly stained with blood. *Did she stab a guard to get here?*

Swiveling at the waist, Mitch moved reflexively in the opposite direction of the knife attack. Thankfully, the shank caught a flap on the inside of Mitch's tweed blazer, causing it to rip as he lost his balance. With the blade stuck in the coat fabric, the weapon pulled free from Darla's grasp as Mitch fell to the floor. A sharp stab of pain blasted into his right shoulder, but it wasn't severe enough to keep him out of the fight.

She may have called herself Eve in here, and had switched to Ruby before this attack, but in Mitch's mind it was still Penny who Darla had come to kill. With one long stride, Darla stepped over Mitch to get to her target, who was slow to react because of the ketamine. In no time at all, she had her hands wrapped tightly around Penny's throat, and Mitch heard the strangled sound that followed.

Momentum from Darla's forward burst carried enough force to tip Penny's chair backward. It balanced on two legs before it went over, and Penny went with it, Darla landing on top of her. Somehow, Penny managed to stay seated when she hit the floor, but with no leverage to wiggle free, Darla's weight advantage kept her pinned in place. Strangled noises from Penny were quiet at first, but became increasingly desperate as Darla's hands tightened around her throat.

Rolling onto his stomach, Mitch pushed to his hands and knees, getting off the floor with a grunt of effort. He needed only a single step to grab hold of Darla's green uniform at the shoulders, bunching the fabric into two little balls as he pulled with all his might. She didn't budge, so he let go with one hand to start hammering heavy blows against Darla's back with a closed fist.

"He's my husband . . . you had no right! No right to sleep with him. You whore! You bitch!"

"Darla," Mitch screamed. "Stop!"

This began a desperate tug-of-war, Mitch pulling on Darla, Darla pulling in the other direction so she could keep her hands white-knuckled on Penny's throat. Kicking wildly, bucking with her hips, Penny tried desperately to free herself, but to no avail. Darla came into this fight phenomenally strong, and rage had made her even more formidable. She was crazed, snapping her head back at Mitch with her teeth bared like the fangs of an angry dog. Penny could not hold on much longer.

There was little for Mitch to use as a weapon. While the shank was in sight, he wanted to keep it out of play. If something went wrong, Mitch feared, someone, probably himself, would end up on the business end of that blade. Best he could do was to pull as hard as he could, get himself back on the floor, and hope that Darla came with him. *Where are the damn guards?*

With a loud grunt, Mitch drove his legs into the ground and essentially threw himself backward with all his might. His plan worked. Sort of. He landed on his back, and Darla's back landed on him. Her crushing weight made it nearly impossible to breathe, though Mitch's arms were free, and soon he had one of them wrapped around Darla's neck.

He had a passing thought that this was the exact hold he planned to tell the guards in his seminar *not* to use on a patient. In a life-and-death struggle, he was seeing firsthand that rules were things to be forgotten.

Darla tried to bite Mitch's arm, but given the odd angle, she couldn't latch on. Instead she kicked frantically as Mitch tightened his hold. His hope was that she'd lose consciousness before she lost her life. Fortunately, it was a race that needed no winner, as a crush of correction officers finally burst into the room. They swarmed Darla, ripped her off Mitch, grunting orders that were difficult to hear in the sudden cacophonous din.

In a furious cluster of motion, the security team had Darla facedown on the floor. A female guard sat on her back, pinning her to the ground with her knees. Another guard delivered blows to Darla's head as she futilely resisted efforts to wrench her arms behind her back.

Mitch heard a hiss as someone fired pepper spray point blank into Darla's face. The room quickly filled with a terrible stench that made his eyes water and his stomach do loops. Clambering past guards who continued to fill the tight quarters, Mitch grabbed hold of Penny, whom he found curled in a ball on the floor near her chair. With a grunt of effort, he managed to pull her out into the hallway, away from the poisonous air. There, he checked her pulse. A little rapid and weak, but steady. She was probably more in shock than anything else.

Strobe lights flashed. Guards were everywhere now. Sirens continued to blare, but they failed to drown out Darla's screams.

"She slept with Charlie! She screwed my husband!"

A thought came to Mitch, several really. *Are Darla's meds off? Is she even taking them?* Something felt wrong about the attack. *Why Penny? Was it just a coincidence that Darla previously targeted Grace, or . . . was it something else?*

CHAPTER 33

Buttery late-afternoon light filtered through the tall office windows, casting a glow on Whitmore's tight expression. Seated around the conference table in her spacious office were Mitch, Grace, and Greg Navarro.

After Grace got the call from Mitch about Penny, she rushed to Edgewater, phoning Navarro on the way. To his credit, Navarro dropped everything to join this emergency meeting with Whitmore at the facility she oversaw. He was there to deal with the legal fallout from the attempt on Penny's life, while Grace's concerns were those of a mother.

"Can I visit her?" Grace asked Whitmore in an anxious voice.

"By 'her,' you mean . . . Eve? Because Eve is back again, not Penny, not—" Whitmore looked down at her notes. "Not Ruby. And no. I'm afraid you can't. Your daughter's fine, I promise, but she's still in the ER and visitors are not allowed."

Grace exchanged a glance with Mitch, recalling the day they'd met and he knowingly broke that rule. "She's a bit banged up, from what I understand," Whitmore added, "but no serious injury. I was just on the phone with Dr. Bouvier and got a full update on her condition. As you know, Darla stabbed a corrections officer on her way to the therapy room, and he is not doing nearly as well. He's in the ICU at Regent's Hospital, and it's touch and go."

"I'm sorry to hear," said Grace, feeling sick to her stomach that somebody else connected to her daughter, no matter how tangentially, had been put in a perilous situation.

"Thank you," said Whitmore, who seemed deeply affected by the tragic event. "I'll make sure to keep Mitch apprised of his situation."

Navarro spoke up. "Grace had told me about her encounter with Darla, and I thought the name sounded familiar. So, I checked my files, and sure enough, a lawyer from my office was her public defender way back when. I remember him complaining from time to time that she was challenging to work with, but never violent. What provoked the attack, does anyone know? And where did Darla get a weapon?"

Putting his pen to his legal pad, Navarro appeared ready to jot down some answers. Whitmore nodded to Mitch, as if to give permission to reveal something of consequence.

"We found a note tucked inside the Bible Darla carries around with her," Mitch began. "The Bible was on her bed. I had to take a picture of the actual note because it's evidence now."

Mitch got his phone out, opened his Photos app, cleared his throat, and began to read.

"'Darla, sorry to tell but Penny Francone calls herself Eve slept with Charles.'" Mitch paused, looked up, and flicked his gaze from Grace to Navarro. "That's the grammar, not quite correct, I know." He continued to read. "'I saw pictures. Can't get to show you'—written with the letter *U*," he clarified, "'but they were doing it. You should do something about it.'"

Mitch handed his phone to Navarro, who showed a look of surprise, his arched eyebrows cresting even higher on a broad forehead.

"It's written in blue crayon," he said.

Navarro passed the phone to Grace.

"Like a child's handwriting," said Grace, making careful study of the image before handing the phone back to Mitch.

"Any idea who wrote it?" inquired Navarro. "Ms. Whitmore, does Penny have enemies here? Obviously, somebody was trying to incite Darla to violence, and I strongly suspect she hasn't made her stance about Charles a secret."

"We're trying to figure that out right now," Whitmore replied. "But you three are the closest to her. Has Penny talked to you about any threats she's received recently, any confrontations with somebody? Anything, anyone we don't know about?"

"Not off the top of my head," said Mitch.

"What about the weapon, the knife?" asked Grace. "Where did Darla get it?"

"We're not sure at the moment," Whitmore confessed. "We're in the early stages of the investigation. We're not even sure how Darla knew where Penny would be."

"Maybe someone was feeding her information," Mitch suggested. "A guard perhaps? CO Blackwood jumps to mind . . . I reported him for excessive force that day when Eve switched to Penny. Did he get reprimanded?"

Whitmore appeared to be in thought.

"Oh yeah . . . suspended three days without pay," she recalled from memory following that brief bout of silence. "Lost out on a promotion as a result."

"Nothing like a punch to the pocketbook to inspire revenge," Navarro said.

"It's an interesting angle," Whitmore agreed. "Easy enough for us to explore. But typically these conflicts are escalated between the guests, not the guards. Any chance that Penny is an instigator, Mitch?"

"Eve can be confrontational, no doubt, but I haven't been here long enough to know if she's acquired a lot of adversaries amongst her peers," Mitch said.

"I'll put that question right back to you, Dr. Whitmore," said Grace. "Who the hell did my daughter piss off?" She didn't mean to come across harshly, but it had been a heck of a day.

Whitmore returned a tight-lipped smile, but did not appear aggrieved. "I suppose we have a lot of potential suspects, don't we?" she said.

"How are we going to keep Penny safe?" Grace wanted to know. "Where's Darla now?"

"At present, Darla is confined to a room for twenty-two hours a day," Whitmore said. "And she'll be moved to a secure adjustment unit soon enough. So, back to Penny. Is she the type to push someone hard enough to want to do her in? The more personalities, the more chances there are to rub someone the wrong way, I suppose. She upsets someone and that someone uses Darla as a proxy, a weapon so to speak."

"Could be," said Mitch. "There's a potential here that she doesn't have DID, but rather a complex presentation of an antisocial personality disorder with a disregard for right and wrong, compulsive lying, arrogance, superiority complex—I could go on."

"If that's the case, I'm less inclined to put much focus on CO Blackwood," Whitmore replied.

"That day in the interview room, Penny told us she was a very bad girl—well, Chloe did," Navarro reminded everyone. "Maybe she was talking about this other alter of hers, the one with the chaotic personality state Mitch was hoping to reach. Could be that's the alter who upset Darla."

Grace, who thought she'd have been inured to the harsh realities of her daughter's condition by now, inwardly cringed at the black-and-white terms Navarro used to articulate the situation.

"Got it," Whitmore said. "So right now, all we know is Darla got a note that caused all sorts of problems."

"That note . . ." Navarro spoke softly, as if talking to himself. "Does anyone find it interesting it was written in crayon?" he asked.

Whitmore seemed indifferent. "Access to our computers and print-ers is more limited than our art supplies," she said.

"I suppose," said Navarro, who inhaled deeply as he sank into thought. "It's just a bit coincidental, isn't it?"

"Are you talking about the drawing Chloe made?" Grace asked him.

Navarro nodded. "Mitch reached one of Penny's alters and she makes a picture using crayons, and then this note shows up, done in blue crayon, and—" He shrugged. "And I don't know . . . just a coin-cidence, I guess."

Grace read the troubled expression on Mitch's face.

"That's an interesting point," he said.

"How so?" asked Grace, shifting uneasily in her seat.

"Chloe could be lingering . . . I think there's this leaking of one al-ter into another that might be taking place," Mitch said.

"The bleed thing you told me about?" asked Grace.

"Yes, that . . . we can call it consciousness leaking for lack of a bet-ter term. It's possible that Chloe didn't completely go away, that she's still present in Penny's subconscious."

"What's the significance of that to the note?" Grace wanted to know.

"I don't have proof, of course, so it's all conjecture at this point, but it's conceivable that Penny herself wrote the note and gave it to Darla, or rather slipped it into her Bible so she'd find it later."

Wonderment sparked on Whitmore's face. "Are you saying that Penny wrote a note that would obviously incite Darla? Why in the world would she do that?"

Navarro pursed his lips and Grace could almost see his thoughts flickering.

"Guilt," Mitch said. "She has a guilty conscience—bad girl, right? She knows what she did, knows it was wrong, and she's trying to pun-ish herself for it. Penny knew when she'd be in the therapy room. She could have easily dropped Darla plenty of hints."

Whitmore looked at Mitch, aghast. "Are you suggesting that Penny *wanted* Darla to come after her?"

Grace keyed in on Mitch's hesitancy.

"Maybe not come after," he said, following a weighty silence. "What Greg said might not be far-fetched. Penny's guilty conscience is surfacing, perhaps even from the work I'm doing with her, and she gave Darla the note not to get punished, but as something of a suicide attempt."

CHAPTER 34

GRACE AND ANNIE WERE bone-tired but not about to give up. They had spent the day locked in a stuffy back room at Navarro's law office, much to Ryan's continued displeasure, sifting through the cartons of evidence that included depositions, her daughter's fingerprints, DNA analysis, printouts of the twisted correspondence between Eve and Maria, police logs, and a slew of paperwork.

Grace found herself in one of her darkest moments. The crime scene photos she came across in a folder, along with disturbing pictures of Penny after her arrest, were gruesome, and for all the hours spent searching, she'd found nothing that might bolster the defense. Now it appeared her daughter may have become suicidal, as well.

"Eve protects," Grace said to Annie. "That's just what she does. I don't see her wanting any harm to come to Penny."

"But it's not just Eve anymore," Annie reminded her, taking the contrarian position for discussion's sake, as she so often did. She'd been properly debriefed and knew all the theories being bandied about. "Mitch is accessing her other alters, so she might be picking up those thoughts."

Grace shuffled some papers back into a folder with a harrumph that announced her refusal to accept that possibility.

"It's that guard Blackwood, the one who nearly clubbed Penny to death," Grace said, slipping into a scowl. "I know it. Can't prove it, but I'm not going to stop looking."

Annie smiled and went back to work. "If Blackwood knew how tenacious you can be, I doubt he'd get much sleep," she said.

As far as Grace was concerned, her effort for Penny was what any devoted mother would do, but not everyone saw it that way. One misguided friend had recently made an unfortunate remark from which the friendship never fully recovered. She said, speaking in all seriousness, "At least it wasn't one of your biological children facing a lifetime in prison."

Grace didn't know how to respond. She didn't give birth to Penny, that was true, but DNA was hardly the only way to encode parental love. The stability and love Grace and Arthur gave Penny had transformed this cherished child's life—and theirs in the process. Thinking of her family seated around the dinner table—Jack, Ryan, Penny, and Arthur, all together—gave Grace a deep sense of satisfaction, a knowledge that her family had become complete out of choice and love.

Giving birth is a single act, but parenting was the culmination of thousands of acts, large and small, done selflessly each day. It was the sum total of those experiences that had cemented an indelible bond, one that blurred the lines between parenting a biological child and an adopted one. To that friend, Grace had said simply she would do for Penny exactly what she'd do for Jack and Ryan, because she didn't think of Penny as her *adopted* child. She was her daughter.

The archival research had been a demoralizing exercise, so when her cell phone rang, Grace allowed herself to feel a tickle of hope that Jack's efforts had been more fruitful. It isn't easy digging up information on somebody, especially without formal training in the craft of detection, but Jack could be as doggedly determined as Grace (and Arthur) when it came to solving a problem.

The problem he'd set out to address was learning all he could about the victim, Rachel Boyd. She'd never been a priority until this moment, because until a few days ago, Penny's guilt was never in doubt. Now they needed to learn everything they could about Rachel in order to figure out why someone other than Penny might have wanted her dead.

"Got some intel, Mom," he said excitedly.

The only information Grace had on Penny's birth mother was what had been in the news (both when Penny was first found and again after Rachel's death) and what the lawyers had told her. She lived in Lynn, the same city where she grew up. She was a known drug user. She had been arrested before Penny was born, charged with drug trafficking, but was acquitted in court. Four years later she got arrested again after she abandoned Penny in the park, when she was charged with child endangerment and the courts took away her parental rights. She pled out, then got probation on the condition she attend drug treatment. She lived in Rhode Island for a time, but moved back to Lynn for reasons unknown. She had rented the bottom unit of a multifamily home, which is where she was murdered.

Grace didn't know much about Rachel's employment history or her family background, but since dissociative identity disorders aren't hereditary, she hadn't made it a priority to find out. Besides, trying to get that sort of detail would have involved hiring a private investigator to track down Rachel or asking Attorney Navarro to dig it up, both of which would cost money Grace didn't have.

Enter Jack, who had experience with things like doxing—which he had explained was using the Internet to reveal and discover personal information.

"What did you find out?"

"For starters, I got the name of the bar where she worked back then," Jack said into the phone. "That wasn't in the papers." Grace rose creakily from the dusty floor of the cramped little room. Food wrappers littered the wastebasket and a musty odor perfumed the air.

"What's the name?" asked Grace.

"Lucky Dog," he said.

"Fantastic," Grace exclaimed. "Someone there has to know something about Rachel's past. Maybe they'd seen some sort of abuse, who knows? Great work, Jack. How'd you get all that information?"

There was a lengthy pause.

"Yeah, better we don't go there," Jack said.

From what Grace knew of doxing, it had a malicious end in mind, and frequently hackers were the ones who did the dirty work. Perhaps Jack had a friend in the computer science department at Emerson who had put his or her specialized skills to the test. In this case, Grace felt comfortable that the end justified the means, whatever those were, and the fact that her son had discovered something of potential value, an entry point into Rachel's past, lifted her sagging spirits. She had high hopes this single lead would uncover truths about Penny's past.

"Annie and I are going nowhere fast with these files," Grace said. "We'll check in with Ryan at the restaurant, then shoot over to that bar, see what we can learn."

"I want to go with you," said Jack. "I'll find some way to get to Swampscott so we can drive together."

Grace furrowed her brow. "Why?" she asked.

"I'm part of this too, Mom," he said. "The film is one thing, but she's my sister . . . guilty or not, I want to help her any way I can." He spoke in a raw, heated voice. "I think she's trying to tell us something, but she can't. She's afraid for some reason, I feel it. I want to help put that fear to rest. I owe her that. Wherever this ends up, whatever the answers— guilty, not guilty because of insanity, or somehow, some way she's in- nocent—I have to help get that answer." He paused, and Grace heard him take a shaky breath. "And I'm not going to give up until I do."

"Meet us at the restaurant at two," Grace told him. "Better together, as your father would say."

* * *

When two o'clock came around, Jack strode into Big Frank's look- ing quite satisfied, his phone clutched in his hand. He had texted his mother to let her know he'd borrowed a friend's car to drive himself to Swampscott, and Grace wondered if this friend of his was the same one who had helped him dox Rachel Boyd.

"Ready, Mom?" asked Jack.

Grace and Annie were standing near the door, hoping to make a quick exit before Ryan came out of the storeroom. Grace had thought it would be a good idea to check in on her older son, who—despite living at home, sleeping in the same bedroom he had once shared with Jack—was barely on speaking terms with her. Oftentimes, she had to address him through his closed bedroom door, as though she were living with a moody teenager again. Then, what she got from him were mostly curt answers to her plaintive questions.

But when she arrived at the restaurant, Grace found Ryan in an especially foul mood. The fact that she and Annie had made good on their pledge to devote their time and resources to the investigation had upset him enough, but an incredibly low turnout at the lunch hour had sent Ryan over the edge. Grace wasn't about to raise the point that some days business was better than others, or that the cloudy weather and threat of rain might have kept people away. He was being irrational, and anything she said would be like pouring gasoline on a fire.

Jack was holding the door for his mother and Annie when Ryan emerged from the kitchen. Grace froze when she saw the tense look on his face.

"What's up, Jack?" Ryan said derisively. "Stopped by to see what the end of Dad's business looks like?"

"Hey, Ryan," said Jack with evident discomfort.

Ryan approached, his hands balled into white-knuckled fists. "Mom told me you found out a lot of stuff about Rachel Boyd. Good job helping a lost cause. Guess now I can add you to the list of people responsible for our demise."

"Honey, please don't be like that," Grace urged. "It's going to be all right. You'll see. We'll get the business booming again before you know it. All right? We have to go out for a bit; we'll be back soon."

"Don't rush," Ryan said, gesturing to the empty dining area. "I think I can manage fine on my own."

Jack let go of the door he'd been holding open to approach his brother. His breathing turned shallow, and his eyes blinked rapidly. Grace sensed trouble brewing.

"Why do you have to keep being such an ass?" Jack spat out the words. "What's your damn problem?"

Ryan got right in Jack's face. "You know the problem."

"She's your sister."

"She's nothing to me," said Ryan, eyes narrowing. "She let Dad die." Ryan's fierce gaze intensified. Grace went cold inside.

"It's not her fault. Why do you keep blaming her?"

"Bullshit it's not."

"Boys, please, don't—"

Jack gave his brother a look of disgust. "I don't know who you are anymore," he said. "Something is off with you, and has been. Why'd you really quit school? You wait until senior year to drop out? Come on. What happened that you're not telling us?"

Jack poked Ryan in the shoulder. Sensing an escalation, Grace moved to intervene. Before she could put a stop to it, however, Ryan took hold of Jack's flannel shirt, swiveled at the waist, shifted his weight to the right, and took thin Jack with him. When Ryan let go, Jack went airborne, arms and legs flailing. His long hair, free from its ponytail, rose up behind him like a dark, silky wave. There came a thunderous clatter when he crashed hard into a set of chairs around an empty table, sending them, and him, onto the floor.

With startling agility, Jack scrambled to his feet, fury flaring in his brown eyes. He let out an angry grunt before charging at Ryan, leading with his head like a bull targeting a matador. Ryan easily sidestepped the counterattack before seizing Jack in a brutal headlock that reminded Grace of the boys' scuffles in their younger days. Jack threw a series of haymaker punches that failed to make contact.

"Stop it!" Grace yelled as she threw herself into the middle of the skirmish. Ryan, who used a headlock to latch onto Jack's neck, spun his younger brother in an erratic circle that eventually brought him into contact with his mother. Down went Grace, hard, and she let go a loud whoosh as air exploded from her lungs.

Ryan released his grip on Jack the instant his mother hit the floor. Immediately, his rage turned to shock and shame. Righting himself quickly, Jack scrambled over to Grace and helped her to her feet, giving her a good look at the red mark Ryan's hold had left around his throat.

For a few tense moments, nobody spoke. Grace brushed bits of grime off her pants. She rubbed her hands clean on her blue knit sweater before straightening her hair, then checked in with her body, especially the knees, which thankfully felt fine.

"We are a family," she said, breathing hard, her heart still racing. "Your father would be devastated to see this behavior, and I won't tolerate it."

"I'm sorry, Mom," Ryan said, in a sincere apology.

"Sorry isn't enough," Grace answered him sharply. "From this point on, no more fighting, no more anger, no more talking to me through a closed bedroom door, no more disrespecting this family."

"But the restaurant . . ."

"Oh, enough with the restaurant," Grace snapped. "Your father's gone, so he's not here to tell you what I know he'd say. Family first. Do you hear me?"

Ryan shifted his gaze to his feet, stuffing his hands into the pockets of his pants. Jack hovered nearby, trying to catch his breath.

"Your sister comes before the business," Grace continued. "If we have to close this place down because we're out of money, so be it. I'll turn the key in the front lock one last time and won't regret for a single second my decision to put Penny above the family legacy. Not one single second." Grace paused to try and regain her composure, but it was to no avail. Anger swirled inside her like something molten.

"If you so wish, please help us keep the lights on here, as best you can, but you need a big-time attitude adjustment, and it needs to happen starting right now." She pointed her finger in front of his face, using it to punctuate her decree to Ryan, as if the words were floating before his eyes. "No more outbursts or pissing and moaning about any of this." She gestured to the empty restaurant. "Penny is locked up in a wretched place, and she might end up somewhere even worse, for the rest of her life . . . forever. So spare me your attitude. Honestly, I don't have the time or the patience for it."

Without another word, Grace threw open the front door and stormed out into a humid, gray summer day.

CHAPTER 35

"How you doing, Eve?"

Mitch got a thumbs-up sign from the girl in the doorway, along with confirmation that it wasn't Penny or any of her other alters who'd come to see him. He noted how Eve had a slight hitch to her step as she entered the therapy room, and observed the ring of blue-and-red bruises, mixed together in a watercolor palette, that encircled her neck like a collar.

After getting settled in her seat, Eve craned her head back and kept a lookout until the guard gently closed the door behind him. This was her first time in the therapy room since the attack, and Mitch was on high alert for signs of traumatic stress, extra anxiety, any indications she might be suffering PTSD. It was Ruby and Penny, not Eve, who'd been attacked, yet somehow she knew what had happened to her. Naturally, that got Mitch's curiosity radar pinging. Was her memory retrieval conveniently selective or was it another indication of consciousness leaking?

"I told the CO to remain outside until we're through," he said. "Darla is still in restrictive housing, so I don't want you to be nervous."

Eve giggled and gave an eye roll that reminded Mitch she was only a teenager.

"'Restrictive housing'? Are you buying into Whitmore's soft-tone crap? Next you'll start calling us 'guests.'" She cocked her head to one side, stuck out her tongue, and scrunched up her face as if to say everything here was crazy. Her expression reverted to normal Eve. "Really, Dr. Mitch. Call it what it is, please . . . solitary confinement."

"Right, solitary," said Mitch. "I saw you limp a bit coming in. Are you injured?"

"Every muscle in my body is sore," said Eve, slumping in her chair. "But I'm okay otherwise."

"Have you had any PT?"

Edgewater might have been lacking in many areas, but their medical facilities were top-notch.

"No."

"I'll call Dr. Bouvier after our session, get you an appointment for the whirlpool tub. It'll help your muscles to relax. They have suits you can borrow, so you can enjoy a full soak. You'll feel like a new person."

"All of me?"

She sent Mitch a wink he found endearing. Now it was time to get down to business.

Mitch didn't have the pull to get evidence from the investigative unit that handled crimes in prisons, but Whitmore did, and he was in good standing with her. Which is why, by the time Eve came to see him, Mitch already had the note from Darla's Bible upside down on the table ready to show her.

"I want you to have a look at something for me, Eve," Mitch said, respectfully, gently, "and I'd like your honest reaction to it."

Eve cocked her head slightly sideways.

"Have I been anything but?" She sent him a malevolent smile that paired well with the searing look in her eyes.

"Okay, then." He turned over the note, secured inside a clear plastic evidence bag and tagged with case details encoded for the police to understand. "What do you make of this?"

Eve's eyes scanned the paper through the plastic while Mitch scanned Eve. He was mindful that the note, if it had come from her hand or that of another alter, might trigger a switch. Sitting quiet and still, she read the words on the paper, written in blue crayon, first to herself, then aloud, speaking in an affectless voice as though reciting a passage from some classroom textbook.

"'Darla, sorry to tell but Penny Francone calls herself Eve slept with Charles. I saw pictures. Can't get to show U but they were doing it. You should do something about it.'"

Eve glared at Mitch scornfully.

"How does that note make you feel?"

"Pissed off. Like someone clearly wanted Darla to be," she said curtly. "No wonder she came after me."

"Eve, I want you to check in with yourself now . . . with you, and with your alters."

Eve's lips twisted into something of a smile. "You think I know who wrote this . . . somebody here who might want to see me dead, is that it?"

"Something like that," Mitch said. "Go ahead, close your eyes, and check in with yourself. Ask Ruby, Chloe, Penny, any of them . . . does somebody here at Edgewater wish to do you harm? Don't think, just feel, and respond with whatever your subconscious mind has to say."

Mitch knew that for most people, over 95 percent of all brain activity was beyond conscious awareness. For someone with DID, seeking out a conscious thought, a memory, an idea, was an especially difficult hunt.

She contemplated the question quietly with her eyes shut tight, and eventually returned a solemn shake of her head. There was nothing.

Mitch wasn't quite ready to give up. He considered the possibility that writing the note was a state-dependent memory, encoded into her brain and kept from her consciousness as part of a neural defense mechanism. Mitch's hope was that he might be able to stimulate her mind enough to get an answer.

"Imagine you're in your room. Picture it."

"Room at home, or here in my cell?" said Eve.

"Your quarters here," said Mitch.

"Okay, my cell."

"Put yourself there. Sit at your desk and think to yourself, 'I'm a bad girl.' Say it over and over in your mind . . . 'I'm a bad girl.'"

Eve opened her eyes. "You've got to be kidding me."

"I'm not."

"It's like a rap song. I'm baaaad girl. Wicked baaaaad girl." She said it with a hint of melody while doing a wiggling dance move in her chair.

"Please, Eve," said Mitch, trying to keep his annoyance in check. "This isn't fun and games. I need your cooperation here. It's important."

Eve stuck out her tongue a little ways—a childish gesture, but one meant to convey Mitch had no fun in him. Despite her brief protest, Eve shut her eyes, but raised her head so she would be looking at Mitch if they were open.

"Really?"

"Really."

She went quiet, and Mitch could almost hear her reciting Chloe's words of guilt and remorse.

"Keep saying it in your mind. Now, I'm going to ask you a question and I want your honest answer. Let any alter answer this question, okay?

"Did you write that note and give it to Darla?"

Eve went completely still, seemed to be holding her breath. Looking at her, Mitch couldn't help but wonder which alter, into which memory bank, she may have gone. Eventually, her eyes came open. To his relief, she gave no outward indications of physical destabilization or emotional trauma.

"And?"

Mitch took in a breath and held it. For a moment, Eve said nothing. He studied her face, burning with curiosity. Her hard look softened.

"No," she said with assuredness. "I didn't write that note."

The tone of finality in Eve's voice told Mitch that she didn't harbor any doubt. It was true. She did not write the note to Darla. The implications tore through him.

Someone else wrote it. Someone wanted her dead.

CHAPTER 36

ON THAT BLEAK AFTERNOON, Lucky Dog looked anything but. The dark interior had the ambience of a power outage, with the brightest lights coming from a jukebox tucked away in a corner of the room and the guitar-shaped neon fixture mounted to the wall above it. What the place needed was natural light, but the small, square windows fronting the wood exterior simply weren't cutting it.

Four of the nine stools at the dark varnished wood bar were occupied by beefy men, who put the dive in dive bar. The small round tables scattered about were unoccupied, but Lucky Dog had been open only thirty minutes, so that would probably change. Behind the bar stood stacks of bottles that looked sticky even from a distance. The air reeked of booze and cleaners, overlaid by a whiff of desperation.

The woman working the bar, whom Grace put in her late thirties, radiated attitude. She was quite pretty, with tousled auburn hair held together in a loose bun. She wore a cut-off belly shirt, which prominently displayed a muscular physique that no doubt was a tip-generator. All sorts of piercings adorned her—nose and ears, both done many times over—and a host of tattoos that snaked up her well-defined arms. She was dressed all in black, and if the rock and roll coming out of the jukebox could somehow have become a person, it might very well have taken her form.

When the trio entered, the heads of the men seated at the bar swiveled as one in their direction. Truth be told, the three Francones did look decidedly out of place: Annie might as well have crawled out of a Western film in her denim outfit, cowboy boots, and sparkling belt buckle, this one featuring a bucking bronco. Jack, in his signature flannel, looked like he was hoping—for his band's sake—that Lucky Dog featured live music. As for Grace, her arrival here, based on dress and appearance alone, would be explainable only if she'd come to ask for directions to somewhere else.

Grace led the way to the side of the bar closest to the exit, thinking a quick departure might become a necessity. She waved to get the attention of the bartender, who turned and eyed Jack suspiciously.

"Is he old enough?" the bartender asked in a raspy voice that carried a whisper of annoyance.

"We're not here to drink," Grace answered.

The bartender screwed up her face. Maybe she was thinking this was the oddest group of robbers she'd ever encountered.

"Booze is pretty much all we have to offer," said one of the men at the bar, an older fellow with a grizzled face and wisps of silver hair sneaking out from beneath his tweed scally cap. His Boston accent came on thick, so "offer" sounded like "offah."

"We tried karaoke, but that was a bust," another man said, and all chuckled.

Grace pasted on a smile. "I'm here to ask about Rachel Boyd," she said, and the laughing died quickly. The men took on serious expressions, and the bartender kept her distance.

"And who are you?" Scally Cap asked, a warning clear in his voice.

"I'm Grace Francone. I'm . . . Penny Francone's mother."

The four men on their four stools sent Grace looks as hard as granite. Jack, in a burst of overexuberance, blurted out, "It wasn't in the papers, but I found out Rachel Boyd worked here. We're hoping to talk to her friends, family, people who knew her."

Scally Cap pushed his stool back with an audible scrape. When he stood, he gave Grace a look at an ample belly under a black T-shirt with an eagle on it, both of which were only partially obscured by a faded denim jacket. He strode over to their side of the bar.

"And why would you want to do that?" Scally Cap asked. His eyes turned to two slits beneath his bushy white eyebrows. He got close enough for Grace to see the stubble dotting his round, ruddy face, to smell the beer soaking his breath.

Jack held his ground, but to his credit, he refrained from making any threatening gestures. "It's possible my sister didn't kill anybody."

Scally Cap shifted his weight to his heels, assessing Jack anew as if he didn't know what to make of him. "Who the hell are you?" he asked. His voice wasn't quite angry, but it wasn't pleased-to-meet-you either.

"I'm Jack Francone. I'm Penny's brother. And you're Russell Harrison," Jack said quickly. "You own the place. I Googled you. Saw your picture. These guys . . ." He pointed to the other men. "I don't know."

"And why you looking me up, son?" Russell said, this time more threateningly, which inspired the beefiest of his three companions to stand.

"It's my daughter, Penny," Grace interjected quickly, fearing Jack would reveal too much about his doxing expedition. "We've uncovered new information about the murder . . . and as Jack was saying, we think there's a possibility that Penny may be innocent. We're hoping to talk to Rachel's friends, people who knew her, might uncover information for the police that might help them catch the real killer."

A twisted grin curled Russell's top lip, giving Grace a flash of his yellowed upper teeth.

"That crazy girl . . . your daughter . . ." He said it languidly. "She killed my dear, dear friend." Russell's whole demeanor turned two shades darker. "I've known Rachel my whole life. She grew up here;

neighborhood girl. Her father was a union carpenter, damn fine one.
Helped build this bar. She had a job here anytime she wanted it. I
thought of her as a daughter.

"Now, I don't know how you went digging up your information on
Rachel and me, and I'm not going to grace you with any answers to
whatever questions you have. I won't be of any help to you at all. So I
strongly suggest the three of you turn yourselves around," he twirled
his index finger to mimic the gesture he wanted, "and mosey on out of
here. Capeesh?"

He pointed to the door.

"Sir—" Annie began, but Grace gripped her arm—hard.

"Okay, Russell," said Grace as she pulled Annie toward the door,
with Jack following. "We won't trouble you anymore. And I'm sorry
for your loss."

Outside in the gray gloom, which perfectly echoed Grace's mood,
the trio headed for Annie's SUV parked at the end of the block. Grace
was about to open the passenger-side door, when she heard a voice call
out: "Hold up a sec, will ya?"

Turning, Grace laid eyes on the striking bartender, who appeared to
have emerged from the alleyway between Lucky Dog and the adjacent
convenience store. "I was hoping to catch you," she said in a resonate
voice layered with a local accent. "Told Russell I had to do inventory
and snuck out the back." Only now did Grace realize she was breathing
hard and might have sprinted to catch up with them. "Russell is actually a really good guy," she said. "A real teddy bear type, but he can be
a prick sometimes, too."

"His anger is understandable," said Grace. "We're all devastated.
What's your name?"

"Morgan. Name's Morgan." She put out her hand and Grace shook
hello. Annie and Jack did the same. "I . . . um, wanted to catch up
with you." She glanced back to see if Russell or someone was coming
before returning her attention to Grace. "The reason is . . . my sister, Jacqueline . . . Jackie . . . she's got problems, mental problems."

Morgan pointed to her head as if Grace wouldn't know where those problems would originate. "Schizophrenia," she clarified.

"Oh," said Grace, unsure how to respond.

"She's doing okay, I mean . . ." Morgan shrugged her shoulders. "She's not great, but you know, she's got a life. Look, I know about your daughter because of Rachel and all, but . . . but mental illness scares people because they don't really know about it, it's different—the head stuff, ya know?"

Grace nodded. She understood better than most.

"But really, people like Jackie are going to hurt themselves before they'd hurt someone else. I've looked up the statistics. It's just . . . they get judged a lot. I know it looks real bad for your kid, but if you think she didn't do it, I mean, the least we can do is try to answer your questions."

Annie, always one to take charge, asked the first question. "Anything you can tell us about Rachel . . . did you know her well?"

Morgan offered a shrug of her shoulders—how to begin? "I knew her from the bar . . . like, we were friends, but we weren't super close. She's older."

"But you knew her back in the day and she was a bartender at Lucky Dog when she abandoned Penny?"

Morgan nodded. "Yeah, I knew her from the party scene. She'd hang out with my crew now and again, even though we were younger, but she hung out with lots of people from town, especially if they had good stuff. That's why when her kid showed up on the news, everyone knew it was Rachel Boyd's daughter. I don't know who told the police. A bunch of people, probably."

"What about the birth father? Anybody know him?"

Grace noted the way Jack had worded his question—birth father, not father. Arthur was Penny's dad.

"No clue," said Morgan. "I'm not sure Rachel even knew. She was clean when we were working together, or at least that's what she told me. But back then she said she was pretty wild, so I guess it could have been any number of guys. She never gave a name, and nobody really asked."

"Is there anybody who'd want to hurt her? Did Rachel have any enemies?" Annie wanted to know.

Morgan thought a moment. "I mean Vince Rapino, he was her high school sweetheart," she said.

"Vince and Rachel dated before?"

"Oh yeah, their fling was a boomerang thing. What goes around, comes around."

"They broke up?" Grace asked.

"I think it was on again, off again, even after graduation, but they went their own ways eventually. After everything went down with Isabella . . . sorry, Penny, right? That's her name now. I knew her as Isabella. Anyway, after all that, Rachel moved to Rhode Island for a bunch of years, get away from all the reminders. She came back not that long ago, a year or so before . . . you know." She looked away, because everyone knew. "I guess she and Vince started seeing each other again, even though he was married with kids. Maybe things got ugly between them. Vince came into the bar a lot. Not the nicest guy."

"The apartment where she was murdered was rented in his name," Jack revealed.

Morgan seemed visibly disgusted. "He put her up, huh? Yeah, that would piss me off extra if I was his wife," she said. "But I'm not surprised. Rachel was always short on cash. She was talking though about how she could get flush fast, use the money to invest in something that would make her rich. I got the sense she had something on someone, too, that's where this investment money was going to come from—a blackmail kind of thing—but she didn't share any details with me.

"Anyway, if you can figure out that blackmail piece, it's a possible motive for murder. Or maybe someone should be looking into Vince's wife. Woman scorned, know what I mean? Those two are separated, headed for divorce, and Nicole—I think that's her name—blamed

Rachel for everything. Nicole would stop by the bar from time to time when Vince was here, make a big scene."

Morgan gave an anxious glance behind her, telling Grace their time together was coming to an end. But there was still something else she needed to know.

"When Rachel moved back to Lynn, did she ever talk about Penny? What made her reach out to Penny after so many years?"

"I mean, I'd hear her mention it a bit, just on her birthday and stuff, maybe Mother's Day, that kind of thing," Morgan said. "But really, it was in the past. She just hoped she was happy, wherever she was."

"Did you ever see Rachel get violent or angry with Penny—Isabella back then?"

Morgan gave a vigorous shake of her head. "No, never. I mean, look, she wasn't the best mother. Wasn't doting or anything. She was kind of into drugs, partying back then, a lot more than parenting, that's for sure, but I didn't see her ever lay a hand on her kid. Not once."

"Any idea why Rachel would have abandoned Penny, why she left her in the park that day?"

Morgan gave a shrug. "It wasn't a shock to us when it happened. I mean nobody questioned it back then. Rachel was kind of a mess, and caring for a kid . . . it's not that easy. I should know. I've got three. She probably just snapped. But she loved her daughter . . . your daughter . . . I know that much. Like I said, she prayed for her, just like she did her other kid."

Grace's breath caught. "What other kid?" she asked. She shifted her attention to Jack, who seemed unsure.

"I didn't find anything about her having other children," Jack said.

"Penny . . . she was a twin," Morgan revealed. "But her sister died at birth."

Reflexively, Grace touched her hand to her heart. "Oh . . . I didn't know," she said.

"There's a little grave for her at the Pine Grove Cemetery," Morgan said with a touch of melancholy. "Rachel had her faults for sure, but she was a good person, had a proper funeral for her baby and all." Morgan sighed aloud while stuffing her hands into the pockets of her black jeans to warm them. "Look, I've got to get back," she said. "You know how to reach me if you have other questions. I'm happy to help."

Morgan was walking away when Grace called out to her. She turned.

"What was her name?" Grace asked. "The baby who died?"

"Chloe," said Morgan. "Her name was Chloe."

And with that, she disappeared back into the alley.

CHAPTER 37

As ONE OF THE few doctors at Edgewater, Mitch didn't have a moment to meet with Whitmore until that afternoon. He hoped her schedule would be free. After Darla's attack, he knew that Penny needed much tighter security around her—and that CO Blackwood, for obvious reasons, could not be among those providing protection.

A check of Penny's record at Edgewater revealed for Mitch her six stints in solitary for a few scuffles, some more violent than others. Most of her adversaries from those fights continued to reside here, but Mitch's top candidate for sending that note to Darla remained the guard who had almost smashed in Penny's head with his baton. He also recalled that Blackwood was one of the men who led Darla away after her tense standoff in the hallway with Grace.

In Mitch's mind, it was not out of the question that Blackwood knew Darla's triggers and had used them to cause Penny harm. The crayon and odd phrasing of the note made it look like it had been written by a patient, not a guard. The fact that Penny (or rather, Chloe) had used crayons to make a drawing was most likely what Navarro had said: a coincidence.

Mitch had finally sat down in his office and was getting ready to draft an e-mail to Whitmore when his cell phone rang. To his surprise,

Dr. Dan Bouvier, who headed up the emergency room department at Edgewater, was on the other end of that call.

"It's um . . . Penny Francone," Dr. Bouvier said.

Hairs on the back of Mitch's neck rose as he gripped his desk, bracing for bad news.

"What about her?" Mitch asked. "Is she all right?"

"I think so . . . it's a bit out of my depth."

Relief washed over Mitch like a wave.

"She's in the PT room," Dr. Bouvier went on, "taking that soak you'd arranged, and well . . . she started speaking in a British accent, and she's been asking for you nonstop. Look, it's packed in here right now and I can't spare a body to look after her. Can you go straight to PT and check her out?"

Mitch was already on his feet. "I'll be right there," he said.

* * *

When Mitch arrived at the ER, he found it, as Dr. Bouvier said, bustling with frenetic energy bordering on mayhem. Doctors and nurses, outnumbered by patients, scuttled from one curtained bay to the other like a team of first responders triaging an accident. Powerful overhead lights vanquished all shadows, putting additional strain on Mitch's already fatigued eyes. From one of the bays, he heard a howl worthy of a wolf, and a nurse informed him that Dr. Bouvier was in there.

Mitch thought: *Nobody here has an easy time of it.*

The PT room, located off the ER, did not take up much real estate, but it did feature modern equipment including exercise machines, weights, bosu balls, and other apparatuses for improving balance, stability, and mobility. Physical therapy facilities in hospitals, including those in a prison setting, helped improve balance and mobility so that when patients got out they were less likely to slip, fall, and go right back in.

Most importantly, there was the tub: about four-and-a-half feet long and two feet high, made of polished stainless steel, occupying a good portion of the emerald green floor.

The portable motor powering the whirlpool feature was shut off. Penny, without the fiery look or angry eyes of Eve, sat upright in the tub, dressed in a blue one-piece suit that was stamped PROPERTY OF EDGEWATER. Mitch dismissed a female guard who was keeping an eye on things while Penny enjoyed her soak.

"Dr. Mitch."

The British accent was back, and so was Ruby.

"Glad you're here. Would've tried to come find you myself," Ruby said, "but this bath was too delightful, and Dr. Bouvier was nice enough to ring you for me."

"Hello, Ruby," Mitch said, wheeling over a metal stool. "How are you doing?"

"A bit confused, to be honest," said Ruby. "One minute we're talking VSCO girls and whatnot, and then this crazed woman comes bursting into the room, no idea what she's going on about, and the next thing I know, I'm here, enjoying a soak."

Ruby turned the faucet on, letting some hot water flow into the tub. The splashing of the falling water echoed in the quiet room.

"Hold on a second," she said. "Got a little chill."

She dunked her body, head included. Holding her breath, she stayed submerged for some time, her hair fluttering underwater like the tendrils of some great anemone. She surfaced, eyes still closed, and kept them that way.

"Can you hand me a towel," she said to Mitch, who got one from a nearby rack. She dabbed at her eyes before opening them.

"So, Doc Mitch," Ruby said cheerily. "Might you tell me what the *hell* is going on here?"

Mitch speculated that Ruby had fled Penny's consciousness soon after the attack, making it a case of lost time for her. For reasons perplexing to Mitch, she'd reappeared, no explanation given, in this tub. Her tone suggested she wasn't severely disoriented, shocked, or even upset by this turn of events, though Mitch suspected that was probably a mask for her true feelings. Elsewhere in Penny's subconscious lurked fear and confusion, but letting Ruby and her world-be-dammed attitude come through was a bit like taking Tylenol for a fever—she was the perfect alter to suppress those troubling symptoms.

Mitch wondered if he simply could restart his efforts with Ruby.

"We were talking about your birth mother, Rachel Boyd," he said. "Do you remember that?"

Ruby's eyes squinted, probing her mind for that specific memory. She had a habit of twirling her hair, and spun a long, wet strand around her finger.

"Yeah, I remember," she said, and Mitch sensed there was more behind it. Deeper memories, more painful ones, seemed suddenly within reach. He thought of getting his phone and setting it to record, fearing he might miss a chance to document something very un-Ruby-like—malevolence, evil, a psychotic break of some sort—but decided against it. A recording might make her think, and what he wanted from Ruby was to feel.

"What's the last thing you remember, Ruby, the very last memory you have, before you and I were in that room discussing your plans to become a VSCO girl? Can you access that for me?"

Her face was a study of concentration, but there was sadness too, and it was impossible for Mitch not to feel her pain and frustration. She closed her eyes, gave a sigh, and stretched out her legs a bit longer in the steel tub.

"I don't know," she said with defeat in her voice. "It's like a blank canvas . . . it's like I wasn't anywhere . . . like I didn't exist. Is this amnesia? Do I have it? Is that why I'm in a hospital?"

"Yes," Mitch said. "It's something like that."

"Then I can't be of much help, I guess." Ruby looked uncharacteristically irritated. "Was it a car accident? Did I bang my head? Oh, help me, was somebody hurt?" She gasped as if a memory had come to her. "Oh no . . . did somebody *die*?" She whispered, clearly hoping that it wasn't true, "Did I kill someone?"

"Close your eyes," Mitch encouraged. "Think about a car. Burgundy color, a Chevy Caprice. Do you know a car like that?"

Ruby's eyes shuttered and she thought.

"That's my dad's car," she said.

"Do you remember taking it without permission?"

"No." She said it with confidence.

Mitch didn't want to lead her, but Penny and Chloe had each referenced a book they were looking at that night, so perhaps mention of it might trigger a memory for Ruby as well. "Try this. Think long and hard about a book you may have been reading. The *last* book you remember reading."

Ruby did as she was instructed.

"A book," she said, making a delighted *hmmmm* sound as she gave her body a relaxed stretch. "Oh, yeah . . . that's clear. I got it. It's a book with water on the cover . . . boats . . . and water . . . but . . . I can't think of the title."

"Where were you when you were reading it?" Mitch asked.

Ruby shut her eyes tighter, a clear indication she was deep in thought, straining to recall.

"I'm . . . I'm not alone."

The accent. Gone. Ruby gone. The voice that spoke was quiet and sleepy . . . dreamlike and tiny.

"It's not good. Very bad."

Mitch could feel his heart rev up. "What's very bad?" he asked. "Can you tell me?"

"She'll go to prison for what she did."

"Who will? Who'll go to prison?"

"A woman . . . no, Mommy . . . Mommy will go to prison if she doesn't stop. She'll go to prison."

Mommy . . . a young girl's word.

"Is Mommy's name Rachel?" Mitch whispered, afraid anything louder might break this spell.

She nodded—whoever this was, Ruby, Penny, someone nodded— her eyes still closed.

"Yes . . . Rachel is my mommy . . . and my mommy is going to prison for a long, long time if she doesn't do as she's told."

"Do what?"

"I heard them yelling . . . so mad at each other."

"Who's angry at her?"

Mitch was thinking of Grace and her conviction that someone else was involved in Rachel's murder. He thought of the boyfriend, Vincent Rapino, who certainly had a past that included prison. Before he could press this young girl for additional information, she spoke in that quiet, trancelike voice.

"Topeka . . . West Virginia . . . Pasadena . . . Tucson . . ."

She then repeated the names of places she said before.

"Michigan . . . Florida . . . Key West . . ."

And with each name she hit the side of the tub with her hand, like the tapping he'd heard in the 911 call.

Tap. Tap. Tap.

Mitch got out his phone and quickly typed in the new locations she'd listed off, as well as the ones from before.

What do they have in common? he wondered. *What's the link?*

He remembered other names she'd recited.

Alabama . . . Alaska . . . Chicago . . .

Were these places she'd visited? Places Rachel wanted to go?

Before Mitch could ask her any more questions, another howl came down the hall, more animal than human. Whatever was happening to the poor patient Dr. Bouvier had been treating in the ER didn't sound good. The girl in the tub looked as though she'd been roused cruelly from a deep sleep. She stared at Mitch, eyes unblinking like a pair of headlights. He saw her body tense up and then relax. For a moment, she looked as if she were seeing right through him to the wall behind. A shift was taking place, he could see it, could feel a change of energy in the room. A moment later, the harsh look was back, and he knew.

She cocked her head at Mitch and said in a chiding way, "Watching me take a bath, Doctor? Think there may be a few lines being crossed, don't you?" She sent Mitch a wink to go with her haughty smile.

"Hello, Eve," Mitch said, feeling flustered at having lost the opportunity to speak to Ruby for longer. He didn't show his disappointment though. She wasn't the only one who had masks for her feelings. "Long time no see."

CHAPTER 38

OF ALL OF YOUR alters, I have to say Ruby is my favorite. It feels a bit like a betrayal of sorts, like I'd rather she was my sister than you, Penny, but I guess in a way she *is* my sister. I mean the diagnosis of DID might be controversial, but the symptoms sure are real, so I suppose that makes Ruby real, too. Here's a question though, one I still can't answer. Is Ruby like a metaphor for some emotional state, or is she truly an autonomous person capable of her own willful action? Capable even of murder?

Film directors use metaphor in their work all the time. *I, Robot* (a solid action flick, I'd say, starring Will Smith, a solid action actor) is a metaphor for how the technology we depend upon might one day be used to annihilate us. Another, *Groundhog Day,* the Bill Murray film about a self-centered TV reporter who lives the same day over and over again until he becomes a charitable person, is actually a metaphor for Buddhist enlightenment. Professor Warren Brown graciously pointed that out to me in one of his lectures. I'm guessing Ruby is a metaphor for living the unburdened life, but is she also a life force unto herself?

She'd always appear at times when you needed a confidence boost to come out of your shell and have a bit of fun that didn't require Eve's dark energy for protection. Anything slightly unsettling could summon Ruby, like the time you worked up the nerve to ride your first loop roller coaster.

"That was absolute genius!" you exclaimed, your face aglow when we disembarked the Flashback ride at Six Flags. It took a lot of encouraging on my part to get you on that roller coaster, and nobody expected it would be Ruby who got off. But sometime between the steep ascent and the stomach-churning final loop, Ruby appeared. I remember bursting out laughing when I heard you talk.

"What's your problem?" you asked in your Ruby voice, and sent me a nasty look before socking me in the shoulder.

"Nothing," I said, still chuckling. "You're the best, Ruby. That's all."

"Well, you're not so shabby yourself, I suppose," you offered in return. "But let's not ruin a brilliant ride by getting all mushy, shall we?"

Brilliant.

That's you, Ruby, absolutely, utterly brilliant.

I hope some of Ruby, most of her actually, can stick around if you ever become integrated into one personality. She's a blast, that one.

She also knows something about the night of the murder, doesn't she? Something she's not telling us.

But what do *we* know?

There's the million-dollar question, and unfortunately, the answer is: not much. We know the name Chloe came from your life before us. Chloe was your twin sister who tragically died at birth, and that's certainly going to get featured in my film. Though I have to be careful not to turn it into a soap opera or a made-for-TV movie. Cue the *da da dun* dramatic music!

I don't know if Chloe is some kind of subconscious channeling, a weird little psychic link, or if you simply needed a name to use and you remembered Rachel talking about your dead sister. After all this time and effort to sort things out, I feel no closer to any answers about you, or that night.

Why would Rachel go to prison?

That's what you told Dr. Mitch in the bathtub at Edgewater, and that's what Mom relayed back to me.

I don't see how this new information fits in with all the other strange things you've said, or how any of it helps Dr. Mitch prove in court that you were in a psychotic state at the time of the killing. But it may mean something? There has to be some kind of connection.

Then there are those places you keep going on about, places I know you've never visited with us:

Alabama . . . Alaska . . . Pasadena . . . Tucson . . .

We vacationed at the water park on the Cape, never in Arizona. Did Rachel bring you to those places? I know your birth mom was into drugs, that she'd been arrested on a distribution charge, so is that what this is all about, Penny? Drugs? Are these places she took you to pick up narcotics? Was that the reason she got in touch with you, to use you as a drug mule? Did you go to her house that night expecting one thing and end up getting something else entirely?

I have to be honest, these questions are keeping me up at night and away from my schoolwork, which is something I promised Mom wouldn't happen. But I'm obsessed now. We all are, to a certain extent.

Maybe Mom's greatest wish will come true and somehow we'll find out we were wrong and you're not a killer. I don't see how that's possible, but after all this searching I feel no closer to an answer, though I do have a new question. Surprise, surprise, it's about Ryan.

We got into a fight about you, and that fight was my fault. I was needling him intentionally, wanting to see if he'd snap. And oh boy, did he snap, all right. There's got to be a reason he dropped out of school so soon after your arrest. Is there a connection?

I get that Eve protects you, Penny, but my question is this: Are you protecting Ryan?

CHAPTER 39

WITH THE TRIAL LOOMING, Sunday workdays were commonplace, and Greg Navarro gave no objection to coming to Annie's house in Swampscott on what was typically a day of rest so that she and Grace could show him the war room they'd constructed. It had been Grace's idea to convert an available study into a headquarters of sorts. One wall in the room contained note cards, string, newspaper clippings, and various timelines that allowed them to better visualize information they'd gathered about Penny's case. Ideally Grace would have preferred to set up the war room at her house, but since Ryan had cooled off after his altercation with his brother, she didn't want to stoke those fires again.

If it weren't for Mitch, Grace knew they would be heading to trial with the slimmest hope of keeping Penny out of prison. The hope meter hadn't shifted much in a positive direction, though, as Mitch hadn't unleashed some psychotic state that would prove Penny belonged in Edgewater. What he'd done mostly was get them more questions than answers.

Now, thanks to the war room, Grace had a place to keep all those questions and possible answers organized. Her secret wish was to find some evidence, a new connection or possibility, that would convince Greg Navarro to enter a plea of not guilty.

I didn't do anything wrong.

Grace couldn't let go of the idea that Penny's only crime may have been picking up the knife that had been used in the murder. Were it not so symbolic of their inadequacies as detectives, she would have purchased a copy of *Private Investigations for Dummies* at the local Barnes & Noble. Perhaps Attorney Navarro, with his background and experience, would be able to make something of their theories or come up with new ones.

He arrived with a coffee cake from Newman's Bakery, for which Annie could not have been more grateful. Grace noticed some crumbs on his blue oxford shirt, suggesting he may have already sampled some of the bakery's other offerings. Annie went to the kitchen to cut the cake while Navarro studied the index cards pinned to a board.

All of the cards were connected with pieces of string to denote correlations between different possibilities. In particular, the card on the wall with Vincent Rapino's name on it had a line of yellow string connecting him to Rachel Boyd's card.

"We've done the timeline," Grace said to Navarro. "And Vince Rapino is the only one linked to Rachel Boyd both *before* Penny was born and *after* the murder."

A beam of sunshine streaming in through a window across the study lit up Vince's card, as if to spotlight that theory. Annie returned with three pieces of cake, but Navarro, who had his hands on his hips, studying the board, was too busy thinking to eat.

"This is Vince's wife, or ex-wife," Grace said. She traced her finger along the yellow piece of string connecting Vince's card to one with *Nicole* written on it. "We don't have much on her, though, and certainly nothing to call her a suspect just yet."

"And we've got Maria," said Annie, who had joined Grace and Navarro at the board. Navarro took his time to assess everything the way an interested museum patron might read the placards of an exhibit display.

"What do you think of Maria?" Navarro asked. He pointed to three strips of paper below Maria's card, on which Grace had handwritten important details. Clues, Annie called them.

1. *Burned it all up. (Chloe)*
2. *Arrested for attempted second degree murder.*
3. *Weak alibi for night of murder.*

"I think she's sketchy as all get-out," said Grace. "But we don't have more than our suspicions."

"Are Penny and Maria still in contact?"

"They write each other letters," Grace said, answering Navarro's question with a dismayed headshake. "It's inappropriate, I know, but I can't stop it. Those two have shared a special bond—a twisted one, I'll give you that—since they met, which is why I think Maria is somehow involved in all this."

Navarro noted the card with CO Blackwood's name on it. "Any updates on him?"

"Denies it, but what would you expect?"

"Yeah, I'd expect that," said Navarro. "And these?"

He pointed to the card listing all of the locations Penny had rattled off when she went into her trancelike state.

"We don't know," Annie said. "She's never been to any of those places. And we don't know what the name of the book she keeps talking about is either."

Annie directed Navarro's attention to several color printouts of books she had sourced online, all of which featured water and boats on the covers.

"The book means something to her," said Grace.

"So do these," said Navarro, looking at the list of phrases Penny had spoken either as herself or as an alter, which Grace had written out in black marker.

I wasn't alone.

Gone and gone for good.

I'll get the bucket.

"When did she say this?" Navarro was looking at the card that read: *Mommy is going to prison for a long, long time if she doesn't do as she's told.*

"There was a second switch to Ruby," Grace explained. "She was taking a whirlpool tub in the PT room to alleviate muscle soreness after Darla's attack. We don't know why, but Ruby came out, and that's what she said."

"We think this all points back to Vincent Rapino. He's been arrested before—criminal, prison," Annie said.

For Navarro's benefit, Grace reviewed the tidbit of information that Morgan, the edgy bartender, had given them outside Lucky Dog. Grace connected the dots for him.

"So, if Vince and Rachel were together years back, before Penny was born, then it stands to reason that Vince Rapino could be—"

"Penny's birth father," Navarro said in a quiet exhale, finishing her thought. "But why come to Big Frank's and antagonize you the way he did? If he's somehow involved in the murder, why do that?"

Navarro knew all about that unsettling incident, along with Grace's desire that no action be taken, including filing a restraining order.

"He's not stable," Grace said. "I smelled booze on his breath that night, too. Vince is an idiot. Who knows what he was thinking?"

"He wanted to mess with us," Annie suggested. "Grace said it's like arsonists going back to a fire. They get a thrill out of it."

"So what are you two thinking?"

"Paternity test," Grace said. "We want Vince's DNA."

"His DNA?" Navarro looked like he'd been blindsided.

"That's right," said Annie. "If there's a match, I think it would be enough to get Detective Allio from Lynn to give Rapino a much closer look. There'd be a clear connection between the victim, the accused, and the boyfriend. Vince is hiding something, we're sure of it."

"And you want the police to go on a fishing expedition, see what they catch, is that it?"

"Cast as wide a net as possible," said Grace.

"Not a bad idea, not bad at all," Navarro concurred. "Who knows what you might snag that way."

"Can you force him to give it to us?" asked Annie. "He's been arrested. Isn't his DNA on record somewhere?"

"Sure," said Navarro. "It's possible, but it doesn't mean it's accessible to us."

Grace's eyes went to the floor.

"Getting Vince's DNA from police evidence to use for paternity testing would require an emergency motion from family court," Navarro explained. "Just because they dated in high school won't be enough to convince a judge to issue an order."

"Do you have a judge who owes you a favor?" Grace had hope in her voice.

"I'm afraid it doesn't work that way," Navarro said. "It'll take all kinds of time and effort to chase after this—time I don't have to give, and there's no guarantee I'll be successful, either. My focus has to be on the trial. We're so close. Maybe after, Grace, but not before."

"It'll be too late after," Grace lamented.

"If she's found guilty we've still got our appeal," Navarro reminded her. "I get it, I do. It's a good idea, but it's wasted effort, and it will be counterproductive at a critical juncture."

"Well, what do you suggest?" asked Grace.

Now Navarro took the coffee cake. He sat at a small foldout table in the study and ate in silence. He appeared to be mulling something over.

"I know Rapino from outside this case . . . from here, the North Shore, from his rep. Bad hombre." He took a bite and seemed to be chewing harder on some thought. "I can't reveal where I got this information from, Grace. It could get me in a lot of trouble. But I know there's a criminal probe going on about Vince Rapino right now, about his auto body shop, a counterfeit auto parts scam that he's running. A client of mine is caught up in it, and he's contemplating copping a plea. Honestly, I don't want to suggest it."

"Suggest what?" Annie asked. All three were now sitting and having cake.

"Start with the police," Navarro said. "Go to Detective Jay Allio with what you have. Ask him to look into Maria again, and make the DNA ask on Vince. I don't think it'll fly, but it's better than my plan."

"And what's your plan."

A weighty look came to Navarro's eyes and face. "Go get his DNA yourself," he said. "His shop is local. I can't really advise you here, you understand, right? What I'm saying . . . it's all off the record."

"I understand. But how do we get his DNA?" asked Grace. "We can't just waltz in there and ask him for it."

"No, but you may be able to snag something, an object, something he touched."

"Okay," Grace said, mulling over his suggestion, not liking it one bit.

"I get it," Navarro said. "Mitch has done great work, but I don't think it's enough. The hit list, those murder fantasies she and Maria wrote— those are what's really in our way. They speak to premeditation, and we've no proof that Penny suffered a psychotic episode. We are fifty-fifty here, and that's being generous. You could be right. Maybe something with Rapino tips those scales in our favor."

"I'm thinking hell yes," said Annie with her gung-ho spirit. "We got something on him. Forget asking, we could pressure him hard."

"Caution here, ladies," Navarro said, taking in a forkful of cake. "Guys like Rapino are tough to bend, but they're even tougher when they break."

CHAPTER 40

Wʜᴇɴ ᴛʜᴇ ʙᴜɪʟᴅɪɴɢ ᴄᴀᴍᴇ into view, Grace saw that two of the auto shop's garage bay doors were open. Large yellow lettering mounted to a piece of metal siding above those bays read: *Vince's Auto Service*. She pulled her Mini Cooper to the curb. From this vantage point she and Annie could see the garage, while keeping mostly out of sight.

This part of Lynn was not the nicest. Across from a row of crumbling brick buildings marked with graffiti, a dilapidated chain-link fence spread out along the road, crushing an overgrowth of weeds and scattered saplings.

Not thirty minutes ago, Annie and Grace had wrapped up a scheduled meeting at the Lynn Police Station with Detective Jay Allio that had not gone particularly well. It had been over a year since Grace had seen Allio, but he still had the signature paunch and thin mustache she remembered vividly.

Detective Allio was familiar with Penny's diagnosis, her DID, all the basics, but Grace still had to catch him up on what had transpired since they last spoke. Then, she tried out her theory about Vincent Rapino, thinking maybe he'd consider a warrant to get a DNA sample. Soon enough, Navarro's discouraging words regarding police cooperation were confirmed.

"It's an interesting theory, I admit, and I really appreciate your efforts, but you're not giving me enough to work with here. I have to give you a firm no."

Now, it was up to them.

Vince might not have been a stickler for the law, but judging by the number of cars parked in his lot, he was a half-decent mechanic. It was a jumble of old sedans, SUVs, and trucks, but other than a Lexus needing extensive front-end repair, there were few cars on the higher end. Grace wondered how many of the waiting vehicles would be outfitted with counterfeit auto parts.

From inside the garage bays, Grace heard the clank of ratchets and wrenches, along with the hiss of hydraulics. Loud classic rock thrummed through tinny speakers, mixing with occasional spurts of laughter from the men at work. The bright sky blazed cobalt blue, but Grace took no comfort from the glorious day. Her thoughts were jangling like alarms going off in her head. She'd never done a stakeout before.

As a pair, they appeared as utterly out of place here as they had at Lucky Dog—Grace in a light green top with dark slacks; Annie in her usual denim outfit with a flashy rhinestone belt buckle. They couldn't have intimidated a mall cop, but here they were, steps away from Vince's place, and from the owner, a known criminal who could very well be a killer.

As if confirming Grace's fears, two men emerged through one of the open bay doors. She immediately recognized one of the rough-looking fellows as part of the duo who had accompanied Vince into Big Frank's the night he dumped Coca-Cola on the floor. They were dressed in heavy-duty work pants stained like a Jackson Pollock painting. Each had on a brown work shirt with patches saying *Vince's Auto Service* stitched to the left breast pocket. Both were smoking cigarettes.

Moments later, Rapino appeared, and bummed a smoke from one of the men. Vince took a few drags off his cigarette before dropping it on the cement floor just inside the garage. He put it out with the sole of his boot.

"That's our DNA," Annie said, getting out of the car. Grace followed, and seized Annie's arm, pulling her to an abrupt stop.

"You don't have to do this," she said in a whisper—as if the two men still outside could hear them over the racket. "You can wait in the car."

Annie shook her head. "We've come this far," she said.

From her pants pocket, Annie produced a plastic bag to collect the evidence. The bag also contained cotton swabs they'd use if they had to go with a more direct approach.

"Okay," said Grace, like it was a relief.

"I can't believe you talked me out of bringing a gun," Annie grumbled.

"I told you, having a weapon might give us a false sense of security," Grace said as the pair passed the two men continuing their smoke break outside. Annie leered at the one Grace hadn't seen before, who had light eyes the color of a husky's.

"I wouldn't mind a bit of that false security right about now," whispered Annie.

Grace hadn't expected a big scene when she stepped into the garage, but everything came to a screeching halt like a needle pulled across a record.

Vince extracted himself from under the hood of a nearby car to send Grace an assessing stare. He approached. There was no way she could bend down and pick up the cigarette butt without him noticing—and asking questions. He didn't seem to recognize her, and Grace got the sense this man hid his smiles like he did his past. Same as that day in Big Frank's, Rapino gave off an uneasy vibe, the way an unlit firecracker never feels perfectly safe to handle. Grace had to wonder how he had any customers at all.

As he neared, Grace got a good look at his thick black eyebrows and close-cropped dark hair. She didn't see any signs of Penny in him, but Grace looked like her mother, nothing like her father, so she made little of it. Still, there was nothing sweet and gentle about him. Grace supposed some men came out of the womb with a chip on their shoulder and fists to fight for survival. Vince was definitely that kind of man.

"Help you?" he said, still no smile. He came to a stop, his work boot directly over the discarded cigarette they'd hoped to retrieve. His work shirt was unbuttoned, revealing the stained white tank top he wore underneath.

Grace jacked up her resolve like she was the car on that lift. "Hello, Vince," she said.

Vince put his hands on his hips, and cocked his head to appraise her. Eventually something of a smile came to his face, but it wasn't warm or welcoming, not in the slightest.

"Well, look at that, wontcha?" he said, eyeing Grace up and down. He had an accent born of the street, hard-edged as his demeanor. "Grace Francone. Whatcha you doing here, Gracie? Car broke down?"

The smokers returned from outside to flank Vince like a pair of sentries.

At that moment plan A (sneak a sample of his DNA) and B (ask for it directly) seemed to Grace like incredibly stupid ideas, but then she thought of Penny. Desperation trumped her better judgment, and she pressed ahead. "I'm sorry to intrude like this, but there's been a development in the case, Vince," Grace said, biting back her fear.

As Vince stepped forward, a flash of his silver necklace caught in the overhead light. "I've kind of lost track of time," he said. "Isn't the trial two weeks away? Or is it three? I've got that date circled on my calendar in the office." He took another step toward Grace. His eyes were the deep shade of brown that almost looked black. "You must be getting nervous, real nervous, to come here."

"The trial is coming up soon, yes," said Grace. "And yes, I'm very nervous. May we speak in private?"

She was thinking maybe Annie could snatch the cigarette butt while they conferred in his office.

"What you say to me, you can say to them." Rapino gestured to the men behind him.

"Very well," said Grace after taking a readying breath. *Plan B it is.* "The reason we're here is we recently met someone who thinks you might be Penny's father." She didn't bother burying the lead, because small talk with Vince wasn't going to happen.

Vince screwed up his face like she hadn't spoken English. Grace carried on. "You and Rachel were together a long time ago. Boyfriend and girlfriend back in high school, on again, off again after . . . The timing, it works."

Vince spit out a chilling laugh. "Yeah? Ya think? That's a hard no." He kept his gaze locked on Grace; his two closest companions stayed still as statues. Other workers began to gather, thinking maybe this might escalate into a must-see event.

"So you're saying you're not Penny's father?"

"Damn straight I'm not that girl's daddy. I got my kids."

"Are you willing to prove it?" Annie asked boldly, holding up the bag with the cotton swabs in it.

A cracked smile broke over Vince's leathery face. He laughed again, and some of the tension left the room like a tire leaking air. "You going all CSI on me, Denim?" He gestured at Annie's shirt to explain the nickname.

"If you want to prove you're not Penny's father, you can give us the sample and avoid any, ah, investigation into the matter."

The smile that had been on Vince's face faded fast. "Whatcha talking about, investigation?" he said through clenched teeth.

"I haven't told anybody yet about you and Rachel being an item back in the day." Grace found the lie came easily. "The police didn't do much looking into you because they already had their suspect for Rachel's murder: my daughter. Now, well, this new information might be of serious interest to them. Suddenly you're more connected to the victim than anyone knew. That'll raise some eyebrows at a minimum, Vince. All the police need is a motive, no matter how thin, to start looking into you more aggressively. Then, well, who knows what they'll find."

"Are you saying I'm a suspect?"

"I'm not saying anything," Grace clarified quickly. She remembered Navarro's warning about pushing too hard. "I'm telling you that if you're sure you're not Penny's biological father, let us help you prove it. If it's what you say it is, then we don't bring it up to the police, and they don't investigate you and maybe find more than just your . . . DNA."

Grace felt she'd gone as far as she could. She wasn't about to reveal what Navarro had shared regarding Vince's illegal auto parts scam. A strong hint would do the job just fine, she told herself. She rested her arms at her sides. That was it. She'd made her big play, her big bluff, and had nothing more to offer. The smell of cigarettes, grease, and fried food tickled at her nose.

Vince didn't seem to know how to react, but a smile played at the corners of his mouth. He took another step forward, putting himself within arm's reach of both Annie and Grace. The cigarette butt was visible now, but it might as well have been a mile away. Vince's two buddies stayed back, keeping an eye on things like good handlers should.

"You are one gutsy bitch," Vince said, almost with reverence. "I'll give you that."

Grace didn't bother responding.

"Let me get this straight," he said. "I give you some DNA right here, right now, or you go to the police and try to get them to shake me down? And you think shaking that tree's gonna get them something else . . . like my private affairs, that it?"

"That's it," Grace said, lifting her hands like they were two scales for Vince to weigh his decision.

He thought a moment. "I was with my wife and kids the night your crazy bitch-ass daughter killed my girl."

"And you do know you're not supposed to have a wife and a girlfriend at the same time," Annie said to him—like that would make him suddenly sprout a conscience.

"Well, I ain't got no wife no more. Don't see my kids much, either, not after all that shit went down and the news people decided to drag my name through the mud," he snapped at Annie. He raised his hand to show off a finger without a wedding band. But as his arm lifted, Grace saw something else, a better look at his silver necklace, that made her take note.

"You don't know what you're messing with, ladies, but I'll tell you right now, it's not a smart move."

"Rachel needed investment money for something she thought was going to make her rich. That's what she told Morgan, her bartender buddy at Lucky Dog," Grace said, breathing quickly. Every muscle in her body was telling her to go, but her legs wouldn't budge.

She studied the necklace again as the pendant around his neck caught the light. Her resolve strengthened as her fears melted away. Vince scared her, but she had something on him now, something potentially game-changing. It bolstered her confidence to go for broke.

"Now—and I'm thinking out loud here, Vince—but maybe you didn't know Penny was your biological daughter. They'd just reconnected, so maybe Rachel was excited to share the news. But you—you snapped. It happens. You killed her in a fit of rage. Or, I like this even better—you and Rachel had a little falling out. You tried to break it off, but she needs you to keep paying her rent, so she decided you could be her banker instead."

"What would she have on me?" Vince asked.

"You've been before a judge quite a number of times. I'm sure there's something in your closet Rachel knew about, something you're involved in, that you'd like to keep out of the public eye. That was a secret she wanted money to keep.

"You show up at Rachel's place. There's a fight, some altercation, whatever, and you kill her. But you don't know that Penny's also in the apartment, hiding in a closet, because Rachel knew there could be trouble when you showed up, probably unexpected and uninvited. Penny overhears you stuffing Rachel's head into a bucket of ammonia, torturing her with those fumes to get her to back off her threat— maybe that's when you told her to leave town, to 'be gone and gone for good.'" Grace used the same words Penny had said to her, and thought she saw a flash of recognition bloom in Vince's eyes.

"But Rachel's a tough one. She doesn't respond to your intimidation tactics, so out comes the knife. You thought Rachel was dead, but she could still call nine-one-one, even with her throat slit open. Now, the hard part is that the police already did their investigation, and they were happy with your alibi. As far as they're concerned this is in the past. But if you're Penny's father, you get a hard second look, and I get a second chance to make my case to them. Might go your way again, might not—or maybe something else comes of it. Either way, if you're not Penny's birth father, I've got nothing new to give the police, we go to trial, and I hope for the best.

"So why don't you help us help you? Give us a swab."

Taking that as her cue, Annie again held up a cotton swab for Vince.

He got right in Annie's face, showing a flash of anger that Grace sensed could easily explode into extreme violence at any moment. He took the swab from her, bending it in half with his fingers.

"You're using a lot of dangerous language with me," he said darkly. "DNA, blackmail, murder, investigations . . . but hell, I'll give you points for your creativity. Look, I've got a business to run, obligations to take care of. You two show up to my place of work, threatening all that . . . that ain't cool with me." He cocked his head sideways. "Not cool at all."

Vince opened his mouth and tossed the bent swab inside. He swished it around, getting it covered in his saliva, before he spat it onto the floor.

"You want my DNA?" he said to Grace. "Go and get it."

Grace stared at the swab like she would a venomous snake. To get it, she'd have to take her eyes off Vince, but the payoff was too hard to resist. Bending at the knees, Grace sank down, lower and lower, never averting her gaze from the man looming above. She reached for the swab, but had to look away for just a second. A blur of something black streaked into her field of vision, and Grace jerked her hand away a millisecond before the heavy sole of Vince's work boot would have crushed her fingers underneath.

"Actually, I came up with another idea," Vince said as Grace stood up. "Why don't you two ladybirds turn yourselves around and get the fuck out of my garage."

The anger in his eyes, the heat he gave off, told Grace to get out—and fast. She took a single step backward, sending Annie a look that got her to follow. She didn't turn around completely until she felt sunshine hit her face, and then she and Annie hurried to the car. She half expected Vince to come barreling out of the garage with a gun drawn, but instead he and his crew emerged merely to watch them drive away, standing in a line, staring straight at them. Only when the repair shop was out of sight did Grace feel like she could breathe again.

"Well, that was a total fail," said Annie shakily.

"Not exactly." Grace pushed down on the gas pedal, still reeling from what she'd seen.

"Um, what am I missing here?" asked Annie. "We went to get his DNA and we nearly died."

"You didn't see it?"

"See what?"

Grace returned a smile as she left the narrow, crumbling neighborhood for a more populous and prosperous one.

"Are you going to share with me, Miss Mysterious?" asked Annie, sounding annoyed.

"Did you see Vince's necklace?" asked Grace.

"Yeah," Annie said before shaking her head. "I mean no. I was too busy trying not to shit my pants."

Grace sent Annie a fractured smile. "Well, I did," she said. "And it was a silver chain with a large anchor pendant attached."

CHAPTER 41

Ruth Whitmore made time in her busy schedule to meet with Mitch and discuss his lunchtime seminar. Edgewater doctors, nurses, and corrections officers had come together as Mitch introduced alternative approaches to patient restraints including new techniques for de-escalation and improved processes for collaboration. By way of example, Mitch dedicated some portion of his talk to the contrast between his violent altercation with John Grady, the Mountain Man, and the encounter between Darla and Grace, in which words had been enough to calm her.

CO Blackwood wasn't one of those in attendance. Mitch noticed that, but everyone who was there seemed eager to learn, and the concentration and pointed questions from his audience revealed another side of Edgewater. For the most part, the people who worked here were capable, caring professionals. Despite their limited resources, they wanted to do the right thing, make a difference in the lives of patients, and be better than they were yesterday.

He hadn't planned it, but the lecture took place on the day Darla got out of solitary. She'd been arraigned on two counts of assault and attempted murder. Despite curtailing of her privileges, keeping Darla away from Penny would be the correction officers' responsibility, so before Mitch got into any specifics about the seminar, the first item he wanted to discuss concerned CO Blackwood.

Whitmore greeted Mitch in an impeccably styled navy suit, though her short hair, normally coiffed to precision, appeared somewhat unkempt today. Then again, Mitch figured if he had her job, he'd have no hair at all. He had no idea how Whitmore juggled the many responsibilities and constant crises with such aplomb.

However she managed, he'd come to admire her a great deal. He sincerely appreciated her continued interest in his work here, and in Penny's case in particular. Mitch took a seat in a comfortable armchair in her spacious office. Typical of Whitmore, she skipped the small talk, somehow already knowing what was on his mind.

"I've spoken again with Blackwood," Whitmore said, "and he vehemently denies writing the note."

"Of course he does," said Mitch. "Wouldn't you?"

Whitmore responded by clasping her hands together, her thin fingers turning white with pressure. "Naturally," she said.

"So what now?" Mitch asked.

"Conjecture is not enough proof for disciplinary action, Mitch," said Whitmore.

"But I've come to trust your instincts, so I've given Blackwood a bump in pay to keep him content and reassigned him to our max security unit. He'll have his hands full over there, and no access to Darla or Penny. That's the best I can do."

Mitch peered at Whitmore for a moment, mulling it over in his head. Best solution for all, he decided. As long as Blackwood was out of the picture he could assume Penny would be safe from further harm.

"Good enough," said Mitch. "Thank you so much."

"Speaking of Penny," Whitmore said. "How is your assessment going? Trial is coming up, and I'm curious if you think she'll be leaving us to stay elsewhere."

"By elsewhere I assume you mean a prison setting."

Whitmore nodded and peered at Mitch with keen interest. He

recalled what she had said to him that day in her office when he asked her to look at the medical examiner's report detailing the forensics of Rachel's murder. She'd put it crassly—her word—but it made sense to Mitch. If Penny were to have a true case of DID, the sensational nature of the crime and the mystique around her condition would generate publicity for Edgewater. With that as leverage, perhaps she could access much-needed state funds to improve facility operations.

He hated to have to disappoint her.

"Do you believe Penny has DID?" she asked.

"I wish I had a clear answer for you," said Mitch. "I've witnessed Penny experience dissociative states that are uncharacteristic of her known alters three times now. On each occasion she shared some memory from the night of the murder, but I think these are false narratives she's constructed. For instance, she's convinced she wasn't alone that night, that someone threatened to put her head into a bucket of ammonia, and that Rachel had done something wrong or was living under the threat of going to prison. That sort of delusional thinking is typical of borderlines suffering paranoid ideation.

"It's also possible these are stress-induced false memories or inventions to ease a guilty conscience and she is transferring her guilt to her alters. I could be wrong about Blackwood, and Penny wrote that note to Darla herself as a form of self-punishment. And there's also the possibility that, the note, all that she's told us, everything *deliberate* fabrications on her part."

"Deliberate? Why would she do that?"

"To mislead us," said Mitch. "To send us on a wild-goose chase, so to speak. In other words, she's getting a thrill out of toying with us. There's been absolutely no verification that anything she has told us is true. If it's all make-believe and done intentionally, then Dr. Palumbo's diagnosis of antisocial borderline personality disorder is probably the right one, and she went to Rachel's home that night with the intent to murder.

"On the other hand, if I could verify that the things Penny has said in her dissociative states are actually true—if I could corroborate *any* of it—I suppose it would strongly support a diagnosis of DID. These personality states are quite real, so it wouldn't take much for me to flip my position."

"Oh my. Bombshells abound. Are you going to testify at her trial?"

"That's the plan," Mitch said, though he didn't sound happy about it. "Greg Navarro was hoping I'd be able to confirm a DID diagnosis and demonstrate that Penny had a psychotic break."

"And?" Whitmore hit Mitch with an inscrutable gaze.

"And I cannot," he said. "I'll show him my final report and he'll have to make the call as to what he wants to do. If he wants me to take the stand, I will, but I'll tell the truth as I see it. I know Navarro wants to prove to a jury that Penny couldn't control herself at the time of the killing, or didn't think what she was doing was wrong, but I can't say that."

"So are you going to tell Grace about your conclusion?" Whitmore's eyes moved a little.

"She won't take it well," said Mitch. "But as I see it, no matter the diagnosis, without the ability to show a psychotic break, it will be a long shot to prove her not guilty by reason of insanity."

"I think 'won't take it well' is soft-shoeing it a bit," said Whitmore. "Grace wants you to unequivocally denounce Palumbo's diagnosis and go with DID. I spoke to her on the phone the other day. She thinks there's a *hidden* alter that may be an avenger-type personality. That Rachel abused Penny in the past, and seeing her for the first time in years unearthed some repressed memories that caused this alter to come out and, well . . . we all know the rest. Has she spoken to you about that?"

A wave of sadness tore through Mitch. He had wanted to do more for Grace, and he had let her down.

"We've discussed it at length. I have no proof of an avenger-type alter, or of any abuse or traumatic experience that Penny may have suffered that would have contributed to her developing DID. None whatsoever. I'm afraid Grace might be suffering delusions of her own."

That seemed to pique Whitmore's interest. "How so?"

"She called me, too, but with a new theory," Mitch said. "Apparently, she found out that Vince Rapino, Rachel's boyfriend, wears an anchor pendant necklace."

Whitmore stared back blankly.

"Penny has a thing for anchors," Mitch clarified. "She had a necklace that she remembered from when she was a little girl living with Rachel. Grace is quite in tune with her daughter's feelings, and began buying these pendants for Penny as birthday presents and such. It's become something of a totem for her. Chloe, the perfectionist alter, even uses anchor symbols to sign her name on her artwork, which is how we reached her. It's a powerful motif for her, that's for sure."

Mitch didn't have the drawing Chloe made on his person, but he did have pictures of it on his phone. He showed Whitmore the scene she'd drawn: the house; the tire swing attached by a brown crayon-line rope to a tree on a wide green lawn; a woman with Xs for eyes near a jug of what he presumed to be ammonia; and a little girl in an upstairs room getting ready to take a bath. She'd been drawn with an anchor pendant around her neck, holding a blue square—probably that missing book featuring water and boats.

"Grace thinks Rapino might be Penny's birth father," Mitch added. "And she either had a matching necklace like his, or she saw it draped around his neck way back then. If you think like Grace, Penny may have seen it again when Vince was killing Rachel."

Whitmore's eyes widened with surprise. "So she thinks Rapino is the killer?"

"Either that or Penny's friend Maria is somehow involved. She's grasping here," Mitch said. "Not that I can blame her. She's doing what any parent would do, what I would do, fighting for every inch on the battlefield."

"But she's going to lose the battle?" Whitmore's mouth formed a tight-lipped frown.

"No," said Mitch. "She's going to lose the war."

A knock on the office door drew both Mitch's and Whitmore's attention.

"Come in," Whitmore said gruffly.

A correction officer entered, holding a large white envelope in his right hand. "This came into the mail room marked 'Urgent,'" he said, striding over to her desk. "You said you wanted anything marked 'Urgent' brought to you right away."

"Indeed," Whitmore said, taking the envelope from him. He remained standing by her desk.

"This isn't the army. You don't need me to dismiss you."

The CO gave a nod and departed quickly as Whitmore opened the envelope. She took out a familiar file folder, and Mitch remembered her instructions regarding its contents. The Edgewater mailroom wasn't the most efficient, Whitmore had cautioned, so Mitch had the medical examiner reviewing Penny's file send it back to Whitmore's attention, not his. It was also marked "Urgent" to ensure proper delivery of the important documents.

"Give me a moment, will you?" Whitmore said, leafing through the pages. The ME might have been Mitch's contact, but it was Whitmore's prerogative to have the first look.

Mitch took the opportunity to text Caitlyn, who'd gone to Clean Start to have a visit with Adam. If this were old times, they'd have wine with dinner that night and talk about the case. She'd listen carefully, encourage him, and make him feel like everything was going to be okay. But Mitch wasn't so sure—not with Adam, or with Penny. What if his diagnosis was wrong? Could Penny be a true case of DID? Could there be a fourth alter, an avenger type, someone else locked inside her—a boy, a girl, young or old, black or white, a person within a person who carried the darkest of intentions—someone Mitch had failed to reach?

"Well, this is interesting," Whitmore said.

Mitch's attention was on his text chat with Caitlyn, who assured him that things with Adam were as good as they could be. He had talked to her about becoming a master gardener after tending the rosebushes at Clean Start, maybe even starting a landscaping business when he got out. An eye to the future was progress for sure. Mitch promised himself that he'd visit his son on the weekend.

But first, the file.

"What is it?" asked Mitch.

Whitmore removed two photographs from the folder. Mitch recognized them: they were pictures of Penny's arms, taken after her arrest. His medical examiner friend had circled the marks around Penny's wrists (which everyone had assumed were abrasions from the handcuffs) in bright red marker and put a sticky note directly on the photograph next to the circles.

"Have a look," Whitmore said, sliding the photograph across the desk for Mitch's review. "She shared my assessment—doesn't believe those marks around Penny's wrists were put there by handcuffs."

Mitch read the note with widening eyes, keying in on certain words that jumped out at him. *Dark brown color . . . red band on both sides of the mark . . . slight bruising visible . . . wearing of the skin . . . indicative of ligature marks.*

"She was tied up," Mitch said with a gasp. He peered at Whitmore over the top edge of the photograph.

"Tied up," Whitmore repeated. "I'm not surprised the police and forensics missed it. Handcuffs can leave marks so it's natural they'd have dismissed them, but I'm nothing if not observant, have to be in this job, and I hadn't seen marks like those before. What is it that Penny told you?"

"She wasn't alone," Mitch said breathlessly.

"Wasn't alone," Whitmore repeated. "Meaning maybe Penny's telling us the truth, Mitch. I guess there's the proof you were after. Assuming she didn't bind her own wrists together, she wasn't alone that night."

"I'll get this to the lawyer and call Grace right away, let her know. This has the potential to change everything."

CHAPTER 42

When Mitch called with the shocking news, he was more excited than Grace had ever heard him. His explanation was so breathless and quick that it took her a moment to grasp what he was saying.

"So if your medical examiner is right, and Penny's wrists were bound, then Mitch—that means she's been telling us the truth all along." Grace felt light on her feet and in her head.

"So who was with her?" she asked.

"That I don't know, and wish I did," Mitch said.

He offered to meet in Swampscott to discuss the ramifications, and they settled on the war room at Annie's house. Mitch got there before Attorney Navarro, giving Grace just enough time to review the ME's report and the photographs for herself before the fireworks started. No defense attorney would welcome an entire strategy being blown apart days before trial.

"Look at these marks," Grace said, waving one of the photos like a pennant before Mitch's eyes. "The rope had to have been very tight to leave marks like these. Is there any way to access Penny's memory to find out who tied her up? Hypnosis? Another dose of ketamine perhaps? Anything?"

"Might be worth a try, but she's got strong defenses, so I wouldn't get your hopes up," Mitch said. "I will concede that this cements for me that Penny isn't delusional. I had no proof that what she's been telling us was true. Honestly, I thought she was playing us for fools or engaging in magical thinking. But now . . . now it's a different story. She's not role-playing here, she's not using alters as an excuse for her behavior. I'm not flat out rejecting Dr. Palumbo's take, as there are aspects of Penny's mental illness that align with borderline personality disorder, but right now I fully support Dr. Cross's diagnosis."

Grace's face broke into a bright smile that Mitch mimicked to a lesser degree.

"Are you saying . . . ?" Her voice was full of hope.

"My official diagnosis for the trial will be that Penny has a dissociative identity disorder . . . meaning she has more than one personality state. Even if Dr. Palumbo was partially right, he was wrong to have assumed an antisocial aspect to her disorder. Your daughter is not depraved."

Relief washed over Grace and gratitude flooded her heart, so much so that she strode over to Mitch and gave him a long, warm embrace. When they broke apart, a thin film of tears coated her eyes.

"I can't even tell you how relieved I am to hear you say those words," she said, her voice rife with emotion. "We need you on our side, Mitch, and now I feel like you're really with us all the way."

Despite the praise, Mitch's expression remained downcast.

"Even with a diagnosis of DID, Grace, I cannot say in court that Penny was suffering a psychotic break when the murder took place."

"I don't think you have to now," said Grace. "How could she have killed Rachel if her hands were bound?"

"You still think she's innocent?" Mitch sent a hand running through his mane of silver hair. "Grace, how do you explain her being covered in blood, holding the murder weapon?"

"She was there," Grace said. "Penny was there, of course. But she was tied up. Then . . . well, she was untied. Simple as that."

"And she was standing close to Rachel when someone else killed her," Annie added. "That's how the blood got on her."

"*After* the murder," Grace clarified. "And that's when Penny went into a fugue state, like she did the night her father died . . . no memories for us to access."

"Or she has trapped memories," Annie said. "Memories she's parsed out to her alters and we're getting them from her in dribs and drabs. You've said that's a possibility."

"Right," said Mitch. "But that still doesn't answer: Who did the killing?"

Mitch was looking at the board that Grace and Annie had constructed, with the cards and yellow string connecting various suspects with different theories.

"Either Vince or Maria," said Grace with definitive authority.

"Motive?"

"Vince to stop Rachel from blackmailing him. Maria because . . . well, she's the firebrand psychotic," said Annie, who had her answers at the ready.

"What about these?" Mitch tapped a finger on the cards with locations written out. Places like Topeka, Alaska, and Chicago. Grace had all the names memorized. All in all, Penny had listed off fifteen unique locations while in a dissociative state of mind.

"We don't know," said Annie. "They mean something to Penny. Jack thinks they could have something to do with drugs. Locations where Penny went as a kid when Rachel was plying that trade, or they could be places she and Rachel talked about on the night of the murder. We just don't know."

"Same as with the book," said Mitch.

At ten past the hour Navarro showed up. He draped his suit jacket over the back of a bridge chair at the foldout table that Grace had helped Annie assemble. Grace wasted no time getting right to it.

"She was tied up that night," she said, showing Navarro the report and pictures from Mitch's medical examiner contact. "It changes everything."

Navarro, who had been preparing for an entirely different defense, looked as though someone had sucker punched him in the gut.

"This is potentially great news," he said, not sounding at all elated. "But I don't think it's the game changer you think it is."

"Why?" asked Grace.

"A jury won't go for theoretical," he said. "They'll follow the evidence. She was tied up, so what?"

"Who tied her?" asked Annie, hitting her closed fist against the table. "Someone else was involved. Had to be."

Navarro did not look convinced. "Maybe Rachel tied up Penny, Penny escaped, and then she killed Rachel. Possible? Justification for murder? I think not. Either way, a rope mark isn't going to convince a jury this was self-defense, not with all the forensic evidence to the contrary, and we don't have another suspect on trial." Navarro's hands went to his hips as he struck a defiant pose. "Is that enough reasonable doubt to acquit? That's what you're after now, right? This is not an insanity defense. You're talking about going all the way to a not-guilty verdict. She was covered in blood, holding the murder weapon. I don't see how we get there."

"Grace raises a good point: How could Penny have untied herself, with rope marks like those? Hard to believe. And how could she have killed the way she did if she was bound?" asked Mitch. "It was a violent, frenzied murder. Hard to pull off if you can't bend your wrists."

"I don't know," Navarro admitted with a shake of his head.

Grace's whole face lit up as a thought came to her. "We have to show it," she announced excitedly.

"Show what?" asked Navarro, trepidation entering his voice.

"Show that she couldn't have killed with her hands bound."

"And how do we do that?" Navarro's eyes widened.

"Simple," said Grace. "We need a demonstration like they did at the OJ trial."

"If it doesn't fit, you must acquit," said Annie in a singsong voice.

"That's right," said Grace. "If we put Penny on the stand, show her hands tied up with rope, do it in a way that would leave these marks." She pointed to the photograph on the table highlighting Penny's discolored wrists. "Hand her a prop knife with her hands bound. Give the jury that visual. She couldn't be the killer if she couldn't wield the weapon. Then we'll play the videos of what Penny's alters each revealed, talk about how she's parsed out her memories of the real killer for safety purposes—that's a defense mechanism, it's what the brain uses DID to do—and we hope for the best."

Navarro appeared utterly shell-shocked. Dazed. Face slack.

"You want me to put Penny on the stand? Tie up her hands? Holy shit." He turned to Mitch. "What's your take on this?"

"The rope marks suggest to me that Penny's not engaged in any sort of deceitful make-believe. These are real, repressed memories that are coming from different personality states. Not only can I testify to her dissociative states and a DID diagnosis," Mitch said, "I can also speak to the possibility of a fourth alter, one we haven't accessed, an avenging type that could have been unleashed during a psychotic break when she saw Rachel for the first time, releasing a torrent of painful memories that triggered the attack. Perhaps Rachel tied up Penny to try and save herself and somehow Penny got free. No matter the scenario, I'll testify that she has no memories from her dissociative states and I can provide a medical explanation as to why she has no memory of the murder."

Navarro lifted his head out of his hands, still looking agitated. "Mitch, without us documenting it—without proof, some recording, something—pitching a fourth alter nobody has met is going to look like we're grasping at straws here," he said.

"We have recordings of Penny when she goes into those trance-like states," Mitch countered. "Even if it appears she can conform to the law, she's still extremely fragile. You can see it on the recordings. Given that, I'd be willing to testify that Penny, or any one of her alters, could have experienced a psychotic break under the stress of meeting her birth mother for the first time."

This seemed to please Navarro.

"That's our win," he said, nodding vigorously. "You being on board with DID, talking about her emotional fragility . . . saying it's possible that there was a snap, a break—that's our best shot at the verdict we're after."

"Why not say there are two possible versions of events for the jury to consider," Annie suggested. "Someone else killed Rachel and the rope marks prove it, *or* Penny was in an altered state and unable to conform to the law. Either way, she's not guilty."

Navarro looked seasick at the thought. "You're trying to have your cake and eat it, too," he said. "This is one or the other. Besides, you don't put defendants on the stand in a murder trial. She'll be utterly eviscerated on cross. She'll fall apart. I know Jessica Johnson. She's a bloodthirsty prosecutor.

"If Penny's nervous, which she will be because her life is on the line, it'll put doubt in the jury's mind," Navarro insisted. "A nervous defendant is a guilty defendant. You want the jury to remain unbiased, not the other way around. We'll be handing the DA's office a victory if we do this."

Grace stood up and pressed her palms firmly against the table. She glared at Navarro and spoke with her teeth clenched.

"Penny is innocent. She wasn't alone. She was tied up. She was afraid for her life. Someone was going to torture her with chemicals. I want the jury to acquit my daughter," she said. "If you don't put her on the stand and argue for an acquittal, I'll find a lawyer who will."

Navarro bowed his head. When he looked up again, he saw the fierce determination in her eyes.

"Grace . . . listen to me, listen to my words very carefully." He spoke in a soft voice, pausing to give her a second to settle. "We argue it's a rope, she couldn't have done the deed with her hands bound, the prosecution will get their expert to say handcuffs *could* leave a similar mark. They may have to ask several experts before they get the answer they want, but somewhere out there"—he pointed to a window—"is someone in a position of authority who will contradict us under oath, and in the minds of the jury it'll be a push. There were no fibers taken from

Penny's wrists to bolster our case. None. So it's all based off a picture. Believe me, Grace, it's not enough evidence to hang an entire defense on. We will lose, and we will lose big."

"Wait, Grace, Greg." It was Mitch who spoke up. "I think we can do both."

Navarro winced. "Both? How?"

Mitch said, "If you put Penny on the stand, the jury will see one of two things, I'm certain of it. They'll see Eve, who will be ice up there, not one bit of nervousness. And seeing icy Eve up there will add credibility to your claim. Or . . ."

Mitch held up a finger as a point of emphasis.

"Or she enters a dissociative state while she's on the stand, not saying it'll happen, but it could, and the jury can see for itself what I have on video. Seeing Penny out of her mind, not really cognizant of her surroundings, will be an even more convincing demonstration than a rope would be. It's a win/win either way."

Mitch folded his arms across his chest in a "case closed" gesture. Grace nodded emphatically.

"Yes, yes, that sounds good to me," she said, that determined look still in her eyes. "I want Penny to take the stand, Greg. Let the jury see what Mitch just said. Fine. We can't go for an acquittal. But Penny on the stand could be the make or break we need. I'm not beyond my threat of going to the court to try and get another lawyer here. This is my daughter's life at stake. The judge may not like it, but I'm sure she'll listen."

Tense moments passed in silence.

"Okay," Navarro said with a huff of air. "Penny testifies. We'll put her on the stand. Defendants can always testify on their own behalf. But Grace . . ." He fixed her with a cold stare. "If she gets convicted, if she gets life, don't say I didn't warn you."

CHAPTER 43

GRACE CAME TO A stop in front of her house, her body a jangle of nerves, a mix of highs and lows. She'd gotten her wish, got Navarro to agree to her demand, but now the implications were setting in and the weight felt heavy on her shoulders. What if the plan backfired? What if the jury came back with a guilty verdict *because* Penny testified? She'd never know if Navarro's approach might have been enough on its own.

Still, the rope marks were proof that Penny couldn't have committed murder, not one as violent as the attack on Rachel had been, not with her hands bound tightly enough to cause ligature marks. Penny was bright, but she wasn't Houdini. Someone else was there that night. She believed it. Mitch believed it. But if Navarro was to be believed, it wasn't enough to convince a jury. Grace vowed to fight on appeal. *Someday, somehow,* she promised herself, *Penny will be acquitted.*

As was her habit in the warmer months, Grace parked in the driveway instead of the garage, where Arthur's car remained during all seasons. It was the same car Penny had taken without permission on the night of the murder, the one that had been impounded and eventually returned, and soon it would be sold to a dealer to help fund her daughter's defense. At least she didn't have to hurry up and get a new lawyer.

Tomorrow, Grace, Jack, and Annie—Ryan too, if he wanted to

come—would go to Edgewater together to tell Penny, tell Eve, tell all of her alters, about the new plan. Tonight, however, was for resting and recharging.

Grace exited into total darkness, having forgotten to leave any house lights on, inside or out. She couldn't see the paving stones of the walkway beneath her feet. No stars out tonight. She managed to get the key into the front lock and open the door. The alarm beeped to be disarmed. She keyed in the code, using the illuminated buttons as her guide, before turning on a hall light, sending a blaze of brightness into her eyes. Her vision quickly adjusted. It was quiet inside.

Ryan was at the restaurant. Jack was back at school. Annie was home cleaning up after the meeting. And Grace was alone again. These were the moments when she felt Arthur's absence most profoundly. The hole he'd left behind in her life followed her like a cruel shadow. What would Arthur tell her to do about the trial? Take Navarro's advice? Hope for the best?

No, he'd say what she said to herself: *Trust yourself.* She'd pushed Mitch on accepting the DID diagnosis, and he did. Pushed Navarro to put Penny on the stand, and he did. She'd been pushing hard every minute of every day, just like her marathon training, only this race never ended.

She'd call Navarro in a bit to make sure there were no hard feelings. First though, she needed some tea.

Some thirty minutes later, Grace still hadn't picked up a phone. She'd changed into her pajamas and put her hair up in a loose bun before finding a comfortable spot on the couch from which to watch, of all things, a nature show. It made her think of happier times, of Arthur and a much younger Penny doing the same.

Eventually, Grace shut off the television. She sat on the couch a few minutes longer, drinking her tea and finally thinking about nothing at all. If the house hadn't been so quiet, Grace might not have heard someone turn the knob on the front door and bump it hard, twice.

She sprang up from her seat, heart lodged firmly in her throat. The noise had startled her. Was it Ryan? Had he forgotten his keys? How had she not heard his car coming down the driveway? Seen his head-lights?

She pulled back the living room curtain. In her distracted state, Grace had forgotten to turn on the front porch lights for Ryan as she usually did, so when she peered outside she could see nothing but darkness. She heard another loud bang, someone at the front door. There was a Stay mode on the alarm, meaning any open door would trigger it, but she didn't set that mode until Ryan got home. She'd left her phone somewhere in the kitchen, and there was no way to sum-mon help from the TV room. *Is there time to run to the kitchen?*

Gingerly, Grace closed the curtain, not wanting anyone to know she was at home. Alone.

Another bang.

Fear and hope made her cry out, "Who's there? Ryan? Is that you?"

Her heart thumped wildly. *He forgot his keys,* she told herself encour-agingly. *It's nothing.* She had all those thoughts as her eyes raked the room, searching for something she could grab to use as a weapon. She tensed, her breathing shallow and quick. Moving away from the win-dow, Grace sought some kind of cover behind Arthur's favorite arm-chair, hoping and praying the noise would go away.

Instead she heard a loud pop, along with a scrape of metal on metal. Her eyes weren't deceiving her when she saw the front door swing open. She always engaged the deadbolt when she set the alarm, but she hadn't done that yet, and the flimsy lock built into the doorknob was easy for someone to breach.

Two large men, both dressed in black, hoods covering their heads, entered her room like panthers on the prowl. The men split up. One went left, toward the TV room and Grace's location, while the other headed down the hall to the kitchen. It would be seconds before she was spotted. Instinct sent Grace scurrying out from behind the arm-chair to her left, heading for the living room and the glass doors that opened onto a stone patio. If she could get outside, Grace thought she could sprint across the lawn, maybe reach a neighbor's house.

A presence loomed behind her as Grace bolted for the patio door in slippery socks. "Get out!" she screamed, her voice drenched in panic. Her house was set far back from the road, so the chances someone would hear her desperate plea stood at slim to none.

With a hurdler's stride, Grace leapt over the coffee table fronting her plush brown sofa. As she went up and over, her right foot clipped a vase, sending it to the hardwood floor with an explosion of glass in every direction. Choking on fear, she glanced to her right, only to see one of her attackers coming at her from the kitchen.

A black bandana covered his face right up to his ice blue eyes—eyes like a husky's. She didn't need to waste one second checking behind her to know the other man was closing in fast. Her best hope, really her *only* hope, was to get outside, where her screams might have a chance at being heard and her legs might carry her to safety.

The brown sofa was all that stood between Grace and the patio door. She couldn't hurdle the sofa, but she could get over it faster than going around, saving two steps, maybe three. Grace's right foot sank deeply into a plush cushion. The cushion functioned as a springboard of sorts, launching her up and over the back end of the sofa, but with too much velocity. Momentum carried her forward, sending her shoulder first into the patio door. She heard a crack, but the glass held. The force of the impact sent her reeling backward, and her lower half connected hard with the couch's solid back, which sent her forward again like a ricocheting pinball. She hit the glass door for a second time, stabbing her abdomen on the doorknob. Her head banged the glass hard, and down she went to the floor in a heap.

Footsteps thundered in her ears, and she heard both men grunt loudly as they landed on her, pinning her to the ground. A blur of black fabric swam in and out of Grace's vision. One man seized hold of Grace's arms, yanking them over her head almost hard enough to pull her shoulders from their sockets. Grace yowled in pain when his gloved hands clamped over her wrists—strong, so strong that she feared he'd break bone.

The other assailant placed his knees on her chest, pressing into Grace's ribs, putting pressure on her heart. He leaned toward her, close enough so the corner of his bandana tickled her face. His light skin and those blue eyes, so familiar to her, glowed in the dim light of the house. Someone reeked of cigarette smoke. She had a flash of the men smoking outside Vince Rapino's auto shop.

She thrashed and bucked to free herself from the man on top before he could crack her rib. "Get off me!" she screamed.

The man with the ice blue eyes placed a gloved hand on Grace's throat as he reached behind his back with his other arm and brought forward a massive knife. Pressing his knees hard against Grace's side to keep himself stabilized, he removed his hand from her throat to set the blade there. He used his free hand to cover her mouth. The other attacker, still holding Grace's arms above her head, dug his fingers into the bones of her wrists, sending sharp, shooting pain down her arms.

"You bite me, I'll slice you," said Blue Eyes. "Stop screaming."

She thought: *I'm going to be raped.* Paralyzing fear hollowed her out. Try as she did, Grace couldn't move a muscle.

How many times had she watched a movie, or read a book and thought: *If it were me, I would have* . . . But it was her, on the floor of her own house, no longer fighting her attackers because the knife to her throat had changed everything. She saw Rachel Boyd's throat slashed open, reimagined the gruesome wounds Rachel had suffered to her body. She went numb, all sensation blocked as she waited for a tug on her pants that didn't come.

The man on top leaned in close. She knew those eyes. They had watched her once, hadn't they?

Rapino. He works for Vince Rapino.

"You stop now," the man said in a whispered voice. "Stop looking in places you don't belong."

"Keep going and it gets ugly for you fast," the man holding her arms warned as Blue Eyes removed the hand covering her mouth. "Next time, we don't leave you breathing. Do you understand what we're telling you?"

"Yes . . . I understand . . ." Grace croaked out the words.

With each hitched exhale, her throat pushed against the meaty part of the knife's blade. "Please . . . don't . . . hurt me," she pleaded.

"Say it," said the man holding her wrists.

"Yes . . . I'll stop. No more."

"You don't know us," said Blue Eyes. "One cop stops by—and we mean one—and we'll be back here to finish you off. That clear?"

"Please, just go," pleaded Grace. "I won't cause any more trouble, I promise."

Blue Eyes pressed the full weight of his body against Grace, still keeping the blade to her throat. He whispered, "If you do it, I'll have fun with you first."

At last, he got off her and she could breathe again. The pressure on her wrists let up, and she could move her arms freely.

"Call the cops, and we'll know," said Blue Eyes. "And we'll be back. Stay on the floor for ten minutes. We'll set a kitchen timer. Don't be a hero."

She heard them in the kitchen, heard them set a spring-wound timer. They left through the front door, and Grace waited a few minutes, not ten, unable to move even if she wanted to. Finally, she got up, her legs supporting her like stretched rubber bands. She staggered to the front door and secured the deadbolt. Her shaky hand managed to push the correct buttons on the alarm, setting it to Stay mode. Anyone coming in or going out would alert the police.

You call the cops, we'll know.

They had gloves. They had masks. She had Detective Jay Allio. He might help her. Probably not. She went to the kitchen and picked up her phone. The timer went off. She sank to the floor, hugging her knees to her chest. She keyed in a number from memory.

Annie answered. "Hello?"

Grace couldn't speak.

"Hello? Grace, are you there?"

A sob escaped Grace's throat as tears of relief came pouring out.

"Grace?"

"Come . . . here . . . now . . ."

Three words, the only words she could manage between choking sobs, but it was enough. Family understood.

"I'll be right there," Annie said. "I'm calling the police."

Grace got out one more word.

"Don't."

CHAPTER 44

Annie and Grace sat together at the kitchen table with an open bottle of wine, now half gone. They'd exhausted talk about Grace going to the hospital for an exam (not going to happen) and getting the police involved (also not going to happen). The feeling of dissociation that Penny knew so well, that Grace had experienced during the attack, persisted as if she were in a dream—or a nightmare—from which she couldn't awaken.

"So, what do you want to do now?" asked Annie.

Grace paused. What *to* do?

"Now I want to drink the rest of this wine and take a long, hot bath and cry," Grace said.

Annie went to inspect the patio door for a second time. She ran her hand over the cracked glass with concern in her eyes. "What are you going to tell Ryan?" she asked.

"That I tripped and fell," Grace said. Her head hurt something awful, but she didn't have any signs of concussion, and her ribs were bruised, but she didn't think any were broken. "He doesn't need to know . . . he shouldn't know."

Annie returned to the table to retrieve her wineglass. "I suppose he'll have no trouble believing you're extremely clumsy." Her quip was meant to defuse some tension. "You'll stay with me tonight." Annie's suggestion came out as an order. "Ryan too."

"No, I'm going to stay here," Grace said with authority.

"What? You can't!" Annie sounded utterly aghast. "What if they come back?"

"They won't come back," Grace answered assuredly. "Not unless I do something stupid."

"How can you be so sure?" asked Annie. "You play stupid games, you win stupid prizes."

It was a favorite saying of hers, but never before had it been so applicable. They *had* been careless, reckless even, and it had cost them dearly. Going after Vince Rapino without support, without so much as a plan, had been utterly foolish, and now Grace had a choice to make. She could pursue Rapino at risk to her own life, find evidence tying Vince directly to Rachel's murder, prove that he was the one who bound Penny's wrists, or she could let it go—and with it, her daughter's best chance at change of plea and full acquittal.

"They don't want me dead, or I would be," said Grace. "Tonight was a warning, nothing more."

"I'd call it a pretty effective one," Annie noted.

It had not been easy for Grace to relive those terrifying moments of her attack for Annie's benefit, but she pushed through her reluctance, and talking it out dampened her lingering terror. When it came time to sleep tonight, though, Grace had no doubt those ice blue eyes would be there, waiting in the dark, peering out from above a black bandana.

"So what now?" Annie asked again, pouring more wine into her glass.

"We can't let Ryan or Jack know what's going on," Grace said in a way that left no room for debate.

"Are you going to tell Ryan that you're taking one of my guns and keeping it in your bedside dresser?"

"I don't want a gun," Grace said, hoping Annie wouldn't press her on it.

"These are dangerous people and you have to protect yourself."

"It's nonnegotiable." Grace said it forcefully, knowing Annie wouldn't back down.

"It'll be a small gun," Annie insisted, proving her right. "I've got a Glock 19, it's a compact model, easy to handle . . . we'll go to the range tomorrow, practice with it."

"No," Grace said, raising her voice.

"May I ask why you're so against it?"

Grace could lie, of course, but Annie might keep pressuring, and the only surefire way she knew to shoot down the idea (pun intended) was to tell the truth.

"I don't want a gun in this house, even a small one, because . . . well, because of Ryan." It came as a surprise to Grace when her voice quavered, but she held back the tears.

"Ryan?" Annie sounded perplexed.

Grace took a deep breath but couldn't quite settle herself. "I don't know what's wrong with him." He was her heart as much as Penny and Jack were. "He's not well. Something . . . there's something off with him and—" She couldn't bring herself to say the words, but Annie said them for her.

"Do you think he'd hurt himself?"

Grace's eyes sank to the floor. "I think it's possible," she admitted. "He hasn't been right, not since Penny's arrest, and I've no idea why. He was going to become a lawyer, acing all his pre-law classes at Northeastern. Now that's gone, or at least put on hold. I've asked him time and time again what happened, why the sudden change, but he won't open up to me about it. You know what can happen if people keep their feelings bottled up."

"He's old enough to buy a gun," Annie said, not ready to let it go. "If he wanted to."

"Annie, please," Grace said sharply, interrupting her. "I can't take the chance. He might go looking for something, anything, and he could find a gun and . . . and then get an idea."

Annie puckered her lips. "No gun, no hospital, no police, no telling anyone about tonight—that doesn't give us a lot of options here."

Grace sighed before cradling her face in her hands. When she closed her eyes, she saw the man on top of her, could feel his hot breath brush against her face, the weight of him pressing down on her. Her wrists ached with a phantom pain as if the other man were there, squeezing the bones. Grace took a deep breath to purge the feelings, and when she opened her eyes, the attackers were gone.

"Are you sure you're okay?" Annie asked, reaching across the table to give Grace's hand a gentle squeeze.

"I'm fine. It's been a real hell of a day." Grace managed a weak smile.

"It's Vince," Annie said. "Tonight just proved to me he's Rachel's killer . . . someone with that kind of violence in him. His alibi worked great because he sent his goons to do it for him."

"Tonight wasn't their first rodeo, I can tell you that," Grace concurred. She rubbed her temples. The wine was giving her a headache. "And you do realize we don't have enough to go after Rapino," she added, feeling dispirited. "Penny knows what really happened that night, and we can't reach her. It's all scattered, dissociated thoughts that are not going to help in the slightest."

Grace needed to decompress, and for that she thought a hot bath might do the trick.

"Annie—"

"Do you want to take a bath and need me to stick around?"

"Hmmm . . ." said Grace suspiciously. "I've got one family member with DID and another with ESP." Grace's slight chuckle felt like a major release.

"Sorry, nothing supernatural. I would want the same, is all," Annie explained. "Anyway, I'm not going anywhere. I'll spend the night. I'll spend the week. Hell, I'll move in. No weapon, I promise."

Grace got up to give Annie a long, hard hug. "Thank you . . . thank you for everything," she said, feeling the sadness in her chest bloom in her eyes. "I couldn't ask for a better sister."

"Arthur couldn't have had a better wife," said Annie. "I miss my brother so much, but I know he's looking after us. We're going to win in court, Grace. It's going to happen, I feel it in my bones."

"I hope more than anything you're right," Grace said.

Some minutes later, Grace found her way upstairs and filled the tub halfway with warm water. She got undressed, letting the faucet run while she climbed in to begin her soak. Annie was in the bedroom just outside, reading a book on the bed, but Grace had no doubt that her purse with some sort of firearm inside was within reach.

Stretching out her legs, Grace flicked her toes in and out of the warm water spilling from the faucet. Feeling more at peace, she let her arms drift to her sides as she closed her eyes. She was safe here; no memories came at her in the dark. Grace could feel herself drifting off . . . letting it go . . . letting everything go . . .

Tomorrow she'd see her daughter. Would Penny be frightened to take the stand in her own defense? What if she refused? There'd be no way to help her then. Grace's thoughts went to Annie—specifically, to the gun she wanted her to have. A frightful vision of Ryan came to her, his skull caved in by a bullet.

What was wrong with him? Why did he suddenly go off the rails after Penny's arrest?

Another question came to her, the same one Jack had raised at the restaurant before the big fight, this one quite possibly the most troubling of all: What secrets might he be keeping?

CHAPTER 45

IT HAD BEEN A long time since I visited you at Edgewater, two months, maybe three. I was a bit anxious, to be honest. It's the not nicest place for a get-together, but I was there to support Mom, who was more nervous than anybody. Would you be willing to take the stand in your own defense? That's what we came to find out. We couldn't force you, and my bet was no, but Mom was counting on a yes, so I had my fingers crossed. Even so, a good filmmaker always has a backup plan in the event a particular shot can't work out, so I had mine.

I wasn't done looking into your life, or into Rachel's past for that matter. There were questions that still needed answers. Did Rachel abuse you? Is she the reason you developed DID? Did an avenging alter of yours (that fourth alter theory)—did he or she do in Rachel because of something monstrous she'd done to you?

At least I had one question now firmly in the answered column.

You are not evil, Penny.

You have a full-blown, true case of DID. This wasn't a game for you. But DID and dissociative states don't make you a killer, so if you did in fact murder Rachel, you did it during some kind of a psychotic episode you suffered. Too bad a jury probably won't see it that way. They'll see the mountain of evidence against you, the hit list with

Rachel's name on it, pictures of Rachel's cut-up body, and other photos of you bathed in her blood.

Guilty on all charges. That's what they'll say, I'm sure of it.

Can we change that outcome by putting you on the stand? Mom
is counting on it. Navarro isn't so sure. He couldn't be here today.
Had to be in court, but said he'd be available by phone for questions.
Questions are not something we have in short supply, but I'm not sure
there's any that he can answer better than we can.

Mom took the lead, guiding us through the prescreening process
before armed security ushered first Annie, then Mom, then me past
a massive steel door. Beyond that door stood Dr. Mitch, awaiting our
arrival. The guard exchanged handshakes and paperwork with Mitch
before stepping off to the side so we could all meet and greet. I hadn't
met Mitch before, but I liked him right away. Seemed like a nice guy to
me. Think: Tom Hanks worked for PBS. I got good vibes from him. For
sure, he was someone you'd want on your team.

I'd decided to forgo my usual flannel attire and came dressed in
khaki pants and a blue oxford shirt, which I wore under a tailored
blazer Mom didn't realize I owned. I also had with me a road atlas with
pages marked to places you'd listed off in your dissociative state.

I was curious if you'd have any reaction to seeing those places in map
form. I wasn't yet done with my drug mule theory—that somehow these
were locations Rachel took you to when you were young. All I knew was
that they were important to you, but I didn't know why. I was worried
I wouldn't be allowed to bring the atlas inside, but Mom had some pull
here, so if there were a rule against it, someone bent it in our favor.

No surprise, Ryan didn't come. He opted for the restaurant instead.
Don't take it personally. He's got issues.

I can't imagine how you've adjusted to living here, Penny. The per-
vasive dull hum and incoherent announcements over the loudspeak-
ers, the strange smells pervading the hallways, the starkness of the
concrete walls—it was sensory deprivation and overload all at the
same time.

"Eve's waiting for us in one of the visiting rooms," Mitch told us. Annie's cowboy boots clomped like horse's feet on the concrete floor.

We came to a stop in front of a steel door painted the color of a battleship. When Dr. Mitch opened the door, I saw not you, Penny, but Eve seated at the table. A lone guard stood off in a corner, as animated as a houseplant.

You noticed me right away and looked sort of pleased.

"Jack," you exclaimed, a bit loudly, but that's typical for Eve. "It's been ages. And Aunt Annie—really, really glad you could come." Your honey-drenched voice came out quite caustic. "So the gang's all here." You clapped your hands together, looking past Dr. Mitch and Mom to the open door behind us. "What? No Ryan?" You made a *tsk-tsk* sound with your tongue. "Such a surprise. He's been so supportive." Your mouth crinkled into a tight smile.

"Hello, Eve," I said, trying to ignore the grand, regal persona you exuded.

"So what brings you all here today?" You cocked your head sideways.

"We need to ask you an important question," Annie said, coming around to give you a quick hug and a peck on the check, which coaxed out a grimace. Mom bent over to hug and kiss you as well and received an equally chilly reception.

"Fine, then," said Eve. "Let's get it over with. Tuesdays we get to do arts and crafts in the rec room, and I'd hate to miss it for . . . well . . . this." You gestured to us, your family.

"Damn," I said. "You're cold as ever."

"You've always looked after me, Jack, even when I was sugar or spice."

We had a code, you and I, and I knew you meant no disrespect. You were telling us, in your special Eve style, that it hurt to be together because we couldn't do it in the way that you remembered and missed.

"Let's get on with it then," said Annie.

"We think there's a chance you didn't kill anybody," I said. You eyed me coolly.

"Well, I guess that settles it," you answered. You glanced at your wrist, feigning a watch. "Checkout is at five, but hoping we can eat somewhere other than Big Frank's? It's the only food I haven't been craving."

Mom stepped forward.

"We have new evidence that shows you were tied up. The marks around your wrists were caused by a rope restraint, not handcuff irritation. Do you remember that Pen—Eve—do you remember someone binding your wrists?"

You looked up at the ceiling.

"Hmmm . . . that's a no. Sounds kinky though."

"We can't argue it in court because we'd have to change your plea," Annie said. "But it gave us an idea that you should take the stand in your defense. It's not common, but in your case, we think it will help."

Mom chimed in here. "We think you'll be very persuasive for the jury. Attorney Navarro will go over your testimony with you in detail, but he's available by phone now if you'd like to ask him anything."

You smiled and shrugged. "I don't have any questions. Do whatever with me. Put me on the stand. I don't really care anymore. But it would save everyone a whole lot of time and hassle if you'd just find the rope that was around my wrist and tie it around my neck."

"Don't say that," Mom said. "This could work."

"You'll be cross-examined," I said. "The prosecutor will come at you hard. Attorney Navarro is worried you'll crack, that you'll be nervous up there, and juries equate nervousness with guilt."

"Do I strike you as the nervous type?" you said.

"No," I said.

"What's in your hand?" you asked, pointing at the atlas. I'd almost forgotten about it.

"I want to show you something," I said.

I opened the atlas, and flipping to the first marked page, showed you the state of Alabama in all its glory.

"Does this state mean anything to you?"

You said, "Sweet home," and I smiled.

It took a few minutes, but I went through every place you had rattled off in your prior dissociative states. The last one I revealed to you was Virginia.

You looked at that page for quite some time, your head at a tilt, and you said in a quiet voice—unlike Eve's, unlike anyone's I'd heard before:

"Boats and water . . . it has a blue cover . . . I love that book."

"What book?" I asked. "This one?"

You looked at me wide-eyed with fright. "There's a picture on his arm. I can *see* the picture."

Your voice was very small, sounded so far away. Tiny. Little. Frightened.

"Picture? What picture? Whose arm?" I asked.

You blinked . . . once, twice, three times . . . and then your whole body stilled, and your eyes blinked no more.

"Eve?" I asked with some alarm. "Are you all right?"

No response.

"Eve?"

You shook your head as if coming to from a blackout. You assessed me, Annie, and Mom, with your familiar darkness.

"Are we done here?" you asked, pointing to the atlas. "I said I'm fine to take the stand, but it's a waste of everyone's time. I'm going to prison for the rest of my life, and there's not a damn thing you can do about it."

* * *

A heavy sadness followed us out as we climbed into Annie's SUV. Nobody knew what to make of what we'd just seen.

"That damn book with the water and boats," Annie said.

"She definitely switched," Mom said. "I don't know to whom, but I know a switch when I see one."

"What did she mean a picture on his arm?"

"A picture on an arm . . . it's got to be a tattoo," said Annie.

Almost simultaneously Annie and Mom said, "Vince."

I powered on my phone as soon as I was in my seat. After we'd passed through security, after the guards had checked to make sure we weren't smuggling someone out, I announced that I had information to share.

"My friend at school . . . my doxing buddy . . . she found something new on Rachel," I said, feeling quite excited.

Mom and Annie craned their necks backward to look at me.

"What?" Mom asked eagerly.

"She found an address in Lynn where Rachel and Isabella used to live," I said.

CHAPTER 46

GRACE, ANNIE, AND JACK were no more than a quarter mile from the spot where Rachel Boyd's murder had taken place. Duke Street, a narrow, one-way road in Lynn, featured a mix of multi-family units and single-family homes, most of which had yards with no landscaping of any kind. These homes had tired exteriors that would never make a magazine cover, but inside were the real stories, the ones of love, joy, sadness, and triumphs of the families who resided there. 17 Duke Street, where Rachel and Isabella—as she was known back then—once lived, was a small, box-shaped home with a pitched roof and vinyl siding, but it appeared to be one of the newer and nicer homes on the block.

Grace imagined Rachel standing on the wooden stairs of this tiny house, which someone had painted light blue with dark blue shutters. She could picture her making a visor with her hand, checking to see that her baby girl was playing safe and sound in the front yard styled after Edgewater: a dirt patch with some tufts of grass.

After undoing the latch on a rusty, waist-high chain-link fence encircling the property, Grace followed a well-trodden path up a narrow staircase that carried her about four feet off the ground. She rang the doorbell while an American flag flapped in the breeze near her face. She had a passing thought that one of Vince Rapino's cronies lived here, or maybe somewhere on this street, that he'd see her ringing the doorbell and she'd get paid another visit, this one much worse than the last. She let go of that fear and rang the doorbell a second time.

A window in the white house next door opened up and a woman's hard-bitten face appeared. She had jowly cheeks that moved independently from the rest of her, and Grace put her age anywhere from a stunningly old forty-five to a far sprightlier sixty-five. Even from a distance, the woman's blue eyes shone with bright inquisitiveness. She wore no makeup, which made her thin lips appear more compressed. When she stuck her head out farther, Grace got a good look at her mane of straw-colored hair that grew in the same untamed manner as the shrubs dotting her yard.

"You Jehovah's Witnesses?" she asked in an accent that was unmistakably Boston.

"No . . . we're not," Grace said.

"Good, 'cause my neighbors ain't home and I was about to tell you screw off," said the woman.

"Do you know who lives here?" asked Grace.

"You're ringing the doorbell. Don't you?"

Grace came down the steps, crossed the yard, and went to the fence separating the two properties. Jack and Annie joined her there.

"I'm Grace. This is my son, Jack, and my sister-in-law, Annie."

"Yeah, all right," said the woman. "Wicked happy to meet ya." It was apparent she couldn't have cared less who they were, so long as they weren't from the sect of Jehovah.

"I'm wondering about this house," Grace went on to say.

The woman poked her head out farther and made a show of looking around the yard. "No For Sale sign," she said.

"No, not to buy it . . . but . . . have you lived here long?"

The woman pulled back a bit, and Grace worried she had scared her off.

"What's it to you?" she asked.

"I'm wondering if you knew . . . Rachel Boyd?" Grace inquired.

A sad look came to the woman's face. "Everyone knew Rachel."

"She lived here?" Jack asked, pointing to the blue house.

"Yeah, she was my neighbor for a bit. Like fourteen years ago."

"Did you know her well?"

"What do you care?"

Grace's mind went blank, but Annie's thankfully did not. "We're relatives, actually. We did one of those DNA test things and found out Rachel is Grace's half sister. We looked her up and, well . . . saw the terrible news."

"Terrible," the woman agreed.

"We really do appreciate your help," said Grace. "We didn't get your name." She prayed this woman didn't have a great recall for faces and wouldn't remember seeing hers on TV back when Rachel's murder broke on the local news.

"Bonnie," the woman said. "Bonnie Blakely, born and raised right here in beautiful Lynn, Massachusetts." She leaned her substantial body out the window and stretched her arms wide as if opening herself up to receive not only the goodness of a cloudless day, but also all of the beauty that lovely Lynn had to offer.

"We've been trying to learn about Rachel," Annie said. "We did a public records search and this address came up, so we stopped by hoping to talk to neighbors, people who knew her, see if we could learn more about her, maybe connect with other family."

"Well, don't go looking for her crazy daughter," Bonnie warned.

"Yeah, we read about that, too," said Grace, hoping she did a good job masking her emotions. "Terrible."

"Did anyone else live here with her?" asked Annie.

"Nah, she was on her own. Single mom kind of thing."

"No boyfriends?" Grace didn't know how the question would go over, but she was hoping to hear that Rachel and Vince had been an item back then. It would bolster the theory that Rapino was Penny's biological father and Rachel's murder was some sort of retribution for attempted extortion.

"Supposedly there was a guy . . . that crazy girl's father . . . but I don't know. We keep our private affairs private around here. Heard things, though, you know?"

"What kind of things?" Annie asked.

"Fights . . . yelling . . . screaming . . . but eh, that's like birdsong on this damn street."

"Do you think she was . . . battered?" Annie thought to ask.

"Only so many times a person can fall down the stairs," Bonnie said, which was answer enough.

"Did you know Vince Rapino?" Grace decided to go for broke. "Was he around much? Was he the boyfriend?"

"Rapino? The auto guy? Hell if I know. Whoever it was didn't want to be seen, that much I can tell you. Came and went mostly at night. Didn't want to be a part of that kid's life, and I only know that because Rachel would complain about him, but she'd never tell us his name. Nobody knew who that kid's father was, and really what business was it of ours, anyway?"

"So why'd she move away?" Jack asked.

Bonnie produced a hearty laugh. "Hard to live in a place when there's no house."

"No house?" asked Grace.

"Look around ya," Bonnie said, motioning to the tired-looking homes lining Duke Street. "That house there might be small, but it's the newest on the block."

"Why's that?" asked Annie.

"Because a bunch of years ago, the house on that there lot was nothing but a pile of ash."

"A fire?" Jack asked.

"Arson," said the woman. "That crazy girl who killed her mama? She put a curtain inside the toaster and let it heat up until it caught fire. Burned the whole place down. Miracle my house didn't go up in flames, too. I thought DCF would get involved, but the police chalked it up to shit happens. Look, I gotta go. Sorry I can't be of more help."

Bonnie slipped back into her dark house, closing the window before Annie could say good-bye. Grace wasn't thinking about issuing a polite farewell. All her thoughts were on the single sentence Chloe had uttered . . .

Burned it all up, but she didn't go away.

CHAPTER 47

WHEN MITCH GOT HOME from work that night, he tried to distract himself with some mindless television, but it was to no avail. He was still ruminating on his dinner yesterday with Adam and Caitlyn at the rehab facility where his son remained a resident. The conclusion of his thirty-day program was in sight, and he wished to extend his stay another thirty, a request to which Mitch readily agreed.

If he wasn't thinking about Adam, and his failures as a father, he was thinking about Penny and worries that he was going to fail her, too. The trial was fast approaching, and he knew the verdict was very much in doubt, but at least now he could take the stand and answer Navarro's questions about DID and the case with something of a different mindset. He understood it was within his power to do everything he could to help this girl, but just as with Adam's recovery, the ultimate outcome was not within his control. He was free to fail, which meant he was free to try his best, time and time again—and what more could anyone expect or ask of him?

He wished he had more to give Navarro. Something was missing from Penny's story, something vital. He was sure of it. In their work together Penny had revealed much to him, but not the most important information. What happened that night?

He went to his desk in the study, which was really Adam's bedroom, and spread out the drawing Chloe had done. His focus went to the billowing smoke pouring out of the toaster.

Grace had shared with him the shocking discovery she'd made on her trip to Duke Street. Young Penny, or Isabella, age three and a half, or four, had burned down her house by putting a curtain inside the toaster.

Grace had used the drawing and what Chloe had said—"Burned it all up, but *she* didn't go away"—to target Maria, but now he thought it was conceivable, probable even, that it wasn't symbolic at all. It was an *actual* memory from her past.

So who is she? Mitch asked himself. *Is she Rachel? Or was Penny trying to rid herself of an alter?*

Was the fire an attempt to escape from some peril, or did it mark the initial appearance of an uncontrollable rage within?

Questions . . . questions . . . questions . . .

Mitch recalled what Penny and her alters had said about her birth mother while experiencing episodes of dissociation.

She'd get the bucket.

She'd go to prison.

She'd be hurt.

Those weren't fears of Rachel. They were fears *for* her, Mitch realized with growing excitement.

She didn't want Rachel to suffer. She wanted Rachel to leave Duke Street . . . but she didn't get away.

The bucket of ammonia.

Mitch considered the possibility that it wasn't some torture on the night of the murder as they'd all believed, but rather, like the drawing of a smoking toaster, it was a specific memory from the past.

Abuse. Fear.

Penny wanted her mother to get away from her abuser. Grace mentioned some violence in the Duke Street home.

"But she didn't go away." Rachel didn't leave. That happened all the time, he knew. Abused women stay. They're too frightened to leave, or they have no place to go. Maybe Rachel didn't abandon Penny as everyone was led to believe . . . maybe Rachel had left Penny in the park that day to get her to safety.

A realization struck Mitch hard. If the memories that Penny and her alters shared with him were recollections from her distant past, why then did she need to be in a dissociative state to access them?

The answer was both obvious and elusive. He recalled Grace's words regarding the day they found Penny—how the little girl in the sweet yellow dress wouldn't talk, wouldn't say anything about what happened, wouldn't even answer to her name, so Jack named her Penny.

She was traumatized, they were told.

They found her. They picked her up. She was their good luck.

Why wouldn't she talk about what happened? Why didn't she pine for her mother, who she had wanted to help, to save?

The answer came to Mitch in a flash, and with it a fierce chill ripped through his body. He saw it now and couldn't believe he hadn't seen it before. The Duke Street fire had opened his eyes. He had to call Grace. He needed to meet with her right away.

Everyone needed to hear what he had to say.

CHAPTER 48

AFTER HOURS AND THEY were back at Big Frank's—all of them, Ryan too—gathered around a large table, eating pizza and waiting for Mitch. He'd called, but wouldn't say over the phone what he wanted to talk about, only that it was important to the case and better discussed in person. Grace had been working a shift, trying to appease Ryan, and Mitch had offered to meet there.

Her sons were being icy with each other, but Grace noted how Ryan seemed extra annoyed when Jack brought up the dissociative state Eve went into while looking at the atlas.

"'There's a picture on his arm. I can see the picture,'" said Jack, reciting Eve's words.

"We think it's Vince Rapino," Annie said for Ryan's benefit.

"That man has more paint on his arms than anyone," said Grace.

Pushing his chair back, Ryan rose quickly to his feet, a fierce look on his face. "I've had enough of this for one night. Actually, for one lifetime," he announced. "I'm going to help Sarah clean up and get out of here. Mom, you've got the keys, so you can lock up. I've got the cash. I'll make the deposit in the morning. It's not a windfall, but business has picked up a bit the last few days. Guess the pretrial buzz is helping out." He gave a wave in everyone's general direction. "Later, all." And off he went to the kitchen.

Jack watched him go, waiting until he'd disappeared through the swinging door before he spoke. "You know," he said, whispering in a conspiratorial way, "Ryan was pre-law before he dropped out of school. Someone like that knows how to put a person in prison."

A flash of anger struck Grace hard, turning her cheeks bright red. "What are you saying, Jack? Are you accusing Ryan of . . . of what?"

"I'm saying what I said before. Ryan blames Penny for Dad's death, and he's been acting very strangely since her arrest."

"Do you think Ryan killed Rachel? For . . . for God knows what reason—and that he's letting his sister take the fall for it? Is that it, Jack?" Grace spoke in a sharp-edged voice.

"I don't know," Jack said, sounding defensive. "It's just weird, is all— the timing of him dropping out of school, his anger toward Penny . . . you know. I'm just saying, we shouldn't close ourselves off to any possibility."

"Well, I'm not going to consider that one," Grace said forcefully, trying to block out the image of her son plunging a knife into the belly of an innocent woman—his sister's birth mother, at that.

"What about what Chloe told us?" Annie asked, delivering a needed change in subject. "'Burned it all up, but she didn't get away.'"

"Burned it up like the house on Duke Street," said Jack.

The discovery had left Grace wondering if those burn scars on Penny's forearms, which the doctors had noted way back when, weren't in fact from a curling iron but from the fire that had consumed her home.

"That is a bit of a sideways turn," Annie admitted. She blew on the tip of a second slice of cheese pizza before giving it a bite. "I thought the fire in that drawing had something to do with Maria," she said while chewing.

Grace still had her doubts about Maria's innocence, but didn't have time to voice them. Mitch arrived with apologizes for running late. To

Grace, he looked breathless and out of sorts; nervous, too. He took a seat and got caught up on the earlier discussion.

"It could be Penny's subconscious is at work here, and the fire in the picture Chloe drew is symbolically connected to Maria, not a specific reference to Duke Street. The subconscious mind works in symbols because it's the most efficient form of communication. So it's possible, but I don't think that's the case. I think the drawing and fire are *strongly* linked."

Grace nodded her head. "I do too, Mitch."

"But here's where it gets tricky," Mitch said. "Penny, Ruby, Chloe, Eve—they've all experienced a dissociative state in Edgewater that's characteristically been the same. I'd call it dreamlike, trancelike, either way—different from the prior personality state, correct?"

Grace nodded. "That's right," she said. "So when she's in that trance-like state, is that the fourth alter, the one we've been thinking is hiding from us?"

"I don't think so," Mitch said, and something in his eyes, his voice hinted at trouble.

Grace studied him with curious intent. "What is it then?"

"We thought it was Chloe who told us she burned it up, but she didn't go away. We also thought it was a memory from the night of the murder, but now we know it was from her distant past. What if it wasn't *Chloe's* memory we were accessing, and what if all the recollections we heard—'she'll go to prison' . . . 'I wasn't alone' . . . the ammonia, even—what if it *all* came from Penny's distant past, same as the toaster on fire?"

Grace sat back in her chair, stunned. "Are you suggesting everything we've learned, everything Eve, Ruby, Chloe, and Penny herself have told us, is *all* from the same time period?"

"What I may have done here—unwittingly, I'll give you that," Mitch said, "is help Penny tap into her subconscious mind to access memories she's blocked out, maybe even memories of the traumatic experience or experiences that caused her personality to splinter in the first place."

Grace's mouth hung open. She'd never considered that possibility, and the implications felt shattering.

"If it's all from the past, then what Penny told us about her not being alone is from the past, too. That means she was most likely alone that night and she *killed* Rachel."

"Maybe," Mitch said. "We still don't have a good explanation for the rope restraints."

"She tied herself up to stop herself from committing murder," Jack suggested. "She was at war with her own self."

"Possible," Mitch said. "Or Rachel tied her and somehow she escaped. But that's not what I called you all together to discuss. Penny, and each of Penny's alters, needed to be in a dissociative state to access these memories. Why? That's the question I've been asking myself, and the answer I think was there all along. They weren't *Penny's* memories."

"So it *is* a new alter?"

"But these are memories from the *past*," Mitch clarified. "Think about the park. You found Penny. She couldn't tell you anything about what happened to her . . . who dropped her off . . . why . . . she wouldn't even answer to her name. And, she didn't cry for Rachel. Why is that?"

"She was traumatized," said Jack. "That's what the psychologists and social workers said. She wouldn't tell us anything because the abandonment was traumatic for her and Rachel probably abused her."

Annie's expression turned unsettled. "Oh God," she said, putting her hands to her mouth.

"Are you suggesting . . . ?" Grace fumbled for the words, her color blanching.

"I'm suggesting that Penny couldn't answer your questions that day, or the day after, or the day after that—couldn't tell you what happened to her, didn't know who put her in the park, didn't respond to her name, didn't miss Rachel—because *she* had no memories to share. Because Penny herself . . . is an alter."

Everyone went silent. The air seemed to still. No one moved. No one spoke. Grace sat a moment, her mind a blank. Soon, thoughts collected and she found her will to engage. She'd lost a husband already, and now, in a way, a daughter as well. She was a woman hardened from experience, so perhaps that's why Mitch's revelation, startling as it was, would not get her down and keep her there.

"So what now?" Grace asked.

"From a therapeutic standpoint, nothing changes," Mitch said. "The goal is still integration. And it doesn't change our strategy at her trial, though I imagine Navarro would have to confirm that."

"But we don't know who she is, really . . . who is the real girl? Who is my daughter?"

Grace sighed as she looked around the table for answers.

"I think she's Isabella Boyd," said Mitch. "Has to be. Penny's kept her under wraps for years . . . she picked a shy, uncertain, and modest persona to adopt because it gave her primary self a buffer zone from which she could keep people at a distance.

"Then adolescence brought on a volcanic change of hormones that may have triggered the emergence of her other alters. The work I did with Penny helped open up a pathway to the primary self. That's what I think we've been seeing. Honestly, it's a very positive step toward integration."

"What about all the things she told us?" Grace asked. "The bucket of ammonia—she wasn't alone—gone and gone for good—what about all that?"

Mitch shook his head glumly. "I don't have all the answers . . . can't say how it fits together to be honest," he confessed. "But I am sure of one thing: that mysterious fourth alter we've been searching for has been with us all along."

CHAPTER 49

THAT WAS A SHOCK, Penny.

I should keep calling you that, right? You're still my sister, even if you are an alter. I surprised myself with how quickly I adjusted to the idea that you aren't really you. I know it was painful for Mom to think the child she'd raised, loved, and nurtured from age four was a mask of sorts for your true self. When I came up with the name Penny, it must have felt good enough for you to embrace as part of this new identity you'd assumed.

And it was Penny who was on trial for murder.

The first day of your trial happened on the first day of August. We were in the old brick courthouse, not the new glass-and-steel addition that had working air-conditioning.

Your trial took place in Salem, Massachusetts, a city notorious for its witch trials. I wonder if you felt a deep kinship to those poor souls. If you'd been born back then, if people knew of the others occupying your body, no doubt you'd have been found guilty of witchcraft and executed by hanging or left to rot in some rat-infested cell.

But on this day, you were in a carpeted courtroom that smelled like a new car. Under the fluorescent lights, the wood benches in the spectator section gleamed with heavy applications of varnish. The air tasted sweetly scented, a mix of colognes and perfumes. You'd been told it was best to be as understated as possible in court, don't stand out in any way—a tall order for someone who was the featured attraction. Even so, you looked appropriately subdued in clothes Mom brought from home. I'd seen you wear that outfit to church before, but now, with all the weight you'd lost, the pants no longer fit like they once did. I know you didn't like the white top, but the line pattern was done in neutral grays.

"Black gives the impression of power, not humility," Navarro had advised.

You were being tried as an adult, but cameras were not permitted in the courtroom. Ironically, video was allowed, but the gaggle of reporters occupying a large section in the back had to share a single feed from the lone video camera. I'm sure everyone in our hometown, former friends and neighbors, were streaming the trial online, gawking at you like a freak in a circus sideshow.

I could feel leering eyes boring into the back of your skull. A soft murmur filled the room with white noise, which made me think of an audience talking before a show begins.

To settle your nerves, Attorney Navarro gave you clear instructions.

Keep your emotions to yourself.

Don't smile.

Don't frown.

Don't look away in disgust.

Don't nod your head.

Don't shake your head.

"The jury will make assumptions about everything you do," Navarro warned. "'She's too remorseful, she's not remorseful enough, she's too sincere, she's not sincere enough'—everything gets judged in here, so sit as perfectly still and calm as you possibly can, don't react to anything you hear, do exactly as I say, and you'll do just fine."

These directions, given quite clearly, kept Eve away and Penny in the courtroom. Quite a wily defense system you've constructed in that marvelous head of yours. When you needed ferocity, you had Eve, and when you needed quiet and stillness, you could be Penny.

So who were you when Rachel died?

I guess that's the question everyone wants answered.

On the opposite side of the aisle, seated at the table across from you, was the assistant district attorney, Jessica Johnson. She had dark hair, expressive eyes to match, and mocha-colored skin. I know little about Jessica other than she graduated from Suffolk Law School, has a seven-year-old daughter, and at one time was a competitive tennis player.

The sounds of the courtroom filled my ears: the groan of a wood bench as a spectator shifted in her seat, the snap of a purse closing shut, the chirp of a phone powering down.

I watched the judge enter the courtroom with purposeful strides and take her seat at the bench. The nameplate in front of her read: JUDGE CLAIRE A. LOCKHART.

Judge Lockhart was about Mom's age. Her face was bronzed in what couldn't be a natural shade, and her eyes were ringed darkly with mascara so they stood out on her face. Dark roots were visible on her stylish shoulder-length hair, which she proceeded to tuck behind her ears. The attention she called to her ears, to her eyes—it's like this judge wanted to make sure everyone knew she would see and hear everything that happened in *her* courtroom. Her dark robe was more like a cloak, and she radiated authority like a regal presence.

"Please be seated."

All retook their seats. I felt like I'd drunk rocket fuel that morning instead of coffee.

"All right, good morning, everyone," Judge Lockhart said in an officious voice.

Attorney Johnson spoke from a standing position at her table, papers and binders strewn in front of her. "Good morning, Your Honor. This is the State of Massachusetts versus Penny Isabella Francone, 2277 CR 1011, first-degree murder. The state is ready to proceed, Your Honor.

We do have some pretrial motions from both sides. We will take those in whatever order the court pleases."

The motions were settled quickly. No issues there.

The prosecutor's opening statement was blistering and brutal.

"When this trial is over, ladies and gentlemen of the jury, you will have no doubt that Penny Isabella Francone, this defendant"—and Attorney Johnson pointed to you—"intentionally and savagely slaughtered her birth mother, Rachel Boyd, murdering her in her home." She gave the jury Rachel's address in Lynn. "The defendant had the opportunity to be alone with Rachel that night, and used a knife taken from Rachel's kitchen to stab the victim twenty-three times in her arms, chest, and abdomen before brutally slashing her throat."

Attorney Johnson didn't move around a lot, but occasionally she'd glance at her notebooks.

"The evidence will show that the defendant was completely aware of her actions, had fantasized about killing before, had made threats to kill before—even made written threats to kill the victim—and was completely sane at the time of the murder. You will hear from an expert witness on dissociative identity disorder, who will testify that Penny believes she possesses multiple personalities. Let me repeat the key part of that: Penny *believes*.

"But these beliefs, as the evidence will show, do not—let me repeat—do not meet the legal definition of insanity. Through the defendant's own words and actions, you will learn, and the evidence will show, that the defendant was completely aware of her actions and knew exactly why she did it. Rachel Boyd, the victim here, was a symbol for this defendant's anger and resentment at the world. The defendant acted in retribution for being abandoned by her birth mother years ago in a park, and that fermenting anger, combined with her dark desire to kill, led to this atrocious crime for which the defendant now stands accused.

"Ladies and gentlemen, we may never know exactly what was going through the defendant's mind at the time of the killing, but not knowing *why* the defendant slaughtered Rachel Boyd does not mean the defendant is not responsible for the murder. It merely means that there is no good answer.

"As you know, the defendant has entered a plea of not guilty by reason of mental disease or defect. Judge Lockhart will instruct you on the elements of the law pertinent to this case. If you find the defendant not guilty, you will have to believe that the defendant was unable to understand or control what she was doing at the time of the killing, and lacked awareness that what she was doing was wrong.

"But, ladies and gentlemen, what the evidence will show is that the defendant acted cruelly and deliberately when she murdered Rachel Boyd in cold blood, that she understood what she was doing, and that she knew what she was doing was terribly wrong."

She paused to take a breath.

"I expect you'll hear testimony from a doctor who has only recently begun treating the defendant, that she has no memory of the murder, and that she's inhabited by other personalities, including the one who has expressed dark and violent fantasies, written about them extensively, and that these personas—or alters, as they're referred to in the evidence—will make her not guilty of any crime. But the evidence will show that this diagnosis is in reality nothing more than an elaborate fantasy world created out of convenience and used as an excuse for this defendant to live out her deepest, darkest, and most depraved desires."

And we were off.

CHAPTER 50

TRIAL DAY 11
STATE OF MASSACHUSETTS VERSUS PENNY FRANCONE

SHE'S SITTING IN HER seat at the counsel table designated for the defense team. Her attorney, Greg Navarro, occupies a chair to her right. She's waiting for the big moment when she'll be called to the witness stand to testify in her own defense.

She knows her name is Penny Francone, that she's been accused of killing Rachel Boyd, and that Rachel Boyd is her birth mother. She knows this from flickers of memories of conversations she's had with her mother, Grace, in a place called Edgewater, and because Attorney Navarro has told her so. She's been told that Eve was the mainstay at Edgewater, which explains all of her memory gaps—those weren't her memories to retain. But there's something else feeding her awareness. It's like a strange voice prattling inside her head, less of a whisper and more like a *knowing,* as if she's experienced things she has no recollection of ever having done.

She doesn't remember much of the time she spent locked up in Edgewater, but that *knowing* tells her she has lived there for quite a while. She knows she has multiple personalities inside her, and that the memories of her life inside Edgewater, possibly the memories of the murder itself, belong to one of her alters—probably to a girl named Eve. She's the dark one. She also has no recollection of plunging a knife time and time again into Rachel's body, but then, she's lived with lost time for most of her life. It's always so confusing that really anything feels possible, even herself committing a brutal murder.

She is wearing gray pants and a slim-fitting white blouse that her mother brought from home. She misses home, misses her mother, her family, her life. She looks behind her and sees her mother sitting in the front of the courtroom along with Jack and Aunt Annie.

To her surprise, Ryan is there, too, even though she knows he doesn't like her. Ryan still blames her for their father's death. *Maybe he's over it,* she hopes, *and that's why he's come.* She wants to wave to her family, but knows that's something she cannot do. Anything she does might influence the jury, Attorney Navarro warned. She's been told to sit still and be quiet like a good girl, so that's what she does. She is that girl.

She sees Dr. McHugh in the row behind her mother. The courtroom lights make his silver hair shine and his neatly trimmed beard glow. She has only a few memories of Dr. McHugh from Edgewater—for example, she can recall meeting him on the day she found out she was living in a special hospital that kept patients in handcuffs. That *knowing* feeling returns to tell her that Eve has spent a lot of time with Dr. McHugh.

There is much she can't remember.

But she remembers this trial. Every day of it she has been Penny Francone.

The trial started on August 1, with twelve jurors selected plus two alternates. The prosecution called thirty-two witnesses to the stand. There were a number of police officers. Several of them had investigated Rachel's murder, and others arrested her for that crime. The jurors saw diagrams and pictures of Rachel's home. There was evidence—bloodstained clothes that belonged to her; her anchor pendant necklace, also bloodstained—all kept safe and contamination-free inside sealed evidence bags.

A medical examiner working for the prosecution testified about the wounds to Rachel's body, and Maria Descenza shared murder fantasies that she claimed to have written with Eve, which is why Penny has no memory of them. A doctor who never treated her testified that DID wasn't a real diagnosis, and a terrible man named Vincent Rapino glared at her angrily from the witness stand. He looked like he wanted to kill her.

Rapino told the jury that he and Rachel were going to get married and live happily ever after, until someone took her life. He said "someone" while glaring across the courtroom right at her, and there was nowhere for her to hide.

Then the prosecution rested its case, and now it was Attorney Navarro's turn to present the defense.

He called eleven witnesses over five days in court. Mom, Jack, Ryan, and Annie all testified about her mental illness. They told stories of her life, including things about a cat, a rock, a girl named Ruby, and a boy named Troy. She remembers the day Troy came to the house, but only because she was so scared. He pointed at her and called her Chloe. He was so sure of it, too. Back then she didn't know what was happening, but now she knows—she and Chloe are different but the same.

Dr. Mitch testified that she has DID, and that DID is a real condition. He said it was possible she was in a dissociative state when she killed Rachel, and played videos of her saying things she has no memory of saying. He used the words "brief, transient psychosis," and talked of her medications. He showed the jury a drawing she made as Chloe—a drawing she doesn't remember making.

She wishes the jury could climb into her mind, experience lost time the way she does. Then they'd believe, and they'd never want to go inside her head again. It's so lonely and confusing in there. She wants to cry just thinking about it, but she knows the rule: don't show any feelings.

She does have a vague awareness of being in the apartment on the night of Rachel's murder, that knowing feeling at work, and looking out the window at a figure standing across the street. She checked again, and the figure was gone. Somehow she knows that figure was familiar to her. But who was it?

Now it's her turn to talk. It is sweltering in the courtroom, no air-conditioning, a hard to breathe kind of hot. Sweat beads up her neck and drips down her back. The jury will think she's nervous and they'll be wrong. She's not nervous. She's utterly terrified. She wants Eve, the knowing tells her that she'd handle this better, or Ruby, but they won't come. For reasons she doesn't understand, they've abandoned her when she needs them the most. She looks back at her family. Jack sends her a thumbs-up sign. She looks at her attorney. He does the same.

The time has come to finally tell her story.

What little she knows of it.

Attorney Navarro, dressed in a sharp-looking blue suit, rises to his feet and says, "Your Honor, the defense calls Penny Isabella Francone to the stand."

A murmur rises from the gallery that stops as suddenly as it starts with one strike of the judge's gavel.

Attorney Navarro, too, has sweat on his forehead, and the collar of his shirt is stained with sweat as well.

This is a moment she thinks she'll never forget—the tap of her shoes against the carpeted floor; the heat on the back of her head not only from the still air but from all the eyes watching her as she gets settled in the witness box.

"Please stand," says a clerk.

She stands.

"Raise your right hand. Do you promise that the testimony you shall give in the case before this court shall be the truth, the whole truth, and nothing but the truth, so help you God?"

"I do," she says softly.

Attorney Navarro starts asking her questions. "Please state your full name for the record."

Her heart is beating like a bass drum, so hard and fast she can't believe the microphone isn't picking up the sound. She says, "Penny Isabella Francone." She answers each of Attorney Navarro's questions one by one, mindful to keep her emotions under control just as she'd been told.

"I live at Edgewater State Hospital."

"The court ordered me there."

"I've been accused of murder."

"I've been accused of killing Rachel Boyd."

"Rachel Boyd is my birth mother."

"Yes, I remember exchanging messages on Facebook with my birth mother."

Those messages are put on a screen, and she confirms the ones she wrote and what Rachel wrote back.

"Yes, she invited me to come to her apartment and asked that I come alone."

"I remember driving to Rachel's on the night of the murder."

"I took the car without asking. I had my driver's license."

"No, I don't remember getting into any arguments with Rachel. I don't remember seeing or talking to Rachel that night."

"I don't know if someone else was in the apartment with me or not."

"I don't remember standing in the middle of Rachel's living room, covered in blood."

"I don't know if I checked my body for cuts."

"I can't say what my state of mind was, or if I was confused."

"I don't remember hearing sirens or going to the window to look outside."

"I sort of have a *feeling* that I saw someone familiar-looking standing across the street under a streetlamp, but I don't remember telling that to anybody. Maybe an alter has that memory."

"The next memory I have after going into Rachel's apartment is my mother showing me a pepperoni pizza she bought for me even though I don't like pepperoni pizza."

"Yes, I realize that was a year and a half later."

"I think that's because an alter of mine named Eve took over to protect me, and she had all the memories of the arrest and Edgewater, not me."

"I don't remember telling Dr. McHugh I wasn't alone."

"I don't remember telling him I was scared about having my head put into a bucket full of ammonia."

"I think I was talking about the night of the murder when I said those things, but I don't really know."

"I don't recall ever having my head forced into a bucket full of ammonia."

Attorney Navarro asks more questions and she answers them. He looks pleased.

The judge suggests a recess before the prosecution starts their cross-examination. Everyone agrees. Attorney Navarro talks to her at the counsel table, drinking water because it's so hot. He takes his jacket off to cool off, and unbuttons his shirt sleeves. She watches him wipe the sweat off his brow and forearms using a cloth towel. He doesn't have an extra towel, but he offers to get her some paper ones from the bathroom. Her gaze is locked on him, and she can't look away. She stares blankly, nods her head, answering his question, but she feels funny now. Not faint from the heat, just . . . funny. Off.

"Do you need something to eat? Want a Coke? Anything?"

The last word repeats, then fades out until she can't hear what's being asked of her at all. Attorney Navarro's lips are moving, but she hears only a loud ringing in her ears, a high-pitched piercing sound, and soon her head begins to throb, powerful and pounding, like a sledgehammer thumping inside her skull.

The strangest sensation washes over her. She feels her body become weightless, but her eyes are heavy, and she fights off a strong urge to close them. She feels dizzy, as if she's stood up too quickly. Then a sensation like she's heading into a tunnel, with a point of light up ahead that beckons to her. The feeling is quite strange, but vaguely familiar. The knowing voice returns to tell her that the vanishing has begun.

Oh no, she thinks.

And that's the last conscious thought she has.

CHAPTER 51

JACK, SWEATING FROM THE HEAT, his long hair looking damp as if he'd showered not long ago, leaned over to his mother and whispered, "Something is wrong."

Grace agreed. Every day of the trial had been a blessing as well as a curse, because every day Grace got to spend time with Penny. She didn't understand why Eve had let Penny take the stand; Mitch couldn't explain it either.

"Edgewater is Eve, and outside its walls is Penny" was the best he could offer.

But now it wasn't Eve, or Penny, or Chloe, or any alter Grace knew of who'd taken the witness stand for her cross. When the judge resumed the trial, Penny didn't immediately move when she was called back to the stand. Navarro had to guide her to her seat, and she seemed utterly out of sorts getting settled in the box.

Grace glanced back at Mitch, who sat two rows behind her. He looked puzzled. Her eyes scanned the back of the courtroom, and they settled on Vincent Rapino on one side of the gallery, and Maria Descenza, with her mother Barbara accompanying, on the other. Their presence here was all it took to make Grace's skin crawl, but there was nothing she could do about it. Both Vince and Maria were as free as anyone to attend these sweltering-hot proceedings. No doubt they had come to court to hear Penny's testimony. But was it Penny who was about to testify? Grace wasn't so sure, and judging by Mitch's baffled expression, neither was he.

A vacant look invaded Penny's sweet eyes, as if she were under a hypnotist's spell, and her whole demeanor changed. In what Grace could only describe as an *Alice In Wonderland* moment, either the witness stand had grown larger, or her daughter had shrunk four sizes smaller.

Attorney Johnson began her cross.

"Ms. Francone, you say you had no memory of going to Rachel Boyd's house on the night of the murder. Tell me, what do you remember from that night?"

To Grace, it remained unclear if Penny could hear or understand what was being asked of her, and those were concerns the prosecutor appeared to share.

"Are you okay, Ms. Francone?" Attorney Johnson asked. Her tone was harsh, unaccommodating.

"I want to go home," came Penny's strangled response. From a distance, Grace could see tears well in her daughter's eyes.

"You're in a court of law. You can leave when court is adjourned for the day."

"I want to be with Mommy." Penny's voice sounded tiny and sad.

"Please don't offer commentary. Answer my questions directly."

Attorney Johnson showed Penny no compassion. She was there for one purpose only—to put the witness away for life. To win.

"What is the last thing you remember?"

"I was in my bedroom looking at the book my daddy gave me. The book I loved. The water made me want to take a bath so I asked Mommy if I could take a bath. So Mommy put me in the bathtub and she left to go talk to Daddy. They were fighting."

"Your mother put you in the bathtub?"

Navarro was on his feet in a flash. "Objection, Your Honor! This is badgering my witness!"

"Your Honor, I'm just following up on the witness's own statements with a logical next question. I find it curious that a then sixteen-year-old girl has her mother put her in the bathtub. I suspect she's not telling the truth and hasn't been telling the truth since the start of her testimony. This is helping to prove my case."

Grace thought otherwise. This girl on the witness stand was being perfectly honest, and Lord help her, she thought she knew why.

"Overruled," said the judge. "You may proceed."

"What is your mother's name?"

"Objection!" Attorney Navarro rose to his feet again in a huff. "Relevancy. We know this defendant's origin story."

"Overruled," said Judge Lockhart. "I'd like to hear the answer, but Counselor, this is your cross, so please, keep it under control."

"I'm not sure I can, Your Honor," Attorney Johnson warned, looking frazzled and uncertain. "Can you please tell us your mother's name?"

Silence.

Grace's heart thundered in her chest. Jack, Ryan, and Annie also had looks of deep concern.

"Can you please tell us your name?" Attorney Johnson said in a much kinder voice.

"Isabella," she said softly. "My name is Isabella Boyd, and I want to go be with Mommy now."

CHAPTER 52

GRACE GASPED, ALONG WITH everyone around her. Once again, Judge Lockhart banged her gavel hard.

"Order, order in my courtroom," she demanded.

"I want to go home," Isabella lamented sorrowfully in a shaky voice that portended tears.

"If you're Isabella Boyd, where do you reside?"

Her daughter did not answer. With a look of annoyance, Attorney Johnson placed her hands on her hips and repeated her question in a terse tone like she was scolding her.

"I said where do you reside? Please answer."

Grace understood the purpose now. Johnson was using language a child wouldn't understand, but Penny—no, not Penny, Isabella—looked bewildered and scared. She had no idea what was being asked of her.

"Where do you live?" Attorney Johnson said, sounding flustered that the trap she'd set hadn't sprung.

"I live with Mommy," said Isabella.

"In what town?"

"In Lynn."

Grace's fingers dug into her thighs. She could see Navarro shifting uneasily in his seat. He knew his client was in trouble, deep trouble, but he had no control now, this wasn't his witness, and his words of warning to Grace about putting Penny on the stand came barreling back at her. Grace was stunned, unsure how to feel. She worried for her daughter, but she also desperately wanted to know what book she'd been reading that she seemed to love so much.

* * *

Mitch had his phone out, hidden in his lap so the court officer wouldn't see it. He wanted to record everything being said, because now it was Isabella addressing the court. Something had triggered a switch, but what? And why to Isabella? The demeanor was similar to the dissociative states he'd observed. Quiet. Dreamy. Childlike.

He was right: she had switched to a new dissociative state in Edgewater several times, and they were slow and careful transitions to the little girl, Isabella Boyd. In those sessions, it had been the primary self, emerging like a butterfly from a chrysalis, bit by bit, and now, here in the courtroom of all places, the whole of the creature had at last appeared.

Mitch pondered the implications, and the possibilities got his blood tingling. He thought of Chloe. If she'd used advanced materials, acrylics or oil paints, to create her work, she might have presented at a more advanced age. The crayons, however, reminded her of the earliest days of her artistic pursuits and for that reason she presented much younger, with memories limited to that specific time period of her life. What did Isabella have for memories to choose from? A very limited supply, Mitch realized.

Then it came to him, a stunning conclusion that tilted his world.

Penny was the girl who'd gone to school, gotten an education, learned to read and write, gained all variety of skills, attained a host of expected developmental milestones and passed those along to her alters. Isabella, poor sweet child, had remained locked away like a prisoner in Penny's mind, trapped in something akin to a state of suspended animation. Isabella had gone into hiding as a four-year-old girl who'd been abandoned in a park, and a four-year-old girl she had remained.

She hid to escape some sort of abuse. But what exactly had Isabella endured? And, perhaps more importantly, who was the perpetrator?

Sweating profusely, Attorney Navarro shot back to his feet. "Your Honor, we need a recess! My client clearly isn't well."

"Your Honor, I admit this is a bit . . . unplanned," said Attorney Johnson uneasily, "but I do have the right to cross-examine the witness and see where it goes. To my mind, this appears to be very relevant to my case."

"Proceed, but I'm shortening your rope, Attorney Johnson."

"I know about rope," Isabella spoke up. "Daddy used rope to tie my hands when he was mad at Mommy."

"What do you mean, when he was mad at Mommy?" Johnson asked.

"I demand a recess," Navarro barked loudly.

Lockhart's expression hardened. "You may have enjoyed a military career before you became an attorney, Mr. Navarro, but here in my courtroom, you do not outrank me. You may ask for a recess, but I alone will make that determination."

Navarro slumped back into his seat, so apoplectic about the turn of events that he slammed his fist gavel-like on the counsel table. Judge Lockhart did not take kindly to his behavior.

"That will do, Counselor," she snapped at him. "One more outburst like that and I'll consider a contempt charge."

"Do you need to take a break?" Judge Lockhart asked the witness.

"I don't have to stop if you don't want me to," Isabella answered politely.

"Good. I'm curious now," Attorney Johnson said.

"I think we all are," Judge Lockhart concurred. "Proceed."

"You say your daddy tied up your hands?" Johnson continued.

"Yes," Isabella answered.

"Who is your daddy?"

"Objection!" Navarro shouted. "Your Honor, we are making a mockery of these proceedings. This is a murder trial!"

"I know what this trial is about, Attorney Navarro," Judge Lockhart shot back. "You needn't remind me—though it appears I need to remind *you* that it's not your turn anymore. The prosecution has a right as set forth in our rules of law to question her witness now in a manner she sees fit. And if she wants this young woman to name her father, then by all means, I'd like to hear the answer."

Navarro slumped back into his seat. He looked around the courtroom, as if in search of a fire alarm to pull. Sweat rained down his face. He took off his suit jacket, rolled up his sleeves, and dabbed his brow dry with the towel.

"I don't know his name. I called him Daddy," Isabella said, answering the judge. "But I couldn't call him that when he was in the house because he didn't like me, so I didn't call him anything. That's what Mommy said. She said Daddy didn't want me . . . he didn't like me."

Grace moved back a row to sit with Mitch. He could see the pain in her eyes. This poor sweet child, to be rejected that cruelly by a parent, to think she wasn't wanted or loved—when all Grace had ever wanted was a daughter to raise, to give her a place to call home forever and always.

"Daddy never came for Christmas or birthdays or anything . . . but he did give me something once."

"Oh, he did? What was it? Do you remember?"

"It was a book . . . it was the only present he ever gave me. I loved that book because I loved my daddy, even if he didn't love me."

Grace whispered to Mitch, "A book with boats and water on the cover?"

Mitch returned a shrug, but he assumed it was so.

"Who's your mommy? Do you know her name?" Johnson asked.

"Rachel . . . Rachel's my mommy."

"Do you remember hurting the victim?"

Mitch noted how she didn't use the word "murder," and called Rachel either "Mommy" or "victim"—all very intentional, he thought, all designed to trip her up, blow the cover, expose the lie. *This is a girl playing games,* Johnson was thinking. But Mitch knew better.

Isabella returned a blank stare, not because she was refusing to answer, but because, as Mitch had speculated, "victim" was not a word she'd learned by age four.

Instead, Isabella gave what she thought would be a pleasing response. Children that age want to please figures of authority, attorneys included.

She said, "I wanted Mommy to move away from Daddy because he was always mean to her . . . he hit her. He hated her. That's why I set the fire. I thought we'd have to go away, far away, but Mommy said Lynn was home so she got a new place to live close by."

"Your daddy hit your mommy?"

Navarro snapped to his feet. "Objection! This is a mockery!" he shouted.

"You will lower your voice, sir, and sit down," Lockhart scolded.

Isabella said, "He did. He hit her. He made her scared."

"Did he ever hit *you?*" Attorney Johnson asked.

Isabella's gaze went back to her lap and she nodded solemnly. "Yes," she said softly.

"So you know hitting and hurting someone is wrong?"

She was still trying, Mitch had to give her credit for that.

"Yes, I know it's wrong, you shouldn't ever hurt someone."

"But you hurt your mommy?"

Isabella shook her head vigorously. "No, I did not," she said, sounding on the verge of tears, her lips pressed together in a pout, cheeks sunken in. "I love my mommy. I wouldn't hurt Mommy."

"Did your daddy love your mommy?"

She shook her head again. "He said he hated her. He said it all the time."

"Did your daddy live with you?"

"No. He only came over when Mommy made him come see me, or she wanted money from him. He never wanted to see me."

"Do you know why your father didn't like you?" Johnson asked.

"Because I was alive," Isabella said woefully. "He said he didn't want me."

"He didn't want you to be alive?"

"He didn't want me to be born. He told Mommy that. That's why he never gave me a birthday present. Chloe was my sister. He didn't want her either, but she died in Mommy's belly and he said he was glad. He said he wished it happened to me, too. That's why when he came to get me, I thought he was going to kill me."

"Why did you think that?"

"Mommy and Daddy were yelling and fighting about money using loud voices. Daddy came to get me when I was in the tub and he said I was a very bad girl and he wished I was never born."

"Why did he come to get you?"

"He wanted to take me to Mommy. He let me put on pajamas and he pulled me by my arm and it hurt. He took me to Mommy in the basement. She had blood all over her face. I think he hit her. He told Mommy that she made him do it because she wouldn't do what he wanted. Then he put her head in a bucket of poison."

Mitch thought: *Ammonia. A common cleaning supply stored in a basement and easily accessible.*

"He made me watch. He said he was going to do it to me, too, if Mommy didn't leave for good. Mommy couldn't breathe right. So I hit my daddy on his back and told him I hated him and he got really mad and he hit my face. He called me a bad girl again. He tied up my hands with rope and said he'd put my head in the bucket next if Mommy wasn't gone and gone for good. Then Mommy started to cry."

Grace looked like she'd had her head put in that bucket as well, and Attorney Johnson appeared out of sorts, her attack failing.

Navarro was back on his feet, incensed. "Objection!" he shouted, his face smeared with rage. With his suit jacket off, Mitch could see the V-shaped sweat mark running down his back. It was hot as Hades in here, but Mitch's blood felt ice cold.

"This is completely out of control," Navarro shouted.

To Mitch's utter surprise, Navarro came out from behind his table to approach the witness in a threatening manner. This got Jessica Johnson's attention, and Judge Lockhart's as well. A court officer, wearing a crisp white shirt like those of the Edgewater guards, even took a step towards Navarro. There was a fire in Navarro's eyes, a simmering rage that seemed out of proportion to his frustration over the proceedings. He should have been pleased, because as hard as Johnson was working to trip up this witness, the jury was getting a firsthand look at someone, a teenage girl talking like a four-year-old, who clearly was meeting the criteria for criminal insanity.

"You will retake your seat this instant, Counselor, or I will hold you in contempt, do you hear me?" Judge Lockhart said, sending Navarro back to his proper place while Isabella, unaffected by his outburst, continued with her testimony.

"Mommy was crying . . . she wanted him to stop. She couldn't breathe with her head in the bucket. She said it burned her eyes and her throat. The rope hurt, but I couldn't get it off to help." Isabella's breathing became rapid and shallow.

"Oh my . . . okay . . . what happened next?" Attorney Johnson sounded less like a lawyer questioning a witness and more like a concerned police officer trying to ascertain facts from a traumatized victim. She appeared stunned and shaky on her feet. Her questions were losing focus and intent. This testimony had to be as shocking to her as it was to everyone else in the courtroom, but nobody more so than Grace.

"Daddy said he'd send her to jail forever if she didn't leave and take me with her."

Mitch thought of what Ruby had shared.

He said he'd put her in jail . . .

Other phrases from those sessions jumped out at him.

I wasn't alone.

Gone and gone for good.

I'd get the bucket too.

He was right. All of it, every dissociative state she'd experienced with him, brought up memories from her distant past. Which meant the state names she'd listed were from the past as well. But how? Everything Isabella shared appeared to belong to the same series of memories, a grouping of memories. Mitch had only asked her about each city and state individually, but didn't think of them as a group, or a pattern.

He took out a yellow legal pad from his workbag, as well as the black marker he used to sign prescriptions. In big letters, he wrote on a page:

HAVE JACK SEARCH THE CITIES AND STATES AS GROUP. LOOK FOR A PATTERN.

He handed the note to Grace.

Grace gave the note to Jack and returned to her seat beside Mitch.

"Did you try to get help for your mommy?"

"I couldn't help Mommy. I couldn't!" Isabella cried. "He hit her all the time. He wanted her to go away. He wanted me to go away. So I ran upstairs when he had her head in the bucket. I ran upstairs and went to my hiding place under the bed, the place I went to when Mommy and Daddy fought. Not under it . . . I hid *in* it."

"*In* it?" Attorney Johnson said. "Like you crawled under the covers?"

"It was a box. I crawled under the box. My hands were tied but I could move the boards to climb in. I laid down on the boards under the box and you couldn't see me even if you checked under the bed."

"You hid in the bed's box spring?" Attorney Johnson asked.

"It's a box. That's where I hid."

Grace's eyes went wide. She whispered to Mitch: "Penny did the same thing when she came to live with us. We couldn't find her. We thought she'd run away."

"How long did you hide in there?" said Attorney Johnson.

"I heard him coming up the stairs. I heard him looking for me." She stomped her feet on the floor of the witness stand.

Stomp. Stomp. Stomp.

"He was looking for me, but he couldn't find me."

Stomp. Stomp. Stomp.

Mitch had heard *tap, tap, tap* and figured it was a reference to the 911 phone call Rachel made, but that was wrong. It was Isabella remembering her father's heavy footsteps coming up the stairs . . . looking for her.

"I heard Mommy calling for me, too. But she couldn't find me either. They thought I'd gone outside, because I tripped and my necklace got caught on my finger and it broke. It fell by the front door, but I didn't stop to pick it up because I had to get upstairs to my hiding place."

"What necklace?"

"A necklace Mommy bought for me and said it was from Daddy, but I knew that was a lie because I heard her tell Bonnie that. Bonnie is our neighbor. Mommy told Bonnie she bought it for my birthday because Daddy never gave me presents."

"What was the necklace?"

"It was a necklace with an anchor.

"I heard Daddy come upstairs and he told Mommy that she better run. She better leave right now. Right now! Or he'd put her head back in the bucket and make her breathe that horrible stuff until she died. Mommy saw my necklace by the door and she thought I'd gone outside . . . she didn't know I was under the bed. But I was too scared to come out."

Jack got up from his seat, came to Grace, and handed her the piece of paper she'd passed to him.

There was a look in his eyes, and something passed between them. Grace unfolded the note and read what he'd written. Mitch couldn't see what was on the page.

When Isabella paused to catch her breath, Grace turned to Mitch. "I know . . . I know who it is," she stammered.

Mitch gazed back at her, stunned.

"I know who killed Rachel," Grace said urgently. "And he's here, Mitch. Help us all, he's been here all along."

CHAPTER 53

MITCH KEPT HIS GAZE locked on Grace as she rose from her seat to approach the bar. She took purposeful strides that drew the attention of Ryan, Annie, and Jack, who had to be wondering what the heck she was up to. When she glanced over her shoulder, Mitch got a good look at the rage in her dark brown eyes, and he knew whatever she was about to do, an earthquake was coming.

He unfolded the piece of paper. On it Jack had written:

Searched all the cities and states in a group. First result was a national defense book from 1996. There are boats and water on the cover. These aren't cities. These are ships. Navy ships.

Mitch looked up when Attorney Johnson asked, "When did you finally come out from under the bed?"

"I heard Mommy's car start up. She drove away. Then I heard Daddy's car start up. He drove away, too. So I went downstairs after everyone was gone. But I couldn't get my hands untied." She held up her hands once more to show Attorney Johnson as if they were still bound.

"I could turn on the TV. So I watched TV and I waited for Mommy to come get me."

"Did Mommy ever come home?"

Isabella shook her head slowly.

"No. She went away and didn't come back so she wouldn't get the bucket. But I went to the basement and poured the bucket into the toilet so she wouldn't get it again. I poured the bucket with my hands tied up, I could do that, but Mommy still didn't come home because she didn't know the bucket was gone."

Mitch read the last line of Jack's note.

> *Guess who has an anchor tattoo on his forearm? I saw it when he rolled up his shirtsleeve.*

"Who came to get you?"

"He did," Grace shouted in a booming voice that drew everyone's attention to her, but not only to her. Grace leaned her body over the bar separating the front of the courtroom from the gallery. With an outstretched arm, she aimed an accusatory finger across the courtroom, pointing it directly at Penny's attorney, Greg Navarro.

CHAPTER 54

Grace kept her distance from Navarro, but leaned over the gallery bar to make certain he knew she had him in her sights.

"You came back to the house to make sure Rachel was gone, didn't you . . . didn't you, you son of a bitch?" she raged.

Judge Lockhart slammed her gavel hard. "You . . . you're out of order!" she screamed. Navarro was on his feet, looking about the courtroom like a cornered animal. Court officers were on the move, closing in on Grace from both sides, several with their hands on the butts of their weapons.

"Did you cut a deal with Rachel, is that it?" Grace continued, undeterred despite the advancing threats. "Rachel got arrested for drug trafficking, and you were working in the public defender's office back then. You were her damn attorney. So what was the deal you made? You'd intentionally throw her case if she didn't sleep with you? Did you forget how babies were made, Navarro? She got pregnant with Isabella and Chloe, your twin daughters, and you . . . you did what? Tried to keep her quiet, keep it all contained, is that it?"

Judge Lockhart slammed her gavel, repeatedly demanding Grace be silenced.

"Daddy found me sitting on the floor watching TV," Isabella said as if nothing were going on around her. "He said Mommy was always asking him for money for me . . . and he was tired of paying . . . he told her to stop asking but she said she'd tell everyone who my daddy was . . . that's why he got so mad and made her go away and leave me . . . he took me to the park and he left me there.

"He told me if I said anything to anybody about what happened, if I ever told anyone his name, he'd come for me, and he'd put my head in the bucket, and he'd kill me in it, and he'd find Mommy and he'd kill her too. And he put a cloth to my face with that horrible stuff on it and I breathed it until it hurt my throat, so I knew he wasn't lying. He took me to the park and he left me there . . . he left me in the park . . . he left me all alone . . ." Isabella raised her arms as though her wrists were bound by invisible rope and pointed to Greg Navarro. "And I never told anyone my name. . . . I never broke my promise to Mommy that I wouldn't tell on him so he wouldn't hurt her. I went away, too. I got gone and was gone for good."

Grace sidestepped a lunging court officer, moving sideways toward the prosecutor's table.

"Why'd you kill Rachel?" she shouted at Navarro. "She came back, didn't she? You didn't expect it, but she came back to Lynn and threatened to expose you. She was blackmailing you, wasn't she? How many others are there? How many other female clients did you extort so you could get what you wanted? How many?"

"Grace . . . Grace, calm down now . . . you don't know what you're talking about," Navarro said with his back to the judge and witness.

Two guards came at Grace from both sides, and given the limited space in which to maneuver, there was nothing she could do to avoid them.

A male court officer jammed his foot into the back of Grace's knee, causing her body to buckle as if it were made of paper. As she went forward, a second officer cupped her right elbow with one hand and her neck with another, making it a controlled descent down to the floor. Ryan was on his feet in a flash, coming at the court officers like a charging buffalo.

A male court officer with the build of a trash can stepped in front of Ryan to block his way. The officer instinctively put his left leg back, widening his stance to give him more stability should Ryan try to go low. Indeed, Ryan did lower his shoulders as he barreled forward.

When the moment of contact came, Ryan had few options available to him. He grabbed the guard's front knee, but with one leg behind him, the court officer easily maintained his balance. With his hands free, the officer struck Ryan repeatedly with several forceful blows to the back of his head.

Ryan endured the pummeling as he attempted to stand. He managed to right himself, taking the officer's leg with him, when a second officer hit him from behind, dumping all three of them in a tangled heap on the ground.

Utter pandemonium broke out. Mitch sprang from his seat in time to see Vince Rapino fleeing through the rear doors of the courtroom. Through the crush of bodies packing the front of the gallery, he could see court officers snapping handcuffs around Grace's wrists. She somehow managed to keep her head turned so that her focus stayed on Navarro, who had wisely decided to sneak out with the crowd exiting from the rear of the courtroom rather than try one of the side doors, through which more court officers were arriving.

"Don't let him get away!" Grace cried out, in a pleading, desperate voice, and by "him" Mitch knew she meant Navarro. The mass exodus afforded Navarro plenty of cover in which to make his escape. He crossed over into the gallery section without attracting much attention—except from Mitch, who had sidled to the end of his row to ready himself for engagement. He stole a glance at the front of the courtroom and Attorney Johnson, who had had the foresight to go to Isabella.

Mitch rose up on his toes in an effort to locate Navarro, whom he saw pushing and shoving his way through the crowd. As fortune would have it, he was headed his way. Mitch waited until Navarro got three steps from him before he stepped out from his row and put his body in the center of the aisle, effectively blocking the only exit. He had expected Navarro to pause and think about his next move, but such was not the case.

Without hesitation, Navarro locked eyes on Mitch before sending a punch to his face that came with such speed and ferocity as to be completely unavoidable. The closed-fisted strike connected hard with Mitch's nose. He heard a crack and felt a stab of pain that turned his vision white.

Blood poured out of his broken nose like a pipe had burst in his head. His brain rattled violently in his skull, leaving him dizzy, his vision blurred, eyes watering. It was no use trying to stay upright. Mitch went down to his knees with a thud, but his body continued to block Navarro's way out. With effort and determination, he tried to stand, but did so with all the grace of a prizefighter failing the ten count.

Navarro effortlessly shoved Mitch aside, but before he could take another step toward freedom, a blur of motion behind Navarro's head caught Mitch's eye. He saw it a moment before impact, a silver streak cutting through the air at an incredibly high rate of speed.

An instant later, Mitch heard something hard, something metallic, smack into the side of Navarro's head with a satisfying thwack. It wasn't until the man went down to the ground beside Mitch that he realized it had been Annie's belt buckle that had felled him. Standing in the aisle was Annie herself, holding her leather belt like she was gripping the butt end of a whip in her hand. A large silver-and-gold-toned buckle, decorated with the scales of justice, dangled from the end of her belt, swaying back and forth, looking as heavy and lethal as a medieval mace.

Annie gave Navarro a second strike with the buckle to the back of his head for good measure as he tried to get up. Behind them, Jack came over the top of the gallery rows, leaping each with a hurdler's grace. When he got close enough, he dove with his arms outstretched onto Navarro's back. Momentum drove them both hard to the ground, Jack landing on top. He kept Navarro pinned until two guards came to pry them apart.

"He assaulted this man," Annie told one of the guards, pointing first to Navarro then to Mitch and his bloody nose. "I saw it happen."

The court officers seemed a bit uncertain as to what to do given Navarro's status. Luckily Navarro was too dazed, perhaps concussed, to offer any defense. Mitch was ready to make his case, but he didn't have to, because he heard Judge Lockhart's booming voice over the courtroom speakers.

"Do not let Attorney Greg Navarro leave this courtroom. I want that man under arrest for contempt of court! And God help us all, that's just the start."

Three courtroom officers joined together to wrench Navarro's hands unceremoniously behind his back. Mitch was thinking of Penny and Grace when he heard the click of the handcuffs being locked into place. He smiled a big, toothy grin as Navarro was brought to his feet and hauled away. Through it all, bloodied and battered, Mitch's smile never faded.

CHAPTER 55

GRACE WAS BACK IN Detective Jay Allio's office, at his invitation, to get an update on the case against Greg Navarro.

The big man looked out of sorts to Grace, baggy-eyed in a wrinkled shirt, but it was not surprising. Greg Navarro must have been keeping him and lots of detectives quite busy.

After Grace declined his offer of something to eat or drink, he started things off, appropriately enough, with an inquiry about Penny.

"She's doing great," Grace said. "Thank you for asking. It's good to have her home."

It had been a relatively peaceful time since Penny's homecoming a week ago. Ruth Whitmore came with Mitch, and she brought a jade plant as a gift for Penny, along with an invitation to the Massachusetts State House. Whitmore got what she had wanted—so much attention for Edgewater that the governor had no choice but to increase funding for the failing institution. The governor himself had requested a meet and greet with the star patient to show the public how much he truly cared.

"That man has less class than an empty schoolhouse," Whitmore quipped to Grace at Penny's party. "But I feel obligated to give him his photo op, so I deeply appreciate your willingness to participate."

"Since it was Eve most of the time, Penny doesn't really remember much about Edgewater," Grace told Whitmore that day, "but she wants to help the patients who are there; she feels a kinship. If it takes meeting the governor to secure your funding, she's happy to oblige."

There were plenty of tears and hugs that day, and lots of photos taken, including one of Penny, Mitch, and Grace. One photo Annie took had a streak of light near Penny's head. Annie remarked with a sad smile: "I bet you anything that's Arthur."

The most important thing was that Penny was home, safe and sound, where she belonged. She was back in her room, sleeping in her bed—one that didn't have a hiding place under the box spring.

Now that the party was past and the family had had time to settle into a new normal, there were other matters to address. She was curious to know what Allio had to share.

"Seven more women have come forward to accuse Navarro of using threats and coercion in exchange for sex. This guy was a piece of work. Word is he got shoved out of the public defender's office because of whispers. If it happened a few years later, he'd have been all swept up in the Me Too movement. Instead, it was Navarro who got swept under the rug. But I wanted you to hear it from me—the DNA test came back. Greg Navarro is your daughter's biological father."

"Thank you. I knew it, but it's good to have confirmation."

"Grand jury has indicted him on first-degree murder charges. You're not going to have to worry about him ever again. He's going away forever."

"I'll be happy to see him go," said Grace.

"Forensically speaking, this guy knew his business. I guess you get enough cons off the hook, you pick up a few tips and tricks along the way. Wasn't quite as good with the digital footprint."

"How so?"

"Those messages Rachel sent Penny? Navarro sent them from a dummy account he made."

Grace had suspected as much, but it still felt like a fresh betrayal to think that this monster, this monster with no conscience, had manipulated her daughter.

"Surprise, surprise, our forensics team found inconsistencies after examining Rachel's laptop and couldn't find any digital communication between Penny and Rachel. It was an inconsistency Navarro was told about in the discovery materials, not a case-breaking bit of evidence, lots of explanations for it, but I guess now we all know why he told you the opposite, and why it wasn't part of Penny's defense."

"I'm sure he wishes Dr. Dennis Palumbo never quit his job."

"I'd say you probably owe Dr. McHugh a debt of gratitude."

"Do you know how Navarro learned about Penny?"

"Two theories," said Allio. "As a public defender, he probably got wind of the pending case of two teen girls up on murder charges. He may have seen the backstory and put it together. Or, more likely, he came across the post Penny made after her arrest, the one that went viral. Either way, he found his biological daughter and when he decided he had to kill Rachel he had someone who could take the fall for his crime."

Navarro's machinations proved so devious they left Grace both horrified and awestruck.

"So when Penny got to the apartment . . . where was Rachel?"

"We think she was already dead," Allio said. "Our working theory is that Navarro lured Penny to Rachel's house using those Facebook messages sent from his phony account. He greeted Penny inside the home, maybe pretended to be someone in Rachel's life. Imagine him saying something like, 'Rachel's in the bathroom. She'll be out in a minute. She's so excited to meet you. Can I get you something to drink?'

"That drink came with a tranquilizer. Roofies, GBH—plenty of options, according to Navarro's Internet search history, which we got from his service provider thanks to a warrant. Guess he wanted to make sure Penny was completely immobilized while he cleaned up his crime scene, so he bound her wrists with rope. His one big mistake."

"Roofies . . . GBH . . . but he ordered a toxicology screen and—" Grace caught and corrected herself. "He said he ordered a tox screen, but he didn't."

"And the prosecutor didn't order one either. Why bother? They had their case in the bag."

"Wasn't Navarro worried about Penny remembering him?"

"He knew how we, the police, would take that . . . she's covered in blood, alone in the apartment, and she's got some story about a mystery man there. We'd do a lot of head nodding, and not a lot of digging. As for remembering her father . . . assume he wore some disguise in case she somehow recalled that face. She was so little when she last saw him, and with aging . . . it's unlikely she would."

"She had some memories of that time."

"Common in trauma," Allio said. "Certain things stick. It's a field of constant discovery for the forensic psychologists we work with. No matter what she recalled, Navarro knew she wouldn't be the most credible eyewitness. He covered her in Rachel's blood when she was passed out—went for the dramatic, because he knew how a jury would see it. They'd be hard-pressed to believe any other story than a crazed girl snapping in a moment of murderous rage."

"That son of a bitch," Grace said under her breath.

"Oh, that wasn't all. We found several notes in his home, written in blue crayon."

"Darla," Grace said. "Of course he wrote those notes." Bitterness rose up Grace's throat. "I had told Navarro about my scary encounter with Darla at Edgewater and he remembered her from his time at the public defender's office. He must have arranged a meeting with Darla that none of us knew about. Who knows what enticement he used, but he'd have had an in with her nonetheless, and he knew about Penny and her drawing. I remember now . . . it was Navarro who led us to believe that Penny may have written the note herself. He was trying to make sure there was a plausible explanation for the attack so we didn't go looking very hard for one."

"What he knew was that Dr. Mitch was scratching in the right spot and he tried to end it."

"I think he tried to end me, too," Grace said. "Remember we talked about Vince Rapino?"

"Sure."

"He told me Rapino was under investigation for a counterfeit auto parts scam he's running."

Allio looked surprised. "Yeah . . . well, I can neither confirm or deny that."

Grace took that to mean: *bingo*. Navarro hadn't been lying about that, at least.

"I thought Vince was Penny's birth father because of his past with Rachel, so Navarro, instead of helping us get his DNA, he gave us information about Rapino that he knew we might use, which we did. When we couldn't get the DNA, we threatened him with a court order to give it up—and dropped plenty of hints that it could lead to a bigger investigation."

"Yeah, with a guy like Vince Rapino, that's like picking up a rattlesnake by its tail. You're going to get bit."

Grace didn't tell him that she did.

"Why did Rachel die? What was his motive?"

"Don't like blaming the victim in these matters, but I think Rachel may have played a role. We found some pretty hard evidence to suggest she was blackmailing Navarro, and we think it might have been to help out Vince."

"What do you mean?"

"Rachel came back from Rhode Island, for whatever reason. Fizzled-out romance, change of scenery, we don't know. We do know that she and Vince started it up again at Lucky Dog. He got her a place to live and things were good for a time I guess, but he wanted money to get some new parts pipeline up and running. Illegal shit. We're looking into it. Anyway, Rachel wasn't shy about trying to get her man some cash. She went right to Banco de Navarro. We've got the correspondence to prove it. Now the Me Too movement was coming back for

Navarro, and Rachel had the goods. A paternity test would screw him, expose his whole sordid history. He knew it. But instead of giving up the green, he came up with another way of dealing with it."

"I'd say."

"But a guy like Navarro . . . he couldn't stomach having a potential murder charge over his head. So he picked your daughter to be his out. He made sure he'd get on this case somehow, smear any attorney you hired if you didn't pick him at the outset, offer you a huge discount on his fee. One way or another, he was going to be Penny's lawyer so he could control every bit of the case."

"Yeah, he hit my car intentionally so I'd have his card," Grace said again.

Grace told Allio about the fender bender that got her Navarro's apology and business card.

"He became a regular at my restaurant. Ingratiated himself with me and my family. He knew I'd call."

"Devious bastard," Allio said.

Navarro may have been a bastard, but Rachel was not. Grace thought of Rachel and how readily she'd condemned her. She didn't abandon her child. She saw the anchor pendant necklace near the door and believed her daughter had run outside to get away, so she did the same. Later on, when news broke of a little girl found in the park, Rachel had made the painful decision to put her child's interests ahead of her own. She willingly gave up her parental rights in exchange for leniency from the courts, allowing her to live the life she wished, drugs and all, while Isabella would be safe, cared for—and most importantly, kept far away from Greg Navarro forever.

Grace had a thought that perhaps the anchor pendant she saw around Vince Rapino's neck had been a gift from Rachel. Probably was, she decided. She could see Rachel equating that symbol not with Navarro, but with her daughter, with love.

Allio looked a bit uncomfortable shifting in his seat.

"I guess now I should tell you about your son, Ryan."

CHAPTER 56

I haven't shown anything I've written to my film professor. That was our deal. But I think it's come together well, and now I'm at one of the final scenes of my movie—*our* movie, Penny.

```
Scene Heading: INT. Our House—Night
```

We were all gathered around the kitchen table like one big happy family. But there was a drumbeat of tension in the air. Something big was about to go down, but I think only Mom and Ryan were in on it.

"Ryan, it's time to tell Penny what you told me and the police," Mom said. Ryan had on his Big Frank's polo shirt, but unlike the cheery, embroidered man spinning a stitched pizza on his extended finger, his face was downcast and serious.

"I've been spying on you," he said. "I put a key logger on your computer and got access to your Facebook, your e-mail, everything that you were doing online."

He didn't confess his sins to me, but to you, Penny. You looked utterly shattered, as if Ryan had reached across the table to slap you in the face.

You were Penny again. There'd been no trace of Eve since you got out of Edgewater. I guess she'd done her job and finished it admirably.

She had protected you when you needed it most. You have no memory of Isabella or what happened in the courtroom; how you yourself took down the man who had tried to destroy your life. But in Ryan's moment of confession and cleansing, I swear I saw a flicker, a hint in the eyes and shoulders, of Eve's return.

But it was you, Penny, not Eve, who responded to Ryan in your sweet, quiet voice. "Why would you spy on me?"

Ryan lowered his head. "Because I wanted to get you on something, get you in trouble, like you got in trouble before with Maria. Everyone keeps secrets, and I figured since there were more of you, there would be more secrets."

"I don't understand."

"I was angry at you," Ryan said, sounding deeply remorseful. "I was angry from the moment you moved in with us, got all the attention after your diagnosis—you know, stupid kid jealousy. When Dad died and I didn't think you did enough to help save him . . . then . . ." He took in a shaky breath, unable to get out the words. "From that moment on, I didn't just dislike you . . . I hated you."

I'll never forget how your face crumpled as tears flooded your eyes. "I should have called nine-one-one," you said, your voice breaking. Tears poured into Ryan's eyes as well. "I knew he was dead, but still, I should have called. I remember calling his name, checking his pulse, listening for a heartbeat, but he was gone. I don't remember anything after. For all I know, I could have switched to Isabella, and she didn't know what to do."

"The doctors said it wouldn't have made a difference."

Mom felt she needed to remind everyone that no one at the table was at fault.

"I know," Ryan said. "I just didn't want to believe it . . . I needed someone to blame because I missed Dad, and you were there with him. All of my earlier resentments got this new energy, and I put all the blame on you, and that wasn't fair. I'm not proud of what I've done." He shut his eyes tightly, turning his head because he couldn't stand to face her.

"I don't have a real memory of seeing someone outside Rachel's window, Eve did, but somehow I knew it had happened," Penny said, putting it together now. "It was you, wasn't it?"

Ryan lowered his head. "I'd make these regular checks on your stuff online," he said. "That's how I knew you were back in contact with your birth mother, or at least that's who I thought it was. So I followed you to Rachel's house, and I watched you go inside. I brought my camera to take pictures and show Mom, because that kind of secret and betrayal would hurt. And I wanted to hurt you. The curtains were closed, so I stayed outside waiting for my good shot.

"I didn't think you had done anything like what happened. But before I heard the police sirens, I saw Navarro leave the apartment. It was dark, and I didn't get a great look at his face, but now, looking back, knowing what I know, it was him, I'm sure of it. I just didn't put it together before. I saw him stuffing something into his jacket pocket, and I guess, thinking back, it could have been rope. Navarro must have called nine-one-one, tapped on the phone instead of speaking to the dispatch operator, and then he left the house, knowing the police would trace the call.

"Eventually I heard the sirens. You must have heard them, too, because you glanced out the window, saw me. That's when I ran. You see, Penny, I knew somebody else was involved, but I believed in my heart—or tricked myself into believing—that he came from the apartment above, that you were the only one in Rachel's place that night, that you snapped and did those things you wrote about with Maria. I wanted it to be true so you'd be punished. That's why I didn't say anything. So many times . . . so many times I thought about coming clean, but every day that went by, my self-deception rooted deeper. I was disgusted with myself. I couldn't concentrate at school . . . I saw Mom, so brokenhearted, and I thought about killing myself, but the lie I was perpetuating took on a life of its own. It all got so out of hand. The longer it went on, the harder it got to tell the truth."

"You damn jerk," I snapped at Ryan, looking at him incredulously.

"Somebody else being in the house that night would have changed everything! Penny might not have been charged."

"I doubt that," you said, surprising me by coming to Ryan's defense. "I was covered in blood, holding the murder weapon. I might not remember it, but I know what I've been told. The police would have been looking for a mystery accomplice, and they wouldn't have realized that he was defending my case."

"That's probably true," Mom concurred.

"So the guilt got to you," I said.

Ryan nodded pitifully. "I let you down," he said, swallowing hard. "And I'll never forgive myself for that. But I'm hoping—make that praying—you'll forgive me."

Ryan templed his hands together in a prayer position. You reached across the table to cup your hands over his. You locked eyes with him and said in an assured voice that didn't belong to the Penny I knew, "Ryan, you're my brother. I forgive you."

Our mom placed her hands over yours and Ryan's. Then she turned her attention to me, but my hands were interlaced on the table, defiant. Mom said nothing, because she knew these decisions had to come from within.

Several moments passed in stillness, until eventually my hands unclasped like a flower coming into bloom. I placed my hand on top of Mom's. And this will be the final shot of my film. Mom looking into the faces of her children, the many faces of them, seeing in each flickers of hurt, joy, anger, sadness, regrets—a plethora of emotions, moods, and attitudes that are merely projections of one self, one person, one family.

"Better together," Mom said, reciting Dad's favorite saying.

And we all responded, "Better together," as though it were a sacred mantra.

EPILOGUE

Hope Starts Here.

Someone had etched Clean Start's inspirational motto in gold lettering on a black plaque, displayed prominently next to the front entrance of the rehab facility where Adam and dozens of other opioid addicts lived. Located in a leafy part of Massachusetts, where the only distractions were the rose gardens and walking paths, Clean Start featured beautifully manicured lawns with lush greenery and gorgeous landscaping designed to evoke a sense of calm.

Unlike Edgewater, the single-story main structure had plenty of windows to let in lots of natural sunlight, and the red clapboard siding gave the building the appearance of a rambling farmhouse. Mitch sat alone in the airy, nicely appointed reception room waiting for Adam to arrive. It was Caitlyn's idea that Mitch and Adam have some alone time, a little father/son bonding, to see if he could be more successful than she'd been at assuaging his fears. With his release day only a week away, Adam was getting quite nervous about his future.

Mitch had rehearsed his speech on the forty-minute drive to the facility, but when Adam appeared from around a corner, he lost his words. Instead, Mitch focused on how strikingly handsome and healthy his son looked. Adam was blessed with a dimpled chin, now covered with a dotting of scruff, and prominent eyebrows. His rugged face no longer bore the gauntness typical of addicts who prefer drugs to food. During his stay at Clean Start, Adam's tousled dark hair had grown to a moppish length, but his sunken eyes held the same haunted, fearful look that would have made him fit right in wandering the corridors of Edgewater.

Mitch knew the many pitfalls awaiting Adam out in the real world—joblessness, lack of purpose, a sense that he was doing time in life and there had to be a way to pass it more pleasurably. And there was a way, of course—a little pill he could take, or a shot in the arm, anything to make it all seem better if only for a while, until the world crumbled in on him again or he exited this existence entirely.

Mitch and Adam shared a hug to go along with their hellos, but conversation was limited to superficial observations: you look well, so do you, a recap of the drive, that sort of thing. They made their way to the dining hall, which had the ambience of an upscale Denny's, and got their food at the salad bar. Mitch found a table for two in the back of the room where they'd have plenty of privacy. Now, he just needed the right words to say.

"Read the *Globe* article about you," Adam said as he buttered some bread.

Mitch gave a slight chuckle. "Oh, yeah . . . I haven't seen it. Heard it's a long one though."

"You're a celebrity now, Pop," said Adam. "They even printed the drawing she made . . . the one you helped her make, in color, too."

"I didn't realize that," said Mitch. "I'd given the drawing back to Penny. I guess she gave her permission to print it."

"It's cool that all the triggers that caused Penny to remember what Isabella Boyd knew . . . the anchor pendant, the running bathwater, the book of ships, the ammonia, even the rope that Navarro guy used on her, were all in that drawing," he said. "Pretty wild stuff. The article said Penny's legally changing her name to Olivia Francone, dropping the Isabella even. Did you know that?"

Mitch might not have read the report in *The Boston Globe,* but he knew that detail. Grace had called to say hello, check in, and in the course of conversation she'd shared the news. It made sense to Mitch that Penny, as he thought of her, would want to give her alters a place to go, a blank canvas, a fresh start.

"How's she doing?" asked Adam.

"She's good from what I hear. But I'm not her doctor. She's not in Edgewater anymore. How are *you*? That's more my concern. Mom says you're nervous about leaving here."

Adam looked down at his salad, stabbing a tomato with his fork.

"I'm not like you, Dad. I'm not strong enough."

Mitch held back a laugh. If only Adam knew how he had held himself in such low regard as a doctor and a father.

"You're stronger than you know," said Mitch. "Trust me . . . I've learned from experience."

"You? You don't have problems like mine, Dad." Adam wiped tears from his eyes. He looked like he had more to say, but needed a moment to gather his composure. Eventually, he found his voice. "You know, when you're driving down some street and it takes you, I dunno, say a minute to make that drive?"

Mitch nodded his answer.

"Well, every second of that minute, I'm craving heroin. So imagine you're on a road that doesn't end, Pop, doesn't change, same mailboxes, same houses, same people walking their same dogs, over and over again, and no matter how much you want to turn, you can't get off that damn road.

"Every single second of every day, I want a fix like I'm driving on that forever street. If it's not the only thought I have, it's tingling in the back of my mind like an obsession I can't shake. You end up needing the drug like you need air, and that's how it traps you and doesn't ever, ever want to let you go."

Mitch peered into his son's eyes, again seeing the pain smoldering there. How could he expect him to beat this beast? The odds seemed as stacked against Adam as they were against Penny. But Penny did triumph over her adversity, thanks in part to Eve. Eve's anger, that cutting sarcasm she wielded like a weapon, all the loathing and guarding she did to protect her psyche, all that was done with a purpose.

What Eve was really asking for with her caustic remarks and standoffish persona was to be left alone, to be forgotten. It made sense to Mitch that this would be her desire. She fully expected to be found guilty of murder, to spend her life in prison, so naturally she'd rebelled against those trying to convince her otherwise. Hope hurt, so it was better to keep everyone at arm's length and take control of her destiny by accepting her doomed fate. Adam didn't have an Eve to help him keep out the world, but he knew he could push another needle into his arm, and it would tell him exactly how he should think and feel.

Eve was Penny's safety net. Heroin was Adam's.

Mitch felt compelled to say something profound to his son—be the father his father never was to him—but even with all his training in psychotherapy, he couldn't think of what to say. He kept seeing a bleak future for his boy. Either he'd boomerang back to Clean Start, or far, far worse.

A plea Adam had made to Mitch during a prior visit came back to him. *Be there for me . . . I need your support, not your expectations . . .*

Mitch had helped save Penny, saved Eve, saved them all from a doomed future. In a way, Edgewater had been Mitch's safety net, as it had given him a renewed sense of purpose. His short time there not only opened his eyes to the value of his work, but of himself as well. With Penny (or Olivia) now exonerated, Mitch felt free to leave that place behind forever, and thanks to his newfound notoriety, he had his pick of jobs. Recruiters hadn't stopped calling, and the *Globe* article would certainly keep the interest going. The reality was that Mitch felt compelled to stay at Edgewater, much to Ruth Whitmore's delight, so he could help others like Penny find their way home.

If he could be there for Penny, Mitch knew he could there for Adam, right here, right now. Mitch took a sip of seltzer water. He closed his eyes briefly, and a flash of Adam as a boy hit him so hard it took his breath away. He could see his son's sweet smile, feel his tiny body curled up against him as they sat on the couch watching a movie, feel the weight of him as Mitch carried him up the stairs to his bedroom after he'd fallen asleep. He couldn't carry Adam now, but he could still hold him in high regard, be proud to tell others that this was his son, what a wonderful person he was, what a blessing—and mean it.

Mitch set down his drink, dabbing at his beard with a cloth napkin. He held his son's gaze, and the connection they shared at that moment was, for once, real and honest.

"I'm sorry," Mitch eventually said. "I'm not talking about what's happened to you—Lord knows, I'm so sorry about that." His voice shook, so he took a couple deep breaths to get calm. "What I mean to say is, I'm sorry I haven't always been there for you . . . not in a way that's served you best."

"But you have been," Adam said assuredly. He tossed his hands in the air as if he'd tossed away any debate about his father's dedication. "You saved my life. Narcan? Remember?"

"Yeah, I did, and I'm so damn grateful, I can't tell you. But I've been angry, too. I thought this disease . . . that it's your fault . . . that you did this to yourself and you could have stopped it. Or I'd ask myself, why'd you do it to me, to your mom? And I held on to those thoughts and that anger, and I let it eat me up inside, and then I'd feel guilty and hate myself for not giving you what you need, what you deserved, which was my support and love. I know you're sick, same as Penny—" Mitch hadn't meant to bring up her name, but she'd been so embedded in his consciousness it came out almost like a reflex.

"So what are you saying, Dad? That I've got multiple personalities?" Adam sounded amused.

"No . . . I'm not . . . well—" Mitch paused as a thought came to him. "Actually, yes, I'm saying that, but in a different way. There's the You Adam and there's the Drug Adam, and they are—in certain respects—one personality fractured into two, battling within the same self. But just like with Penny, that split is not your fault." Mitch paused to collect his thoughts. Eventually, the words came to him, and he hoped they were the right ones.

"I get that people think addiction is a choice, not a disease. But I *know* better. My depression isn't a choice. You said it, Adam—the way the drugs make you feel, all those heightened senses, the beautiful emotion that flooded you . . . there's a chemical reason why the drugs connected with you the way they did . . . a lack of dopamine receptors in your brain, I suspect, so you were always predestined in some way, shape, or form, to seek out pleasure in other, less natural ways.

"And the more you used drugs, the more your brain chemistry changed—your prefrontal cortex shrank, and it affected your decision-making drastically. But the good news is that recovery *is* a choice, same as loving you unconditionally is one, as well. I won't abandon you, son, not now, not ever . . . so when you get out there—" Mitch pointed a finger to the dining hall window, just like he'd done so many times at Edgewater to indicate the vast, unknowable world beyond its secure walls—"know that you'll never, ever walk alone. I haven't done my best by you, but I'll be there every time to lift you up if you fall down, and that's my promise. It's the best I can do."

Adam sat with it a moment, then rose quickly and came toward Mitch with such purposeful steps that he worried he'd angered his son. To his great relief, Adam bent over and wrapped his father in a tight embrace as thick tears came streaming down his face. When they broke apart, Mitch saw it in Adam's eyes, on his beautiful, battle-weary face—those were the exact words his boy needed to hear.

Those were perhaps the truest words Mitch had ever spoken, for they came straight from the heart.

ACKNOWLEDGMENTS

This is always one of my favorite bits of writing to do, and it comes at the end of the line, after the book has been edited, copyedited, and reviewed with a fine-tooth comb. Here, I get to say thanks.

These books are a team effort, and many people lent their time and expertise to help me get the details right. If there are any failings here—oversights, misrepresentation of facts or procedures—the error is mine and mine alone. To that end, I want to extend my deepest thanks to Attorney William J. Bladd, for his advice on all legal matters. Dr. Joel Solomon, my first cousin (do you see a theme here?), provided me with a good primer on dissociative identity disorder and helped me immensely with Mitch's character and the work he does. Dr. Ethan Prince, yet another highly accomplished cousin, was similarly helpful with my medical-themed questions.

As always, I need to thank my mother, Judy Palmer, for her many reads, suggestions, thoughtful edits, and encouragement along the way. Thanks to Sue Miller, for her proofreading skills, Danielle Girard, a bestselling thriller writer and fellow client of my literary agency, for her thoughtful and insightful feedback, and Zoe Quinton for the same. And special thanks to Barbara Wright and Donna Prince, my eagle-eyed readers who helped catch the errors I missed. Early drafts often look quite different from the final version, and in the case of *The Perfect Daughter*, that difference was especially pronounced. To that end, my appreciation goes to my agent, Meg Ruley, and Rebecca Scherer, who helped me to see areas for improvement. But nobody made more contributions to this novel than my brilliant editor, Jennifer Enderlin, who has a remarkable gift for seeing what might bog down the story and suspense. Fixing it is my job.

Behind the scenes at my publisher, St. Martin's Press, Danielle Prielipp and Sarah Bonamino as well as others in the marketing, sales, and public relations departments, have done everything possible to make sure *The Perfect Daughter* finds its readership, and have done so with the added challenge of a global pandemic. I wrote this novel before the pandemic struck, and I believe the book is going to be read long after we've returned to more familiar ways of living. To that end, I intentionally did not modify the story to reflect the current times.

One thing that won't change with the years is the struggle many people have with mental illness. Dissociative identity disorder, which features prominently in this novel, is a very complex and multifaceted condition that is often incorrectly dramatized in books, TV, and the movies. I did a substantial amount of research on the disorder and prioritized portraying the character with DID as true to life as possible. Where I took too many liberties, I did so for the sake of the story, and to anyone who feels I fell short of my goal, I offer my apologies.

A heartfelt thank you goes to Jessica, for taking care of everything else as I was busy writing, as she's done for many years, and to my children, for being constant sources of joy and inspiration. For me, the satisfaction comes when I hear from delighted readers. It is a privilege that people take time out of their busy lives for my story, and they do so with the expectation that I will take them on a journey that will be thrilling, surprising, and a blast to read. I hope I have wildly exceeded your expectations.

—D. J. Palmer, New Hampshire, 2021

D. J. PALMER is the author of numerous critically acclaimed suspense novels. He received his master's degree from Boston University and after a career in e-commerce, he shifted gears to writing full time. He lives by the ocean in Massachusetts, where he is working on his current novel. Besides writing, D.J. enjoys yoga, songwriting, and family time with his two children and his ever-faithful dog.